Yesterday
Once More

To: Earlene + Anna

Thank you so much!

Enjoy the book.

Karen D. Badger

7/31/08

BLUE FEATHER BOOKS, LTD.

To Babs:

Here's to scar-ified pavement, raise-ified drains and hole-ified tires! Thank you for making me laugh and for teaching me to believe in myself again. Never doubt that our time together was anything but phenomenal. You made me feel treasured. You made me feel loved. You made me feel beautiful. Thank you for all of those things, and so much more. You will always own a special piece of my heart. I love you, and miss you. Be happy. You deserve that and so much more.

ALSO WRITTEN BY KAREN BADGER AND
AVAILABLE FROM BLUE FEATHER BOOKS:

❖ ON A WING AND A PRAYER

COMING SOON:

❖ THE COMMITMENT: THE BILLIE/CAT
   SERIES, BOOK I

www.bluefeatherbooks.com

Yesterday Once More

A BLUE FEATHER BOOK

by

Karen Badger

This is a work of fiction. All characters, locales and events are either products of the author's imagination or are used fictitiously.

YESTERDAY ONCE MORE

Cover design by Ann Phillips

A Blue Feather Book
Published by Blue Feather Books, Ltd.
P.O. Box 5867
Atlanta, GA 31107-5967

www.bluefeatherbooks.com

ISBN: 978-0-9794120-3-5

First edition: July, 2008

Printed in the United States of America and in the United Kingdom.

Acknowledgements

So many people… So many strong, beautiful women contributed to making this work the best it could be. To my beta readers: Barbara, Bliss, Mom, Cindy, Pat, Carol, and Brenda, you ladies rock! Thank you so much for your diligence in reading, commenting and correcting my errors. Your unique views and perspectives added great depth and validation to the story. Barbara, you are an awesome editor and a fantastic taskmaster! To Sher, for verifying and scrubbing (pun intended) the medical situations and terminology—I love you, Big Guy. A special thanks to Joan for tying to make the editing process as painless as possible, and to Andi for your awesome comments and suggestions. To B for putting up with my foul temper during the edits, and loving me anyway—ILYWAMH! To my sons, Heath and Dane and their lovely ladies Kacie and Daisy for believing Mom can do anything… and expecting nothing less. To my babies Ky and Ari for reflecting in your eyes the belief that Nona is the coolest grandmother on earth. You keep me young. Many thanks to my entire family for looking beyond *what* I am, and for unconditionally loving me for *who* I am. Finally, to all of my friends who love me regardless of the fact they think I'm whacked. I love you guys!

PROLOGUE

"911—What is your emergency?"

"Please! Send an ambulance! My daughter's been injured!" The woman's voice was almost indiscernible as she sobbed hysterically.

"Let me confirm your address, ma'am. Are you at 1029 Pheasant Hill Road, Shelburne, Vermont?"

"Yes, please hurry!"

"Help is on the way, ma'am. Please tell me the nature of your daughter's injury so it can be relayed to the emergency response team currently en route to your home."

"I… I don't know. We found her lying in the north pasture. It looks like she was thrown by her horse. So much blood! We don't dare to move her. Please… please hurry!" The woman gasped for air as she choked on her own tears.

"Calm down, ma'am. We'll be there as soon as we can. A unit has already been dispatched. Could I have your name, please?"

"Kathleen Lewis."

"And your daughter's name?"

"Jordan Marie Lewis."

"How old is Jordan?"

Kathleen began to sob once more. "She's sixteen. She's just a baby. Oh, God—please let her be all right!"

"Is Jordan conscious?"

"She's been drifting in and out."

"Help is on the way, Mrs. Lewis. I will stay on the line with you until the ambulance arrives."

* * *

Raymond and Kathleen Lewis clung to each other in the waiting area of the emergency room at the Fletcher Allen Medical

1

Center. After four hours of waiting, Raymond intercepted the next person who exited from the trauma unit.

"Excuse me, but you have our daughter in there. Is there anyone who can tell us what's going on?"

The resident frowned at Raymond, and then looked at the clipboard he was holding in his hands. "Is your daughter's name Jordan Lewis?" he asked.

Kathleen rose from her seat and approached from across the room. "Yes. Yes, Jordan is our daughter. Please, how is she?" Kathleen wrung her tear-dampened handkerchief between her hands.

The resident looked around the room, nervously avoiding the gaze of the concerned parents. "Ah... why don't you have a seat," he suggested. "I'll let the attending physician know you're waiting." A moment later, he was gone.

After what seemed like an eternity, the attending physician emerged from the emergency room and approached them. "Mr. and Mrs. Lewis?" He extended his hand. "My name is Dr. Lindale. I've been treating Jordan since she was brought in."

Kathleen grasped Dr. Lindale's arm. "How is she? Please tell me she's all right."

Dr. Lindale cleared his throat. "Maybe we should step into a consultation room. Please, have a seat," he urged.

When the Lewises were seated, Dr. Lindale positioned himself in the chair opposite them and began paging through Jordan's chart. It was obvious that he was stalling for time.

Unable to contain his frustration any longer, Raymond spoke. "Look, Dr. Lindale. You've had our daughter in that room for over four hours. We want to know how she is, and we want to know now."

Dr. Lindale glanced at the Lewises, then closed Jordan's file. Finally, he spoke. "Jordan's injuries are more extensive than we thought. "I wish I had better news for you, but I'm sorry to say that Jordan has a complete spinal cord injury at the L1 vertebra."

"What exactly does that mean?" Raymond asked.

Dr. Lindale sighed deeply then looked at the Lewises once again. "It means that Jordan is paralyzed from the waist down."

A high-pitched wail erupted from Kathleen's throat.

"She will heal from this, won't she? She'll be okay, right, Dr. Lindale?"

"Jordan will survive, but I'm afraid she will never walk again."

CHAPTER 1

Dr. Jordan Lewis reached into her pocket for a remote control as she walked across her office. She tucked her shoulder-length brown hair behind her ear and pointed the remote at the computer on the desk. Her three-dimensional holographic image appeared over the projection plate in the desk. Her students across the world would see her this way, while lecture notes appeared on the screen. Her hips swayed as she paced back and forth across the room.

"Welcome back from the break. Now, let's resume our lecture. As first-year medical students, I am sure you all realize that what you see here is a healthy spinal cord. When functioning properly, it coordinates all movement and sensation in the body. Considered an organ, it is a type of switchboard between the brain and the body." Jordan stopped and acknowledged an inquiry from one of the students in her multinational audience. An instant interpreter relayed the student's question to Jordan in English.

"Dr. Lewis, why is it that spinal cord injuries cause varying degrees of immobility in the patient? I mean, disability can range anywhere from lack of coordination to total paralysis."

Jordan crossed her arms in front of her chest. "That is a very good question. Actually, the answer is quite simple." Jordan advanced the hologram to display a three-dimensional figure of a human being with the central nervous system highlighted. "Keep in mind that each part of the spinal column is responsible for a different neurological area of the body. The type of disability resulting from a spinal cord injury greatly depends on where the injury is, the severity of the injury, and how much damage is caused to the nerve fiber pathways."

Another student asked a question. "Dr. Lewis, an injury to the spinal cord seems only to affect the area of the body below the injury. Why is that?"

Jordan walked once more across the room. "Well, imagine the spinal cord as a sheathed wire and the brain as a battery. An electrical system depends on a closed loop to work properly. As long as the wires remain intact, all functions between the brain and foot will react to commands given by the brain in the form of electrical impulses. If you cut the wire, say, just above the lower back, the neck, shoulder and arm will continue to receive the impulse, but the hip, knee and ankle will not. By cutting the wire, you no longer have a closed loop to the foot. Mobility ends at the point where the wire was cut. Does that make more sense?"

Jordan scanned her monitor for negative responses from her students. When she received none, she moved on. "Now, let's discuss varying degrees of injury. Injuries to the spinal cord are categorized as either complete or incomplete. A complete SCI results in a total loss of function and sensation below the affected vertebra, and an incomplete SCI means only partial loss of function or sensation. Loss of function depends on the level of damage to the neural pathways between the body and the brain."

Another student submitted an electronic inquiry. "Dr. Lewis, does it matter how soon a spinal cord injury is treated? I mean, are the chances of recovery better if the injury is treated immediately?"

"Yes and no," Jordan responded quickly. "Complete SCIs rarely heal to the point where mobility returns; however, for incomplete injuries with a lower level of severity, the speed at which the injury is treated absolutely plays a factor in the degree of recovery. Speed is an important factor in minimizing neuron death. It makes sense that the lower the rate of neuron death, the greater the chances of reestablishing sensory channels."

Jordan scanned the monitor for more inquires. "Are there any more questions?"

A student beeped in. "Dr. Lewis, is there any hope for victims of severe trauma, for example, complete severance of the spinal cord?"

Jordan listened intently as the student spoke, allowing for an intentional pause as she considered the student's question. The students watched her holographic image as she walked from one end of her office to the other and then back again. Finally, she stopped and looked at her watch. "We only have a minute or two left in this session, so let me try to answer your question in the time we have." Jordan spread her hands and inhaled deeply. "Yes, there is hope. I stand before you—a paraplegic."

A barrage of inquires flooded the control panel of Jordan's monitor just as the two-minute warning appeared at the bottom of the screen.

Jordan grimaced as she realized they were out of time. "I'm afraid class is over. Perhaps we can resume this discussion at the beginning of tomorrow's session?"

As soon as her class had ended, Jordan powered down her computer and headed home. Her announcement had caused such a stir among the students that several of them sent urgent emails begging her to continue the dialogue. Fortunately for Jordan, she was able to put off responding to the inquiries simply by turning off her computer. Normally, she would feel guilty for dismissing students that way; however, she did promise to review her case in detail in the next session.

She pulled into the driveway of her home and dragged her weary body into the house.

Jordan's roommate, Kale Simmons, was stretched out on the couch watching a three-dimensional football game on the holographic projector. Jordan dropped her briefcase on the floor, then collapsed next to her friend and snuggled into his shoulder. "Damn, it's cold out there. It's hard to believe spring is just a month away."

Kale turned his head and kissed Jordan's forehead. "Rough day?"

"Long day. After spending the entire morning working on the new implant, I covered spinal cord injuries in my kinesiology class."

Kale glanced at her before looking back at the ball game. "Don't tell me. They found out about your injury."

Jordan grimaced. "I kind of told them about it with only two minutes left before the end of class."

Kale looked at her. "You're kidding, right? Damn, woman. They must have mobbed you after class."

"Mobbed is an understatement. They filled my inbox in a matter of seconds." Jordan dropped her face into her hands. "You'd think I'd have learned by now not to divulge that particular piece of information without adequate time to discuss it."

Kale rubbed Jordan's back. "You can't blame them, you know. If I were a rookie in that class, I would have followed you home and forced you to tell me the details."

Jordan smiled. "Pray tell, just what do you mean by force?"

Kale grabbed Jordan by the waist and pulled her onto his lap so that she rested across his legs with her head on his shoulder. He ran his free hand across her cheek. "First, I would turn on my irresistible charm."

Jordan chuckled. "It wouldn't work, and you know it."

Kale grinned. "Well, then I'd resort to bribing you."

Jordan's eyebrows arched. "What makes you think you have anything to bribe me with? If I didn't feel for your sorry ass, you'd be living on the street."

Kale clutched at his heart. "Ouch. That hurt."

Jordan punched him lightly in the chest. "You know I'm just kidding. I kind of like having you here."

Kale grabbed Jordan's chin. "What you like is my cooking."

Jordan patted her stomach. "Now that you mention it," she teased.

"Why, you little imp." Kale began to tickle her.

Jordan squirmed with all her might, trying to escape the attack. "Okay! I give. You win."

Jordan settled back into his embrace. Once again, Kale trailed his fingertips across her cheek. "Now, if I could only get you to fall for me, I'd be all set."

Jordan reached up and cupped Kale's face between her hands. "Sweetheart, I love you dearly, but we've had this discussion before. You are just not what I need in my life."

Kale smiled. "Not even for my spinach soufflé?"

"Kale," Jordan warned.

"I know, I know. You can't fault a guy for trying. So, ask me about my day."

"Okay. How was your day?"

"Wonderful. We had a breakthrough."

Jordan climbed off Kale's lap and sat on the coffee table in front of him. "Are you serious? Tell me about it."

"We finally have proof that electrical impulses can actually stimulate cell growth in the spinal columns of rats."

Jordan placed her hand on Kale's knee. "That's wonderful news," she said excitedly. "Are you sure? Are the results conclusive? Are you ready to test it on human subjects?"

"Whoa, slow down, partner. What we know is that by using a continuous wave electrical impulse in the area of the injury, we were able to simultaneously activate thousands of genes. The first genes to activate were those that promote cell growth, similar to the type that repair skin wounds in humans."

Jordan began to speak but Kale interrupted her. "Before you say anything, you have to realize our testing is just in the preliminary stages. It may take years before we know if we can repair a complete spinal cord injury. The results are encouraging, but they're preliminary."

Jordan's shoulders slumped, but to lighten the mood, she forced a smile. "I know, I know. I'm a scientist, too. I know how long the research and development period can be. It's just that I've been living with this for sixteen years, and it wears thin after a while."

Kale sat up straight. "What? Sixteen years? Wow. You're getting old, my friend."

Jordan slugged him in the shoulder. "I'm only thirty-two. You talk like I'm ninety-eight."

"And what a beautiful thirty-two you are. Are you sure I can't convert you to men?"

Jordan laughed. "Not a chance, Kale. Not a chance."

"What if I grew my hair really long and wore falsies?" he teased.

Jordan pretended to consider it, but then shook her head. "If you would consider changing your equipment, I might think about it."

Kale crossed his legs. "I don't think so."

Jordan grinned. "Then, I guess you're out of luck."

Kale opened his arms. "Oh, well. Come here and watch the game with me."

Jordan allowed herself to be wrapped in Kale's arms as they lay entwined together on the couch. Soon, Jordan had fallen asleep. Kale worked his arms under her knees and then carried her to her bedroom, placing her gently on the bed. He rolled Jordan onto her side and lifted her shirttail, exposing her back. He paused for a moment, tracing the long scar that ran nearly the entire length of her spine. Kale reached inside her trousers and pulled out a small wire with a round access port on the end. He plugged this into the cord of a solar power receptacle. Then he pulled Jordan's shirt back down.

Kale leaned in to kiss Jordan on the head. "Sleep well, honey."

* * *

Jordan loved horses. Her favorite was a mustang, Sally, a gift from her parents. On this particular day, Jordan planned to take Sally on an all-day ride across the rolling hills of the family farm. After several sprints across the wide plains, Jordan carefully led Sally through the dense forest. The light was fading; Jordan had gotten a late start, and she'd ridden for a long time. She was careful to steer Sally away from fallen tree branches. Within moments, they had cleared the forest and emerged at the edge of the open pasture between the trees and Jordan's home.

A broad smile spread across Jordan's face. She leaned down and rubbed the horse's neck. "Okay, girl, are you ready?" She jabbed her heels into the horse's side.

Sally erupted into a full gallop across the north pasture. Jordan felt the liquid fire of adrenaline racing through her veins. A rush of heat washed over her, and she surrendered herself to the momentum and speed as she became one with the horse. Jordan felt like she was flying as the horse rapidly closed the distance between the forest and her house.

Suddenly, Jordan felt a violent jerk. Her body snapped backward and then abruptly forward. Sally was no longer beneath her. The impact was terrible. All of the air was knocked from Jordan's lungs, and her mouth and nose filled with blood. Jordan struggled to breathe. She forced herself to calm down and willed her muscles to relax, hoping to stop the painful contractions in her stomach. Soon, her breathing returned to normal.

Jordan closed her eyes. There was a thunderous pounding in her ears. She remained face down in the grass as the twilight descended around her. She could feel warm blood flowing from her nose, but curiously, she felt no pain.

Some time later, Jordan opened her eyes and realized that night had fallen. The reddish-gold glow in the distant sky had been replaced by utter darkness. A chill had set in, and the night air cooled her skin. She was shivering. Now, Jordan felt pain. As she awkwardly lifted her head, she fought against the terrible ache in her neck and looked around her. It was too dark to see.

The skin on Jordan's face felt tight. As she reached up to brush the sensation away, she discovered a large swelling on her cheek. She winced at the awkward and uncoordinated movements of her hand.

What happened to me? Where am I?

Suddenly, Jordan heard a sound. She tried to control her ragged breathing as she fought to distinguish the familiar sounds of crickets and critters from the unusual noise that had caught her attention. She listened carefully as the noise returned. "Sally? Sally! Where are you girl?" The noise was louder this time. Jordan lifted her head and caught a small movement to her right. "Sally?"

Jordan braced her hands on the ground and tried to push herself up, but she was only able to lift her shoulders before she fell back. "Oh, my God!" she said as a wave of pain rushed through her head.

Desperately worried about her horse, Jordan rested her forearms on the ground and lifted her upper body off the grass. With all her strength, she dragged herself to the fallen animal. She reached out to touch Sally, who released a long, painful whinny, and then stopped breathing. Jordan froze.

"No!"

"Jordan! Jordan, wake up. You're having a nightmare."

Jordan sat up abruptly, panic-stricken and disoriented. She was bathed in sweat, her hair plastered to her forehead. It took several moments for her to focus on the person in front of her.

"Kale?"

Kale sat on the edge of Jordan's bed and cupped the side of her face with his palm. "You had the dream again, didn't you?"

Jordan nodded. Tears spilled onto her cheeks.

Kale opened his arms. He held Jordan close and rocked her. "You know, you really should see someone about these dreams. They seem to be coming more and more frequently. How long have you been having them now?"

Jordan lowered herself back onto the pillow and reached for Kale's hand. "I had them all the time when I was a kid. They started right after the accident, and they continued pretty regularly right up until I left for college. They've only come back since I've been home again—since Mom and Dad died and left the house to me."

Kale grinned to lighten the mood. "Maybe it's the house. Maybe there's a ghost calling to you."

"Get out of here!" Jordan said. She pushed hard on Kale's shoulder. He threw himself backward, eyes wide, pretending to flail. Jordan tried unsuccessfully not to laugh. "There's nothing wrong with this house. It's a great house. I grew up here."

"No, nothing's wrong with the house," Kale agreed. "You're right, it's great. It just seems odd that the nightmares only happen here."

"I'm sure it's because this is where the accident happened. It's a hard memory to shake." Jordan was interrupted by the sound of the oven timer. "Oh, goody, it sounds like dinner's ready. I'm starved."

"Oui, Mademoiselle. Allow me to escort you to your table," Kale said in a poorly faked French accent.

Jordan took his hand. "Oui, oui, Monsieur." As she swung her legs over the side of the bed, she felt a tug at her back. "Oops, Forgot to unplug. Do you mind?"

Kale unplugged the solar charger and tucked the wire back into Jordan's pants.

"Merci. Now, garçon, to my table." Jordan braced her feet on the floor. As she pushed off the bed into a standing position, her knees gave out. She fell back onto the bed. "Goddamn it! That's the second time it's happened this week."

Kale climbed onto the bed behind her. "Bend forward," he instructed. He pulled the waistband of her pants down to reveal a small, oval-shaped bulge. It was under the skin and just above Jordan's right buttock. He placed his palm over the device. After several long seconds, Kale pulled her waistband back up and climbed off the bed. "It seems to be working. I can feel the vibration."

"It must have a short in it or something."

"Maybe," he said. "You've got to remember that the device is a prototype. I'm actually surprised it's worked for this long. Come on. Let's see if you can stand now." He wrapped his arm around her waist, and, in one swift movement, they stood up. "How does that feel? Do you think you can walk on your own?"

Jordan took a few tentative steps. Then she walked across the room and back again. The worried look on Kale's face was touching. She reached for his arm. "It seems to be okay. Now be a gentleman and escort this lady to dinner."

CHAPTER 2

Jordan was pouring a thermal decanter of coffee to take with her to class when Kale emerged from his bedroom, ready for work. Jordan took one look at him and laughed. Kale Simmons was good-looking. Roughly the same age as Jordan, he was just under six feet tall, thin, with boyishly handsome features.

"Kale, don't you ever comb your hair? You look like a mad scientist."

Kale stopped and ran his hand through his unruly blond mop. "What's wrong with my hair?"

Jordan sipped her coffee. "It's sticking up in a zillion different directions. It looks like you went to bed with it wet."

"As a matter of fact, I did. You know how I like to shower in the evening. It gives me more time to sleep in."

"I just think you're lazy and can't get your butt out of bed in the morning."

"I plead the fifth." Kale batted his eyelashes. "Pour me a cup of java, would you?"

Jordan reached for the carafe and a clean cup. "You're lucky you're so cute. Otherwise, I'd have to beat your ass."

Kale grinned. "Now there's one beating I'd gladly endure."

Jordan shook her head. "You are impossible."

"No, ma'am, I'm pretty easy. Show me even the slightest interest, and I'll jump your bones in an instant."

"Argh." Jordan advanced on Kale, who jumped to the other side of the kitchen table. Jordan chased him around twice with no luck. Finally, she gave up and grabbed her briefcase.

"Okay, imp-boy, I've got a class to teach. Will I see you at the lab later?"

"Count on it. Oh—we need to talk to Peter today about your malfunctions. Don't forget to remind me."

* * *

11

As part of her research grant, Jordan taught a class in kinesiology at the University of Vermont Medical School. The class met on Monday, Wednesday, and Friday at 3:00 p.m., and at 8:00 a.m. on Tuesday and Thursday. The 8:00 a.m. classes invariably suffered from poor attendance. However, after Jordan's stunning announcement, word spread quickly, and this morning's class was full.

Jordan said, "It's nice to see such wonderful attendance this morning." She paused at the chuckles and murmurs. "So, where did we leave off yesterday? Oh, yes. We were talking about restored mobility for patients with a severe spinal cord injury."

Jordan leaned against the desk. "I mentioned yesterday that I am a paraplegic, yet here I am, walking as if I had a fully intact spinal cord. I don't. For fourteen years, I was confined to a hover-chair. My legs were totally useless."

Jordan called on a student, who asked, "I assume your injury was not catastrophic then?"

Jordan grimaced. "No, it was catastrophic. My spine was completely severed at the L1 segment. In other words, total and permanent paralysis from the waist down."

Several students began to ask questions at once.

"Whoa, slow down. One at a time," Jordan said.

"How did it happen?"

Jordan took a deep breath and related the details of her accident. "I was sixteen. I had taken my horse out for a run on our family farm. It was nearly dark when we started for home. We were running at full gallop when my horse stepped onto an old dried well, covered with a piece of rotting plywood. My horse's front legs went into the well, and I was thrown several feet. The impact severed my spine. My horse, unfortunately, did not survive the fall."

After several long seconds, another student chimed in. "Dr. Lewis, how are you able to stand and walk? Did your spinal column regenerate? I thought that was impossible."

Jordan stopped pacing. "I wouldn't say it was impossible. I would say that we are still learning how the body works, and we're moving closer every day to understanding how to force regeneration of the spinal cord. Two years ago, I volunteered for trials aimed at restoring mobility. My implant allows me to walk, but it doesn't repair the injury. The work I've been involved in restores mobility by artificially inserting functional connections at the injury site. It's not a permanent fix, and heaven forbid your power supply should run out while you're on the dance floor!"

Jordan waited for the laughter to subside. "I have a surgically-implanted device that emits electrical impulses into the severed region of my spinal column. Fortunately for me, my parents insisted on a regular regime of physical therapy, which I objected to at the time but am now quite thankful for. That kept my muscles in good shape, allowing me to participate in mobility studies."

"Did the surgery work right away?"

"It has taken the better part of those two years for me to relearn basic walking skills."

"Dr. Lewis," said another student, "it seems like a remarkable breakthrough."

"We've come a very long way, but there is still a significant amount of work ahead of us. We need to perfect the implant. There are still moments when it misbehaves, but we have learned a great deal by carefully monitoring my progress." Jordan paused. "Okay, we really do need to cover new material today, so I'm going to move on."

By the end of class, Jordan was fighting a splitting headache. Kale found her sitting at her desk with her head in her hands. She looked up at him.

Kale knelt by Jordan's side and rubbed her back. "Not feeling very well, huh?"

"My head is killing me. I haven't had a headache this bad in almost two years."

Kale frowned. "Have you taken anything for it yet?"

She shook her head. "No."

"Maybe you should go home. I'll give you a ride, if you like."

Jordan sat back in her chair and massaged her temples. "No, I have way too much work to do. My class is taking up so much of my time. I'm not contributing as much as I'd like to on the new implant. I'll just take a cranium pressure stabilizer. I'll be all right in a few minutes."

Kale looked skeptical, but he said, "Let me get it for you. Don't move, okay?"

Jordan dropped her head back into her hands. "I'll be right here."

Kale ran to the infirmary as fast as he could. When he stepped back into Jordan's office, he found her lying on the floor. "Jordan!"

Kale rushed to her side and carefully checked her pulse. He breathed a sigh of relief when he found it to be strong and regular.

Kale activated his communication device and notified security. "Hello? This is Kale Simmons in the lab. I have a medical emergency. Jordan Lewis's office. Please, hurry. She's unconscious."

Kale heard sirens in the distance. Minutes later, Jordan was strapped to a stretcher and loaded into an ambulance. The EMT addressed Kale.

"Are you riding to the hospital with us? We'll need someone to talk to Admitting."

"Yes, I'll go." He climbed into the back of the ambulance and sat on a bench while the paramedics collected Jordan's vitals and transmitted the information into the emergency room.

"Does she have any special needs, Mister…"

"Simmons, Kale Simmons. Special needs? She's a paraplegic."

The EMT looked surprised. "A paraplegic? Where's her hover-chair?"

"It's a long story," Kale said wearily. "She has an experimental spinal implant. She's had it for two years and… Oh, my God. I wonder…" He looked up at the EMT. "When we get to the hospital, we need to contact Dr. Peter Michaels right away. He's the surgeon who placed the implant."

*   *   *

Peter Michaels looked at Jordan's holographs.

"Is she having any problems with the implant, Kale?"

"As a matter of fact, yes. Last night, it malfunctioned. She collapsed. Do you see something in these holographs that might indicate what caused it?"

Peter pointed to a shaded area. It was one of the many points where the electrodes were inserted into Jordan's spine. "This area right here indicates an abnormality. Most likely swelling due to the malfunction."

Both men were focused so intently on the holograph that they didn't hear Jordan enter the room. "So, Doc, am I going to make it?"

Peter swung around. "Jordan, how are you feeling?"

"Better now, but still a bit headachy. So, let's have it, Peter. What's the verdict?"

Kale led Jordan to the table. He pulled out two chairs, forcing her to sit beside him. "Jordan," he said, "can you tell us what happened? I went to get your meds. When I came back, you were on the floor, unconscious."

"You found me on the floor?"

"You're damn right I did. You scared the shit out of me."

Jordan sat back. "I needed a drink of water. I remember standing up, and then... nothing. I woke up in the emergency room."

She looked at Peter. "Tell me, what's happening here?"

Peter walked over to the holograph and pointed to the abnormalities he had noted earlier. "Jordan, I think we need to take the implant out."

Jordan jumped to her feet. "Oh, no you're not! I am not going back to that hover-chair! I won't, Peter. I can't."

"Jordan, I think you should do what Peter says. There's no telling when the implant will stop functioning altogether. Hell, you could be driving when it happens. Listen to him," Kale urged.

Jordan was furious. She leaned close to Kale's face. "You don't have to be confined to a goddamned chair for sixteen hours a day. You have no idea what it's like!"

Peter watched the exchange, leaning against the table, his legs crossed at the ankles. He waited until Jordan had finished speaking. "I understand your reluctance, but there is another reason this may be necessary. You blacked out. That might be an indication that the implant is affecting your cerebral spinal fluid. The last thing you need is an infection that might result in a stroke and further paralysis in your upper body."

Jordan knew he was right. As she absorbed this information, she wilted before their eyes.

* * *

Two days later, Jordan awoke in the hospital, lying face down in a suspension bed. As she opened her eyes, the first thing she saw was Kale sleeping on the floor beneath her bed. Tears filled her eyes and dropped directly onto his face.

Kale snapped awake. "Hey! Turn off the waterworks up there."

Jordan smiled down at her friend. "I'm sorry. I can't help it."

Kale reached up and wiped the tears from her face. "How are you feeling, kiddo?"

Jordan searched her heart before answering. "Drained... scared... angry. I don't know if I can live my life in a hover-chair. I just don't know."

Another tear fell, hitting Kale squarely on the forehead. "I'll be right back," Kale said. He rolled out from under the bed and popped into the bathroom. He returned with a handful of tissue.

As Kale swabbed her eyes, he told Jordan about a conversation he'd had with Peter Michaels. "Of course, we'll need your approval before we can move ahead."

Jordan frowned. "My approval?"

"Yeah. I... uh... I suggested we try the new implant on you."

"The new implant isn't ready yet."

"It's further along than you think. Don't forget that while you've been playing teacher, I've been working my butt off on this thing. If I put in extra hours, I think it can be ready in about a month." Kale studied Jordan's face.

Jordan closed her eyes. "What if it doesn't work? I don't know if I can bear the disappointment of a second implant failing."

When she opened her eyes again, Kale was gone.

*   *   *

Two days later, Jordan was transferred to a standard hospital bed. She was lying there, absorbed in self-pity, when Peter Michaels paid her a visit.

"Okay, we're going to test your reflexes. I don't expect any reaction from the waist down. I'm more interested in the reflexes in your arms and neck."

Jordan endured the tests and tried not to show her disappointment when there was no reaction in her lower extremities.

Peter looked at her. "I'm sure that Kale has discussed his plan for the new implant."

Jordan turned her head to the side and closed her eyes.

"I'll take that as a yes," Peter said. "What do you think?"

Jordan sighed. "I don't know. I'm afraid to set myself up for more disappointment. What if it fails again in a year or two? I don't know if I can deal with that."

"That's a valid concern. The decision is yours, but I hope you'll consider it. Even if you decide to go ahead, neither you nor the implant will be ready for another month or two."

Peter made several notes on Jordan's chart before he addressed her again. "We should be able to release you this afternoon. You'll need to come back in about a week for a follow-up. You need to pull yourself out of the funk you've been in these past few days. It may sound corny, but a positive outlook is part of the healing process. You, more than anyone, know life in a hover-chair is not a death sentence. You're among the lucky ones."

Jordan narrowed her eyes. "How can you possibly say I'm lucky?"

Peter leaned over her. "Because there's a possibility that we can fix this. You have an entire team of research scientists willing to help you. Not everyone is that fortunate. Think about that, Jordan. Think about it long and hard."

CHAPTER 3

Jordan stared out her bedroom window at the light snowfall. She could summon neither the energy nor the desire to get up. In the two weeks since her surgery, she had shown little interest in rejoining the human race—a fact that she knew greatly worried Kale.

"Hey," Kale said from the doorway to her room. "How about getting your ass out of bed and going for a walk with me?" Jordan shot him a venomous look. "Very funny, asshole. Where do you propose I get a pair of functional legs on such short notice?"

Kale sighed. "Damn it, you know I didn't mean it that way." He walked over to her bed and held out his hand. "Come on. It'll do you good to get outdoors this morning, even if it is only thirty-two degrees."

Jordan turned her head, refusing to look at him. "Leave me alone. I'm busy."

Kale crossed his arms over his chest. "Yeah, I can see that. You're busy writing a thesis on self-pity."

Jordan's head snapped around. "Don't you dare judge me. You have no idea how I feel. No idea!"

Kale shoved his hands deep into his pockets, his shoulders slumped. "No, you're right. I don't know how you feel. But I do know how you're making me feel, and that's pretty shitty. If you don't want to go for a walk with me, then I guess I'll go to the lab. I have a lot of work to do. The visiting nurse will be here shortly to take care of things. Is there anything I can do for you before I leave?"

Jordan still refused to look at him. "No. Just leave me alone."

Jordan could see the defeat in her friend's shoulders as he walked away. Part of her felt sorry for the way she had treated him, and part of her felt justified that someone else should suffer as she did. She listened intently until she heard the door close. Then she closed her eyes and wept.

* * *

When Kale arrived home that evening, he found Jordan sitting in her chair, staring out the window. He put his briefcase on the couch and walked over to place a kiss on top of her head.

"Hey, there. How was your day?"

Jordan continued to stare silently out the window, ignoring his greeting.

Kale decided to lighten the mood by speaking for both of them. He changed his voice to a higher pitch. "My day was fine, Kale. How was your day?"

He dropped his voice. "My day was great, Jordan. Thank you for asking. We made a lot of progress on the implant. We now have a prototype ready for testing on non-human subjects."

"Oh, that's wonderful," Kale squealed. "I can't wait for you to try it out on me!"

Jordan looked directly at him and shook her head. The disgust was clearly evident on her face.

Kale sighed and threw up his hands. "Okay, I've had enough partying for one night." He turned on his heel and headed for the door.

"Where are you going?" Jordan called out.

"I'm going where the atmosphere is a little more friendly. Out to the barn, with the horses. I'll be working on my invention. If you need me, use the intercom."

Jordan was seething inside, extremely envious of Kale's ability to pick up and go whenever and wherever he wanted. "Sure, go. Go and leave me here to rot. You're wasting your time on that stupid invention, Kale. You must be out of your mind if you really believe it will work. If time travel were possible, don't you think it would have been done by now?"

The loud banging of the screen door ended Jordan's tirade. She guided her chair over to the door and watched Kale stride purposefully across the yard to the barn.

"Damn you, Kale Simmons. Damn you to hell!"

Kale kicked the barn door open. "Damn it, Jordan Lewis. Why do you have to be so fricking stubborn? You're not the first person in the history of the world to be confined to a hover-chair."

The horses looked at Kale. He made a conscious effort to calm himself. He cleaned the stalls, putting in fresh water and feed. The barn was cold but the physical exertion warmed him. When Kale had completed his chores, he looked around and inhaled deeply.

He turned up the thermostat on the solar heater at the far end of the barn. Then he reached for the cloth tarp that covered a large object in the center of the room. Kale set the tarp aside and slowly circled his creation. The object consisted of a series of concentric rings, each of which moved on a different axis, creating a large sphere when the rings were in motion. Along the inside circumference of the globe, parallel to the floor, was a shelf approximately two feet wide, and in the middle of that was a four-foot square platform. Kale smiled as he felt a surge of confidence. He switched on the light above his workbench, illuminating a mound of paperwork. He thumbed through the papers on top of the stack, speaking out loud as he read.

"Okay, let's see. To travel faster than the speed of light I need a black hole." Kale looked over the top of the paperwork and gazed at the device. "The trick will be generating enough energy to create one."

Kale retrieved an old boot from the tack box and placed it on the platform. The boot was so worn that it barely stood. "Let's give it a go." He pulled a second tarp from a console beside the desk, revealing a panel containing an array of buttons and switches.

Kale looked once more at the device. Taking a deep breath, he toggled the first switch. A loud hum resonated and the rings began to rotate, slowly at first, but soon with increasing speed. Kale watched the boot carefully. When the rings reached critical velocity, he toggled a second switch. The velocity of the rings increased exponentially, as did the volume of the hum coming from the center of the object. Kale threw a third switch, and a surge of blue, yellow, and red electricity lined the inside of the rotating rings.

Kale's heart pounded wildly in his chest. His hand hovered over the large red accelerator button on the control panel. Struggling with a sense of urgency, Kale forced himself to wait for the velocity of the spheres to reach critical value. Finally, his hand came down hard on the accelerator button. A blinding flash of light exploded through the barn as a powerful energy force knocked Kale off his feet and slammed him into the wall behind the console. The room suddenly dimmed, illuminated only by the lights hanging from the rafters of the barn.

Kale lay motionless for several moments as he regained his bearings. The console was between him and the device, blocking his view. With great anticipation, he climbed to his feet and clamored to the center of the room.

The boot was still on the platform. He had failed.

Kale slammed the door. He shrugged his way out of his coat and tossed it on a chair. Throwing himself on the couch, he crossed his arms tightly over his chest and glowered.

Jordan looked at him. "You're in a good mood."

He looked at her sharply. "Kind of matches yours, huh?"

Jordan was taken aback. "Want to talk about it?" she asked softly.

Kale rubbed his brow. "I failed. It didn't work."

Jordan maneuvered her chair across the room. "What didn't work?"

"The boot. The boot was still there."

"The boot?" Jordan asked, confused. "A little more information, please?"

Kale rose to his feet and paced the room. He gestured broadly with his hands. "I found an old boot in the tack box and tried to send it back through time. The machine seemed to be operating okay, but when it reached critical momentum and I pressed the accelerator button, the entire thing just blew up in my face. The boot was still there."

Jordan raised her eyebrows. "The boot was still there?"

Kale leaned forward and placed his hands on the armrests of Jordan's chair. "The boot was still there. It didn't work. What part of that don't you understand?"

Anger burned in Jordan's chest. She looked at Kale through narrowed eyes. "Doesn't feel very good to be helpless, does it? Try living with that feeling every day."

Kale pushed off the arms of her chair and stood up. He stared down at her for several moments before he spoke. "The difference between you and me is that I plan to try again. I will not let this failure defeat me. You, on the other hand, have chosen to remain helpless."

Jordan looked away, embarrassed. "I don't know what you're talking about."

"Bullshit. In a few weeks, the new implant will be ready for testing on human subjects. You are the perfect candidate, yet you sit in that chair stubbornly feeling sorry for yourself. I've always admired your spunk and determination, but lately, I've been sorely disappointed in your behavior. Get a grip on yourself, woman. Do something with your time while you wait for the implant, something other than wasting away in this chair. You need to get on with your life, Jordan."

Jordan lowered her chin to her chest and closed her eyes to hide the tears. When she opened them again, Kale was gone.

* * *

When Kale returned home from work the next day, the driveway was full of trucks. It took him a few moments to maneuver his vehicle into the driveway. Once the landing gear was lowered and the nuclear power supply was switched off, Kale made his way through the maze of boards and tools and climbed the stairs to the front porch. As he reached for the door, it flew open, nearly knocking him down.

"Oops. Sorry, Bud."

"No problem." Kale caught the swinging door and held it open for the carpenter, who was carrying a large piece of worn plywood.

Kale made his way inside. He found Jordan sitting in her hover-chair, directing another carpenter's efforts. Kale grinned. The old spark of authority had returned to his friend. "Hey, girlfriend. What's going on here?"

Jordan maneuvered her chair in Kale's direction. "Hey Kale, you're home."

Kale kissed Jordan on the cheek, noting with pleasure her rosy glow. "It looks like a battlefield in here. What's up?"

"I'm getting on with my life."

Kale grinned. "This isn't exactly what I had in mind."

"Hey—it beats sitting here feeling sorry for myself." Jordan reached for Kale's hand. "Thank you for being so tough with me. I needed someone to kick my ass. I'm glad it was you."

"No problem. Any time you need your ass kicked, just let me know. I look forward to any excuse to touch that lovely ass of yours."

Jordan slugged Kale in the stomach. "You are such a pig."

"Oink! Oink!" Kale replied. They both laughed. "So, what's with the demolition?"

Jordan looked around at the rapidly growing mess in her kitchen. "Well, I thought as long as I was stuck at home for a while, I could do something productive like remodel the house. Starting with the kitchen seemed like a good idea. These are the same cupboards that were here when my parents bought the house almost forty years ago."

Kale looked at the sheetrock and plaster that littered the floor. "That's really old stuff. What are you planning to replace it with?"

"I know photosensitive synthetic wallboard is easier to work with, but in order to preserve the historic nature of the house, I'm going to restore it to its original form. That means sheetrock, plaster, and tiles."

"Makes sense to me. Once this kitchen is finished, I'll fix you some real gourmet dinners. How's that sound?"

"Sounds great. I thought I'd start on my bedroom, too. Then we'll take the other rooms one at a time. You get to choose the next one, okay?"

"Sounds good to me," Kale said. "Since the kitchen is torn to shreds, how about I take you to dinner?"

"Okay. Give me a few minutes to clean up. I'm covered with dust and dirt."

"All right," Kale said. "I'll be in the barn. Just give a shout when you're ready."

* * *

Jordan smiled at the waitress who refilled her coffee cup. "Thank you," she said sweetly. The waitress gave her a coy smile and walked away from the table, her hips swaying suggestively.

Kale's gaze passed from Jordan to the waitress. "How do you do it?"

Jordan sipped her coffee. "Do what?"

Kale leaned forward. "You know what I mean. How on earth do you pick them out?"

Jordan frowned. "Really, Kale. I don't know what you're getting at."

"You were flirting with the waitress."

"And your point is?"

Kale rolled his eyes. "My point is, how do you know they're interested? How do you, well, you know... how do you know they're lesbians?"

Jordan smiled. "I don't always know they're lesbians."

Kale nodded his head toward the waitress. "Is she one?"

"Is she one, what?"

"Damn it, don't make this any harder than it has to be."

Jordan chuckled. "Are you asking me if the waitress is a lesbian?"

"Duh! Of course I am, and you know it."

The waitress, who was busy clearing a nearby table, looked up at Jordan and smiled. Jordan smiled back before looking at Kale. "I haven't a clue," she replied quietly.

"You've been flirting with her all evening, and she's been flirting back with you."

Jordan shrugged. "That doesn't make her gay, you know."

Kale was clearly frustrated. "Okay, clue me in here. Heaven knows, I could use a few pointers. If you can't always tell, then how do you know which ones to flirt with?"

Jordan covered Kale's hand with her own. "You just don't get it. Women like attention. They like it when someone notices how attractive they are. It doesn't matter if the person who notices that is a man or a woman."

Kale watched her closely. "Good point. I'll keep that in mind. But how do you know? I mean, say you were looking for a new relationship. How would you know who to flirt with seriously? Damn. This is harder to explain than I thought it would be."

Jordan covered her mouth with her hand to hide her grin. She inhaled deeply and tried to adopt a serious air. "How do I know? I know it sounds stereotypical, but if there's a chance that she'll be interested, my gaydar kicks in."

"Gaydar?"

"Gay radar," Jordan explained. "It's a feeling we get when we're pretty certain the other party is of the same persuasion."

"Is it ever wrong?" Kale asked.

Jordan sat back in her chair and laughed. "Oh, yeah! I've hit on several straight women."

"That must be pretty awkward."

"No more than when you hit on a woman and she turns you down. It's not nearly as bad for women as it is for men."

Kale frowned. "What do you mean?"

Jordan wrapped her hands around her coffee cup. "I think women are cooler about it."

"That's a pretty sexist thing to say."

Jordan leaned forward. "What would you do if you were in a bar and a gay man hit on you? What would your reaction be? Be honest."

Kale looked into his coffee cup. After a few moments, he met Jordan's eyes. "Honestly, I think I would become defensive, maybe even angry."

Jordan nodded. "I guessed as much. A woman hitting on another woman, gay or straight, is taken as a compliment but, sadly, a man hitting on a man is seen as a threat. Society may have moved beyond expecting gays to be closeted, but mistaken identity can still be uncomfortable."

Kale shook his head. "Man. I'll never understand women."

"Don't feel bad. You're in good company. Men and women have been on this earth for millions of years and have yet to figure each other out."

"I think I'll stick to science for now."

Jordan changed the subject. "Speaking of which, you went to the barn this evening while I was getting ready for dinner. I assume you were going over what went wrong with your experiment last night?"

Kale ran his hand through his hair. "I don't know what went wrong. I've been over and over it, but I can't figure it out. My calculations appear to be correct. There's something missing, something so simple that I'm sure it is staring me in the face, but I just can't see it."

"What makes you believe that time travel is possible? I mean, it's the year 2105. Don't you think if it were possible, someone would have figured it out by now?"

Kale sat back in his chair. "It's attitudes like that, Jordan, that discourage people from trying."

Jordan touched his arm. "I really am interested in your theory. Please, humor me."

Excitement flooded Kale's face. "Okay, here's what I know. Hundreds of years ago, Albert Einstein's theory of relativity proved that time is not constant. It's affected by direction, motion, and gravity. In 1971, the well-documented Hafele-Keating experiment, using four atomic clocks, proved that point. It appears that time passes faster if you travel back in time than it does if you travel into the future."

Jordan was captivated by Kale's description. "What role does gravity play in all of this? Wouldn't you have to defy gravity to travel through time?"

Kale grinned. "Actually, gravity is an essential part of the equation. We need to travel faster than the speed of light to break the gravitational attraction of the earth. The only thing known to science with that kind of power is a black hole."

"A black hole? Isn't that the result of a dying star? Is it really possible to create a black hole?"

"I believe it's totally possible. I've been working on a design that emulates the gravity produced by a dying star, but for the life of me, I can't figure out what I'm doing wrong."

Jordan's eyes grew wide. "Are you saying you've produced a black hole right out there in our barn?"

Kale looked Jordan squarely in the eye. "That's exactly what I am saying, or, rather, that's what I'm trying to do."

"Get out of here," Jordan exclaimed. "I don't believe you."

"You've seen what I've been working on out there for the past two years."

"That pile of junk in the barn?" Jordan sat back in her chair. "No way."

Kale ran his hand through his hair. "Well, considering it hasn't worked yet, you might be right. But, yes, that pile of junk is going to create a black hole."

Jordan tried hard to hide her grin. "Forgive me for laughing, but your time machine is just a collection of spinning rings. How on earth can that produce a black hole?"

"In theory, if I can generate enough energy while they're spinning, the centrifugal force should generate enough gravitational pull away from the center to create a black hole. An object in the center of that black hole will be sucked into the space-time continuum."

"In theory," Jordan pointed out.

Kale nodded. "In theory."

Jordan was about to question the stability of Kale's ideas when the waitress approached with their check. Kale paid for their meal. When he returned, Jordan was staring at a slip of paper.

"What's that you've got there?"

"It's her airwave code," she replied.

Kale's eyebrows shot up. He looked from Jordan to the waitress.

Jordan grabbed the front of Kale's shirt and dragged his face down to hers. "Say one word and you're dead meat, you got it?"

Kale grinned. "No clue, huh? Did you forget to turn your gaydar on?"

Once in the parking lot, Kale turned to Jordan. "So, why the hit and run?"

"What?"

"You were flirting with her, but when she gave you her airwave code, you ran like a scared rabbit."

Jordan looked down at the paper in her hands. "I'm too busy with our research to engage in a relationship."

"No, Jordan. You're too busy avoiding another heartache. This one may turn out to be different. She seemed nice. Why don't you give it a try? Not everyone is like Susan."

"I don't know. I'm in the middle of remodeling, and the new implant will be ready in a few weeks. I don't have time for a new relationship."

Kale brightened. "So, you've decided to go for it? The new implant, I mean."

Jordan saw his excitement and smiled. "A few weeks in this chair, and I'm more sure than ever that I can't spend my entire life like this. Not if I can get myself up and walking and maybe ensure that no one else has to spend his or her life in this contraption."

"Hallelujah!" Kale said.

CHAPTER 4

Jordan sat patiently in Peter's office, waiting for him to return from his lecture. She glanced at the medical degrees that adorned his office walls and thought about what an unlikely trio she, Kale, and Peter made. They'd become a team four years earlier, working on the spinal implant prototype. Jordan had lost both of her parents in an accident two years before, and she'd been living alone on the family farm. The only significant person in her life was her girlfriend, Susan Daley.

Jordan sighed as a familiar wave of sadness washed over her. She and Susan were together for two years, until the first implant. Once Jordan had her mobility and independence restored, Susan ended their relationship. Two more years had passed since then. Two years of avoiding serious relationships. Two years of "hit and run" encounters.

Jordan thought about her relationship with Peter Michaels. Peter was quite a stuffed shirt in the beginning, very prim and proper. It wasn't until they were working together in the lab that he began to loosen up and show what Kale called his human side.

Jordan's thoughts were interrupted by Peter's entrance. Peter immediately bent at the waist and enveloped Jordan in a fatherly hug. "Good afternoon, Jordan. I'm thrilled that you've decided to proceed with the implant. Kale called me at home last night with the good news."

Peter circled his desk and sat down.

Jordan said, "I have to admit that I'm nervous. Finding myself back in this chair after two years of freedom was a pretty devastating blow. If it were to happen again, I don't know if I could survive psychologically. I'm scared and more than a little skeptical."

Peter nodded. "That's understandable." He leaned forward. "My turn to be honest. I have to admit that I'm surprised the first implant lasted as long as it did. After all, it was only a prototype. For you to realize two years of use from it is truly amazing."

"How long do you expect the new implant to last?"

Peter stood and walked around his desk. He sat on the corner facing Jordan, his arms crossed in front of him. "We're hoping it lasts for several years, long enough to perfect the regrowth of synapses. Our goal is to give you uninterrupted mobility while the electrical stimulus prompts the regeneration of your spinal column. We have a lot to do between now and then, but I believe this new implant will go a long way toward helping us in the regeneration process."

Jordan leaned forward. "Will this second implant restore feeling as well as mobility? The first implant allowed me to look and move and live something close to a normal life, but I had no feeling in my lower extremities, nothing beyond an awareness of when I needed to relieve myself, and I only felt that because of the monitor in my bladder."

Peter squeezed Jordan's shoulder lightly. "The new implant is designed to restore connections to all nerve cells, not just those associated with mobility. If we succeed, we'll be light-years ahead in figuring out the regeneration process. It's my personal goal to help you live a totally normal life, Jordan. If I can do that for you, it will be my greatest accomplishment. The biggest drawback will be recharging the energy source."

"That's a small price to pay for mobility. With the adapter Kale developed, I've got access to all kinds of energy sources. The worst part has been learning new sleeping habits."

Peter rose to his feet once more and sat at his desk. He opened Jordan's chart. "It's only been a few weeks since we removed the last implant. You'll need additional time to heal, say, three or four more weeks. After that, we'll evaluate how far the new implant has developed. We'll make a decision based on that and on your post-surgery test results. Sound okay to you?"

Jordan exhaled deeply. "Okay."

Peter closed the folder and tossed it aside. "Until then, you need to give yourself ample time to heal—no overdoing it. Kale tells me you've started remodeling your home. That's a good thing, as long as you don't take over and start doing the heavy work yourself. Don't you give me that indignant look, young lady. I know how stubborn you can be."

Jordan didn't answer. She turned her hover-chair and made for the door.

"Jordan…" Peter said in a warning tone.

Jordan glanced over her shoulder, fighting to hide her smile. "All right. Nag, nag, nag."

Peter smiled back as she turned and glided down the hall toward the lab.

* * *

Kale pulled Jordan's hover-chair from the trunk and guided it to the passenger door. He pushed the chair in as close as possible and stood behind it, holding it firmly in place as Jordan placed her hands on the armrests and hoisted herself into the chair in a single smooth motion.

"You're pretty good at that," Kale said.

"Unfortunately, practice makes perfect. I just hope it's one trick I can put behind me."

Kale pushed Jordan toward the house. "What did Peter have to say about the implant?"

"We've agreed to approach it with guarded optimism. We're both hopeful, but I'm not going to set myself up for a huge disappointment if it doesn't work."

Jordan opened the front door, and Kale pushed her through and into the house. They stopped short as they entered the kitchen. "Holy shit! Look at this place."

Exposed beams and insulation hung from the walls and ceiling, and a thick layer of dust covered everything. Kale was dismayed. "It's going to take some work to get this kitchen clean enough to cook in."

"Well, better break out the cleaning supplies 'cause I'm starved."

For the next hour, Jordan and Kale worked to clean the construction residue from the counter tops and appliances. Before long, they were seated in front of the holovision, enjoying grilled cheese sandwiches and tomato soup. Partway through the meal, Jordan picked up her bowl of soup and clumsily spilled it in her lap.

Kale jumped to his feet and grabbed the bowl from her hands, cursing as the hot liquid burned his fingers. "Damn. Quick, get those jeans off."

"Kale! Kale, it doesn't hurt. Really."

In the immediacy of the accident, Kale failed to register that Jordan's condition made her indifferent to the burning soup. He scooped her up in his arms and laid her flat on the couch, pulling off her jeans.

"Kale! What are you doing?"

He grabbed the cuffs and tugged hard, yanking the jeans cleanly off Jordan's body. He threw the jeans on the floor and pointed at Jordan's legs. "I'm saving you from blisters. See?"

Jordan raised herself with her forearms and looked down. Large red blotches covered both thighs. "Help me to sit."

Kale grabbed her ankles and swung her legs around while Jordan pushed her upper body erect. She reached down and ran her hands over her burned thighs. "Wow. It still feels hot."

Kale found a cold pack and placed it on Jordan's reddened skin. "I hope we caught it before it caused too much damage."

Jordan touched the side of Kale's face. "Thank you. I really appreciate your looking out for me."

Kale blushed under her praise. "Nothing to it. Sorry if I was a bit rough. I guess I acted before I thought."

Jordan grinned. "Oh really? I thought you liked forcibly stripping helpless women."

Kale turned bright red. "Ah, gee, Jordan. I…"

Jordan laughed. "Relax, I'm just teasing. You did a good thing here. Thank you. Now, could you do one more thing for me?"

"Sure, anything."

"How about finding a blanket to cover my scantily-clad ass?"

* * *

The next morning, Jordan was up and dressed before the contractors arrived. When Kale emerged from his room, she was in the kitchen removing a pan of muffins from the oven. She smiled up at him. "Good morning, sleepyhead."

Kale bent over the muffins and inhaled deeply. "Hmm, that smells heavenly, but I thought I was supposed to do breakfast on weekdays."

"I was up early and too hungry to wait for you. Pour the coffee?"

"You got it." Kale poured two cups and carried them to the table. He placed one in front of Jordan, grabbed two muffins, and sat down. "How are your legs?"

Jordan shrugged. "I suppose if I could feel them, they'd be tender, but so far, no blisters."

"That's good. Sounds like we caught it in time. So, what's on the agenda for today?"

"The contractors are supposed to start ripping out my bedroom walls today, and we've got a second crew coming to begin restoring the kitchen. Would you mind helping me pick out cabinets? The contractors will need them in a week or so."

"You want me to pick out cabinets?"

"Sure. You use the kitchen more than I do. My culinary skills are pretty much limited to soup and muffin mix. We might as well design the layout around what's convenient for you. I don't really have a preference other than to keep it as original as possible."

"Cool. I could probably be home by three o'clock. We're making the final adjustments to the sensory connections on the new implant. Our goal is to have it ready for the first test subject tomorrow morning. I'll call you before I leave the lab so you can be ready when I get here."

Jordan sat back in her chair and nodded. "Sounds like a plan. Now get going before Peter calls out the National Guard. Oh, and take a few of those muffins with you so I won't eat them."

Kale finished his coffee and took two more muffins. "All right then, I'll see you this afternoon. Have a great day." Kale kissed her on the cheek.

"You, too. Good luck with the final sensory tests."

No sooner had Kale left than she heard a knock at the door. She maneuvered her chair to the door and welcomed the contractors. The foreman took off his baseball cap and greeted her formally. "Good morning, ma'am."

Jordan touched the man's arm. "Tom, didn't I ask you yesterday to call me by my first name?"

Tom twisted his cap between his hands and blushed. "Well, to be honest, ma'am, for the life of me, I can't remember what you said your name is."

Jordan laughed. "I applaud your honesty, Tom, truly I do. My name is Jordan."

Tom grinned. "Jordan. So, do you still want to give us a hand with the demolition, ma'am... I mean Jordan?"

Jordan clapped her hands excitedly. "You bet I do. Just let me know how I can help."

Moments later, baseball hat perched on her head, Jordan sat in front of one of her bedroom walls, polarizer in hand. For the next half hour, she used the tool to extract nails from the sheetrock. She freed the lower half of one sheet, pushed the elevation button on her hover-char, and floated up so that she could reach the top of the sheetrock. Once it was loose enough, she grabbed it with both hands and pulled hard.

Jordan watched the wallboard fall to the floor. "What a mess. Look at all this junk between the walls. I wonder how it got here." Jordan reached for the polarizer once more and poked at the objects she found resting near the floor between the studs. "Insulation, an old sock, shredded paper... critters must have dragged all of this stuff in here."

She moved on to the second piece of sheetrock. When she grasped the wallboard and pushed it aside, an object fell forward, hitting her on the legs. "What the hell is this?" she exclaimed. It was rectangular-shaped and wrapped in cloth. Jordan pushed it off her legs, and it fell to the floor with a clunk.

Intrigued, Jordan reached down and retrieved the object from the floor. She removed the cloth wrapping. It was a book. Jordan opened it and read aloud.

"This is the private diary of Maggie Downs, age sixteen." Jordan held her breath as she felt a surge of warmth spread through her. "2004," she whispered. "Well, I'll be! That was a hundred years ago."

A noise behind Jordan startled her. "How are you doing in here?" Tom's voice boomed.

Jordan quickly snapped the book closed and looked up at the man. "Oh, you scared me, Look at what I found inside the wall." Jordan held out the book. "It's a diary."

Tom took the book and fanned the pages. "I can't tell you how many times we've found odd things between the walls of an old home. You can learn a lot about the former residents that way. Is this the only one you've found?"

Jordan took the book back from Tom. "Do you think there might be more?"

"Let's see," Tom said. He picked up the polarizer and removed the next wallboard.

By the time all of the boards were removed, they had discovered five more diaries.

* * *

Jordan was waiting outside in the driveway when Kale arrived home to take her cabinet shopping. She waved her hands at him, signaling that she wanted him to hurry. Kale glided the vehicle to a stop and climbed out. As he reached for the passenger door, Jordan moved her chair close and prepared to transfer herself to the vehicle. Kale noticed the wide-eyed look on his friend's face. "You seem quite excited this afternoon."

Jordan seated herself and fastened her seatbelt. Kale looked at her as he climbed into the driver's seat and fastened his own seatbelt. "In fact, you look like you're about to explode. Want to share?"

Jordan turned in her seat, her hands moving quickly as she spoke. "You won't believe what happened this morning. It was incredible."

Kale guided the vehicle down the driveway. "Whatever it is, it must be big. I've never seen you this animated."

"You bet it's big. Tom and I were—"

"Who's Tom?" Kale asked.

"The foreman of the construction crew. Anyway, Tom and I were tearing down the sheetrock in my bedroom and guess what we found hidden in the walls?"

"You were tearing down sheetrock? You're not supposed to be overdoing it," he scolded.

Jordan's frustration was evident. "Will you please shut up and listen? I wasn't overdoing it. All I did was pull a few nails. Tom did the rest. Anyway, guess what we found?"

Kale thought for a moment. "I haven't a clue."

"We found six diaries hidden in my bedroom walls. Can you believe it?"

Kale frowned. "Six diaries? Who wrote them?"

Jordan tucked her hair behind her ears. "I only looked closely at the first one. It was written by a girl named Maggie Downs in the year 2004. She was only sixteen. How cool is that?"

"2004? Wow. That was over one hundred years ago. What kind of shape are they in?"

"Actually, pretty good. The print is a little faded, but structurally, all six of the books are pretty much intact. Each one was wrapped in cloth, so they were shielded from the dust."

Kale glanced at Jordan. "Were they all written by this kid, Maggie?"

"I don't know. I assume they were. Like I said, I haven't looked at all six books yet. By the time Tom and I finished ripping down the wallboard and clearing out the mess, it was time to clean up to meet you. I'll take a closer look at them after dinner."

Kale let out a sigh of relief. "Good. I was feeling guilty about leaving you alone tonight while I worked on the machine."

"There's the specialty cabinet shop, Kale. Turn right here."

Kale parked and retrieved Jordan's chair from the storage compartment. Within moments, they were perusing the aisles, looking at various styles of kitchen cabinetry.

"May I help you find something?"

Kale shook hands with the salesman. "Yes. We're restoring the kitchen of an old farmhouse, and we'd like to keep things as original as possible. Authentic hardwoods."

"I think I have just what you need," said the salesman. "Follow me."

*　*　*

Kale slammed the trunk lid and climbed into the driver's seat. He glanced at Jordan. "I really like the cabinets we picked out. Thank you for allowing me to choose them."

"No problem. You do most of the cooking anyway." Jordan glanced at the time projected on the vehicle's console. "Hey, it's only 4:00 p.m. I wonder if the town records office is still open?"

"It should be," Kale said. "I think most of the town offices are open until 5:00 p.m. Why the sudden interest in the records office?"

"I want to research the history of my farm from the time Maggie Downs lived there until now. I looked online, but the records are so old that I couldn't find anything of substance. After finding those diaries this morning, it's all I can think about."

CHAPTER 5

My name is Maggie. I am sixteen years old. This is my first diary. I am amused with myself as I sit to write these words. You see, I have never been very comfortable expressing my feelings, and I will not allow myself to become caught up in the typical emotional frenzy of so many girls my age. So why am I writing now? Well, I'm getting ahead of myself. Let me start at the beginning.

I was born Margaret Michelle Downs on April 16, 1988 to Gary and Sharon Downs at the Fletcher Allen Medical Center in Burlington, Vermont. I really hate the name Margaret. I was named after my grandmother. Don't get me wrong—I love my Nana, but her name sounds so old-fashioned. I prefer to be called Maggie.

We live on a 250-acre farm in Shelburne, Vermont, with miles of waterfront on Lake Champlain. We raise Mustang horses. I've made it clear to my parents that when they are ready to retire, I'm interested in buying the farm from them. Someday, I hope to start a riding school here for underprivileged and handicapped kids. We have about fifty horses right now, which is plenty for Mom and Dad and me to handle.

Many of our horses have won blue ribbons and national titles. We take them to competitions all around the country, but my favorite shows are right here in Vermont at the Champlain Valley and Tunbridge Fairs. The awards aren't huge, but there's something wonderful about a small country fair. Cotton candy, sausage and peppers, and fried bread dough are among the things I look forward to the most. There is nothing like it anywhere.

I am currently a sophomore at Mt. Mansfield Union High School. My plan is to graduate in two years, then go to the University of Vermont in Burlington to study agriculture and animal husbandry. When I graduate from UVM, my parents have agreed to allow me a more active role in planning programs for the horses and running the basic functions of the farm. I will have to be ready to take on more responsibility around the farm before they're ready to retire.

Well, I've been rambling here, and I haven't explained yet why I started this diary. I guess one reason is because I don't know how to find the words to say out loud what I am about to put down in print. You see, I'm not like the other kids at school. I'm different in a lot of ways. The girls I go to school with are all about acting silly, making an impression on the boys, and competing with each other for attention. They are so immature! There is so much jealousy and name-calling and so many cliques. I almost hate to admit that girls can be so brutal to each other. I always thought guys were rough and tough, but the girls have them beat by a mile!

The girls think I'm pretty weird because I don't care what the boys think. I'm not into wearing makeup and dressing up in trashy-looking outfits like most of them do. That's such a waste of time. Quite frankly, I find the boys boring. Their immature macho behavior pretty much makes me sick. I... damn—this is hard! I sometimes wonder what's wrong with me. I just don't get it. I mean, what is it they find so attractive about sweaty, sex-crazed boys? I actually went on a date with a kid in my class this year, and he couldn't keep his hands off me. He made me feel used and dirty. By the end of the evening, I felt nothing but disgust for him, yet the other girls I hang out with think he's "to die for." I just don't get it!

Jordan was fighting to keep her eyes open. She glanced at the clock on the bedside table. It was 11:30 p.m. She was exhausted. She'd spent nearly the entire day working with Tom, ripping out the old tile floor in her kitchen. Jordan yawned loudly as her eyes closed once more. Forcing them open again, she looked at the book in front of her. "Okay, I give up. Got to get some sleep." Jordan placed a bookmark in the diary, closed the book, and placed it on her nightstand. She was asleep as soon as her head hit the pillow.

The alarm clock beeped loudly. Jordan rolled over and groaned. "Why did I stay up so late last night?"

She pushed her upper body forward until she was sitting with her legs dangling off the side of the bed. Transferring herself to her hover-chair seemed more difficult than usual. The muscles in her shoulders were sore.

The aroma of muffins drew her down the hallway. "Wow—that smells great, Kale."

At the end of the hall, Jordan stopped and stared. "What the hell is going on here?" Jordan looked around at the unfamiliar furnishings: tan sectional sofa, oak coffee tables, and a very large entertainment center with a widescreen TV. Sunlight flooded the room through lacy white curtains. Jordan frowned.

"Kale, what have you done to my house? Kale?" Jordan moved her chair toward the kitchen. "Huh. He must have left for the lab already."

The smell of muffins and coffee grew stronger. "Something isn't right here," she mumbled. "Kale wouldn't leave without waking me first."

As she reached for the kitchen door, it suddenly swung open and a middle-aged woman poked her head out. "Maggie, time to get up. You'll be late for school."

Maggie? Did she say Maggie? What the hell was going on here?

Jordan reached again for the kitchen door. A young redheaded girl came up from behind and brushed by her. The girl pushed the door open and burst into the kitchen, leaving the door ajar.

The girl grabbed a muffin and said, "Mom, why did you let me sleep so late? I'll miss the bus."

The woman placed a kiss on the girl's cheek. "You're so dramatic, Maggie. The bus won't be here for another few minutes. Sit down and have some juice with your muffin."

Maggie sat at the table and tucked her unruly red hair behind her ears. Her mother handed her a glass of orange juice. "Thanks. Is Dad calling the vet this afternoon? I'd like to be here when the mare gives birth."

Maggie's mother poured herself a cup of coffee and sat at the table. "If she lasts that long. With any luck, you'll be home before anything happens. The vet doesn't believe she'll foal until later tonight."

Jordan sat in the doorway, not believing the scene before her. She inched her way into the room. "Ah, excuse me," she said. "Excuse me, but what you are doing in my kitchen?"

"Your bus is coming, sweetie," said the woman. "Have a good day at school."

Maggie smiled at her mother and grabbed the backpack that was sitting on the end of the table. "I'll see you this afternoon. Let's hope the mare waits for me to get home. Love you, Mom," the girl called before the door closed behind her.

Jordan sat there, incredulous. The woman carried her coffee cup and Maggie's juice glass to the sink, rinsing them before placing them in an old-fashioned dish washer. *What happened to the sonic cleanser?* It was then that Jordan realized the kitchen was intact. The walls, the ceiling, even the floor that she had just spent the previous day scraping—everything was in order.

"What's happening here?" she asked aloud.

A searing pain shot through Jordan's head. She grasped her head between her hands. "Oh, my God, make it stop! Please make it stop." The woman remained oblivious to Jordan's presence as the pain increased and her throat began to seize. Jordan jerkily moved her chair to the sink. She needed a glass of water. She stretched to reach the glasses on the bottom shelf, but in her haste, she neglected to stabilize her chair. Before she realized what was happening, the chair tilted forward and slipped out from under her. Unconscious, Jordan fell to the floor.

Jordan awoke to an incessant pounding on her bedroom door. Kale called, "Jordan, get your carcass out of bed. The contractors will catch you in your skivvies if you don't get moving. It's not like you to sleep so late."

Jordan looked over at her clock. It was 7:00 a.m. She blinked to clear her vision and then pushed herself into a seated position. She felt disoriented.

"Come on, get a move on. There's coffee and muffins waiting for you in the kitchen. If you don't get up soon, I'll feed them all to Tom and his crew."

Jordan looked at the closed door. *Coffee and muffins? The dream. It must have been the aroma of muffins, but it was so real.* Jordan pushed the remnants of the dream aside and called to Kale, "I'll be right out. Don't you dare give my muffins away."

Jordan eased into her hover-chair and made her way to the kitchen. She slowed as she approached the living room. She stopped and looked around at the familiar Victorian and Queen Anne furnishings. Back to normal. She sighed with relief. It was only a dream. Jordan muttered to herself, "I don't know what you ate last night, Lewis, but whatever it was, you'd better avoid it like the plague from now on. It gives you nightmares."

As Jordan approached the kitchen door, it swung inward. A feeling of déjà vu washed over her. She half expected Maggie's mother to appear. Instead, Kale's familiar face poked out.

"Ah, there you are. I was just about to yell at you again. I hope you're hungry."

Jordan grinned. "Good morning to you, too, and yes, I'm famished."

"Good. Blueberry muffins and fresh coffee await, my lady."

Jordan laughed. "Lead on, fair knight, or risk skid marks on your face."

Kale chuckled and held the door open for Jordan. He followed her into the kitchen and grabbed a sanitary wipe to clean the dust from the table. "I'll be glad when this room is finished. It's kind of tough to produce an edible meal in the middle of all this mess."

Jordan looked around and readily agreed. She looked at the floor, stripped clean of the old faded tile. "I knew I stripped this floor yesterday."

Kale frowned. "Are you all right?"

"Huh? I'm sorry. What did you say?"

"I asked if you were all right. You seem a little preoccupied this morning."

Jordan moved her chair closer to the table and grasped her coffee cup. She sat and stared into the dark liquid. "I'm fine. I had a really strange dream last night. Kind of creeped me out."

Kale sipped his coffee. "A dream, huh? Want to talk about it?"

Jordan shrugged. "It was nothing, really. You're just going to say it's a bunch of mumbo jumbo."

He touched her hand. "If it creeped you out, it wasn't nothing. And for the record, I happen to believe dreams have meaning."

"Really? I've always thought dreams were your subconscious thoughts brought to life, so to speak. You know, your hidden thoughts, fears, and dreams."

Kale nodded. "I can see where that would make sense. You must have some pretty scary thoughts if this particular dream made you so uncomfortable."

Jordan frowned. "I'm not really sure how it made me feel. It wasn't creepy in a scary kind of way, it was just... I don't know. In every dream I've had since I broke my back sixteen years ago, I have never been in my chair. I'm totally intact and totally unharmed, walking around like the accident never happened. Every dream, that is, until the one I had last night."

"You were in your chair in the dream?"

"Yeah. It was way too real. It didn't feel like a dream."

"Well," Kale said, "I've got to get to work. Promise me you'll tell me about it tonight?"

Jordan nodded. There was a knock at the kitchen door.

Kale rose to his feet. "That would be Tom," he said.

"Good morning, Mr. Simmons."

Kale placed his hand on Tom's shoulder. "Please, call me Kale. My dad is Mr. Simmons. Help yourself to some coffee and muffins. I'm off to work."

Kale grabbed his briefcase, took another muffin, and bid them both a good day. Seconds later, he was gone.

Jordan moved her chair to the cupboard and poured a cup of coffee for Tom.

"Okay, Tom, fill me in on the plans for today."

* * *

Kale noticed the new ceiling as soon as he stepped in the door. "Wow, that looks great!"

"Kale, is that you?" Jordan called.

Kale made his way into the living room where Jordan was curled up on the couch, reading Maggie's diaries. He dropped his briefcase on a nearby chair, kissed Jordan on the cheek, and said, "Hey, you. How was your day?"

Jordan smiled and patted the sofa beside her. "We got a lot done today. The kitchen ceiling was first, but since the cabinets won't be here for another week, we put up a new ceiling and walls in my room. My room is a wreck right now—the bed is in the middle of the floor—but Tom thinks it will only take a few more days to finish the floor and trim work."

"You aren't being too much of a pest to the guys, are you?"

Jordan punched her friend in the arm. "When am I ever a pest?" she demanded, quickly adding, "Don't answer that. I didn't realize home repairs were so much work."

Kale nodded. "Judging by what's already been done, it will all be worth it in the end."

"I think you're right. So, tell me about your day."

Kale grinned and repositioned himself on the couch so that he was facing her. "We've been banging our heads against the wall trying to figure out how to make the synapse connections. Today, it all came together. We'll try our second test with the lab animals tomorrow. If things work out the way we hope, the implant should be ready in about two weeks."

"Wow. I see Peter again on Monday. Everything should be fine. I'm feeling great."

"I think you should talk to Peter about coming back to work. You really should be involved in the final testing and preparations. After all, you've put a lot of work into this thing as well. It would be great for you to be there and have a voice in the wrap-up."

"I agree. Being out of the loop for the past few weeks has been hell. I've missed being in the middle of the action. I'll talk to Peter about it on Monday."

Kale stood up. "Okay, sounds like a plan. So, what do you want for dinner?"

* * *

"Mmm, this is good. You're a great cook."

Jordan and Kale were sitting side by side on the couch with plates of spaghetti balanced on their laps. Large pillows were positioned on each side of Jordan, propping her up.

"My grandma taught me well."

Jordan looked over at him and grinned. "She forgot to teach you how to comb your hair."

Kale tried to keep from smiling. "What do you mean by that?"

Jordan coyly covered her mouth with her hand and batted her eyelashes. "Did I say that out loud?"

"Very funny, Jord. Very funny."

She grinned at Kale. "I thought so. Are you doing the dishes tonight or am I?"

Kale rose to his feet and took Jordan's plate from her. "You go ahead and read your old diaries. I'll do the dishes. Then we'll talk about this dream of yours, okay?"

Jordan looked up at Kale. "How about you rinse, I'll load the sonic cleanser, and we'll talk about the dream while we work?"

"Okay then. Let's do it." Kale scooped Jordan from the couch and gently placed her in her hover-chair. "Lead the way."

Kale handed the first dish to Jordan. "Tell me about the dream."

"Well, I dreamed that I woke up at 6:00 a.m., just like I do every morning. I got up, got dressed, and headed for the kitchen. The moment I opened my bedroom door, I could smell muffins and coffee. I thought you were treating me to breakfast, but when I got to the living room, it was all changed. My furniture was gone, and in its place was this stuff that looked like it was from the early 2000s. That really freaked me out. I thought you might be responsible, so I went to the kitchen looking for you—so I could kick your ass. But when I got there, the door opened and a middle-aged woman poked her head out. She called out for Maggie. Can you believe it?"

Kale handed Jordan another dish. "Maggie? You mean the Maggie from the diaries?"

"Yes, or at least, I think so. Just then, this young red-haired girl breezes by me like I'm invisible and goes into the kitchen."

"What did she look like?"

"She looked to be fifteen or sixteen years old."

Kale frowned. "I can see why the dream creeped you out. What happened next?"

"The kid left for school and I asked the mother why they were in my house. She ignored me, and when I tried to get her attention, a really sharp pain shot through my head and my throat started to close up. I tried to reach for a glass of water, but my chair tilted forward and dumped me. The next thing I knew, you were pounding on my bedroom door."

Jordan loaded the last dish, and Kale rinsed out the sink. "It was obviously a dream, Jordan. When you came out of your room after I woke you up, things were normal, right? I'm sure reading the diaries put those thoughts in your head."

"I'm sure you're right. But it seemed so real. I could actually smell the muffins and coffee, and I was in my chair."

"Do you think you'll be all right alone tonight? I'd like to get back to work on the machine."

Jordan smiled. "Sweetie, you don't need my permission to go off on your own. Please, don't feel you need to entertain me. We've had this discussion before, remember? Sheesh. Sometimes we act more like an old married couple than roommates. Go work on your invention. I've got some reading to catch up on, okay? Now scoot."

CHAPTER 6

Kale walked around the time machine several times, hoping that through close examination, he would find the flaws in the system. After several moments, he returned to his desk in the corner and shuffled through the blueprints he'd used to build the machine.

"Okay. If I've designed this right, the spinning rings should cause gravity to be pushed away from the center, and voilà! A black hole. So why was the boot still there?" Kale stared at the machine. "There must still be some gravity in the center of the sphere. How do I prove that? I wonder if it would help to use a tracer."

Kale placed a bucket densely packed with paper in the center of the sphere and lit the paper on fire. When he was satisfied with the quantity of smoke it emitted, he walked over to the control panel and powered up the sphere. As the sphere began to rotate and then pick up speed, the smoke moved toward the outer edges of the sphere. Kale waited several minutes until he was satisfied that conditions within the system had become stable. He carefully inspected the interior of the orb. There was a small trace of smoke in the center.

Kale powered the sphere down and released a long sigh. "Now I know what's wrong. Either the rings aren't spinning fast enough, or I need some counteractive force."

He sat back in his chair and sighed. "Oh hell, I need some time to think about this." He looked at his watch. He had been in the barn for three hours. "Damn. Time sure flies when you're having fun. I think I'll call it a night."

Kale returned to the house to find Jordan still reading in the living room. He threw himself down on the couch, the air of defeat hanging over him.

Jordan closed her book. "No luck, huh?"

"Am I that transparent?"

"Clear as glass. Want to talk about it?"

Kale rose to his feet and began to pace. "I figured out that I still have some gravity in the center of the sphere. That's why the boot was still there. I need zero gravity in the center for this to work."

"How do you do that?"

"That's what I need to figure out. I need to create a counteracting force of some sort."

Jordan tilted her head to one side. "What about a second set of rings? You know, a smaller set in the middle that spin in the opposite direction?"

Kale looked at Jordan for several long moments. A parade of emotions marched across his face. "I need to think about this. Look, I'm going to bed. I'll see you in the morning, okay?"

"Okay, sleep tight."

Jordan threw her soiled clothing into the laundry basket then slipped a nightshirt over her head. She settled in the bed, lying on her back, close to the edge. Within moments, she felt herself drifting off to sleep.

She snapped awake when the door to her room flew open. A young woman with unruly red hair stormed in and slammed the door behind her. Jordan watched the girl pace the room, gesticulating wildly as she walked.

"How dare she? How dare she call me such names? I'm so angry I could spit nails!"

Jordan lifted a hand to get the girl's attention. "What are you doing in here?"

"She called me a lezbo. I'll show her who's a lezbo. How dare she?" The girl continued to rant and pace, then she suddenly threw herself onto the bed next to Jordan. The girl stared up at the ceiling. "Why on earth would she think I'm a lesbian? Because I don't have a boyfriend? Because I don't wear dresses and makeup? So what if I don't like boys. So what if I feel more comfortable with girls. So what if I dress like a tomboy. That doesn't mean I'm a lesbian, does it?"

Jordan looked at the girl. "Are you attracted to women?" she asked.

The girl continued to stare at the ceiling. Suddenly, she sat up. "Am I attracted to women? Am I?" Her hand flew to her mouth to cover the gasp that escaped. "Holy smokes! I am. I am attracted to women. She was right." The girl threw her legs over the side of the bed and sat with her back to Jordan. She dropped her face into her hands and sighed deeply. "What am I going to do?"

Jordan propped herself up on her elbow and faced the girl. "It's not a death sentence, you know. All it really means is that you love women. Love is love, regardless of how it's packaged," she said soothingly.

The girl stood up and began to pace again. "How will I tell my parents? What will they say? God, my life is over." The girl looked around with a panicked expression on her face and then headed toward the bedroom door. "I need some fresh air." A moment later, she was gone.

Jordan fell back and stared at the ceiling, confused. *What the hell is going on here? This can't be real. My mind must be playing tricks on me, or it must be another dream. Yeah, that's it, another dream.*

She paused for a moment and thought about the girl. She thought about how it felt to have her in such close proximity. *She certainly is attractive. I could feel her touching me, and she smelled really good, like patchouli.*

She realized where her thoughts were headed. *Jordan, get a grip. She's a child for Christ's sake—and she's dead. She lived in the past. Yes, she's gorgeous. Yes, that wild red hair is very sexy. Yes, if she were here today, and closer to your own age, you might be interested in pursuing her, but Jesus, woman, she lived one hundred years ago. Go to sleep, Jordan. She's a ghost. Get her out of your mind.*

Jordan closed her eyes and soon, with some effort, she drifted off to sleep.

* * *

It was Saturday, and Jordan was feeling refreshed, the best she'd felt in the few weeks since her surgery. She was sore from her work on the house the previous day, but it was a good kind of sore. Soon, she was showered, dressed, and in the kitchen, making breakfast.

When it was ready, she knocked on Kale's door. There was no reply. She knocked again. Nothing. She gently pushed the door open. Kale hadn't slept in his bed.

"Kale?" she called. There was no answer. Jordan returned to the kitchen just as Kale came through the back door. "Where the hell have you been?" she asked, a little gruffer than she intended.

Kale's face was wild with excitement. "In the barn. Jordan, you gave me a lot to think about last night. I couldn't sleep, so I worked on your theory all night."

"You stayed up all night? Are you crazy? When do you plan to sleep?"

"Right after I eat this wonderful breakfast." Kale smiled warmly as he carried the food to the table. He retrieved the coffee carafe and poured a cup for Jordan.

"Thanks," she said. "You worked on the machine all night? Any progress?"

Kale sat down. "Lots. Hmm, this is good," he said through a mouthful of scrambled eggs. "Before I went to the barn, I did some research on your idea about the internal rotating sphere. According to my calculations, the second set of rings would also rotate the black hole, which should generate the energy we need for time travel. You're a genius, Jord!" Kale grinned. "I worked all night to retrofit the machine with a second set of rings. We now have our black hole containment device. All that's left to do is testing."

Kale yawned. Jordan reached for his empty dish and placed it on top of her own. "Now that we've established that I'm a genius, my next scientific theory is that you need some sleep. You look exhausted."

"Let me help with the dishes."

Jordan slapped his hand as he reached for a dish.

"I don't think so. Go to bed. I'll take care of these."

"Are you sure? I hate leaving you alone while I sleep the day away."

"I'm a big girl. Go to bed."

Kale kissed Jordan on the cheek and retired to his bedroom. Jordan loaded the dishes into the sonic cleanser before settling in the living room to resume reading the diaries.

The first diary covered Maggie's sixteenth year. Most of the entries described life on the farm or made comments about school. There wasn't much that Jordan found exciting, but having made the commitment to read all the diaries, she pushed on. When she finished, she set the first diary aside and opened the second. The first entry was dated June 12, 2006. Maggie was eighteen years old.

I am a lesbian. There, I've said it. As I reread this, it looks odd in print, but it feels good to admit it. I am a lesbian. Realizing this fact came as a shock to me. I knew I was different, but I didn't understand how different until Amy Gokey pointed it out to me today at school. She called me a lezbo. I was shocked to hear that word used to describe me.

Jordan gasped. Maggie was describing Jordan's dream. She read on.

I was furious with her. My first thought was, how dare she? I couldn't wait for the school day to end. I couldn't wait to get home. I marched right to my bedroom and paced the floor, trying to understand why Amy would say such a thing. Finally, I threw myself on the bed and had a real good talk with the ceiling.

Jordan's heart began to beat rapidly. She closed the diary for a moment to calm her nerves. When she picked it up again, she read,

I explored the various reasons Amy might have come to that conclusion. It's true that I don't have a boyfriend, and I don't wear dresses or makeup. Hell, I don't even like boys that much, and not at all in a sexual way. I feel much more comfortable with the girls. Amy said I dress like a boy. I've always been a tomboy. I see nothing wrong with that. All of these things don't necessarily mean I am a lesbian— at least I didn't think they did.

But as I was lying there on my bed, I thought hard about it. Was I attracted to women? A wave of heat rushed over me as I really thought about that question. I have never felt anything like it in my life. Then realization dawned... it could only mean one thing. I am attracted to women. I am a lesbian. Amy is right. Now what do I do? What will my parents think? What will they say? How do I tell them? At that moment, I felt like my life was over.

Unexpected tears filled Jordan's eyes as she continued reading.

As I stared at the ceiling, I felt overwhelmed, confined by my secret. I needed to get out, to escape. I needed fresh air, so I went for a walk. When I returned, I felt immensely better. I realized that being a lesbian is not a death sentence. All it really means is that I love women. What's wrong with that? Love is love. Does it really matter how it's packaged? I feel liberated. I feel good about who I am. I am Maggie Michelle Downs. I am eighteen years old. I am a lesbian, and I am okay with that.

Jordan's vision blurred as she replaced her bookmark and closed the diary. A mixture of fear and tenderness filled her heart as she thought about Maggie. The dream was real! Was Maggie trying to talk to her? A warm feeling filled Jordan's stomach. Did she find the diaries by accident, or did Maggie want her to find them?

* * *

On Monday morning, Jordan rode to the lab with Kale. She waited with apprehension for her appointment with Peter, balancing herself on the edge of the examination table, her legs hanging limply over the side.

Peter came in and hugged his patient. "Hey there, Jordan. It's good to see you. Do you have any questions before we begin your exam?"

Jordan leaned forward. "Tell me about the new implant. How do you propose to reestablish the synapse connections in order to restore feeling as well as mobility?"

"Our immediate goal is to restore mobility, but, long-term, we believe the implant will stimulate nerve growth and permanently repair the synapses."

Jordan nodded. "Okay. How?"

Peter picked up a stylus and drew a diagram. Jordan leaned forward to afford herself a better view. "The device has six electrodes. Three are implanted above the injury, three are implanted below. The alternating current between the upper and lower sets of electrodes will encourage the nerves to grow toward each other. At some point, they will grow close enough to close the gap over the injury site and reestablish spinal function."

"Are you sure the new implant will restore all sensory response? Will I actually be able to feel things like heat and cold, pain and pleasure?"

Peter nodded. "The new implant will significantly change your life. Are you sure you want to do this?"

Jordan's head snapped up. "Yes," she responded immediately. "Yes, I am very sure. When will the implant be ready?"

"In about three weeks, maybe four. We'll need to prepare your nerve endings above and below the L1 vertebra to accept the new electrodes, and you'll need about two weeks to recover before we place the new implant. We'll need to schedule that in the next week or so. Any more questions?"

When Jordan didn't respond, Peter continued. "How are you feeling?"

Jordan perked up considerably. "I feel great. Don't get me wrong—it's been really frustrating being stuck in this chair again, but physically I'm coping quite well. I've even been able to help my contractors work on my house."

"You aren't overdoing it, are you? You had strict instructions not to do any heavy lifting."

"No, I've been taking it easy. I'm anxious to come back to work. Kale tells me you need to release me before the institute will allow me to return."

"Let's take a look at you and see if you're ready. We can do the tests for the electrode placement surgery at the same time."

Over the next quarter hour, Peter performed a battery of tests to gauge Jordan's strength and responsiveness to external stimuli. As expected, she had superior strength and responsiveness in her upper body but none below her waist.

Peter turned off the reflex probe and turned to Jordan. "I'm not surprised by the results so far. I really didn't expect any response from your lower body. Everything else looks good. All we have to do now is some blood work and a thoracic holograph. You can go to the lab today. We should have the results tomorrow."

"Can I go back to work?" Jordan asked anxiously.

"On one condition. You work only an eight-hour day. Understood?"

"Understood."

CHAPTER 7

When Kale and Jordan got home from work that afternoon, a transmission was waiting for them from the Shelburne Hall of Records. Jordan anxiously opened it and scanned its contents.

"It says here that the farm was owned by Gary and Sharon Downs from 1985 until 2019. Then a woman named Janneal Safford owned it from 2019 until 2031. It was purchased next by Leland and Marion McKenzie who owned it until 2048, when the deed was transferred to Carl and Rachel McKenzie... probably their son. Carl and Rachel sold the farm to my parents in 2071. I was born two years later. When my parents died, the deed passed to me."

"Let's see," Jordan continued. "Maggie was sixteen in 2004, so that means she was born in 1988, and she was my age in 2020. She was born eighty-five years before me. Hell, if she were still alive today, she'd be one-hundred seventeen years old."

"You know, Jordan, if she were born today, she might well live to be that old, but back in 1988, life expectancy couldn't have been more than eighty or eighty-five years for the average female."

Jordan sat back and contemplated Kale's remarks. "I wonder when she died?" Jordan clicked on the link marked Deaths. "Here it is. Margaret M. Downs, born April 16, 1988. Died, March 29, 2019. Cause of death: severe C-spine fracture and traumatic aortic dislocation sustained in a horse riding accident. Kale, she died so young!"

Kale reread the cause of death. "Severe C-spine fracture and traumatic aortic dislocation. She must have had a pretty bad impact injury to cause that much damage. If her aorta was torn, she would have bled to death in a matter of minutes."

Jordan narrowed her eyes. "Don't you think it's odd that she died from a horse riding accident on this very farm? I survived my accident, but only just barely."

"What do you mean? Accidents happen on farms all the time. I don't think it's that unusual."

"I don't know. I can understand how my accident happened, but an injury like Maggie's must have been caused by a catastrophic impact. I wonder how it happened. She couldn't have sustained that injury just by falling out of the saddle. Was she thrown from her horse? Something doesn't feel right. Don't ask me why, but it just doesn't."

"Maybe we can learn more from her obituary," Kale suggested.

Jordan clicked on the link to the Burlington Free Press obituary page and searched the records for Maggie's name. A three-dimensional holograph of a woman emerged from the computer. Jordan was stunned. The woman had creamy white skin, green eyes, and long, wild, curly red hair. Her face was heart-shaped with a finely chiseled nose and well-defined lips.

"She's beautiful," Jordan whispered.

"She *was* beautiful, you mean," Kale said. He read aloud. "March 29, 2019, Shelburne, Vermont. Margaret M. Downs, 'Maggie' to those who knew her, was killed in a horseback riding accident yesterday, just two weeks shy of her thirty-first birthday. Her body was found by a stable hand at the bottom of a cliff by the shores of Lake Champlain on the western fringes of her property. Although it appears she was thrown from her horse, the cause of the accident is still unknown. She was declared dead at the scene and taken to the Fletcher Allen Medical Center."

Tears flowed from Jordan's eyes. "She died on the farm, Kale. She died on my farm."

Kale lifted Jordan's chin and looked into her tear-stained face. "Are you all right?"

Jordan met Kale's eyes. "I'm okay." She looked back at Maggie's holograph. "She's more than beautiful. She's breathtaking. It's such a pity she died so young. I wonder if she had a partner."

Kale frowned. "Partner... as in female? How do you know she was gay?"

"Let's put on a pot of coffee and chat for a while. I have something to tell you."

Jordan continued to look at the holograph of Maggie while Kale made coffee. He sat down at the table as he waited for it to brew. "What is it you have to tell me?"

"There's something odd going on in this house."

"What do you mean, odd?"

"Do you remember when we talked about my nightmares, and you joked that maybe a ghost was trying to contact me?"

Kale sat back and looked at Jordan with wide eyes. "I was joking. You didn't take me seriously, did you?"

"At the time, no. But now I'm not so sure."

"Come on. You're kidding, right?"

"No, I'm not. I don't think it's a coincidence that I've had this particular dream in this particular house, and I don't think finding the diaries is a coincidence either."

Kale's brow furrowed. "What are you getting at?"

"I think Maggie is trying to contact me."

"Oh, for Christ's sake. Do you hear yourself? Maggie died a hundred years ago."

"Then how else can you explain this? The diaries? The dreams? You're going to think I'm nuts, but I really think this is some type of paranormal experience."

Kale nodded "You are absolutely correct. I think you're nuts!"

"Hear me out. I did some research on paranormal experiences. There are dream experts who believe the mind experiences different levels of consciousness, that it can receive input from different spiritual realms. I think Maggie is asking for my help. I think she's putting visions in my mind before I read about them in the diaries to convince me they're real—and that she's real."

An uncomfortable silence fell between them. It was interrupted by a faint beep signaling that the coffee had finished brewing. Kale rose, poured two cups, and returned to the table. He placed one cup in front of Jordan and sipped from the other. After a few moments, Kale placed his hand on Jordan's arm. "Let's say that you're right. Let's say that Maggie is trying to contact you. You've lived in this house all your life. Why now?"

Jordan looked at Kale, a faint mist clouding her eyes. "Don't you get it? She isn't just contacting me now. I've had the same dream ever since my accident at age sixteen."

Kale sighed deeply. "If you've had the dream for years, why are you only making the connection now?"

"I didn't realize Maggie was behind it until now. I think the fact that we were both involved in equestrian accidents has somehow linked us through time. Each dream has become increasingly real, so real that I can't believe they're just dreams. I don't remember them being this vivid when I was a child."

"Did you say dreams, as in more than one?"

Jordan nodded. "I had another dream a few nights ago. You asked me how I knew Maggie was gay. I know because she told me so herself."

Kale was visibly agitated. "You're starting to scare me. How could she have told you she was gay?"

"Remember when you worked on the machine all night because you couldn't sleep? I went to bed and drifted off. Next thing I knew, the door flew open and in came Maggie, in a rage because some kid at school had called her a lezbo. She went on and on for several minutes, ranting and raving until she suddenly threw herself down on the bed right next to me. Kale, I could feel her touching me! I swear on my life, I could feel it. Anyway, she continued to jabber away and finally came to the conclusion that she was indeed attracted to women."

"Jordan, I'm sure that dream was prompted by something you read in the diaries."

"No. No, it wasn't. The next morning, I read the second diary, one I hadn't started reading yet. The first entry was an exact description of the scene with Maggie the previous night. Don't you see? I had the dream before I read about it in the diary."

Kale ran his hand through his hair. "You're really scaring me. There has to be a good explanation for all of this."

"There is. I'm telling you, Maggie is trying to contact me."

Jordan touched his arm. "There's a third reason I believe Maggie is trying to contact me now. You see..." Jordan's voice trailed off as she searched for the right words.

Kale leaned forward. "What?"

She looked up at Kale. "Third, the timing is right. We haven't had the means to help her until now."

Kale looked at Jordan for several long moments. He shook his head. "Tell me you're not thinking what I think you're thinking."

"We have the technology. You have the technology. You said yourself that you were close."

Kale jumped to his feet. "No. Are you out of your mind? It's totally untested. Hell, it doesn't even work yet. No. Out of the question." Kale paced back and forth, his hands planted on his hips, clearly agitated.

"Kale?" Jordan said tentatively.

"I can't deal with this right now, Jordan. I'm going to the barn."

While Kale worked, Jordan sat in the house and sulked. Her stomach rumbled. She looked at her watch—it was almost 7:00 p.m. Tired of waiting for Kale to come back from the barn, she went to the kitchen and threw together a sandwich. She ate that and a bag of chips in front of the holovision. When she was done, she clicked off the set and rested her head on a cushion. Jordan couldn't get Maggie out of her mind. *Who are you, Maggie Downs? Why are you haunting my dreams and invading my thoughts?*

Suddenly, Jordan's attention was drawn to the kitchen as an unfamiliar voice rang out. "Maggie? Maggie, where are you?"

"I'm in the bedroom, Jess. I'll be right out."

Jordan's head snapped around to the direction of Maggie's voice. *Maggie?*

The door between the kitchen and the living room swung open, admitting a slim young woman with short-cropped, bleached-blonde hair. Maggie emerged from the bedroom. Her beauty took Jordan's breath away. Her unruly red hair was pulled loosely into a ponytail. She wore cutoff jeans and a tank top with no bra. A rush of heat in Jordan's chest made her feel lightheaded.

Maggie smiled brightly. "Hi, Jess."

The woman sauntered up and wrapped her arms around Maggie's waist. "Hey, baby. I missed you after class. Hmm, you smell good." The woman nuzzled Maggie's neck. Maggie giggled and pulled away. She walked over to the mirror above the fireplace and began putting on her earrings.

"I had to leave as soon as class was over to get my parents to the airport on time."

Maggie's visitor groped her from behind. "That's right. I forgot they were going to Florida today. That means we have the whole house to ourselves." She turned Maggie around and pressed her against the fireplace.

Maggie pushed her aggressor away. "Jess, is that all you ever think of? There's more to life than sex."

Jordan watched the scene from the couch, wishing desperately that she could walk over and teach Jess a lesson.

Jess looked surprised. "There is? You could have fooled me. Come on, Maggie, you know you want this as much as I do." Jess pressed her against the fireplace once more.

Maggie pushed Jess harder this time. "I said no. Jess, I don't know if I'm ready for that yet. I need time."

Jess advanced on Maggie again, this time roughly pinning her shoulders to the fireplace. She leaned in so that their faces were nearly touching. "Maggie, you're a twenty-two-year-old virgin. Get with the program, will you? What you need, little girl, is a good lay."

Maggie stared directly into Jess's eyes. "Not by you," she said vehemently.

An angry mask descended over Jess's face. She grasped Maggie's neck and hissed, "You'd better listen to me good, Maggie. You've known about your sexuality for what, six years now? Don't you think it's about time you acted on it? You've been leading me on for nearly a year, and I'm getting tired of waiting."

Maggie strained against Jess's weight. "I'll only say this one more time—let go of me!"

"Or what? Face it, Maggie, I'm stronger than you are. Now, I'll say *this* one more time. Like it or not, you're going to give me what I want."

Jess released Maggie's neck only to grasp two handfuls of T-shirt, which she proceeded to rip from Maggie's body.

"No! Jess, stop. Please!"

"Shut up." Jess raised her right hand and backhanded Maggie across the face. Maggie fell to the floor. Jess straddled her waist, roughly grabbing Maggie's creamy white breasts.

"No! Get off me." Maggie struggled against her attacker, but to no avail.

Jordan watched in horror as she transferred herself to the hover-chair. Several times, she tried to move her chair forward, but for some reason, it wouldn't move.

"No! Leave her alone," Jordan screamed as Maggie continued to struggle. Jordan's efforts to move her chair forward were futile. In one final, desperate attempt to get to Maggie, she pushed herself out of the chair and landed in a heap on the floor. Using her arms to drag herself to the fireplace, Jordan got close enough to grab Jess's calf muscle. With strength born of desperation, she dug her nails in as hard as she could. Jess howled out in pain and rolled off her victim.

Jess lay on her side, gripping her calf with both hands and moaning in pain. Maggie scrambled to her feet and picked up the fireplace poker. She held the weapon in front of her like a sword.

"Get out of my house right now, Jess, and don't ever come back again. Do you understand?" Anger radiated from her as she waved the poker back and forth. Maggie lifted the poker and slammed it down on Jess's injured calf. "I said get out. Now!"

Jess howled in pain. "Fuck! You hit me, bitch. You fucking hit me."

Maggie shifted her weight from foot to foot as she waved the poker. "I mean it, Jess. Now get out before I do it again."

Jess crawled to the nearest chair and used it as leverage to climb to her feet. With a final venomous look at Maggie, she limped from the room. Maggie stood rooted to the spot as she listened to the sound of the door closing and the squealing of car tires. When she was satisfied that Jess was gone, she calmly put the poker back into its holder and pulled the tattered pieces of her shirt together. Then she turned around and slowly walked down the hall to her bedroom.

Jordan watched the scene from the floor. She was concerned about the emotional state Maggie was in, but thankful that she had been able to influence the outcome. As she watched Maggie walk away, she pushed herself into a seated position and dragged herself back to her chair. Exhausted, Jordan laid her head down to rest.

*   *   *

Kale sat back and studied the diagram on the screen. Satisfied that he had a workable design, he saved the file and then shut down the computer. Before calling it a night, he circled the machine once more and admired the upgrade he'd installed. *It just might work.*

Kale opened the kitchen door and called out. "Jordan?"

There was no answer. He ran to the living room and found Jordan lying on the floor, unconscious. "Oh, my God. Jordan!"

CHAPTER 8

Kale knelt by Jordan's side. He rolled her onto her back and gently patted her cheek. "Jordan, Jordan, wake up."

Jordan's eyes fluttered open. "What... Kale, what is it?"

"You're on the floor. Are you all right? Did you fall from your chair?"

Jordan grabbed Kale's arms and pulled herself into a seated position. She looked around in confusion. Slowly, she recalled the events of the evening. "Kale... Maggie... she was attacked. The chair wouldn't move. I... I climbed out of my chair to help her."

Kale sat back on his heels and looked at her. "Maggie?" he said in disbelief. "Jordan, I'm worried about you."

"She was here. I swear to you." Jordan was disoriented. She looked around the room for Maggie.

Kale rose to his feet. "Okay, wait a minute. We need to get you off the floor." In one movement, he lifted Jordan from the floor and gently placed her on the couch. Then he sat down beside her. "I think you need to get some help. You've become obsessed with this dead woman. I'm really worried about you."

"No. It's real. I swear to you, it's real."

"Jordan..."

Jordan placed her hand on Kale's arm. "Stop. Please. Let me prove it to you."

Kale looked skeptical. Jordan retrieved all the volumes of Maggie's diaries from the end table. She shuffled through the books until she located the one she was currently reading and handed it to Kale. "Okay, before you open that, let me tell you about this last vision. I was sitting here reading the diary you're holding, and my eyes started to droop, so I decided to quit for the night. I closed the book, placed it on the end table, and I laid my head on the pillow. Seconds later, this woman comes into the house and calls out for Maggie. The woman was obviously a lesbian—"

"How do you know?"

58

"She was very butch. Anyway, she came into the house looking for Maggie. Maggie came out of her room and the woman—Maggie called her Jess—this woman started to grope Maggie, trying to convince her to have sex. Maggie said no, but Jess wasn't taking no for an answer. She started manhandling Maggie. She pushed her against the fireplace and started ripping her clothes off. Maggie struggled, but Jess wrestled her to the floor and pinned her there."

Kale interrupted Jordan's description. "Let me guess. This is where you come in."

Jordan grew animated. "Yes, it is. I tried to move my chair toward them, but for some reason, it wouldn't move. Maggie was obviously in distress and needed help, and Jess was stronger than she was. I tried several times to reach her, but I couldn't. Finally I gave up on the chair and climbed down to the floor. I dragged myself over to them, and when I was within reach, I grabbed Jess's leg and dug in with my nails as hard as I could. When Jess couldn't stand it anymore, she yelled out and released her grip on Maggie, who was able to free herself. Jess lay on the floor holding her injured leg while Maggie got up and grabbed the fireplace poker. After one good whack to Jess's leg, she convinced Jess to leave. Then Maggie went to her bedroom. That's all I remember."

Kale looked skeptical. "How is that explanation supposed to convince me you aren't losing your marbles?"

Jordan pointed to the book in Kale's hands. "Open the diary. What's the date on the entry where the bookmark falls?"

Kale looked at the diary. "July 9, 2008."

Jordan did the calculations in her head. "So that means Maggie was twenty at the time she wrote that particular entry, right?"

Kale nodded.

"Okay, now scan through the books until you find the year 2010."

Kale threw his hands up. "For crying out loud, Jordan, what exactly are you trying to prove here?"

Jordan inhaled deeply to contain her frustration. "In the vision, Jess said that Maggie was a twenty-two-year-old virgin. If she was twenty-two, it would have been the year 2010. The bookmark is on an entry dated 2008. Don't you see? I haven't gotten to the year 2010 yet."

Kale closed the diary and threw it onto the table in obvious frustration. "Listen to me. All this proves is that you haven't read past the year 2008. You said yourself that you became drowsy while reading. You could have easily fallen asleep and dreamed the attack."

"Bullshit. Why don't you believe me? Remember the last dream? Remember there was an entry in the diary that described the dream in detail? I didn't read that entry until after my dream. Give me some credit here. I'm not some crazed whacko obsessed with a dead woman!"

Kale looked concerned. "Jordan..."

She interrupted him, tears shimmering in her eyes. "Please, keep an open mind... for me."

Kale looked at the diary, took a deep breath, and smiled at Jordan. "All right, I'll give you the benefit of the doubt. I'll read the diary tonight. Okay?"

Jordan smiled, wiping the moisture from her eyes with the back of her hand. "Thanks."

Kale leaned in and kissed her forehead, then lifted her chin with his fingertips. "You're welcome. Now it's time for both of us to call it a night. I'll see you in the morning."

"Good night." Jordan watched Kale retreat to his bedroom. Then she transferred herself to her chair and headed to her own room.

* * *

Jordan was awakened by a movement at her side. Convinced it was Maggie, she lay as still as possible and feigned sleep. Suddenly, she found herself wrapped in strong, male arms. She opened her eyes to look at Kale. "Is something wrong?"

Kale met Jordan's gaze but remained silent for a long moment.

"Kale, you're scaring me. Is something wrong? Why are you in my bed?"

"I owe you an apology."

"An apology? Why?"

Kale switched on the lamp on her bedside table.

"Listen to this." Kale held the diary between them so Jordan could follow along as he read.

August 10, 2010. My day really sucked. It started out okay. I went to class and then drove Mom and Dad to the airport. They flew to Florida today to make sure their condo is in order before moving down there for the winter. I had just gotten home and changed my clothes when Jess arrived. The second she realized I had the house to myself, she was all over me. She ridiculed me for being a twenty-two-year-old virgin. She thinks it's odd that I've known about my sexuality for six years now but have yet to have sex with a woman. Hello? Just because I knew at age sixteen that I liked girls doesn't mean I want to jump into bed with every lesbian I meet. I just haven't found the right one yet. Giving myself to someone is a sacred thing for me. It has to be the right someone, and Jess just isn't it.

Anyway, Jess wouldn't take no for an answer. She got pretty rough and pinned me against the fireplace, and then she tore my shirt open. Before I knew what was happening, she'd wrestled me to the floor and started groping me. I thought she was going to rape me right there and then, but all of a sudden, she got a really bad cramp in her calf muscle and let go of me."

Jordan said excitedly, "That cramp! That was me digging my nails into her calf."

"Jordan," Kale said carefully, "listen to yourself. This happened almost one hundred years ago. You couldn't have been there to influence the attack. I'm ready to admit there is something odd going on here, but we need to be realistic about this."

"I was there. I know I was. Look, I can't explain it." A silence descended over them as they lay side by side on their backs looking at the ceiling. Their reverie was broken by Jordan's body shaking as she sobbed.

Kale tossed the diary onto the nightstand and took her into his arms. "Please don't cry."

Jordan burrowed her face into Kale's shoulder. She gasped for breath. "I feel so helpless. She died so young. Why? Why did she have to die? She was my age, Kale. She had so much life yet to live. My heart is breaking for her. It's just not right." Jordan's shoulders shook violently as Kale held her close.

"It's okay. I've got you. Let it out, baby. I've got you."

Several long minutes later, Jordan relaxed in his arms. He loosened his grip on her. "Are you all right?" he asked softly.

Jordan took a deep breath and nodded. A shudder ran through her body. "What's wrong with me? I feel like I'm losing my mind."

"You're not losing your mind, Jordan. You just have the softest heart of anyone I know."

Jordan started to cry again. "I swore I would never let myself feel like this again. After Susan left me, I vowed never to open my heart again."

62

"Talk to me about Susan."

Jordan wiped the tears from her eyes. "There's not much to tell that you don't already know. She was a nurse at the physical therapy office."

"I have to be honest with you. I didn't like her very much. I watched her pretty much run your life for two years. I guess I don't know what you saw in her."

"It wasn't as bad as all that. In the beginning, she made me feel special. I'm disabled—my dating opportunities are pretty limited. There aren't many women out there interested in a relationship with me. Susan was different. Who'd have thought she liked me being dependent on her? As you know, she split after the first implant was successful. She broke my heart. I loved her, I needed her, and she deserted me. So I decided to never open myself up to that kind of hurt again."

"Never say never, Jord. There's someone out there for you, someone who will treat you with the love and respect you deserve."

"I don't know. Look at me. I'm infatuated with a ghost."

"Come here, you," Kale said.

Jordan snuggled into his shoulder. Kale pulled the blanket over them both and kissed Jordan on the temple. "Go to sleep, Jordan."

Within moments, they were both snoring softly.

* * *

The research team was waiting when Kale and Jordan arrived at the lab in the morning. The department head had scheduled a briefing in the conference room to update Jordan on the status of the new implant. As they entered the room, the other members of the team stood and cheered. Peter Michaels walked to the front of the room and shushed the group. He smiled at Jordan. "Dr. Lewis, I think I speak for everyone when I say that we're glad to have you back."

Applause broke out again. Peter waited patiently until the room was quiet. "As I was saying, welcome back, Jordan. In your absence, we've been working hard to perfect the new implant. I think we're less than a month away from testing it on a human subject."

"That would be me," Jordan said firmly.

Kale chuckled. "Tell her yes, guys. Take it from me—you don't want to make her mad."

The team members laughed, and Peter assured Jordan that she was indeed the test subject. "All right," he said, "let's get down to business. Jordan and I have briefly reviewed the new implant's function. Now it's time to iron out the details. Lights, please."

For the next two hours, the research team talked about the status of the new implant and worked out a detailed roadmap for developing the self-powered energy unit. At the end of the meeting, each team member had been assigned a task and a strict schedule.

Peter closed the proceedings. "Okay, party over, folks. Let's get back to work. You too, Jordan."

Jordan grinned, happy to be working with the team once more.

Jordan spent the rest of the morning running tests on the prototype implant in a lab monkey. Around mid-afternoon, Peter stuck his head in the lab. "Jordan, do you have a moment?"

Jordan smiled at her mentor. "Sure. What's up?"

"I'd like to talk to you in my office."

Jordan frowned. "Okay, but I feel like I'm being called to the principal's office. Are you giving me detention?"

Peter's smile looked forced. "Now, Lewis," he said with mock sternness.

Peter closed the door to his office and sat down. There was an open folder on his desk. He picked it up and pulled out a piece of paper. "Your test results came back this morning. Your thoracic series looks very good, but your white blood cell count is elevated. As you know, that generally indicates an infection."

"An infection? But I feel fine. What do you think might be causing it?"

"I don't know, but we need to find the cause and treat it before it gets out of control. None of us can afford for you to be ill right now."

"Okay. What would you like me to do?"

"I need you to go to the hospital for a complete workup."

"When?"

"Now. It's all set up. I'll be going with you to supervise the examination."

Peter watched as the medical staff performed a thorough examination of Jordan. All cardio, respiratory, and digestive systems tests were negative. Despite her high white cell count, Jordan was healthy.

Peter crossed his arms in front of his chest. The test results made no sense unless... he had a thought. "The implant site—I wonder if that's inflamed? That might be causing the high white cell count."

Peter watched carefully as his team inspected the site. "There it is," he exclaimed.

Jordan strained to see what Peter had found. "What is it?"

"I think it's the beginnings of a pressure ulcer. The area is red and warm."

"A pressure ulcer?

"Yes. Too much time in the hover-chair, or it could have been caused by you sliding yourself in and out. I'm sure you're well aware how dangerous this type of wound is."

"It's not like I'm a rookie at this hover-chair thing. Yes, I'm aware of the dangers of a decubitus ulcer. After two years on my feet, I forgot to protect myself. Is it infected?"

"It hasn't broken the skin yet, but it's red and warm." Peter stripped off his rubber gloves and reached for his phone.

"Who are you calling?" Jordan asked.

"I'm going to admit you for a few days."

"What? Aren't you overreacting? It's an infection. I don't need hospitalization."

"It's a pressure sore. Left untreated, it could develop into sepsis." Peter reached for Jordan's hand. "Look, Jordan. Your paralysis makes this a special case. This ulcer could be life threatening without proper treatment. If the implant schedule weren't on the line, I might agree to treat this on an outpatient basis, but if this infection doesn't respond to antibiotics, it could put the entire project in jeopardy. If we can get this cleared up quickly, I'll see if we can move the electrode placement surgery up a week and do it while you're in the hospital. Okay?"

"It sounds like I don't have a choice," Jordan said.

"Not if we plan to stay on schedule with the implant," Peter replied.

Jordan sighed in resignation. "You're the boss."

CHAPTER 9

Kale poked his head into Peter's office. He wasn't there. As Kale turned to leave, Peter rounded the corner at the far end of the hall. "Kale, I'm glad you're here. I need to talk to you." Peter pushed open his office door and urged Kale inside.

"Do you know where Jordan is? I've been looking for her everywhere. The guys in the lab said they haven't seen her since just after lunch."

"Have a seat. That's what I wanted to talk to you about. Jordan is in the hospital."

Kale was instantly on his feet. "What?"

"We found the beginnings of a pressure sore at the base of her spine. We would never have looked except that her white cell count was elevated."

"So it's the beginnings of an ulcer?"

"Yes. It hasn't broken through the skin yet, but I thought it was best to hospitalize her for a few days. We'll administer an aggressive regime of antibiotics before it develops into something serious."

Kale shook his head. "Will it never end with her? Damn."

Peter grinned. "She is quite a handful, isn't she? If it makes you feel any better, I admitted her as a precaution. I see no reason why the infection won't react well to the antibiotics. She'll be fine in a few days. Feel free to visit her any time, she has no restrictions."

Kale sat back in his chair. "Peter, we promised she could be the test subject for the implant. We can't take that away from her now. Regardless of how long it takes, we have to wait for her to recover."

Peter nodded. "I agree. I wouldn't dream of implanting the new prototype in anyone else. If the infection responds well to the antibiotics, we can do the electrode placement surgery to prepare her nerve endings for the new implant while she's hospitalized. That will save time later."

Kale leaned forward, "That would be great. Will she be home for the recovery period?"

"Yes, but I'm not sure I trust her to stay in bed." Peter steepled his fingers. "How would you feel about working from home when she's released?"

"We could move the next phase of the trials out to the farm. With a few modifications, the barn would be perfect." Kale smiled. "I'll check it for feasibility tonight and bring the specs tomorrow."

* * *

Jordan was sitting up in bed when Kale entered her room. "You're going to be the death of met yet. What the hell are you doing in here?"

"Kale, thank God you're here. I am so bored."

"Don't try to change the subject. Christ, woman—a pressure sore? I knew you were pushing yourself too hard."

"Don't get your panties in a wad. It could happen to anyone," Jordan said defensively.

"No, not anyone. You spent fourteen years in a hover-chair. You know how to prevent pressure sores. Are you trying to kill yourself? Are you trying to sabotage the implant project?"

Jordan was silent while she waited for Kale to vent his frustration.

"Are you finished?" she asked sweetly, batting her eyelashes.

"That won't work," he said. "I'm serious."

"Could I ask you for a favor?"

Kale put his hands on his hips. "And what would that be?"

"Could you run home and bring the diaries back? I'm bored out of my mind."

* * *

Six in the morning. Jordan reached over to silence the beeping alarm clock. As she rolled back into bed, she noticed a hollow in the pillow beside her—someone had been sleeping with her. She frowned. The pillow was still warm. Jordan grasped the edge of the blanket and threw it aside. She swung her legs out and stood up. Jordan froze. *Wait. What's going on here? Am I dreaming again?*

Jordan looked down. She was totally naked. *Okay, this is disturbing. I haven't slept in the buff since Susan.*

Jordan tested her legs by taking two small tentative steps. When they continued to support her, she grabbed a robe from the back of the bedroom door and headed for the kitchen. "Kale? Where are you?" When she reached the end of the hall, Jordan found herself in unfamiliar surroundings. It was the same furniture she'd seen in her first dream about Maggie. *Okay, now I know I'm dreaming. Get a grip, Jordan.* She walked into the kitchen. It was also the kitchen of the past.

She decided to confront the dream directly. "Maggie? Maggie, where are you?" Jordan waited patiently for a reply that did not come. Finally, she gave up and returned to the bedroom. "Okay, so where are my clothes?" She rummaged through the dresser. After a moment, she found a pair of jeans and a flannel shirt that seemed to fit her okay. Next came footwear. Beside the bed was a pair of cowboy boots that fit her suspiciously well.

She returned to the kitchen, the sound of her boot heels echoing on the tile floor. She looked around the room and noticed something she hadn't seen before—a note on the countertop near the stove. It was folded in half and addressed "To Jordan." She picked it up with shaky hands and brought it to her nose. It smelled of patchouli. A surge of warmth spread through her abdomen. She gasped at the unfamiliar feeling, which quickly spread to her lower extremities. She leaned against the cabinet to steady herself and her emotions. When the strength returned to her shaky legs, she whispered, "What's happening here, Maggie? Why do you enchant me so?"

The note shook in her trembling hands. She closed her eyes and inhaled deeply to calm her nerves. Finally, she opened her eyes and began to read.

My Dearest Jordan,

I awoke this morning and saw your beautiful face beside me. Last night was so incredible. How did you have the energy to make love after working so hard yesterday filling the well? I wanted desperately to wake you with kisses and make love to you all day long, but I knew you needed to sleep. Thank you for filling the well. You were right. Putting it in the middle of the north pasture was a bad idea. How did you become so wise, lover? I have decided to take an early morning ride along the west ridge. I anticipate making love with you upon my return.

I love you with all my heart, Maggie.

Jordan's was filled with confusion. She read the note a second time and felt the burning ache in the very core of her being. *She loves me? We made love? Why can't I remember?*

Jordan carefully folded the note and placed it in her back pocket. Then she looked around the kitchen for clues about Maggie's personality. The room was decorated with a decidedly country flair, not unlike the décor she and Kale had chosen for their new kitchen. As she admired Maggie's taste, her eyes fell on a calendar hanging on the back of the kitchen door. Jordan frowned as the date came into focus. March, 2019.

Jordan took a step back, her brow furrowed in thought. Why was that significant? *March, 2019, March... oh, my God! Maggie died on March 29, 2019!* Jordan began to pace, a panicky feeling invading her heart. *What should I do? I'm not even sure what day it is. How do I find out? Wait! The holovision.* Jordan ran into the living room. *Shit! This is one of those old fashioned televisions. How do I turn it on?* She sat on the edge of the couch and struggled with the remote control until she managed to turn it on. She clicked through the channels until she found one broadcasting the local weather. On the bottom-left side of the screen were the numbers 6:50 a.m., 3/29/2019.

Jordan gasped. *Oh, God. What did the obituary say? Maggie Downs died yesterday... early morning ride... found at the bottom of a cliff on the western fringes of her property.*

Jordan pulled Maggie's note from her pocket.

I have decided to take an early morning ride along the west ridge.

Panic clenched Jordan's heart. "I've got to stop her!"

Jordan jumped to her feet, grabbed a canvas barn jacket from a hook by the door, and ran out into the yard. She ran to the barn and flung the door open. She searched desperately for a horse, finding only empty stall after empty stall. Finally, she came to a magnificent mustang steed. Maggie owned the very same kind of horse that Jordan had had as a child.

She spoke soothingly to the animal as she threw a blanket and saddle on its back. "Come on, big guy. We've got a job to do." Jordan climbed into the saddle. A quick jab to the horse's ribs and she was racing over the snow-covered fields at a full gallop. As she rode, Jordan anguished over how long it was taking to cover the distance from the house to the lake. In her desperation, she was oblivious to the biting cold that chafed her cheeks. *I've forgotten how large this property is. God, please let me reach her in time.*

Nearly half an hour later, the frozen lake came into view. The sight encouraged Jordan to dig in her heels and push her steed to its limits. *Maggie, please stay away from the edge. Please! I'm coming, my love, I'm coming. Please let me reach her in time.* Suddenly, a shot rang out. As Jordan crested the last knoll separating her from the cliffs, the sight below robbed her of breath like a punch to the stomach. A riderless horse. Jordan's heart fell. "Maggie! Maggie! No!" she screamed. She dug in her heels, bringing the horse to an abrupt stop at the edge of the cliff. Jordan jumped out of the saddle, the impact causing her to tumble into the snow and, in the process, twisting her right ankle. She grabbed her injured limb. "Goddamn it!"

She climbed painfully to her feet and limped to the edge. Throwing herself to the ground, she peered over the side. At the bottom, among snow-covered boulders and rocks, lay a woman's body. Her arms and legs were at odd angles, and her long red curls were splayed out around her head.

"Maggie," Jordan screamed.

She looked around desperately for an easy way down the cliff and spotted a worn trail about thirty yards away. She scrambled to her feet and limped along the edge of the cliff until she reached the path. Clumsily, she began her descent, falling several times as her injured ankle refused to support her weight on the slippery slope. Jordan was terrified that she was already too late. "Maggie, baby, please hold on. I'm coming. Please hold on."

It felt like an eternity before Jordan reached the bottom. She struggled to climb over the icy rocks and boulders. Finally, Maggie was only a few feet away. Jordan called out to the injured woman as she closed the distance between them. "Maggie! Maggie, talk to me, sweetheart. Say something, please." Maggie's breathing was ragged, her chest rising and falling unevenly.

Jordan knelt by Maggie's side, taking special care not to move her. She gently brushed the curly locks from Maggie's brow. Placing her shaking hands on either side of Maggie's face, she leaned close and whispered, "Maggie, I'm here. Hold on my love. Please, don't leave me. The stable hand will find your horse. Help will be here soon. Please hold on."

Maggie's green eyes fluttered open.

Jordan gasped and choked back a sob. She took Maggie's hand in her own and brought it to her lips. Maggie's hand was bloody. Jordan kissed it tenderly, her eyes never leaving Maggie's.

Maggie smiled as she fought to keep her eyes open. "Jordan," she rasped, her breath steaming in the cold March air.

Jordan leaned closer to hear what Maggie was saying. "I'm here, my love."

Maggie took a ragged breath and her brow furrowed in pain. Her eyes were locked on Jordan. Finally, she summoned enough strength to speak. "Jordan, I love you. I always have... through all time."

Jordan's throat nearly closed with emotion as she held back a sob. "I love you too, Maggie. I always will. Please don't leave me. I need you, my love. Please don't leave me." Tears cascaded from Jordan's eyes and fell onto Maggie's cheeks. She placed a tender kiss on Maggie's lips. As she raised her head, she watched the life ebb from the beautiful green eyes. Still holding Maggie's hand, Jordan fell back onto her knees and a long painful wail escaped her.

"No!"

CHAPTER 10

"Good morning," Kale said as he entered her room. "Here, I brought you some goodies."

"You're a saint," Jordan replied as she accepted the bag of sweets from her friend. "I wonder if hospital food has always been this bad."

"How are you feeling today?" Kale asked.

"I feel great. I felt great yesterday when Peter confined me to this jail."

"I confined you to this 'jail' for you own good, Jordan," Peter said from the doorway.

"Peter," Jordan exclaimed, embarrassed.

"The lab crew will be in later this morning for another round of blood work. I expect it will take a few days to get your white count back to normal. Until then, you're safer here than in a germ-infested lab environment or at home where you're sure not to follow doctor's orders."

Kale grinned. "Peter knows you too well, doesn't he?"

Jordan stuck out her tongue.

"Well," Peter said, "I can see everything is fine here. I'll be back later to review your test results with you. Kale, I'll see you later at the lab."

"I'll be right along," Kale replied.

"Take your time. The less opportunity she has to drive the staff crazy, the better."

"I hear you." Kale chuckled.

"Hey!" Jordan exclaimed indignantly.

After Peter left, Kale sat on the edge of Jordan's bed.

"Thanks for bringing the diaries, Kale. Seriously, I was really bored." Jordan embraced him tightly.

"Kale Simmons?"

Kale looked up quickly. Sunshine from the window obscured his view of the speaker standing in the doorway.

"Yes?" he asked, squinting to see through the glare.

The visitor advanced into the room. "Hi, my name is Andrea Ellis. Peter Michaels told me I would find you here."

Kale was on his feet immediately. He was stunned by the beauty of the woman standing before him. Andrea Ellis stood a little over five feet tall with long, flowing blonde hair and striking blue eyes. The tailored blue business suit hugged her shapely curves as if molded especially for her body.

Kale stammered. "Ah... ah..."

Jordan was clearly enjoying Kale's discomfort. "Where are your manners, Kale? Shake the woman's hand," she said.

Kale shook Andrea's hand. "Miss Ellis. Yes. I'm sorry for being so rude. My friend over there," he nodded his head toward Jordan, "gives me such grief, I'm afraid I was a bit preoccupied. Forgive me?"

Andrea shook his hand firmly and smiled once more. "Only if you call me Andi."

"Andi it is." Kale continued to shake Andi's hand much longer than politeness demanded. Her smile mesmerized him.

"You're going to shake her arm off at that rate," Jordan observed.

"Oh! Oh, I'm sorry. I'm such an idiot. Here, have a seat." Kale pulled a chair over to Jordan's bedside.

"No, that's all right," Andi said. "I just came to introduce myself. I'll be working with you on the power supply for the new spinal implant." Andi turned to Jordan. "You're Dr. Jordan Lewis, right?" They shook hands.

"Jordan, just Jordan. I only use the doctor crap with my students."

"I understand you'll be the recipient of the new implant?"

Jordan looked at Kale. "Yes, I am, assuming there are no complications from this infection. Right, Kale?"

Kale took Jordan's hand and brought it to his lips. "You bet. We promised you. Now you have to keep your promise to behave and get your butt out of here so we can proceed."

Andi watched the tender scene with obvious interest. Jordan smiled. "I'll do my best. I have a redhead to meet. I won't do anything to jeopardize that."

Kale frowned. The only redhead he was aware of in Jordan's life was the long-dead Maggie.

Jordan grinned. "Get your ass out of here. Miss Ellis needs your help at the lab. Scoot."

Kale grinned at Jordan and then at Andi, who smiled back at him. He leaned in close to Jordan and whispered, "If you weren't in this bed right now, I'd kick your ass."

"I can still kick your ass, in bed or out. Better run before I get mad."

Kale promised to come back that afternoon. "I expect to see you running sprints up and down the hallway," he said.

"Well then, I guess you'd better get to work on that implant pronto, so I can do just that."

Kale clicked his heels in mock salute. "Yes, ma'am!"

Jordan watched as Kale escorted a grinning Andi from the room.

*   *   *

When Kale returned, Jordan was engrossed in a diary. He sat on the edge of the bed. "Any news on today's blood tests?" he asked.

Jordan smiled. "It appears the antibiotics are beginning to kick in. My white count is improving. Peter just left a few minutes ago. He's thinking maybe one more day of antibiotics, then the surgery to prep the nerve endings. A couple of days of recovery and then I can go home."

"That's awesome news. If Andi and I can work out the details of the self-generating power pack in the next few weeks, we'll pretty much be on schedule."

"Andi, huh? She's cute."

Kale blushed to the roots of his unruly hair. "Really? I hadn't noticed," he said.

"Like hell you haven't. You are so full of shit, Kale Simmons! You turned into a total pile of jelly when she was here earlier."

Kale rose from the bed and walked to the window, turning his back on Jordan for a few moments. Finally he turned around and threw his hands in the air. "All right, I confess. Yes, she's gorgeous. And you're right—my hormones are kicking in big time. Damn. I've never felt this way before." He sat down once more on the bed. "What should I do?"

"Well, for starters, you need to give it more time. You've only known her for a few hours. Don't go jumping in with both feet until you know her better. She could be a royal bitch."

Kale shook his head. "She could never be like that. She's so sweet."

Jordan smiled. "I'm sure she's very nice, but take my advice. Don't commit your heart until you know for sure."

Kale rose to his feet and paced back and forth. "I'm so inept, I don't know what to do. It's not like I have beautiful women falling all over themselves to date me."

Jordan wondered to herself why that was true. Kale was a good-looking man. A little bohemian perhaps with his unruly hair, and a bit nerdy, too, but good-looking, nonetheless. "Well, is she showing any interest in you? I mean do you get the impression that she likes you, or do you think she's just being cordial?"

"How can I tell?"

"Does she treat everyone the same way or is she especially nice to you?"

Kale shrugged. "I don't know. I guess she treats everyone pretty much the same way."

Jordan was afraid of that. "Okay, okay, we can work with this." She paused to think for a moment before continuing. "Do you remember when we were out to dinner, you know, the night the waitress gave me her airwave code?"

"How could I forget?"

"Do you remember the advice I gave you?"

Kale looked off in the distance for a few seconds. Then he looked back at Jordan, excitement on his face. "Compliments. You said that women like compliments."

"Exactly. If you really like this woman, start off by giving her small compliments. Don't overdo it. Drop subtle lines here and there."

"Like what? Help me out here."

"Okay, try this." Jordan made a picture frame with her fingers. "You and Andi are poring over the blueprints for the new power pack. She points something out to you, you lean in close to see what it is. You look at her and casually comment about how nice she smells. Then you immediately turn your attention back to the blueprints."

Kale's eyes opened wide. "Yeah, I can do that. Anything else?"

"All right. Let's see. Okay, you're already at the lab one morning. When Andi walks in, she's wearing this killer 'I'm-too-sexy-for-my-clothes' outfit. She comes over to where you're working, putting her lab coat on as she approaches. You glance at her and say, 'It's too bad you have to wear that coat over such a beautiful outfit. You look very nice today.' Then, as soon as you drop the compliment, you move on to whatever it was you were doing."

Kale was once again on his feet. "I think I've got it. Drop a quick compliment and then change the subject. Show a little interest, but don't make a big deal about it. Show her I'm interested, but don't overdo it."

"Exactly."

"What do I do if she begins to show some interest back?"

"You invite her to dinner. Or better yet, invite her over to our place. You're a great cook, and I'll be there to help you break the ice. Women just love it when a man can cook. You can use the pretense of discussing the implant to lure her over. How does that sound?"

Kale grinned from ear to ear. "Jordan, you're a genius. Every guy should have a lesbian friend to help him through a first date."

Jordan shook her head. "You're such a nerd, but I love you anyway."

Kale hugged Jordan. "I love you, too. I always will." He released her and headed for the door. "I'm going to run home for a quick shower and a bite to eat. I'll be back after dinner. Is there anything I can bring you?"

"Just you. Oh, and I really want to talk to you about the dreams. I have so much I need to discuss with you."

* * *

"Jordan. Jordan. Wake up, sleepy head."

Jordan slowly opened her eyes "Go away, Kale. Can't you see I'm sleeping?"

"Oh, no you don't. You've slept for ten hours. I think that's quite enough, don't you?"

Jordan's eyes snapped open. "Ten hours? Are you sure?"

"Positive. I stopped in last night around 9:00 p.m. You were sound asleep then. It's 7:00 a.m. now. How do you feel?"

Jordan reached for the remote to raise the head of her bed. Once she was in a seated position, she rubbed her eyes and looked more closely at Kale. "I had the oddest dream last night. In fact, I've had a couple of odd dreams since I've been in here."

"Are they about Maggie?" he asked warily.

"The first one was. The one last night was just weird. I was filling the well that Sally and I fell into sixteen years ago. I was filling it by hand." Jordan touched his hand, a look of urgency in her eyes. "Kale, about that first dream—Maggie knew I was there. She actually wrote me a note." Jordan's eyes misted over. "She died. I wasn't able to save her. I tried to reach her in time, but I failed. We need to help her. We can't let her die."

Kale was concerned about Jordan's grasp on reality, but before he could respond, Peter entered the room.

"Good morning," he said cheerily.

Kale rose to his feet. "I hate to run, but I've got to get to the lab. I'll stop by after work."

Before Kale could leave, Peter said, "How's that new research assistant working out?"

Peter looked at Jordan, his eyes full of mischief. Jordan grinned.

"Andi... I mean Miss Ellis is working out fine. Smart girl." Kale wanted desperately to leave before Peter asked any more questions.

"Good, I'm glad. I'm sure she'll be a fine addition to our staff. I'll see you both in my office at one o'clock this afternoon. I've called a review meeting on the status of the implant."

"One o'clock. We'll see you there." Kale scurried out the door and down the hall.

"Peter," Jordan scolded. "You're awful. Do you have any idea how much you intimidate him?"

Peter looked at her. "Come now, you enjoyed that as much as I did."

"True, but I still feel bad for the guy."

Peter chuckled. "I'm looking forward to this afternoon's meeting. I'm willing to bet he'll be so busy looking at Miss Ellis that he won't hear a word I'm saying."

"You might be surprised. We've been working on a plan for him to woo her without making a total fool of himself."

"Do you realize how lost he'd be without you?"

"That's not a real comfortable place for me to be. I'm kind of glad Andi has entered the picture. He needs someone who can give him the kind of relationship he'll never have with me. He's already infatuated with her. I just hope she's interested in him."

"Time will tell. So, we'll do another round of blood tests this morning, and if the results are normal, we'll schedule the surgery for the electrodes. If that goes well, you could be home in a couple of days. That doesn't mean you'll be off the hook, mind you. A few days of bed rest when you get home, and then you should be as good as new."

"Please tell me that 'bed rest' is only a figure of speech. Don't tell me I really have to stay in bed."

Peter smiled. "Only for a few days. After that, you'll have to be especially careful about getting in and out of your chair. In fact, it would be best if you had help with that."

* * *

Jordan spent the rest of the day reading excerpts from Maggie's diary. At six o'clock, Kale poked his head through her door. "Hey, girlfriend!"

Jordan looked up. Kale had a wide smile on his face. Jordan smiled back at him. She closed the diary and crossed her arms in front of her. "Something tells me you had a good day. You look like the cat that ate the canary."

Kale pulled a chair close to her bed. "It was incredible. I did as you suggested. I complimented her on her perfume and then quickly changed the subject to the power supply. She kind of blushed a little and thanked me. I could see her glancing at me and smiling on and off for the rest of the morning. When it was time for lunch, she asked me to join her. What do you think of that, huh?"

Jordan clapped her hands. "I think it's a great start. Remember not to move too fast. Tomorrow, comment on her outfit and then do little things that might please her, but do *not* overdo it. Take it slow. If she likes you, it'll get easier. She'll start reciprocating with little gestures of her own."

Kale took Jordan's hand. "I can't thank you enough. I really, really like her. She's so smart. We spent the entire day brainstorming ways to integrate the power supply into the body's natural energy-generating capabilities. She's brilliant, and she's beautiful. I struggle to stay focused on the task. During the meeting, I was so mesmerized by her, I hardly heard a word Peter said."

"Peter was right."

"What was that?"

"Oh, nothing. She asked you to lunch, huh? I assume you went?"

"You bet I did. It was only to the cafeteria, but heck, it's a start."

"That it is. Congratulations. Just remember to take it slow, okay?"

"Slow... got it. How was your day?"

"Fairly uneventful. My white count isn't quite normal, but it's improving. Peter is hoping we can do the pre-surgical workup tomorrow, then the electrode prep surgery. I'm so tired of being in the hospital."

"Did Peter say when you can go back to work?"

"It looks like I'll be confined to home for a while. Peter is prescribing a week of post-operative bed rest."

"You'll follow Peter's orders, right?" Kale asked.

Jordan pretended to take offense. "What is it with you and Peter? I do know how to follow orders, you know."

"I know you know how. The question is, will you?"

Jordan picked up the diary and swatted Kale. "Get out of here before I kick your ass," she said. "Go home. Get some sleep. I expect to be waited on hand and foot when I get home, so you'd better rest up. By the way, you forgot one of the diaries. It might have fallen on the floor next to the end table in the living room. If you think of it, bring it by on your next visit."

Kale saluted Jordan as he left the room.

CHAPTER 11

Early the next morning, a lab technician woke Jordan from a sound sleep to draw what she hoped would be the final blood sample. Not long after he left, she fell back to sleep, only to be wakened some time later by the scent of patchouli. As she opened her eyes, she expected to see Maggie sitting by her bedside. Instead, her eyes fell upon a very beautiful blonde. As her blurry vision cleared, she realized the woman was Andrea Ellis.

Jordan ran her fingers through her disheveled hair. "Andrea! I didn't expect to see you here. When I smelled patchouli, I thought you might be someone else."

"Please, call me Andi. Andrea is such a formal name. You like patchouli? It's one of my favorite scents."

Jordan groped around until she found the remote control for the bed and adjusted her position. She looked at Andi's slim, shapely legs, just slightly out of arm's reach. *Damn, she's beautiful!*

Jordan looked around. "Is Kale with you?"

"No. He's in the middle of some critical tests on the implant. He asked me to drop this off." Andi handed a diary to Jordan. "Apparently, he forgot it yesterday."

Jordan accepted the book. "Thanks for bringing it to me. I appreciate it."

"That's a really old book. Kale said you found several volumes hidden between the wallboards of your house?"

Jordan looked at the book in her hands. It was the next diary in the series. "Yes. I was doing some remodeling a couple of weeks ago, and when we tore down the sheetrock, I found them. Thanks again for bringing this to me."

"You're welcome." Andi rose to her feet and hesitated, a series of emotions playing across her face. Finally, she sat back down on the edge of the chair and looked at Jordan.

"Jordan, can I ask you something?"

"Sure."

Andi looked down at her hands and then back up at Jordan. "You and Kale live together, right?"

Jordan could see where this was going. "Yes we do, but—"

Andi interrupted her. "Do you love him?"

Jordan cocked her head to one side. "I love him very much. He's a wonderful man."

Andrea looked down at her hands again. "I see," she said softly, standing to leave. "I guess I should get back to the lab."

"Andi, come back, please."

Andrea stopped and turned around.

"Please, sit. You need to know something about Kale and me." Andi hesitated. "Please." Jordan waited until Andi returned to her seat.

"I'm listening."

Jordan ran her hand through her hair. "Kale and I are just friends. I know how lame that sounds, but it's true. I'm going to tell you something that I don't normally share, because no one really needs to know something this personal about me."

Andi leaned forward. "You don't owe me an explanation."

"No, I don't, but I really love Kale, and I happen to know he's quite smitten with you. I'll be damned if I'm going to do anything to ruin it for him."

Andi smiled. "He's smitten with me?"

"Like a schoolboy. Anyhow, you need to know that even though Kale and I have lived together for four years, we haven't been together. We've been housemates, pure and simple."

Andi frowned. "Don't you find him attractive?"

Jordan grinned. "Kale is very cute. No, he's more than cute. He's a very good-looking man, even though he doesn't know how to comb his hair." Andi laughed and nodded in agreement. Jordan paused to collect her thoughts. "Look, Andi, Kale is great. He can cook, he doesn't mind housework, he's extremely intelligent, and he is a wonderfully nice, loyal, considerate person, but to be honest, I find you much more attractive than I do him." Jordan fell silent as she waited for Andi's reaction.

Please don't tell me you're a dumb blonde. I don't want to have to spell it out for you. Suddenly, Andi's eyebrows shot up. One hand flew to her mouth to hide her surprise. *Okay, you've got it. Good girl. Come on, you can say it.*

Andi rose to her feet and walked across the room. Then she turned to look at Jordan. "Are you telling me that you're gay?"

"Queer as they come, through and through."

Andi sat back in her chair and stared at Jordan, who began to feel uneasy under the scrutiny. "You're making me nervous."

Andi smiled. "I can see why Kale likes you. You're very funny."

"Oh yeah, I'm a barrel of laughs." Jordan paused. "Andi, what I just told you is very personal for me. A select few know. Kale and Peter, and now you. It's not that I'm ashamed of it—and heaven knows, the need to be in the closet ended about fifty years ago, but this is a very sacred thing for me. I don't broadcast it to the world any more than a heterosexual person would. Does that make sense?"

"I understand. Really, I do. Please don't worry. As you said, it's your personal business. I'm honored that you shared it with me."

"I just don't want Kale to be hurt because of a misconception. He deserves so much more."

Andi smiled. "He seems like a very nice man."

"They don't get any better than Kale. The woman who wins his heart will be very, very lucky."

*   *   *

After Andi left, Jordan contemplated the sparse furnishings of her hospital room. She missed the comfort of her home. She longed to be in front of the fireplace, enjoying the warmth as the wind and snow raged outside. She found herself wondering if Maggie enjoyed such comforts on cold winter days. A chill ran through her as she realized that she and Maggie had actually shared the same physical space, albeit at different times in history. Jordan closed her eyes and imagined what it would be like to spend such intimate moments with her dream lover.

Jordan stood at the kitchen table and poured merlot into two long-stemmed glasses. Setting the bottle aside, she picked up the glasses and made her way into the living room, lit only by firelight. She paused just inside the room for a moment to allow her eyes to adjust to the dim light. Then she walked carefully to the pile of blankets and pillows that were scattered on the floor in front of the fireplace. Outside, the snow gently fell, covering the earth in a blanket of white.

She stopped at the edge of the pillows and handed a glass of wine to the woman lying on them. "Thank you, my love," Maggie said as she accepted the glass and brought it to her lips. Jordan gently lowered herself into a semi-reclining position next to Maggie.

Propped up on one elbow, Jordan sipped her wine as she admired the beauty of the woman lying beside her. Maggie was of medium height, with long, slender limbs and a tiny waist. She wore faded low-cut denim jeans and a short-waisted turtleneck sweater, which framed her face like a Victorian lace collar. A mass of unruly, curly red hair cascaded over her shoulders. Jordan couldn't look away as she watched Maggie sip her wine, then run her tongue over the rim of the glass to capture a drop that threatened to escape. A shiver of anticipation ran through her.

Maggie looked at her. "Are you cold?" she asked.

Jordan smiled and transferred her wine glass to the other hand then reached forward and traced the side of Maggie's face with her fingertips. "No. I was just imagining making love to you."

Maggie smiled, and Jordan's insides melted. "My God, you are beautiful." Maggie turned her eyes away to sip her wine while Jordan admired her creamy white skin, tinged pink by the heat of the fire. Maggie placed her glass on the hearth. She then took Jordan's wine from her and placed it beside her own. Jordan's breath caught in her throat as she anticipated Maggie's next move.

Maggie placed her hand on Jordan's shoulder and gently pressed her back into the pillows. She leaned over her and lowered her mouth to Jordan's, delicately tracing Jordan's lips with her tongue. Jordan shivered once more as their tongues intertwined. They shared the sweet taste of wine as they savored each other's mouths for several long moments.

Jordan caught Maggie's face between her hands. "I love you," she whispered huskily.

"I love you too, dear heart," Maggie replied. "Let me show you how much."

Jordan was helpless to resist as she granted permission with a nod, releasing her hold on Maggie's face and allowing her hands to fall to the pillows. She waited patiently as Maggie drank deeply from her wine then set the glass aside once more. Jordan's patience was rewarded when Maggie leaned forward and transferred the mahogany liquid into her mouth.

For what seemed like an eternity, Maggie explored Jordan's mouth with her tongue, flitting in and around its moist depths, and thrusting deeply. Jordan could feel the dampness between her legs increase with each probing thrust of Maggie's tongue. The pungent taste of merlot accented the kiss with intoxicating results.

Jordan's desire raged out of control as her hands flew up to grasp Maggie's bottom. She kneaded the supple flesh until she could feel the heat directly through Maggie's jeans.

Maggie pushed herself to a seated position so that she straddled Jordan's waist. She reached up and grasped Jordan's wrists, pushing her hands above her head and into the pillows. Maggie lowered her face to Jordan's and whispered softly, "No, no, my love. No hands. Just relax and enjoy this."

Jordan fought with herself to keep her hands off her lover as Maggie sat up once more and removed her sweater. Beneath the sweater, she wore a black lace bra which afforded Jordan an up close view of her ample cleavage.

Maggie threw the sweater aside and leaned closer to Jordan. "Do you like what you see, lover?" she teased.

Jordan nodded and allowed the truth to show in her eyes. She couldn't speak.

"Good," Maggie replied. "Now it's your turn." Her hands snaked under Jordan's shirt and pushed it up and over her head. Jordan's sports bra quickly followed suit. "You are so beautiful," Maggie whispered as she traced the outline of Jordan's breasts with her fingertips. Maggie leaned in and captured first one, then the other erect nipple between her teeth and flicked the sensitive buds with the tip of her tongue. Jordan's chest arched high off the pillows as she thrust her breasts closer to Maggie, silently demanding more.

Maggie's eyes met Jordan's. "I want to taste you. I want to fill you, body and soul. I want to make you cry out my name when the passion becomes too much."

Jordan could feel spasms of delight clench at her abdomen and contract in her core as the anticipation of what was to come caused her desire to mount to near explosive levels. "Maggie, please—I need you," Jordan begged.

Maggie smiled as she pushed Jordan's legs to one side and knelt on the pillows beside them. Without breaking eye contact, she reached forward and opened the front of Jordan's jeans. Carefully, she pulled the rough material down over her lover's hips and removed the garment. The jeans soon joined Jordan's shirt and bra in a heap beside the pillows.

Maggie returned to Jordan's breasts and suckled their erect buds, eliciting delightful moans from deep within Jordan's throat. She then moved very slowly down Jordan's abdomen, leaving a delicate trail of kisses and nibbles along the way. Her tongue dipped into Jordan's navel, causing Jordan to squirm as a spasm of desire jolted her core.

Maggie reached inside the waistband of Jordan's panties. She allowed two fingers to slide between the folds, while her palm cupped Jordan's mound. When her fingers encountered the abundant moisture between Jordan's legs, her own body convulsed and she dropped her head to Jordan's abdomen. "Oh, my God, baby… you're so wet. Is this for me?" she asked.

"Only for you, my love. Only for you," Jordan replied.

Jordan bolted awake and sat upright in her hospital bed. As her breathing returned to normal, she covered her face with her hands and tried to control her raging emotions. *I must have fallen asleep. Oh, my God! I'm in love with her. I love her!* Tears spilled from her eyes as she felt an overwhelming sense of helplessness and despair. *What am I going to do? Maggie, why? Why is fate so cruel?*

* * *

Peter Michaels made his rounds before lunch. When he reached Jordan's room, he found her sitting in bed staring at a blank holovision. It was obvious that she had been crying. She barely acknowledged him when he entered the room. Peter sat on the edge of her bed and took her pulse. "How are you feeling?" he asked as he looked at his watch.

Jordan dragged her eyes from the blank screen to Peter's face. "Fine."

Peter raised his eyebrows. "Just fine? Are you sure?"

"I'm sure."

Peter continued his exam in silence. When he finished, he wrapped his stethoscope around his neck and stood up, looking at Jordan for a few moments. It was obvious to him that she was troubled. "Your tests came back normal, so it looks like we'll start the pre-implant workup now. If there are no additional issues, the surgery will be tomorrow night."

Jordan nodded, but said nothing. Peter was confused by her behavior, as she had been so upbeat the last time he'd seen her. He didn't want to leave her alone in such obvious emotional pain. He placed his hands on either side of her reclining torso. "Jordan, I don't know what's bothering you, but your emotional health plays a critical part in your recovery. If you can't talk to me about it, then you need to find someone with whom you can talk."

Jordan turned her face to meet Peter's eyes. Tears spilled onto her cheeks. "I'm sorry, Peter. It isn't you. It's just something I need to come to terms with."

Peter sat on the edge of the bed and retrieved a tissue from the box on her bedside table. He gently wiped the tears from her cheeks. "You know I'm here for you, right?"

Jordan nodded. She took the tissue from Peter and blew her nose. She tried to smile through her tears. "Thanks. Please don't worry about me. I'll be fine."

Peter patted her hand and returned her smile. "All right. I'll be back tomorrow morning, but if you need me before then, don't hesitate to have me paged, okay?"

"I will. Thank you, Peter—for everything."

Peter stood. "You're welcome. I'll see you in the morning."

No sooner had Peter left the room than Kale walked in. The excitement was evident on his face. "Hey Jord!" he said, parking himself on the edge of her bed. His enthusiasm quickly faded as he looked at Jordan's red, puffy eyes. "Jordan?"

She found it impossible to hold it together under Kale's scrutiny. She began to sob. Kale held her close and rubbed her back. She rested her head on Kale's shoulder until the sobbing subsided. Kale looked into her anguish-filled eyes. "Tell me what's wrong."

Her bottom lip quivered as she tried desperately not to cry. "Why am I so hopeless?"

"You're anything but hopeless."

Jordan wiped her nose. "No, no, I'm hopeless." She paused for a moment to collect her thoughts before continuing. "I love her. I'm actually in love with her."

Kale frowned. "Who are you in love with?"

Jordan studied the damp tissue in her hands and indirectly answered his question through her prolonged silence.

Kale threw his hands up in an exasperated motion and rose to his feet. "Oh, for crying out loud. Please don't tell me it's Maggie."

Jordan looked everywhere but at Kale. Her hands became animated and the tears flowed as she spoke. "I didn't ask for this. Believe me, this is one heartache I could live without."

She watched Kale walk to the window and look out over the city. There was a decided slump to his shoulders.

"I can't help myself, Kale. It's like she's reaching out to me from the past. I've been having dreams about her. In one dream, she left me a letter the morning she died. In it, she said that she loved me. I came so close to saving her; so close that she died in my arms. It ripped my heart from my chest. I find myself thinking about her day and night. She's become a part of my life." Jordan sobbed. "Oh, God! I don't know what to do. My heart is shattered. I can hardly bear it."

With his back still to Jordan, Kale reached up and wiped the moisture from the corners of his eyes. When his emotions were under control, he returned to her bedside. "I've got you, Jord. Please don't cry."

"I want to die."

Kale was startled by her words. He pushed her back roughly. "What the hell are you saying?"

"I need to be with her. I don't see any other way."

Kale was never so angry in his life. He leaned in close. "I will not allow you to die. That's the most selfish thing I've ever heard you say."

"But—"

He jumped to his feet. "But nothing," he shouted. He grasped the sides of his head in an attempt to calm his temper. This was a side of him that Kale had never shown Jordan. Finally, he dropped his hands to his sides and sighed deeply in defeat. "Okay, you win."

"I win? I don't see any way to win at this one."

Kale sat on the edge of Jordan's bed and dropped his chin to his chest. He remained in this position until he'd collected his thoughts. *Either way, I'll lose her. This is a no-win situation.* He looked at Jordan. "I'll help you. It's against my better judgment, but I'll help you."

Jordan looked confused. "How?

"The time machine."

Jordan's hands flew to her mouth. "But, but you said no. You said—"

"I said it was too risky, and it is. It still doesn't work." Kale was once more on his feet. He walked to the foot of her bed and turned to face her, his hands spread wide. "Look, there's a lot of work to do. It scares the shit out of me to think about sending a human subject into the past when I can't even send an inanimate object. It's extremely risky."

Jordan wiped her tears with the edge of her bed sheet. "I'm willing to accept the risk. I don't know how to explain it to you. I love her enough to risk dying to reach her."

"I've been thinking about this since you first suggested it. There are so many risks that the thought of it scares me to death, but after mulling it over, I think we might be able to make it work. I'll help you on five conditions."

Jordan frowned. "What conditions?"

Kale held up his left hand and started counting off. "First, the implant. You need to go through with the surgery so if we are successful with the time travel, we're not dealing with the added complications of a hover-chair. While you're recovering from surgery, I'll work on the time machine."

Kale folded down one finger. "Second, even if we're successful, we do nothing until we can establish two-way travel. I will not send you anywhere without the ability to retrieve you. If you can't live with that, we'll end this discussion right now."

Hope began to rise in Jordan's chest. "I can live with that."

"All right. Third, once we're able to send and retrieve an inanimate object, we'll work with non-human subjects until I feel sure the transfers are completely safe. We'll start with rats and work our way up. This is a lab experiment, Jordan. You can't lose sight of that. Agreed?"

Jordan crossed her arms in front of her. "Agreed."

Kale folded down another finger. "Two more conditions. We need to have a very serious discussion about time paradoxes. You need to understand that your presence in the past will change the future—changes that may affect a lot of people. We need to come up with a set of rules to minimize the impact."

Jordan thought about it. "I've never considered that aspect before, but I certainly understand what a time paradox is. I don't think that's an unreasonable condition."

Kale sat on the edge and took her hand. Jordan could see the internal struggle on his face. "What's the fifth condition?" she asked softly.

Kale looked at her, fresh tears in his eyes. "Fifth, if this doesn't work... if I can't send you back, or if you die trying, promise me you won't hate me forever. I couldn't live with that."

Jordan lost all control as she realized that Kale was compromising everything he believed in to help her. She opened her arms to him, her turn to provide comfort. Tears fell from both their eyes as they clung to each other in love and friendship. "I could never hate you. Even if you refused to help me at all, I would never hate you. I love you, Kale. Don't you know that? You're the brother I never had."

Kale pulled back and retrieved two tissues from the box on the bedside table. He handed one to Jordan and dried his own eyes with the other. "I will do everything I can to bring you and Maggie together."

CHAPTER 12

Kale went home that evening with a heavy heart. He found himself constantly on the edge of tears as he came to terms with what he had committed to do. If he was successful, he would lose his best friend to the clutches of time. If he failed, there was a good chance that Jordan would die. Both possibilities were unthinkable, but what he feared most was not knowing what Jordan would have to endure during the transfer, or in what condition she would arrive when she landed in the past. Even exhaustive testing with animal subjects couldn't predict what would happen to a human being. What Kale feared most was losing Jordan in the transfer and never knowing what happened to her.

He went to bed hoping to gain temporary relief from his worries. Unfortunately, when he closed his eyes, he had little else to focus on but the fact that everything could go wrong. After an hour of anxiety, he sat on the edge of the bed and lowered his head into his hands. Resigning himself to a sleepless night, he dressed and went to the barn.

* * *

While Kale was busy working on the time machine, Jordan was engrossed in the fourth volume of Maggie's diaries. This volume began where the previous one had ended, with ordinary descriptions of day-to-day life on the horse farm. Jordan was growing bored when she came across an interesting entry.

I met someone new today. Her name is Jan.

Jordan frowned as a twinge of jealousy touched her heart. She read on.

Jan is unlike anyone I have ever met. She is enthusiastic and brash. She answered an ad placed in the Burlington Free Press for a stable hand. At first, I had doubts as to her abilities, as she is quite petite; however, she laid my fears to rest when she literally picked up a large hay bale and threw it over her head for ten feet. I've been stacking hay for a lot of years and I still struggle with some of the standard sized bales. She also seems to have a natural affinity with the horses. Gentle, but firm. She gained their respect almost instantly.

I have already mentioned that she is petite. No taller than five foot two inches and very slim. She has short blonde hair, almost boyish in style, green eyes similar to my own, and a deep cleft in her chin. I find myself staring at that cleft as it accents her naturally beautiful face.

Jordan felt the anger rise in her chest.

I find myself thinking about her often. In the mornings, I stand by the kitchen window and watch the barnyard, hoping to get a glimpse of her as she exercises the horses. I believe she has caught me staring once or twice. Her smile is very endearing. Now that Mom and Dad have moved full-time to Florida, I'm considering asking her to move into the spare bedroom instead of living in the bunkhouse. It would be nice to have some companionship close by in the evenings.

Jordan slammed the book closed. She took a deep breath. Maggie had a right to have relationships. Still angry, she reopened the book and read the date of the entry. August 20, 2014. That would make Maggie twenty-six years old. She stared at the back-slanted handwriting and for the first time realized that Maggie must have been left-handed. Jordan closed her eyes and imagined Maggie reaching with her left hand to stroke Jan's cheek. She shook her head. *Stop it, Jordan. You have no right to be jealous. This happened years ago.*

Jordan opened her eyes. "I hope she treated you well, Maggie," she whispered softly. She closed the diary and placed it on the bedside table. She reached for the automatic control and lowered the head of her bed. She closed her eyes and chased away images of Maggie and Jan sleeping in each other's arms. It was a long time before Jordan finally fell asleep.

The next day was filled with tests and examinations. Jordan passed the physical examinations with ease, but the lab results were not in yet.

Peter walked into the room with the results, his smile wide, "We're on for surgery tonight. Your lab work looks excellent. Are you ready?"

"You bet I am. The sooner we get this done, the sooner I can get out of here!"

* * *

The next morning, Andi intercepted Kale as they left their daily briefing to head to the lab. "Um, Kale, are you free for dinner?" she asked nervously.

Kale ran his hand through his already disheveled hair. "Oh, I'm sorry, Andi. Jordan had the electrode preparation surgery last night. She's doing so well that Peter is letting her come home tomorrow. I really need to clean the house tonight."

Andi was disappointed. "Oh, well, that's all right. Maybe another time?"

Kale stopped her as she began to walk away. "Andi, wait. What if you come to my place and I cook for you after I clean?"

Andi found the hopeful look on his face endearing. She also found it sweet that Kale wanted to make Jordan's home clean for her homecoming. She smiled brightly and reached out to straighten his collar. "What do you say to this: I'll come over early and we'll cook dinner together. Then I'll give you a hand cleaning the house."

Kale blushed bright red. "You don't need to do that," he said.

"I know I don't, but I want to. What time would you like me to come over?"

"Anytime you like, I guess. You can even follow me home after work if you want to."

Andi smiled. "All right." She looked around as an awkward silence fell between them. "Well, I guess we should get to work."

"Oh, yes, you're right. After you," Kale said, as a smile spread over his face.

* * *

At lunch, Kale left the institute to run to the grocery store. He bought food for dinner as well as a bottle of wine. On his way back, he stopped to visit Jordan.

He pushed the door open. Jordan was gazing longingly out the window. Kale stepped into the room. "Hey."

Jordan turned around, smiling brightly. "Hi! I wasn't expecting you so early."

Kale grinned. "Change of plan. I have a date tonight."

"Oh really?" she teased. "With Andi? What's on the agenda?"

"Housework."

Jordan frowned. "Come again?"

"Housework. Actually, dinner, and then housework."

Jordan shook her head. "All right, run that by me again. I thought you said dinner then housework."

"I did." Kale enjoyed the confused look on Jordan's face. "Andi is coming over right after work to help me clean the house before you come home tomorrow. We're going to cook dinner together first."

"Well, I'll be. How did she react to that suggestion?"

Kale sat on the edge of Jordan's bed. "It was her idea. She asked if I was free for dinner, and when I explained my plan to straighten up the house, she offered to help. I certainly wasn't going to turn her down. I'm looking forward to it."

"You really don't have to clean the house for me."

"Oh, yes I do. I'm afraid I haven't been very diligent about picking up after myself over the past few days. Besides, I want your homecoming to be perfect."

"Just going home is perfect enough. I'm looking forward to sleeping in my own bed again and wearing something besides this ever-so-flattering hospital gown. That reminds me. Could you take that bag of clothing home and bring me some clean things to go home in tomorrow?"

"Sure, no problem. I wanted to stop in to see you on my way back to the lab because I probably won't make it tonight."

"That's all right. I've got a lot of reading to do, though I've come to a point in the diaries that I'm not enjoying very much."

Kale frowned. "What do you mean?"

Jordan opened a diary and handed it to Kale. "Here, read this."

I find myself thinking about her often. In the mornings, I stand by the kitchen window and watch the barnyard, hoping to get a glimpse of her as she exercises the horses. I believe she has caught me staring once or twice. Her smile is very endearing.

Kale looked at Jordan over the top of the page. She was sitting with her arms crossed, her chin lowered to her chest. She was pouting. He said, "It's not like you haven't had other lovers."

Jordan looked at him. "No, I guess not, but it still bothers me. That should be me, Kale."

"You really need to keep things in perspective here. You're acting like Maggie is cheating on you." He held the diary up for her to see. "All of this is in the past. It's already happened. It's history."

Jordan pressed her head back into the mattress. "I know that, but it still hurts to know there was someone special in her life, someone who wasn't me."

"You had someone special in your life too. How does Maggie's relationship with Jan differ from your relationship with Susan?"

Jordan took Kale's hand and held it for a long time. Kale waited patiently. Finally, she raised her eyes and smiled. "How did you become so smart?"

Kale smiled back at her. "From living with you for the past four years."

Jordan chuckled. "You would think someone with your intelligence would learn how to comb his hair."

Kale's free hand immediately shot to his head. "What's wrong with my hair?"

*   *   *

Andi and Kale each carried two bags full of groceries into the house, along with the bag of Jordan's laundry. Kale held the door open for Andi, who smiled at him as she squeezed past.

"Wow, what a beautiful kitchen. It looks new," she said.

Kale placed his bags on the kitchen table then took the ones Andi was holding and placed them with the others. "We just remodeled it. The contractors finished it early this week with the installation of the new cabinets. Feel free to browse while I take care of these clothes," Kale suggested as he left Andi in the kitchen and went to Jordan's room.

Kale emptied the bag of clothing on Jordan's bed and methodically checked the pockets of the jeans before throwing them in the hamper. To his surprise, he found a folded piece of paper in one of the back pockets. He dropped the jeans onto the bed and carefully opened the paper. It appeared to be very old and frayed at the edges. He began to read,

My Dearest Jordan,

I awoke this morning and saw your beautiful face beside me. Last night was so incredible. How did you have the energy to make love after working so hard yesterday filling the well? I wanted desperately to wake you with kisses and make love to you all day long, but I knew you needed to sleep. Thank you for filling the well. You were right. Putting it in the middle of the north pasture was a bad idea. How did you become so wise, lover? I have decided to take an early morning ride along the west ridge. I anticipate making love with you upon my return.

I love you with all my heart, Maggie.

Kale felt sick to his stomach. *Jordan, did you write this letter? Did you write it to yourself? It can't possibly be real... Maggie's been dead for one hundred years.*

Kale rubbed his face vigorously. Then he remembered he had left Andi in the kitchen. Carefully, he refolded the paper and shoved it into the inside pocket of his jacket. Resolving to push his worries into the background until Andi left, he returned to his date in the kitchen.

Andi had started to unpack one bag of groceries. "Is all of this for dinner?"

Kale searched through the bags as he answered her question. "No. We were out of a few things, so I picked them up while I was out. Ah, here it is." Kale pulled a bottle of wine and handed it to Andi. He pointed to a drawer. "The corkscrew is in that drawer, long-stemmed glasses in the cupboard to the left of the refrigerator. How about pouring us each a glass while I put these groceries away?"

"Sure." Andi took the bottle from Kale and promptly located the corkscrew and glasses. "I'm surprised you cook the old-fashioned way," Andi said as she poured the wine.

"What do you mean?"

"It's much easier to just pop a four-course packet into the hydrowave."

Kale looked over his shoulder as he transferred the canned goods to the cupboard. "My grandmother taught me how to cook, and she preferred the hands-on style of preparing a meal. I've tried the pre-packaged stuff, but, quite frankly, you can't beat home cooking."

Andi carried Kale's glass to him as he placed the last can on the shelf. "I agree. How did you come to be so self-sufficient?"

He accepted the glass and leaned against the counter top. "When I was a kid, my grandmother took care of me while my mom worked. She made it her mission to be sure I learned how to cook and clean. I hated every minute of it, but today, I really appreciate her diligence. When I moved in with Jordan four years ago, it became somewhat of a necessity to take care of myself. Between Jordan's independent spirit and her limitations, she forced me to carry my own weight."

Andi sipped her wine. "This isn't Jordan's first implant?"

"No, I thought you knew that. I'm sorry. I should have given you more background when you joined us a few days ago."

"No better time than the present. Tell me about her."

Kale pulled out kitchen chair and offered it to Andi. "All right. Have a seat and I'll give you the details while I start dinner."

"Oh, no, you don't. I said I would help with dinner. Lasagna, right?" Kale nodded. "I happen to make a killer spaghetti sauce."

For the next half hour, Kale and Andi worked together as they talked. "Tell me about how Jordan ended up in a hover-chair," she said.

Kale diced onions as he spoke. "Jordan was sixteen years old. She grew up right here on this farm. They raised horses. She was riding her mare at a full gallop across the north pasture when her horse fell into a dry well. She was thrown quite a few feet and landed in such a way that her spinal cord was completely severed."

Andi cringed. "That must have been very difficult for her."

Kale scraped the onions into the pan. "I'm sure it was. She mentioned once that she seriously considered suicide when she was a teenager. It's tough to be different at that age, and Jordan was certainly very different from her peers—in more ways than one." Kale placed the cutting board in the sink then leaned against the counter next to Andi. He crossed his legs at the ankles and sipped his wine as he watched her cook.

Andi looked at Kale from the corner of her eye. "You mean because she's gay?"

"You know?"

Andi stirred the sauce as she nodded her head.

"How?"

"She told me. Where are your herbs and spices?" Kale frowned. "Third drawer down, next to the stove. She told you? That surprises me. She's usually not very forthcoming with that information."

Andi squatted down in front of the drawer and sorted through the spices. "Let's just say she was protecting someone she loves very much." She continued to search through the jars and cans until she found what she was looking for. "Garlic, basil, oregano, rosemary, cayenne. You have everything I need. Who's the cook in this family, you or Jordan?"

"Jordan burns water. I do most of the cooking. What do you mean, she was protecting someone she loves? Who was she talking about?"

Andi shook spices into the meat mixture. "You," she said without looking at Kale.

"Me? Who does she think I need protection from?"

"Herself, apparently," Andi replied cryptically.

Kale was silent for several moments, digesting their conversation. He was having a problem connecting Jordan's sexuality with his need to be protected. "Are you saying she told you she was gay to protect me? Why would she do that?"

Andi turned to Kale and handed her empty wine glass to him. "Please?" she asked with a sweet smile.

Kale melted. He refilled her glass and handed it back to her.

Andi kissed him lightly on the cheek. "Thanks." She sipped the wine, then turned back to the stove to tend the meat mixture still browning in the pan.

Speechless, Kale didn't notice that the water had begun to boil until Andi tapped him on the arm. He set the wine bottle aside, then loosely arranged the wide lasagna noodles in the water. As he stirred the noodles, his thoughts returned to their conversation. "Why does Jordan believe I need protection from her?"

Andi added several cans of tomatoes and a can of paste to the herbed and spiced meat. She stirred the mixture as she answered Kale's question. "Not from her, but from any potential misunderstanding on my part about her role in your life."

"Jordan is my best friend, Andi, nothing more," he said defensively.

Andi turned toward Kale and lifted a spoonful of sauce to his mouth. "I know that now. Here—taste," she said.

Kale obediently opened his mouth and closed his eyes to savor the sauce. "That tastes great."

"Thanks," she replied. "I think these noodles are cooked enough to drain."

Kale retrieved a strainer from the cupboard and placed it in the sink. Then he fetched the cheeses from the refrigerator. "Okay, my turn. Drink your wine while I layer the lasagna." Kale coated the baking pan with a thin layer of no-stick spray, then diligently added layer upon layer of noodles, cheese, and sauce into the pan, topping it off with a final layer of sauce and a layer of shredded cheese.

Andi watched him work. "It looks good, Kale. I can't wait to taste it."

Kale slid the pan into the oven and set the timer on the stove. He turned to Andi. "Let's sit in the living room while this bakes."

She stepped away from the counter. "Sure. Lead the way."

Kale led Andi to the living room where they sat on the couch. Andi shifted her weight so she was sitting sideways, facing Kale. She leaned her shoulder against the back of the couch and sipped her wine. "I thought you said the house needed to be cleaned. It looks fine to me," she said, looking around the living room.

"It needs a good dusting. The rugs need to be vacuumed, and the bathrooms really need to be cleaned. You're right, it doesn't need much, but I want it to be clean to minimize any unnecessary exposure to germs for Jordan."

"Did you decorate this room? It's very nice," Andi said.

"No, Jordan did. When her parents died, they left everything to her. Painful memories of them were everywhere, so she refurnished the house. It really helped her to heal."

"How long ago did she lose her parents?"

"Six years." His eyes shifted from the wine to Andi's eyes.

Andi placed her wine glass on the table and traced the side of Kale's face with her fingertips. "You're a good friend, Kale Simmons. Jordan is lucky to have you."

Kale grasped Andi's hand and turned it upward to kiss the palm. Her eyes closed at his touch. Kale's desire escalated as he took her face between his hands and kissed her fully on the mouth. Andi wrapped her arms around his neck as their kiss deepened.

Neither of them heard the oven buzzer.

CHAPTER 13

When Kale arrived at the hospital at noon to collect Jordan, she was fully dressed and sitting up in bed, eager to be going home. She hugged Kale affectionately. "Break me out of here. I can't wait to go home," she exclaimed.

Kale grinned. "Has Peter released you yet?"

"I'm just about to."

"Peter, good morning." Jordan held out her hand. Peter took it gently.

"Good morning to both of you," he said. "So, Jordan, are you ready to go home?"

"More than ready. Bust me loose, warden!"

Peter laughed. "All right, but not before you understand your parole conditions." Jordan and Kale chuckled. Peter turned to Kale. "Kale, as her parole officer, I expect you to be sure she follows these rules, understand?"

Kale saluted the doctor. "Yes, sir! I'm really going to enjoy finally having the upper hand over this one."

Jordan crossed her arms and narrowed her eyes at the two men. "Enjoy this while you can, 'cause I'm planning a coup d'état as soon as I'm able."

Peter grinned. "Of that, I have no doubt. Okay, here are the rules: You need to stay in bed for a few days. Next, you'll need some help getting in and out of your hover-chair for the first few days after you're out of bed. The incision looks really good, but for safety's sake, we don't want to do anything to aggravate it. That means you'll need someone there to physically lift you."

"I can do that," Kale offered immediately.

Jordan looked at Kale. "Don't you need to be working on the implant?"

Kale took her hand. "Peter and I have already talked about this. We're at a stage where the testing can be done from our home. In fact, we're in the process of moving a few pieces of test equipment to the farm. We can carry out the next week or two of clinical trials there."

Jordan looked from Kale to Peter. "It seems you two have already planned this whole thing, haven't you?" She tried to sound firm but failed to suppress her grin.

Peter looked at her over the top of his glasses. "Well, someone's got to make sure you behave." He continued. "Finally, I want to see you in my office in a week for a follow-up exam." Jordan and Kale watched Peter as he signed her chart. He handed a copy of the follow-up items to Kale. Peter slipped his stylus into the breast pocket of his lab coat then held the clipboard close to his chest. "All right then. You're released."

Jordan opened her arms to Peter and hugged him affectionately. "Thank you."

Peter stood and cleared his throat. "Well, yes... um... just be sure to follow the regime I've outlined for you so we can get you back on your feet—literally."

"I will, I will. Thank you again."

"You're welcome. Now get out of here."

* * *

As Jordan and Kale turned into the driveway, there were a number of vans in front of the barn, and men were unloading equipment. She saw that one truck belonged to a local furnace dealer. She looked at Kale. "What's going on here?"

"It's just the crew from the lab," he replied.

"But there's a solar furnace truck here as well."

Kale switched off the ignition and turned to her. "Some of this equipment is pretty sensitive to temperature and humidity. We needed to make some improvements to the barn to make this work. I hired Tom's crew to install new insulation, wiring, and solar-absorbing wallboard. We needed a new furnace."

Jordan's eyebrows shot up high on her forehead. "Something tells me these improvements are as much for your benefit as mine." She grinned.

Kale chuckled. "Guilty as charged. I have to admit, the old solar heater is a pain in the neck when I'm out there working on the machine. The far end of the barn is a really large area to heat." He looked once more at the flurry of activity in front of the barn, then back at Jordan. "Okay, let's get you into the house." He climbed out of the vehicle and circled around to the passenger side to retrieve

Jordan. He lifted her into his arms and carried her to the front door. As they approached the door, it suddenly opened and a smiling Andrea Ellis greeted them.

"Andi!" Jordan was surprised and pleased. "What are you doing here?"

Andi stepped aside to allow Kale and his cargo to enter into the kitchen. "Kale wanted so badly to make sure things were perfect for you when you returned, I finished up what we were unable to complete last night."

Jordan looked at the blush rising on Kale's face. He squirmed under the scrutiny. "Ah, let me get you into your bed." He carried Jordan to her bedroom and gently lowered her to the bed.

Jordan kept her eyes glued to Kale's face. She couldn't resist teasing him. "What exactly did you and Andi accomplish last night?"

Kale shoved his hands deep into his back pockets and looked everywhere but at Jordan.

"Kale?" she prompted again, taking a wicked delight in his discomfort.

Finally, he looked at Jordan. "Ah, gee," he said.

Jordan suddenly felt sorry for Kale as she patted the bed beside her. "Sit," she commanded. When Kale settled in beside her, she took his hand. "Look at me." Kale finally allowed his eyes to meet Jordan's. She smiled broadly. "I'm happy for you. Andi seems really nice. I hope things work out for the two of you."

Kale looked away. "She likes you. She really wanted to help make your homecoming special."

"I like her too. I look forward to getting to know her better. I'll have to thank her for helping you."

"You're welcome," Andi said from the doorway. She walked to the bed and stood beside Kale, her hand on his shoulder. "How are you feeling?"

Jordan grinned. "Remarkably well, considering I had spinal surgery a day ago. I'm looking forward to being back on my feet and getting on with life."

"I'm sure you are." Andi looked at Kale. "Lunch is ready if you're hungry."

Jordan's stomach growled, as if on cue. She chuckled. "I'm famished. A little home-cooked food is going to taste great after that mush they served in the hospital."

An anticipatory look crossed Andi's face. "I hope you like quiche and salad."

Jordan's eyes grew wide. "Oh, my God! I haven't had quiche since before Mom and Dad died. I love quiche," she exclaimed.

Andi smiled broadly. "All right then. We'll have our own little picnic right here on your bed. Kale?" she said brightly.

Kale was on his feet in an instant. "Lead the way."

Jordan closed her eyes and smiled. *He's going to be just fine when I'm gone.*

Jordan did her best to stifle a yawn as the trio finished their makeshift picnic. "I'm sorry, guys. I guess I'm more tired than I thought."

Andi collected the dishes and placed them on one of the trays. "Come on, Kale, we need to let Jordan sleep. She needs to heal in order to be ready for the implant."

Kale had been sitting in Jordan's hover-chair by the side of the bed enjoying his lunch. At Andi's suggestion, he handed his empty dishes to her then climbed out of the chair. "Good idea." While Andi carried the dirty dishes to the kitchen, Kale circled Jordan's bed and knelt on the opposite side. "Okay, we need to rotate the tires."

"Rotate the tires? Since when did I become an old jalopy?"

"Since you backfired on us and nearly blew your engine a week ago. Hold on while I roll you onto your side. Peter said he wanted you to change positions frequently to avoid aggravating the incision site." Kale placed one hand on each side of her hips and physically repositioned her while Jordan assisted by grasping the side of the bed with her hands. He bent her top leg at the knee to improve her balance then pulled the blanket up over her. "Are you comfortable?" he asked.

"Very. Thanks, but you know I could do that by myself." Jordan yawned again. "Sorry about that."

Kale kissed her on the head. "No apology necessary. Get some sleep. I'll wake you for dinner."

Kale found Andi in the kitchen loading the sonic cleanser. As he entered the room, his breath waged war with his heart for room in his chest as he felt an overwhelming sense of attraction for this young woman. He quickly crossed the room and captured her in his arms.

Andi wrapped her arms around his waist and dropped her head to the side to allow Kale greater access to her neck. "Oh, God... that feels good."

"Hmm," Kale murmured as he held her close, enjoying the scent of her freshly-washed hair. "You smell good."

Andi stiffened at the sound of a door closing in the yard. "Kale... as much as I'm enjoying this, we have a dozen lab workers crawling around the barn. I'd rather not be caught in a compromising position."

"Damn, you're right." He backed away from her to avoid temptation. "I guess I should go give them a hand, huh?"

"I think we should both go give them a hand. The sooner they're gone, the sooner we'll be alone."

Kale frowned. "What about Jordan?"

"We don't have to be secretive in front of Jordan. I'm not worried about her."

Kale grinned wickedly. "I like the way you think. Come on." He took Andi's hand and led her to the barn.

Andi explored the barn while Kale disbanded the crew. The insulated room was at the far end of the barn, allowing the primary entrance to be isolated from the new room but open to the livestock area. It was here that Kale found Andi after the crew had left.

"There you are," he said. Andi was stroking the mane of Jordan's cherished mustang.

"He's a beautiful horse," Andi said.

Kale rested his arm on the top of the horse stall and crossed his legs. "Do you ride?"

Andi continued to stroke the animal's neck. "I did as a child. I haven't ridden in years. It seems that as we grow older, we allow our priorities to change... oftentimes not for the better," she commented. She glanced at Kale. "Do you ride?"

Kale threw his head back and laughed. "Me? You're kidding, right? I grew up in New York City. I'm a city boy to the core. Jordan got me on a horse about a year ago and talked me into riding to the north pasture with her to show me where she'd had her accident."

"How was it?"

"By the time we reached the old well, my backside hurt so much I was standing in the stirrups. Worst part was I still had to get back to the house. I swore I'd never get back on a horse after that."

Andi looked at Kale from the corner of her eye. "Are you sure I couldn't talk you into another ride? A short one?"

Kale looked around nervously.

"Please?" Andi asked sweetly.

Kale put his hands on his hips. "Oh, all right. But only a short ride, and not until it warms up, okay?"

Andi clapped her hands gleefully. "Deal. Okay, let's make one final check of the equipment and head into the house to start dinner."

Kale took Andi by the hand and led her toward the room at the opposite end of the barn. He held the door open for her to enter before him. Together, they circled the room and powered down the equipment.

When they reached the far end of the room, Andi approached a large object and reached for a corner of the tarp covering it. "What's this?"

Kale lunged forward and prevented her from removing the tarp. "It's nothing. Just a pile of junk."

Andi looked at Kale and then at the tarp. She narrowed her eyes. "What are you trying to hide?"

"Nothing," he said.

Andi crossed her arms. "I don't believe you." She walked a few feet away and then turned to face him. "I don't want to start this relationship by keeping secrets from each other. I feel like you don't trust me."

Kale ran his hand through his hair, frustrated. "Andi, I really wish you'd wait until I have it working. Otherwise, I'll feel like a loser if it fails."

Andi closed the distance between them and stood on tiptoe to kiss his cheek. "You could never be a loser in my eyes. You can trust me."

Kale sighed and dropped his chin to his chest. "All right." He lifted the edge of the tarp and slowly pulled it off the machine.

Andi's eyes grew wide as she slowly circled the device, inspecting it very closely. Finally, she approached the console and reached for the piece of paper sitting on top. As she read the complicated mathematical formulas written there, her hand crept up to cover her mouth. She looked again at the contraption and then at Kale. She seemed awestruck. "It's a time machine, isn't it?"

Kale was stunned. "You know what it is?"

Andi's eyebrows arched. "I'm a physicist. Of course I know what it is. My God, I've always wanted to build one, but I never had the time or the resources." She walked back to the machine and touched the rings. She looked back at Kale. "Have you tested it yet?"

Kale nodded. "Just diagnostic runs. I made an adjustment to the design about a week ago, but I haven't had a chance to test it yet. Jordan and I were about to do that when she landed back in the hospital."

Andi's head whipped toward the door of the new lab. "Jordan!" she exclaimed. "I almost forgot about her. She's probably awake by now." She turned to Kale once more. "We need to go fix dinner. Promise me we can talk about this after Jordan goes to bed for the night?"

Kale grinned, an ecstatic feeling filling his breast as he realized he had found someone who shared his dream. "You bet. How long did you plan to stay tonight?"

Andi looked at him coyly. "Who says I'm going home?"

* * *

Jordan parked the truck in front of the barn and climbed out. She brushed the dust from her jeans and stamped her feet to loosen any dirt she might have gotten on her boots after mending the fences in the north pasture. She headed toward the house and climbed the two steps leading to the porch. She removed her cowboy hat as she pushed the kitchen door open and stepped inside. The first thing she noticed were the freshly-baked cookies cooling on the countertop.

"Jordan, is that you?"

Jordan turned. "In here. In the kitchen." She threw her hat on the table and reached for a cookie just as the kitchen door swung open.

Maggie scolded her. "Hey, you'll ruin your dinner."

"No chance of that happening. I'm famished!"

Maggie approached Jordan and tried to wrap her arms around her waist.

Jordan took a step back. "Whoa. I'm dirty and sweaty from working in the field."

Maggie crossed her arms in front of her chest. "Well then, get in the shower. Dinner will be ready soon."

"Yes ma'am." She leaned in and kissed Maggie on the cheek. "I'll be back shortly. Then maybe you'll let me sample your cookies." Jordan winked at Maggie and headed to her bedroom. She stripped off her dirty clothes and threw them into the hamper.

Jordan pulled the shower curtain back and stepped into the water, soaking her body. She stood there for several long moments, basking in the feel of the needle-like spray massaging her worn muscles. She took a step out of the water and washed the sweat and grime from her body. After she rinsed the soap from her limbs, she soaked her head, lathering honeysuckle shampoo into her hair.

Jordan remained under the spray for a long time with her eyes closed and her hands braced on the sides of the shower as the water rinsed the soap from her hair. She felt a presence behind her. She willed her eyes to remain closed as she felt hands slide across her hips and abdomen while a soft, supple body molded itself against her from behind. One hand slipped downward, finding a home below her navel, while the other hand pressed firmly on her abdomen. She was a willing captive of this creature as she softly moaned her pleasure.

Jordan turned around, took Maggie's face firmly between her hands, and devoured the redhead's mouth. "I love you," she whispered.

Maggie gasped for breath as she broke the kiss. She turned her head so that Jordan could have access to her neck. She realized Jordan had turned the tables on her as she closed her eyes and savored the feel of Jordan's lips sliding down her neck.

Jordan lowered herself to her knees, leaving a trail of kisses from the hollow of Maggie's neck to the triangle of curly red hair above Maggie's treasure. Maggie pressed herself against the shower wall and braced her hands on Jordan's shoulders as Jordan's tongue slipped into her curls and massaged her already swollen bud.

"Oh, my God," Maggie gasped as her abdomen convulsed of its own accord. "Jordan... harder, baby... please."

Jordan obliged as she captured Maggie's engorged clit between her lips and rhythmically sucked, flicking the end of it with her tongue.

Maggie was wild with desire as the tension mounted deep within her core. Jordan slid two fingers into her lover's center and repeatedly thrusted upward as Maggie returned the motion with downward lunges. Maggie tightened around Jordan's fingers as her orgasm began to crest.

Suddenly, Maggie's nails dug deep into Jordan's shoulders as her body first stiffened, then began to convulse uncontrollably. "I'm coming! Baby, I'm coming! Don't stop," she cried out as orgasm weakened her knees and forced her to lean heavily on Jordan for support. Jordan wrapped her free arm around Maggie's waist as she pinned Maggie against the shower wall. She pressed her cheek against Maggie's abdomen and held her there until the spasms subsided and Maggie was able to regain her senses. Jordan released her hold on Maggie, lightly taking the quivering woman into her arms. The two women clung to each other for several moments before pulling apart. Jordan kissed her tenderly then leaned her forehead against Maggie's. "I adore you," she whispered.

Maggie smiled. "You are a beautiful lover. That was wonderful."

A buzzer sounded in the kitchen. Maggie looked at Jordan, her face tinged with regret. "That would be the oven timer. Sorry, baby, but if I don't take the casserole out of the oven, we'll be eating burnt cardboard for dinner." Maggie stepped out of the shower and wrapped a large towel around her. She grinned at Jordan and then stood on tiptoe to place a kiss on her lips. "I'll make it up to you tonight, lover," she promised.

Jordan watched as Maggie spun around and left the bathroom. She then reached for her towel and completely covered her face to mute the scream of frustration she felt rise in her throat. She forced herself to take long deep breaths to calm her nerves. Finally, she realized she couldn't spend the rest of the day in the shower. She toweled herself dry. Moments later, she donned clean clothing and sat on the edge of the bed as she combed the tangles out of her wet hair. Her mind was never far from Maggie. Jordan moaned and threw herself back onto the bed.

"Jordan, wake up. Dinner's ready. Come on, hon, time to get up."

Jordan fought off sleep as she forced her eyes open. "Andi?"

Andi smiled at Jordan. "I hope you're hungry. We've got a tuna casserole waiting for us."

Confused, Jordan raised herself onto her elbows and looked around. "Where's Maggie?" she asked. Her mind felt cloudy as anxiety settled in her chest.

Andi frowned. "Maggie?"

Jordan lay flat on her back again and rubbed her eyes with the heels of the hands. Her heart was beating wildly as she remembered the passionate encounter in the shower. *Calm down, Jordan. Take a deep breath. You were obviously dreaming again.* She opened her eyes once more. Andi was still standing there, clearly confused. Jordan sought to defuse the situation by grinning broadly. "Did you say dinner was ready? I'm famished."

Andi smiled. "Dinner is indeed ready. Kale is dishing it up right now."

A voice boomed from the doorway. "Jordan, are you hitting on my girlfriend?"

Jordan feigned innocence. "Would I do that?"

Andi interrupted the banter. "All right, you two. Enough of that."

Kale grinned. "Dinner's ready. When should I bring it in?"

Andi lifted her face to Kale and accepted a quick kiss. "Right after I check the incision. Peter wanted to make sure the dressing is changed every day. Give us a couple of minutes, okay?"

Kale glanced at Jordan over Andi's shoulder. "Hey—no fair. You wouldn't let me look at your butt."

"That's because you're not a hottie. Only hotties can look at my butt."

"I thought you said I was cute?"

"You might be if you would learn to comb your hair."

Andi laughed as Kale looked offended by Jordan's comment. "We'll be there in a minute," she said to him again as she pushed him toward the door. When he was gone, Andi turned and grinned at Jordan. "You are so bad!"

* * *

After dinner was finished and the dishes cleared away, Kale carried Jordan to the living room and placed her on the couch in a semi-reclined position. When Jordan was settled comfortably, Kale pulled the Victorian settee closer to the couch, and Andi refilled their wine glasses.

Jordan asked about the new lab in the barn. "What does it look like?"

Kale sipped his wine. "The end of the barn that contains the machine has been finished with new synthetic wallboard, new lighting, a raised floor, and a drop ceiling. It's pretty well-insulated to keep the equipment in a clean, stable environment. The entrance to the barn still opens into the livestock area. None of that has changed."

Andi became animated. "Speaking of livestock, Jordan, your horses are absolutely magnificent."

Jordan smiled. "Thanks. Do you ride?"

"I did as a child, but it's been many years. Kale has agreed to go for a ride with me when it warms up."

Jordan looked at Kale, shocked. "You're going to ride? You swore you'd never get on a horse again when you stiff-legged it back to the barn after that ride with me."

Kale shrugged. "Hard to say no to the boss," he joked.

Andi patted his leg. "That's right." Jordan chuckled. "Is your project inside the new lab, too?" she asked tentatively, not sure if Andi was privy to Kale's experiment.

"You mean the time machine?" Andi asked.

Jordan was surprised. "You told her about it?"

Kale grinned. "Actually, she guessed. Apparently, Andi has had an interest in time travel for a long time."

Andi interrupted the conversation. "Hello, I'm in the room, you know!" She turned to Jordan, who was trying hard to hide a smile. "As a matter of fact, I've been studying time travel theories for quite a while. I've just never had the resources to build a machine of my own. I recognized what Kale's machine was as soon as I saw it." Andi turned to look at Kale. "I'd be happy to give you a hand with it if you'd like."

Kale nodded. "Your degree in physics certainly won't hurt. If you'd like to help, that would be great."

Jordan finished her wine and placed the empty glass on the coffee table. A loud yawn escaped as she reclined once more. "Boy, who would have thought just lying around could be so tiring?"

Kale sat up. "Are you ready for bed?"

Jordan yawned again. "Yeah, I guess so."

"All right, then." Kale lifted her from the couch and carried her to her bedroom.

A short time later, as Jordan fought to keep her eyes open, Kale and Andi both kissed her and wished her a goodnight. By the time Kale pulled the door closed behind them, Jordan was nearly asleep.

Andi and Kale straightened up the living room and carried the wine glasses to the kitchen. As Andi loaded the last glass into the sonic cleanser, she said, "Who is Maggie?"

CHAPTER 14

Kale was caught off guard. He looked around nervously. "She told you about Maggie?"

Andi leaned against the cabinet and crossed her arms over her chest. "Actually, no. When I woke her for dinner, she looked around groggily and asked where Maggie was."

Kale frowned. "Humph. I wonder if she realizes she did that."

"Who is she, Kale?"

Kale rested his hands on his hips and took a deep breath. "It's complicated, and I'm not sure I understand it myself."

"Maybe I can help you to understand."

Kale held Andi's gaze for several moments, unsure about whether he should share Jordan's private world with his new love.

"Is Maggie her girlfriend?" she asked.

"Yes... and no," Kale replied hesitantly.

Andi frowned. "Yes and no? What do you mean?"

Kale rubbed his face with both hands and sighed. "Okay. I'll tell you about Maggie, but you have to promise not to judge Jordan. Like I said, I don't quite understand this myself, but I'm willing to give her the benefit of a doubt. Let's go for a walk while we talk."

Kale slipped his jacket on and then helped Andi with her coat. Once outside, he offered his arm as they walked side by side in the brisk dusk.

"This is a beautiful farm. A person could get used to living here."

Kale looked around as the full moon cast muted shadows across the barnyard. "Yes it is. Jordan was fortunate to have grown up here. Vermont is a beautiful state. So beautiful it makes living through the long winters worth it." Kale fell silent as they continued their walk.

Andi looked at Kale, noting the creases on his forehead. He was obviously deep in thought. "Tell me about Maggie."

Kale stopped and looked at Andi. He signed deeply. "What I'm about to tell you is kind of off-the-wall."

Andi blew on her hands to keep them warm. Kale reached for them and tucked them inside his jacket. Then he wrapped his arms around her, pulling her close to him. "Better?"

Andi smiled. "Very much so, thank you. You can trust me. I promise to keep an open mind, okay?"

Kale nodded. "All right, here goes." He looked at Andi. "Maggie is a ghost."

Andi's head snapped back. "A ghost? You're kidding, right?"

"I wish I was. Maggie is the author of the diaries Jordan has been reading."

Andi took a moment to digest what Kale was telling her. "You mean the diaries she found between the walls?"

"Yes. They were written about one hundred years ago."

"So, she's become infatuated with the woman who wrote them. I don't find that so hard to believe. Haven't you ever had a crush on someone unattainable, like a movie star or someone like that?"

"Yeah, I guess we've all had that kind of crush, but this is so much more than that."

"In what way?"

Kale took a step back and began to pace. "This is where it gets weird."

Andi watched him pace and stepped back to give him the space he appeared to need.

"Jordan claims that Maggie has contacted her."

Andi cocked her head to one side. "Really? How?"

"Through dreams—or visions, as she calls them now. Funny thing is, I believe her."

Andi stopped Kale from pacing by standing in his path. She reached up and took his face between her hands. The look on her face spoke clearly of her seriousness. "Sweetheart, you're obviously worrying yourself sick over this. You don't have to share this with me if you're uncomfortable doing that."

Sweetheart? Kale blinked rapidly. "No, it's all right. I really do need to share this with someone. Keeping it a secret from Peter has been hard enough. I can't imagine keeping it from you—especially if you're going to be around here for a while."

Andi smiled. "I don't plan to go anywhere, so why don't you start from the beginning?"

* * *

Andi wiped a tear from her eye. "My God. That is so sad. She was far too young to have died, and so tragically. I don't blame Jordan for being upset."

"She was overwhelmed with grief. She cried about it for days."

"I think Jordan has a very tender heart. Lost opportunity is one of the saddest things in the world. I can see why it would be difficult for Jordan."

"She's more than upset, she's obsessed. I'm worried about her mental state. Worse yet, I'm worried about how Peter will view her mental state."

"How so?"

"She's in love with a dead woman. If Peter finds out, he might think she's not stable enough for the implant. I don't want that to happen to Jordan. She needs to be out of that chair and on the path to a normal, healthy life. She'll never be able to fulfill her dreams if she isn't."

Andi was silent for a moment. "You said you believe Maggie has contacted Jordan through her dreams. Why do you believe that?"

Kale sat beside Andi on the couch, leaning forward so that his forearms were resting on his knees. He looked at Andi. "The first dream came after Jordan and I found that article and obituary." He nodded to indicate the article and holograph. "In that dream, Jordan woke up and the house was all different, with different furnishings, and she was in her chair, something that had never happened in past dreams."

"She was never in her chair in previous dreams?"

"No, she was always walking. Anyway, she saw Maggie in the dream. Maggie as a teenager. Like I said, we both thought nothing of it, except for the presence of the hover-chair. I think we attributed the dream to information Jordan had gleaned from the diaries. Then, the second dream changed everything. At that point, the dreams were no longer dreams, but visions to Jordan." Kale stopped to reflect on how he was going to explain the subsequent dreams to Andi.

"Visions often imply predictions, and predictions imply future events. How could she predict the future of someone who lived in the past?"

Kale looked at Andi. "My thoughts exactly—at the time, anyway. Jordan called them visions because she saw events in a dream prior to reading about them in the diaries. In the next two dreams, she explained in vivid detail what had happened, then showed me the diary entries she had read after she had already had the dreams. The diary entries matched her dreams exactly. How could she have possibly known what would happen in the diary if there wasn't some sort of psychic connection between her and Maggie?"

Andi sat back, thinking about what Kale had told her. For long moments, neither of them spoke. Finally, Andi broke the silence. "Are you sure they were dreams, or visions, or whatever you want to call them?" Kale looked at her, confused. "Is it possible that she was actually there when the event happened?"

Kale looked at Andi as though she didn't understand what he had been telling her. "Andi, she was here all the time, in the year 2105. In her bed. How could she have been both here in the present and there one hundred years in the past—at the same time?"

"Did Jordan actually have any interaction with Maggie in the dreams?"

Kale thought for a moment about what Jordan had told him. "In the first two dreams there didn't appear to be any. Maggie didn't acknowledge her at all in the first dream—the one in which Maggie was a teenager. In the second dream, Jordan implied there was some interaction on her part, but no response from Maggie. In the third dream, Jordan claims to have interrupted a sexual attack on Maggie by Maggie's then-girlfriend." Kale stopped and threw his hands into the air. "Can you see how crazy this is?"

"To the casual observer, maybe, but I'm not so sure. Have there been any other dreams? Specifically ones where interactions have occurred?" Andi asked.

"One more. While Jordan was in the hospital, she dreamt that she awoke in Maggie's bed one morning, fully intact—no hover-chair or anything. She says she found a note, specifically addressed to her, which Maggie left before going for a morning horse ride." Kale suddenly stopped talking and gasped.

The change in Kale's demeanor startled Andi. "What is it?"

"The letter! Wait right here. I'll be back in a second." Kale left Andi sitting in the living room while he ran into the kitchen and retrieved his jacket. Andi watched him closely as he reached into the inner pocket and pulled out a worn, folded piece of paper.

"What is it?" Andi asked.

Kale unfolded the paper. "I found this in the back pocket of the jeans Jordan was wearing the day she was admitted to the hospital."

Andi took the paper from Kale's shaking hands and carefully opened it.

When she finished reading the letter, she looked at Kale through the veil of tears that had filled her eyes. "Oh, my God! Is this the note Maggie left for Jordan?"

Kale shook his head. "I don't know. It certainly looks very old, but if it is the letter, it would have been written long before Jordan was even born. This doesn't make sense. How would Jordan have gotten this note?"

Andi examined the letter once more, noting the apparent age of the document and the faded print before she looked back at Kale. "There's mention here about Jordan moving a well out of the north pasture. Didn't you say Jordan was injured when her horse stepped into a well? I wonder if that's why she wasn't in her hover-chair in that dream." Andi looked up. "What else did Jordan say about that dream?"

"Jordan was alarmed when she realized the date was March 29, 2019—the day Maggie died. She rode out after Maggie but arrived too late. She found Maggie lying at the bottom of a cliff where her horse had thrown her. Jordan reached her in time for Maggie to die in her arms." Kale stopped and inhaled deeply. "She was devastated, Andi."

Andi touched his arm. "You asked me to be open-minded about this. Now I'm asking you to consider the same." She flicked her long hair back over her shoulder as she turned to face him. "Consider the possibility that she may have been in both dimensions at once—here in the physical, and there in the emotional. You're a scientist. You believe in time travel. Open your mind and consider the possibility. Maybe physical time travel isn't possible, but intellectual time travel is? Maybe Jordan was there. Maybe Maggie did write this letter."

"You're kidding, right? Einstein's theories of time travel all involve the possibility of transferring the human form from one dimension to another. There is nothing in his work that suggests the mind is capable of traveling through time all by itself." Kale ran his hand through his hair and walked a few feet away from Andi.

"All I'm asking is that you keep your mind open to the possibilities."

Confusion and concern clouded Kale's features. "Okay. Let's say intellectual time travel is possible. How the hell am I supposed to send only her mind through time and then manage to bring it back when she's ready to come home? Shit! How would we even know when she returned? Would she be in some sort of trance while she was gone? Would she be in a coma? Would she suddenly wake up and say, 'That was cool, let's do it again?' If she did go into a coma, how would we know it was because of time travel instead of something gone wrong during the attempt?" Kale dropped his head back and looked at the ceiling for a long moment before looking back at Andi.

Andi wrapped her arms around Kale's waist. "Sweetheart, everything you say may be true. I don't know if the machine will work. I don't even know where to begin, but I do know that Jordan appears to be very much in love with Maggie, and she must be dying inside knowing she may never get the chance to be with her. If you were Maggie and I were Jordan, I would do everything in my power to be with you. I couldn't bear the thought of never touching you, never seeing you, never holding you in my arms, never knowing what it was like to make love to you."

Tears sprang to Kale's eyes. He blinked rapidly and then lowered his forehead to Andi's. After a few moments, he lifted his head and placed a gentle kiss where his forehead had just been. "You're right. How can I deny her this? Come hell or high water, I will try to bring them together. I promise you, I will try."

"Well, no time like the present."

* * *

Andi watched Kale as he slowly walked around the time machine, explaining his failed attempt to send the old boot back into time. As she watched, she admired the degree of passion with which he applied himself to his work. Once again, she thanked the heavens above that she had been given the opportunity to meet this extraordinary man.

"When the boot failed to disappear, I carried out a controlled experiment with smoke to understand why, and I realized that there was a minute amount of gravity still remaining in the center of the sphere as it rotated. The amount of smoke that remained in the exact center of the sphere was so small it was nearly indiscernible, but still, it was there. In order for the machine to work, there has to be absolutely no gravity within the sphere."

"How do you plan to correct that problem?"

Kale stopped and grinned at Andi. "I hope it's already corrected. It was Jordan who came up with the solution. Can you believe it?"

Andi smiled. "Jordan? Really?"

"Yeah. When the experiment first failed, I was pretty bummed out and went into the house looking for sympathy. Of course, Jordan being Jordan, she was anything but sympathetic. In fact, her lack of compassion made me even more determined to try again. I discussed the results with Jordan, and she suggested I apply a counterforce to the spinning rings. That suggestion led to the idea of internal rotating rings. They should eliminate the remaining gravity, creating a black hole. But they should also cause this black hole to rotate. According to Einstein's energy equation, rotating the black hole would finally give us the amount of energy we need to make time travel possible."

Andi looked skeptical. "You mean to tell me Jordan realized all of that?"

Kale chuckled. "Hell, no! Jordan is a brilliant doctor, and she's a whiz with computers, but she has absolutely no clue when it comes to metaphysical science. Her comments and suggestions did, however, prompt me to do the research I needed to come to these conclusions. Any way you look at it, she deserves a great deal of credit if we get this to work."

Andi clasped her hands together. "I totally agree, but let's not put the cart before the horse. What do we need to do to get started?"

"I've already fitted the second set of rings. The next step is testing."

"Okay, then," Andi said. "Let's get started."

"Before we conduct any experiments, we need to do another smoke test. If you don't mind, I'd rather be fresh to do that. Let's plan to start right after the crew leaves tomorrow. Okay?"

CHAPTER 15

Andi nudged the door to Jordan's room open with her foot as she carried in a tray of breakfast foods. Kale had left early that morning to meet one of the technicians at the lab. Jordan was not only awake, but also not in her bed.

"Jordan? Jordan, where the hell are you?"

"In the bathroom."

Andi put the tray down on the corner of the dresser and ran to the bathroom door. "Damn it, you aren't supposed to be getting in and out of that chair by yourself. Peter will have a conniption if he finds out about this."

Just then, the door swung open. "Well then, I guess he just doesn't have to know." Jordan grinned up at Andi, hoping to lighten the mood and get herself out of trouble.

Andi put her hands on her hips. "And what excuse am I supposed to give him if your incision becomes infected because of foolishness like this, huh?

Jordan grinned wickedly. "You could tell him it happened while you and I were having hot monkey sex."

Andi's eyebrows shot up. "Oh, really? If you keep that up, I'll ask Kale to inspect your incision from now on."

Jordan clutched at her chest. "Ouch! You really know how to hurt a girl's ego."

Andi walked around Jordan's chair and grasped the handles. She pushed Jordan to the bed. "Pull that stunt again, and I'll hurt more than your ego. You got that?"

"You're no fun," Jordan whined.

"Now, how about we transfer you back to bed so you can get dressed before breakfast?" Andi suggested, stooping to move the footrests out of the way. She moved in close and wrapped her arms around Jordan. "Okay, put your arms around my neck," she instructed.

Jordan grinned slyly, knowing full well that she could transfer herself to the bed in the wink of an eye with little to no effort, but she kind of liked the special attention from Andi. She obediently raised her arms, wrapped them around Andi's neck, and held on tightly as Andi deftly lifted her out of the chair and into a standing position.

"Now, don't let go. I'm just going to push your chair out of the way and then swing you onto the bed. Are you ready?"

"Go for it, Captain," Jordan said.

Struggling to stay balanced, Andi pushed the chair away with her foot, then wrapped her arms tighter around Jordan's waist and rotated her sideways. With controlled movements, she slowly began to lower Jordan to the bed.

The most efficient thing Jordan could have done to make it easier on both of them would have been to reach down to the bed behind her and brace herself with her arms as Andi lowered her to the mattress. However, Jordan had other plans. Andi's load soon became unbalanced, and they both toppled to the bed with Andi lying directly on top of Jordan.

Jordan looked into Andi's face, which was a mere hair's breadth away. "Now this is more like it," she exclaimed.

"Ahem! What's going on here?"

Andi's and Jordan's heads snapped around quickly at the sound of the voice coming from the doorway. Jordan was grinning from ear to ear. Andi was scarlet with embarrassment as they lay there cheek to cheek.

"Sure, Jordan, I leave you alone for one hour with my girlfriend, and you manage to get her into bed!"

Jordan's grin broadened. "I'll bet that beats your record." Andi managed to break free from Jordan's embrace. She scurried to the side of the bed. As she straightened her blouse, she looked apologetically at Kale. "I... er... it's not what it looks like," she stammered.

Jordan propped herself up on her elbows to watch the exchange.

Kale was barely able to contain his grin. He knew from the glimmer in Jordan's eyes that his wicked friend had set up an innocent victim. Not wanting to end the fun too soon, he turned on his heel to leave the room and then stopped to look over his shoulder. "Do you want me to close the door so no one disturbs you for a while?"

Andi looked aghast. "Kale!"

Kale turned around and looked at Andi. "Yes? Is there something I can do for you?"

Jordan said, "Yeah, I think she wants a threesome."

"Argh!" Andi reached for a pillow to beat Jordan with. "Shut up! Shut up, shut up, shut up!"

"Whoa, now," Kale said. He grabbed the pillow from Andi, who had already managed to get in a half a dozen good whacks. "Relax. We were just teasing," he said.

"Teasing? Is that what you call it? You two are totally incorrigible."

"Come on, sweetheart. Forgive me?" Kale tried to take her into his arms.

"Yeah, let's kiss and make up—all three of us," Jordan suggested.

Kale and Andi looked at Jordan, then Kale unceremoniously handed the pillow back to Andi. "Go for it," he said.

Jordan's protests could be heard all the way to the kitchen.

* * *

Andi made her way into the kitchen, where Kale was pouring himself a cup of coffee. The morning's interlude had left her shaken and a bit wary. "Do you two always act like that?"

Kale feigned innocence. "Act like what?"

"Never mind." She did her best to straighten her clothing and smooth her tousled hair, and then she poured herself a cup of coffee. Trying to be a good sport, she changed the subject. "Did you get what you needed from the lab?"

"Yeah, Chuck is setting it up now. I offered to bring him a cup of coffee, so I guess I'd better go give him a hand. Are you coming?"

"In a few. Jordan is getting dressed, and I need to help her into the chair again."

"I can help with those things, Andi."

"No, you need to head out to the barn. I'll take care of things here. One of these days... one of these days I'm going to get her back. You wait and see."

Kale wrapped his arms around Andi and kissed her tenderly. "Don't let her get to you. She loves to tease, and she's a huge flirt. Hell, we went out to dinner recently, and by the time we left she had the waitress' airwave code. I don't know how she does it, but she's harmless enough. Just give it right back to her, and you two will get along fine. You'll see."

Andi grinned. "She is kind of cute about it. I do admire how bold she is. Sometimes I wish I were brave enough to be like her."

Kale leaned in and kissed her again. "Don't you dare ever change. I love you just the way you are."

Andi smiled. "Ditto. Now get your butt out there and help Chuck with those lab animals. I'm going spend some time with Miss Pain-in-the-Ass. I'll join you when she's napping. Okay?"

"Okay, but before I go, I want to thank you for your help with the machine last night. I really enjoyed working on it with you. It was almost as though you could read my mind... like we share the same vision. It was pretty incredible."

Andi smiled. "I should be thanking you, Kale. It's been a long time since I've been this excited about a project. It gets my juices flowing."

Kale grinned broadly, eyebrows dancing wickedly on his forehead. "Your juices, huh? Maybe we should use them to christen the machine before we test it."

Andi placed a long kiss on Kale's lips. "That, lover, sounds like a plan. Now get your butt out to the barn before I say to hell with the machine and take you up on that offer right here, right now!"

* * *

Andi sat cross-legged on the side of Jordan's bed. She helped herself to the bowl of fruit salad positioned between them. Jordan apologized to Andi for the morning's antics.

"I want you to know I really do appreciate everything you're doing for me. I just couldn't resist teasing both you and Kale. Kale is such an easy mark—and so fun to toy with. I didn't have any siblings to play practical jokes on, so I guess Kale is the closest thing I have to that. You were simply collateral damage."

Andi looked at Jordan through raised eyebrows. "Collateral damage, huh? I've never been called that before."

Andi looked piqued, so Jordan batted her eyelashes flirtatiously. "You can't possibly stay angry at little 'ole me. Am I forgiven?"

Andi grinned. She chuckled and responded in kind, "You're damn lucky you're so cute, you little shit. Okay, you're forgiven, but I warn you, watch yourself. Payback is a bitch."

"Fair enough. I'll keep that in mind."

Andi speared a strawberry with her fork. "So, are you excited about the new implant?"

Jordan crossed her hands in her lap.

"Are you all right?" Andi asked.

Jordan forced a faint smile. "I'm fine, it's just... well, I have to admit that I have mixed feelings about the new implant."

"How so?"

Jordan reached for a container of yogurt, removed the cover, and dropped several small pieces of fruit into it. She glanced once more at Andi. "I'm excited that I'll get my mobility back and get out of that damn chair, but at the same time, I'm a little wary about it failing again and landing me right back at ground zero. I'm not sure if I can handle a failure like that again. It took some hefty convincing on Kale's part... as well as other things... to talk me into it again."

"What do you mean by other things?"

Jordan frowned and looked down at the yogurt container in her hands. She was quiet for several long moments.

"Jordan?"

Jordan sighed deeply and leaned her head back against the headboard. She stared at the ceiling. "You wouldn't understand."

"I understand more than you realize."

Jordan turned to look at Andi. "No, I don't think you do." Jordan turned her gaze back toward the ceiling and closed her eyes, trying hard to shut out the sorrow that threatened to drown her heart.

"Tell me about Maggie," Andi said softly.

A flash of anger and indignation lit Jordan's eyes. "Kale told you, didn't he?" she said angrily. "He had no right to betray my confidence."

"Don't be angry with Kale. In a way, you told me yourself."

"I don't remember telling you about Maggie."

Andi repositioned herself beside Jordan so that she, too, leaned against the backboard, her legs stretched out before her. "I'm not surprised you don't remember. You were half asleep."

"Okay... you're freaking me out here. Explain yourself."

Andi grinned. "Relax. You didn't give away any juicy secrets or anything. Just before dinner last night, you woke up in a daze and asked me where Maggie was. It was obvious to me that you weren't aware of what you were saying." Andi leaned over and bumped shoulders with Jordan. "Tell me about her, Jord."

"You wouldn't understand."

"Try me."

"I'm sure Kale told you everything you need to know."

Andi frowned. "I promise not to judge you. Please trust me."

Jordan reluctantly turned her head so she could look directly into Andi's eyes.

Andi took one of Jordan's hands and held it between her own. "Kale told me about your dreams, but he doesn't know how you feel about Maggie. As a woman, I understand that you love her with all your heart. I understand that it's painful for you not to be with her. I understand that almost any risk is worth taking to fulfill that love. Tell me about her."

Jordan broke eye contact and looked down at her lap again. "You'll just think I'm off my rocker."

"Not a chance."

"She's dead, Andi. How much weirder can you get than that?"

"She may be dead physically, but she's very much alive in your heart."

For several long moments, the women sat in silence. Jordan laced her fingers with Andi's, gently squeezing their hands together in a bond of friendship. Finally, Jordan spoke. "Have you ever been so in love with someone that you finally realize the purpose of your life?"

Andi's smile widened.

Jordan grinned at her. "Kale?"

"Yeah." Andi wiped her eyes.

"That's how I feel about Maggie. I can't explain it any better than that."

"I understand, Jordan. I understand totally."

CHAPTER 16

"Kale, this steak is perfect. How do you manage to keep it from drying out on the grill?" Jordan asked.

"Easy. I spray it with water as it's cooking. It's a secret my grandma taught me."

"Your grandmother was a brilliant woman. Too bad she didn't teach you how to—"

"Comb my hair. Yeah, I know," Kale interrupted with mock severity. "You're never going to stop reminding me of that, are you?"

"Not a chance. And by the way, you look cute with that napkin tucked into the front of your shirt."

Kale stuck his tongue out.

"Be careful what you do with that tongue. Andi might get jealous."

"In your dreams." Kale laughed.

Andi chuckled.

"I can't remember the last time we actually sat at the kitchen table to eat," Jordan said.

"You don't eat in the kitchen?" Andi asked.

"We eat most of our meals in the living room in front of the holovision," Kale said.

"Sometimes," Jordan added, "we don't eat at the same time. It depends on our schedules. There have been times when I haven't seen Kale for two days."

Andi scoffed. "My mother would never allow that. She was pretty strict about meal times and eating family dinners at the table. Heaven help us if we didn't make it home in time."

"Well, we run a pretty informal ship around here. With our busy lives, we need to be independent and flexible," Jordan said.

Kale pulled the napkin out of his collar and placed it on the table beside his plate. "Speaking of busy lives, we need to get out to the lab and test the machine."

"The machine is that far along?" Jordan asked.

Kale grew animated. "You bet it is! I installed the second set of rings before you went into the hospital, and with Andi's help last night, we modified the algorithm so that they're configured to rotate in the opposite direction with a reverse charge polarization. Our plan tonight is to verify the absence of gravity in the center of the sphere. If we're lucky, maybe we can even give it a test run with an inanimate object."

An unexpected wave of dizziness washed over Jordan. She sat back in her chair and clutched at her chest as it became difficult for her to breathe. She closed her eyes. A vision of creamy white skin framed by a mane of wild red curls filled her mind. Emotion and longing gripped her heart.

Andi was immediately by her side. "Are you all right?"

Jordan shook her head. "Yeah, I'm okay. Just a little dizzy. I'll be fine." She inhaled deeply. "I'm okay. Don't worry about me. I guess the thought of that piece of junk out there actually working is a reality check for me. Why don't you go work on the project while I clean up the dishes? Really, I'll be fine."

"Oh, no you don't," Kale said. "You're supposed to be resting. We're breaking the rules as it is by letting you out of bed for dinner."

"Actually, I thought I'd relax on the couch with the diaries."

Kale stood and walked behind Jordan's chair. He leaned down to talk to her. "Come on, I'll help you onto the couch then come back to help Andi with the dishes. You should relax and enjoy us waiting on you hand and foot because when your hiatus is over, you're pulling your own damn weight around here again. You got that, girlfriend?"

"Nag, nag, nag," Jordan said.

Kale transferred Jordan to the couch and wrapped her legs in a fleece throw. He sat down beside her. "Want to tell me what that was all about?"

"I don't know. Maybe I didn't realize you had made so much progress on the machine. The whole possibility is becoming real to me now."

"Getting cold feet?"

Jordan's eyes opened wide. "Not a chance. I want this more than I could ever explain. I'll admit I'm nervous, but I'm excited as well."

"Well, don't count your chickens before they hatch. This may not work, you know."

Jordan smiled. "You're one of the most brilliant scientists I know. I have faith in you... and in Andi."

"Thank you for the vote of confidence, but there are no guarantees. Even if it does work, we have a long road ahead of us. We'll need to do a ton of testing before I'll be willing to risk your life. You need to understand that."

"Maggie has waited nearly one hundred years for me. I'm sure she'll wait a while longer. I'm more worried about my own lack of patience."

"You and me too, Jord! You and me too."

* * *

Kale and Andi stood by the control console watching a small trail of smoke emerge from the bucket in the center of the sphere. Soon, the amount of smoke increased substantially.

"Okay, I think we're ready to begin. Here we go."

Kale initiated the outer sphere program, slowly turning the speed control dial. He and Andi watched the centrifugal motion of the inner rings pull the trail of smoke into the sphere. Once the rings reached maximum velocity, they carefully examined the space inside the sphere.

Andi had to raise her voice to be heard over the loud hum of the rotating rings. "It's really faint, but I can still see smoke in the center of the sphere. The minute traces of gravity still remaining there should be counteracted by the rotation of the inner rings. Go ahead and start."

"All right. I'm setting them in motion right now."

They held their breath as the velocity of the inner spheres increased. The traces of smoke in the center of the sphere gently migrated to the inner circumference of the rotating rings. Then, an amazing thing happened. The bucket containing the smoking paper began to slowly drift up.

Andi grasped Kale's arm. "Kale, it's happening. The bucket is becoming weightless. You did it! You actually did it!"

Kale held his breath and hoped the anti-gravity state could be sustained and controlled. "We're not there yet. We need to be able to control this before we can claim victory."

Kale slowly reduced the speed of the inner rings. As gravity returned to the center of the sphere, the bucket slowly dropped and resettled on the platform. When Kale increased the speed of the rings, the bucket levitated once more. Kale repeated the process two more times until he was convinced it was consistent and repeatable.

For several minutes, Kale and Andi stared at the bucket on the platform. They approached the machine. Kale tentatively touched the bucket, only to pull his hand back quickly.

"Damn," he exclaimed, shaking his hand sharply.

"What is it?"

"It's hot. Look." Small red blisters were already erupting on Kale's fingertips.

"Damn. Why would that happen?"

"It must be molecular excitement. To generate this much heat, the molecules in the bucket had to have been moving at an enormous speed." Kale walked a few feet away and then turned to face Andi. "Do you realize what this would do to living tissue?"

Andi frowned. "I'm not sure I agree with you. Maybe it has something to do with the material as well. The bucket is metal, and metal is an excellent conductor."

Kale nodded. "Fair enough. Let's repeat the experiment with a non-metallic object." Kale looked around the room and located the boot he had used in his original experiment. "Here—this is the perfect test subject. If you're right, the leather in this boot should remain cool and only the metal rings around the shoelace holes should become hot. Let's give it a shot."

Kale placed the boot in the center of the sphere and once more initiated ring rotation. Again, Andi and Kale held their breath as they watched the boot rise from the platform and hover in the center of the rings.

Kale powered down the system and then gingerly reached for the boot. His brow furrowed as he touched the leather. He removed the boot from the center of the rings. He measured the temperature of each of the materials comprising the boot. "Leather, slightly warm. Rubber soles, hot, but not scorching. Metal grommets, burning hot." He glanced at Andi. "Okay, I'm ready to accept that heat generation has something to do with the conductive nature of the material. The question is, how much heat is too much for living tissue? And how do we dissipate it?"

"That's easy."

Kale stopped pacing and looked at Andi.

"Electricity 101. How do you get rid of a charge? By grounding the object."

Kale thought for a moment then shook his head. "The boot was grounded to the platform. It has rubber soles."

Andi nodded. "That would be true in an equilibrated environment. However, what we have here is an anti-gravity environment. When the object is floating, it's not grounded to anything. We may need to ground both the machine and the object."

"That makes sense. You might be onto something."

Andi looked around the room. "Where did the workmen put the leftover filament from when they wired the lab?"

"It's out in the shed behind the barn. Stay here, I'll be right back."

Kale quickly pulled on his jacket and raced out of the lab. He came back with a large coil of electrical filament. "This should do the trick," he said, shrugging out of his coat. He attached a length of filament to both the boot and the metal table. "We'll have to remove one of the floor tiles to gain access to the ground. What to use, what to use?" Kale paused for a moment. "Got it! Wait here, I'll be right back."

Kale returned with a long metal spike. "This should do the trick."

"All right. I think that's long enough. Power it down and we'll see if it works."

Andi watched the boot drop slowly onto the platform. She and Kale stared at it.

Kale glanced at Andi before reaching into the center of the sphere. "Here goes nothing." He touched the boot. Andi held her breath.

"Well, I'll be damned," Kale exclaimed. He retrieved the boot and unwound the grounding filament. "Here... think quick!" Kale tossed the boot to Andi, who trapped it against her chest in an awkward football catch.

Her eyes opened wide. Every part of the boot, leather, sole and metal loopholes included, was at ambient temperature. She smiled brightly and threw herself into Kale's arms. "We did it!"

Kale squeezed her tight then held her at arm's length. "Yes, we did. I could use a beer to celebrate. What do you say we go share the good news with Jordan?"

CHAPTER 17

Tuesday, August 29, 2017

I am in love. There, I've finally admitted it to myself. I never thought it would happen, but it has. It surprises me that I could be attracted to Jan. She's very boyish and she reminds me in some ways of Jess. After Jess tried to force herself on me, I vowed never again to become involved with someone who could overpower me, but Jan is different. She's gentle and kind, despite the fact that she can throw a bale of hay a country mile. Her strength surprises me, considering she's shorter and slimmer than I am. She is so good with the animals, and has voluntarily taken on the role of horse trainer. Jan has a knack for showing horses, and even managed to earn a couple of blue ribbons at last month's horse show. That's so important to the farm's financial stability. After all, we're in business to raise, breed, and sell Mustangs. She has been a godsend.

Anyway, I digress. I am in love. It's not something I was looking for. It kind of found me. All I wanted when I invited Jan to move from the bunkhouse into the main residence was companionship. It didn't make sense for her to sleep out there all alone while I lived a solitary life in this big farmhouse. I admit that I found her attractive right from the start. She's pretty cute. I find myself staring at the cleft in her chin and wondering what it would be like to trace it with the tip of my finger. Yes, I found her attractive, but I wasn't looking for someone to share my life with when she came to work for me.

When she moved into the main house, she pretty much kept to herself... cooking her own meals and spending her free time in her room. But after a few weeks she began to loosen up and finally accepted one of the many invitations to join me for dinner. I will never forget that dinner. Don't ask me what we ate... for the life of me, I can't remember the food, but I certainly remember spending the entire meal trying not to be too obvious about staring at her. I just couldn't take my eyes off her. Anyway, by the time the evening was over, we managed to consume an entire bottle of wine, but very little else. I couldn't take my eyes off her long enough to eat. I felt quite giddy... like a schoolgirl experiencing her first crush. I'm not sure if it was the wine or her presence that caused the heated flush to color my cheeks.

That was three months ago. Since then, we've spent more and more time together and I have felt myself falling deeper and deeper in love. She walks into the room and my insides turn all warm and mushy. She's on my mind all day long. Earlier this week, in the middle of a meeting of the Shelburne Board of Trustees, I was called upon to voice my opinion and became quite red-faced when I realized I hadn't even heard the question through my preoccupation with her.

There is something about her, something that draws me in. She has an effect on me like no one else I've ever met. We attended the Champlain Valley Fair together last week and in the process of leading me through the crowds surrounding the exhibits in the crafts barn she placed her hand on the small of my back. That simple act took my breath away. I felt as though her hand penetrated my body and grasped deep within my core to the very center of my desire. I was nearly paralyzed by the rush of heat and longing that filled my being. I knew then that I wanted her. I knew then that I had to have her. I knew then that I needed her in my life.

This morning, I am at peace with my soul. I sit here on my bed with pen in hand, recording my most secret thoughts while she sleeps beside me, her arm thrown over the pillow, her blonde hair tussled into a windblown disarray from a night of lovemaking, her cleft chin calling to me, begging me to invade it with my tongue.

"No! Goddamn it!"

*　*　*

Kale and Andi entered the house in time to hear a loud thud in the living room.

"Jordan?" Kale called. "Are you all right?"

"Damn it," came the loud reply.

Kale gently pushed open the living room door. "Jord?" He half expected to find Jordan lying on the floor. "Are you okay?"

The door was stuck. There was something behind it, dragging along as the door opened. Kale peered behind it and saw one of

Maggie's diaries. He glanced at Jordan, who was still lying on the sofa. He stepped completely into the room, followed by Andi, who immediately went to Jordan's side and sat down beside her.

Kale picked up the diary and turned to face Jordan. She was crying. Andi held her, providing what comfort she could. Diary in hand, Kale sat on the coffee table, facing Jordan, waiting for her to compose herself. Finally, the crying subsided.

"Want to tell us what this is all about?" Kale asked.

"I wish I'd never found those damn diaries."

"Jordan, you can't mean that," Andi said.

Jordan lifted her head from Andi's shoulder and looked her in the face. "Yes, I do mean it. My life has been nothing but hell since I found them. I feel like I'm losing my mind. She's all I can think about, all I can dream about. It's impossible—can't you see that? She's dead! She's nothing but a name in the town's historic register. Leave it to me to fall in love with a dead woman. I'm so fricking pathetic."

Kale's heart broke for Jordan. She put her head back on Andi's shoulder and sobbed uncontrollably.

Andi's eyes met Kale's. "Shh, Jordan. It will be all right. I know it will. Don't lose hope." She arched an eyebrow at Kale, who added his assurance.

"Andi's right. There's reason to hope."

Jordan lifted her head from Andi's shoulder. "How can you say that?"

Kale tipped his head back, closed his eyes, and inhaled deeply. As he released his breath, he looked at Jordan. "We had a breakthrough. Andi and I have figured out how to reach zero-gravity in the center of the spheres."

Jordan was suddenly animated. "It works? Are you telling me the machine works?" she asked excitedly, wiping the tears from her cheeks.

"Whoa, slow down. No, I'm not saying it works—at least not yet. What I am saying is that we've accomplished the first step toward making it work." Kale watched as the hope on Jordan's face faded, and she physically shrank back into the fold of Andi's arms.

He reached for her hand. "This is a huge breakthrough. Without this step, we would never be able to accomplish what we're trying to do. Don't give up on us yet. Okay?"

* * *

Andi stood at the kitchen stove the next morning, turning the eggs in the frying pan. "I'm worried about Jordan's emotional state."

Kale leaned back against the cupboard, holding a coffee cup in one hand while the other ran through his hair. "I know. So am I. If she isn't able to hold it together, she risks losing the candidacy for the implant. There's no way Peter will allow her to participate in the study if she's emotionally unstable."

Kale looked at Andi. "I won't risk the time travel experiment without the implant. There is no way I'll attempt to send her through time without her being able to take care of herself. She needs to realize that."

Andi nodded in agreement. "Well then, I guess one of us will have to kick her ass and break her out of the funk she's in."

"Are you volunteering for that job?" Kale asked.

"Volunteering for what job?"

Kale and Andi turned to see Jordan approaching them in her hover-chair.

"Damn it, Jordan. You aren't supposed to be dragging yourself in and out of that chair yet. Do you want to end up back in the hospital?" Kale scolded.

"Don't get your panties in a wad. I'm fine," Jordan responded. "I'm tired of being in a funk. I'm sick of being helpless. I want to help with the machine."

Kale glanced at Andi, then back at Jordan. "I'm not sure you should be spending that much time in your chair. We tend to lose track of time out there, especially if we're making progress."

"Which is exactly why I want in on the action. Do you have any idea what it's like sitting idle day after day unable to participate in life? You wonder why I'm in a funk? Try it for a while."

"She's got a point there," Andi said.

Kale raised his eyebrows. "A lot of help you are," he complained. He looked back at Jordan. "Okay, but only if Peter gives his permission. You need to clear it with him first. You've got some convincing to do. Don't forget that his original instructions had you taking it easy for a few more days."

"I can handle Peter," Jordan said. "Which one of you is volunteering to take me to the office this morning? I can't wait to tell him about the time machine."

"Hold it right there, girlfriend," Kale exclaimed. "You can't be serious. Do you know what Peter will do if he finds out about the machine? First, he'll throw all three of us off the implant project, and then he'll have us committed to the insane asylum. You can say good-bye to any plans you have of dropping in on your dead girlfriend if that happens."

Jordan grinned. She knew her comment would push Kale's panic buttons. Andi smiled.

Kale finally caught on to the teasing. He approached Jordan's hover-chair and placed his hands on the armrests. He leaned in close so that he and Jordan were face-to-face. "You are so lucky that I love you. Otherwise, I'd have to beat your ass."

"Luck has nothing to do with it. I'm just irresistible and you know it." Jordan placed a quick kiss on the end of his nose. "Now, how about a cup of coffee?"

"Grr!" Kale responded. As he poured her coffee, Jordan caught Andi's eye and winked.

* * *

"To what do I owe the pleasure of your company today, Jordan?" Peter asked as he enveloped Jordan in an affectionate hug. "You aren't due for your checkup for another few days."

"I'm climbing the walls with boredom. I want to go back to work."

"Absolutely not. It's only been, what, two, three days? You're not ready to spend that much time in your chair. In fact, you're supposed to be in bed right now."

"Peter, I can't stand it anymore."

Peter sat down behind his desk and leaned forward on his elbows. "You should take advantage of this time and do some reading. Knit. Write. You have a marvelous brain. Surely you can think of something to keep you busy while you convalesce."

"Knit? You want me to knit? Honestly, do you really see me as the knitting type?"

Peter chuckled. "Well, no. I confess I was grasping. But surely you can think of something to do. How about reading those diaries you found?"

Jordan frowned. "I'm not so sure that's a good idea," she replied, thinking about how upset she'd been with the last entry. The last thing she needed was to read more about how happy Maggie was with Cleft Girl.

Peter studied Jordan for a few moments while she sulked. Finally, he spoke. "I have an idea."

Jordan perked up. "Yes?"

"I understand that you're bored, but it's vital for you to allow the incision to heal properly. If you're sitting up, you'll only aggravate it. So let me propose this. What if Kale found a way to set up a computer that would allow you to conduct some of the research from a reclining position? Maybe you could even use a thought projection system while lying prone? It might be possible to set it up inside the new lab so you can actively participate in the development and testing of the new implant. Would that be acceptable to you?"

Jordan was definitely interested. "Hell, yeah. It would be a thousand times better than lying alone in the house every day for the next few days."

Peter smiled. "All right then. I'll talk to Kale this afternoon."

Jordan turned her hover-chair toward the door then looked back over her shoulder. "Thanks. I don't know how I'll ever repay you."

"No thanks necessary. All I want is for you to be happy and to live a full and healthy life. If we can accomplish that and make medical history in the process, the world will be that much better for it. What you need to do is listen to your doctor and do nothing to sabotage our efforts. I know how stubborn you are, so I appreciate you coming in here today to discuss this before going ahead with your own agenda."

Jordan pretended to be insulted. "Would I do that?"

Peter grinned. "That, and so much more. Now get out of here. Go home and get out of that chair."

"Aye, aye, Doc!"

* * *

Jordan was lying on the bed beside the time machine as Kale positioned the boot in the center of the platform and carefully wrapped the grounding hardware around it. "I can't believe you talked Peter into letting you do this."

"He was putty in my hands. What's the filament for?"

Jordan watched as a knowing look passed between Kale and Andi.

"Okay, you're scaring me here. I'll ask again. What's the filament for?"

"It's a ground," Andi said. "We discovered during the first round of anti-gravity testing that a high level of molecular activity within the object made it heat up. We realized that was due to the buildup of electrical charge within the center of the rings. We can dissipate the charge by grounding the object to the platform and then grounding the machine to the earth."

"Holy shit! How did you discover that?"

"Kale burned his hand while retrieving a bucket we had levitated. It was so hot it blistered the skin on his fingers," Andi said. "But don't worry. Grounding the object ensures that it comes out of the machine at the same temperature it went in."

"Okay, ladies. I think we're ready for our first test. Andi, why don't you move Jordan behind the barrier? The first time I tried this, the blast knocked me off my feet and threw me against the wall. I'll join you after I set up the remote program."

Jordan propped herself up on her elbow so she could see the platform through the observation window. She watched as Kale positioned the old boot on the center of the platform and programmed the computer for remote control. He joined them behind the barrier.

"All right. Here we go." Kale initiated the inner sphere program and then slowly turned the speed control dial as they watched the rings begin to spin. "I'm going to start by rotating the outer rings in a counter-clockwise direction."

They watched as the rings gained momentum.

"Maximum velocity, Kale," Andi announced as she watched the speed gauge stabilize. "Go ahead and start the inner ring rotation."

"All right. We're almost there," Kale said.

Jordan watched, wide-eyed.

"Watch carefully, Jord. Once the rings reach maximum velocity, something amazing happens."

Jordan's gaze never wavered from the boot in the center of the platform.

"Maximum reached," announced Andi.

The loud humming from the spinning rings made it virtually impossible for the three to communicate as they watched the boot slowly rise. The boot was very old and the leather so worn that it floated bent in half over the platform.

"It's floating," exclaimed Jordan. "Kale, it's floating!"

"Watch it carefully, Jordan. Let me know when it's dead center," Kale instructed.

For the next several moments, Jordan watched the boot intently until finally it became eerily still as it hovered like a bent old man in the exact center of the spheres. "Okay. Dead center," she yelled.

"Put on the dark glasses. You'll need to protect your eyes from the flash. I'm going to release an energy surge into the center of the rings. If this works, the two sets of rings will produce the amount of energy needed to create and rotate a black hole. In theory, this will open a wormhole to alternate time."

Andi signaled to Kale that they were ready then held tightly to both her companions as Kale initiated the power surge. Suddenly, the barn was illuminated by a blinding flash of light as a wave of energy passed over them. A steady, but gentle tug of gravity pulled them in the direction of the machine while sucking the air out of their lungs. A moment later, the pull of gravity ceased and they were jolted back. The room became still.

Kale looked at his companions. "Are you two all right?" Each nodded her head but continued to stare at the platform in the center of the machine.

"It's gone! The boot is gone," exclaimed Jordan.

Kale powered down the rings and the room quieted. He gathered Jordan in his arms and together, the trio emerged from behind the barrier and walked toward the machine. There on the platform was the filament, and nothing else.

"We did it! I can't believe it. We actually did it," Andi exclaimed.

Kale replied calmly, "Yes, we did. But where did it go? Better yet—can we get it back?"

Jordan massaged her forehead. She looked up at Kale, then back at the computer. "The stats are stored in the computer. We need to record the exact timing and coordinates of the event and then reverse the process to retrieve the boot."

"Of course. We'll have to reverse the direction of the rings and apply the power surge with the exact same timing that was used to send it. Jordan, you're the computer savvy one. Maybe you can search the event logs and find the information we need to reverse the process."

"I can try. Give me a few minutes, and I'll see what I can do."

As Jordan searched the logs, Kale and Andi walked around the lab, inspecting the other equipment that had been exposed to the black hole. Everything seemed to be intact, with the exception of loose papers that had been sucked toward the machine

"Got it," Jordan said. "Everything is here." She handed a list of numbers to Kale. "Here they are. I recorded them exactly as they appear in the log. These two numbers represent the points of maximum velocity for the inner and outer rings, and this number is the point at which you applied the energy surge. That's the one I'm most worried about. I'll need to program the computer to apply the surge at exactly 249.3 seconds after the rings reach maximum velocity. "

Kale looked over the numbers and smiled at Jordan. "Great job. Get back behind the barrier. Let's see if we can retrieve the boot."

The rings were again spinning at maximum velocity, only this time in the opposite direction.

Jordan watched the timer carefully. "Okay. Watch the monitor carefully. The computer will apply the surge when the timer reads exactly 249.3 seconds."

Three pairs of eyes watched the monitor as the seconds counted down. At exactly 249.3 seconds the room filled with a blinding flash of light and a surge of energy washed over them. This time, however, the energy wave pushed against them and away from the machine. Kale powered the rings down. From their vantage point behind the barrier all three strained to examine the results.

"Stay here," Kale instructed as he approached the machine. Andi and Jordan held hands and waited for him to return.

Moments later he did—carrying a brand new boot.

CHAPTER 18

Kale paced back and forth across the living room, visibly shaken by the time travel experiment. "It's over, Jordan. I'm sorry, but I can't risk it."

"It was only the first trial. I'm sure we can figure out what went wrong. Please, don't give up," Jordan begged.

Kale stopped in front of Jordan and fell to his knees. He took her hand in his and looked directly into her eyes. "You saw what happened to the boot. It came back altered. Sweetheart, consider what might happen to you in that circumstance."

Jordan grinned in an attempt to lighten the mood. "Well, worst case scenario—I come back as a baby and you'll have to raise me all over again."

Andi's smirk earned her a glare from Kale.

"Andi, come on. I'm trying to be serious here."

"I'm sorry, Kale, but Jordan is right."

Kale rose to his feet and began to pace again. "How can you say that?"

Andi looked squarely at him. "Love, look at what we've accomplished. Time travel! You did it. You are the first person in history to accomplish that. Sure, there's a lot of work to do to perfect it, but damn, you did it. Don't run scared now. There's a long way to go before we put Jordan into the machine, but damn it—don't give up now. Only a coward would do that, and you are not a coward."

"She's right, you know," Jordan said. "The Kale Simmons I know isn't a coward."

"Jord, I don't want to hurt you. I am so afraid of that. I could never forgive myself if anything went wrong."

"Kale, you know I love you. I am so very proud of you. Only someone driven by love would have been as devoted to this as you've been. I desperately want you to finish the job, but I will always love you, even if you decide to walk away. I will also love you if you continue this and everything goes terribly wrong. This is my decision too, and I'm willing to risk it."

Kale closed his eyes. "I need to think about it. I need time to think about it."

Jordan nodded. "I understand. Really, I do."

Kale rose to his feet, lifted Jordan from the couch, and carried her into her bedroom. Andi followed close behind. He sat her carefully on the edge of her bed and placed a kiss on top of her head.

"I need to sleep," he announced.

Andi wrapped her arms around his waist and placed a kiss in the middle of his chest. "I'll help her get ready for bed. Go. I'll be in soon."

* * *

"Kale... Kale. Wake up."

"What is it?" Kale raised himself up onto one elbow, trying to see Andi in the darkness.

"Listen. Do you hear that?"

Andi and Kale remained as still as possible, trying to hear any unusual sound or movement in the house.

Andi grasped his arm tightly. "There it is again. Did you hear it that time?"

Kale threw back the covers and swung his legs over the side of the bed. "Yeah, I did. I'm going to check it out. Maybe Jordan's in trouble."

"I'm coming with you."

Kale and Andi quietly tiptoed through the bedroom and into the hall. The first thing they noticed was that the door to Jordan's room was open. As they approached, they heard a noise coming from the living room.

"There's someone in there," Kale said.

"No," Andi said. "Wait for me. I want to be sure Jordan is okay first."

Kale stood quietly by the door to Jordan's bedroom, but he kept his eyes fixed firmly on the living room.

"Kale," Andi called from Jordan's bedroom. "She's not in there. Her chair is there, but she's not in her bed, nor in her bathroom."

"Jesus Christ! What's going on here?" Kale said. "I'm going to check out the noise in the living room. Wait here."

"Not on your life. I'm coming with you." Together, they slowly made their way down the hallway toward the living room. Just as they approached the archway at the end of the hall, Kale stepped on a board that creaked loudly beneath his weight. They immediately froze.

"Who's there? Show yourself," came a frantic voice from the living room.

"Jordan?" Kale whispered hoarsely.

"Who are you? I have a weapon." The voice was female, and its owner was obviously very frightened.

"Jordan? Is that you?" Andi asked.

"Jan? Jan? Thank God! It's me, Maggie. Jan, I need your help. I can't walk."

Andi gasped and made a move forward. Kale stopped her. "No. Something isn't right."

Andi pushed Kale's arm aside. "She needs me. It will be okay."

"I'm coming with you," Kale insisted.

Andi placed a restraining hand on Kale's shoulder. "I'll be okay. She's obviously dreaming, and she's frightened. Let me talk to her alone. It might be dangerous to startle her awake."

"I'm not letting you go in there alone. I'll keep my distance, but I'm going with you."

"Okay, but please let me talk to her," Andi insisted. She turned toward the living room. "Maggie, where are you?"

"By the fireplace. Jan, please hurry. There's something wrong with my legs. They won't move."

"I'm coming, Maggie. I'm just going to turn a light on first." Andi switched on the table lamp near the archway and flooded the room with light. Jordan was lying half-reclined against the hearth on the floor by the fireplace. In her hand was a poker that she wielded like a sword. She raised it the moment she saw Kale.

"Who are you? What are you doing in my home?" Her gaze shifted quickly back to Andi. "Jan, who is he?"

Andi moved to Jordan's side and removed the poker from her hands. "It's okay, Maggie. He's a friend. Don't be afraid."

Jordan peered into Andi's face with a look of terror and desperation in her eyes. "Jan... I can't move my legs. Something's wrong!"

Andi took Jordan's face between her hands. "Maggie, sweetie... calm down. It's okay. How did you get out here?"

Jordan was clearly confused. "I... I remember waking up because I heard a noise outside my bedroom door. My legs wouldn't work. I had to drag myself out here. I didn't know where you were." Her eyes suddenly locked on Andi's face. "Jan, where were you? I looked for you but you weren't there. There wasn't even a dent in your pillow. When I went to bed last night, you said you'd join me soon, but you didn't come. Don't you want to be with me anymore?"

Andi looked worriedly at Kale then turned her attention back to Jordan. "Maggie, I'm going to ask Kale to put you back to bed, okay? It's not good for you to be on the floor like this."

Jordan looked at Kale. "Who is he?"

Andi stroked Jordan's face. "Don't be afraid, Maggie. Kale is a friend."

She looked back to Andi once more. Anger suddenly flashed across her face. "You're sleeping with him, aren't you? Is that why you don't want to share my bed anymore?"

Andi was taken aback by the tone in Jordan's voice. Not wanting to upset her further, she played along with the charade. "Maggie, you know that I love you."

Jordan pushed her hand away. "Like hell you do. I could have died in the barn yesterday, but did you care? No! I lay there for hours before the vet arrived and found me."

"Okay, this is creeping me out," Kale interjected. "We need to wake her up."

Andi grasped his arm. "No. The shock may cause her more harm than good. Let's try to get her to bed." Andi turned back to Jordan. "Sweetie, you know how important you are to me. It would devastate me if anything happened to you. It's not good for you to be lying on the floor, especially not after the incident in the barn yesterday. Please let Kale carry you to bed. I promise you'll feel better in the morning."

Jordan looked at Kale, then back at Andi.

"Trust me, Maggie. He won't hurt you," Andi assured her. "I'll hold your hand the whole way."

Jordan finally nodded and allowed Kale to lift her from the floor and carry her back to the bedroom. Andi carefully pulled the blankets over her then sat on the edge of the bed and kissed her tenderly on the forehead. As she rose to go, Jordan grasped her arm.

"Don't leave me. Lie with me. Hold me while I sleep, just like you always do. Please."

Andi cast a concerned glance in Kale's direction and silently promised him that she'd join him as soon as Jordan was asleep. Kale nodded his understanding and quietly left the room. Andi climbed in beside Jordan and took her into her arms. Jordan burrowed into Andi's embrace and whispered, "I love you, Jan."

Within moments, she was asleep.

* * *

The next morning, Andi was in the kitchen making breakfast when she heard Jordan call out her name. She slipped the tray of batter into the oven and responded to Jordan' call.

"Good morning, brat," Andi said cheerily as she entered Jordan's room.

Jordan cocked an eyebrow at Andi. "Brat? What did I do to earn that moniker?"

"Well, I could have called you 'pain in the ass,' but I thought I'd be kind to you this morning, considering the night you put in."

Jordan frowned. "What do you mean by that?"

Andi pulled the covers from Jordan. "No. Bathroom first, gossip later. Come on, let's see if we can get you into the chair without falling into an obscene position today."

"You're no fun. I like the obscene positions," Jordan responded.

"You would. Hold on... ready?" In one swift movement, Andi lifted Jordan from the bed and swung her around to seat her comfortably in the chair. "There we go."

Jordan grinned up at Andi. "You know I can do that myself with much less work, and in about half the time."

"Yes, you can, but doing so requires that you drag your butt across the bed and the seat of the chair, and you know you're not supposed to be doing that for a while."

"Yeah, yeah. Whatever. Clear the way, I'm coming through," Jordan said as she maneuvered the hover-chair toward the bathroom.

Andi watched her go. "Want some help in there?"

"Hell, no. I'll be out in a minute."

"Okay, breakfast is cooking. Join me in the kitchen when you're ready. I'll have a cup of coffee waiting for you."

"I'll be right there."

Andi made Jordan's bed and then returned to the kitchen. By the time she'd poured two cups of coffee, Jordan had entered the kitchen.

"It smells great. I'm famished."

Andi placed the cup of coffee in front of Jordan. "You should be. You worked up an appetite last night."

Jordan's brow knit. "That's the second reference you've made to last night. Spill it."

Andi sipped her coffee then lowered the cup to the table. "What do you remember about last night?"

"I remember having a discussion with you and Kale about refining the time travel experiments." She suddenly sat up straight and looked around. "Where is Kale, by the way?"

"He's in the lab. The crew arrived about an hour ago to resume the implant testing."

"Oh. I guess I should think about showering and getting my butt out there to help them. Anyway, I remember discussing Kale's reluctance to continue the experiments, then all of us going to bed after that."

"You don't remember anything else?"

Jordan looked at Andi. "All right, you're freaking me out. What the hell happened last night?"

"Basically, you sleepwalked. Kale and I found you in the living room on the floor by the fireplace."

"You found me in the living room? Back up. Begin again and don't spare the details."

Andi leaned forward and covered Jordan's hand with her own. "I think Maggie was trying to reach you last night. You were her."

"What the hell?"

"You became Maggie, Jordan. You were frightened when you heard Kale's voice, but when I spoke, you thought I was someone named Jan. I didn't want to startle you, so I played along."

Jordan frowned deeply at the mention of Jan's name. "What did I say?"

"None of it made much sense. You said you had woken up and realized I wasn't in bed with you. I'm assuming Jan was Maggie's girlfriend?"

Jordan nodded absentmindedly. "Please, go on."

"Anyway, you accused me of not caring about you and cited some incident that had happened in the barn a day earlier. Apparently Maggie was in some sort of danger and was finally found by the veterinarian. Maggie was quite upset that Jan didn't seem to care enough to be concerned about her. That's the impression I got, anyway."

"What happened next?"

"It was the middle of the night, and I knew that your lying on the cold floor like that wasn't exactly the best thing in the world for healing, so I urged you to let Kale carry you back to bed."

"Did I allow that?"

"Only after I assured you that I... er, I mean, that Jan wasn't sleeping with him like Maggie accused her of doing. It was kind of freaky. Anyway, you finally did allow him to carry you back to bed, but you insisted that I stay with you while you slept. So, I climbed into bed with you until you fell asleep. Then I slipped quietly out of the room."

Jordan's mind was full of turmoil, but she tried to make light of it. "Are you telling me that you agreed to sleep with me and I don't even remember it? That sucks!"

Andi said, "You snooze, you lose! So... what do you say you get your butt into the shower while I brew another pot of coffee for the lab crew? I'm sure they'll enjoy some of these muffins."

Jordan hesitated slightly, deep in thought. Finally, she snapped out of her trance. "Sounds like a plan. I'll be back in a jiff."

* * *

"Jordan, let me get that." Andi darted forward to hold the door open while Jordan maneuvered her chair into the house.

"Thanks." Jordan guided her chair into the center of the room and then sat back and stretched. "That feels good. It's amazing how tiring lying on your back all day can be."

"I can understand that."

"It's kind of odd to be entering data into the computer while lying in bed, but it beats sitting alone all day in the house. I feel like I'm participating in the work on the implant this way. I felt pretty useless before."

Andi walked up behind Jordan and massaged her shoulders. "We did make a considerable amount of progress today."

Jordan's head rolled forward. "Ah! Can you do that for about two hours? I agree that we've made some progress, but there's still something not quite right with the testing. Did you notice how the prototype implants are causing the rats to move haltingly across the table? They should be moving much more smoothly than that. My gut tells me it's in the computer code somewhere. I just need to find it."

"You'll find it. I have faith in you. Why don't you go enjoy your diaries while I get dinner started? Kale should be in from the lab soon, and then we can all sit down and enjoy a nice meal together."

"Are you sure I can't help you?"

"Nope, got it covered. Go ahead, relax in the Jacuzzi, read."

"You don't need to tell me twice," Jordan replied as she headed for the bathroom.

Jordan eased into the Jacuzzi. She had pulled a stool close to the edge of the tub so she could place her book on it. "Oh, my God, that feels good," she murmured aloud as she felt the warmth spread to her back and chest. Her buoyancy in the water allowed her to position her upper and lower body comfortably in the tub as she placed a rolled up towel behind her head. With the push of a button, gentle jet streams of water pummeled her body in a therapeutic massage.

Jordan reached for the book and began to read.

* * *

September 23, 2018

God! My body hurts like a toothache. I need to speak with the contractor who built the barn. That rafter should not have come apart the way it did. The barn was only built two years ago. And besides, there are other hoists hooked to rafters throughout the barn, and they have never been a problem.

Of course, with my luck, I just happened to be standing beneath the damn thing when it went. Thank God for reflexes. I saw it coming at the last minute and was able to turn so that it grazed me on the back below my shoulder. The doc said if it had hit me on the head, it would surely have killed me. As it is, I ended up with a couple of fractured ribs and a whole lot of black-and-blues.

I swear I lay there for hours before the vet showed up. The thing that puzzles me is where Jan was through all of this. She was supposed to be working on the fences in the barnyard. She should have been close enough to hear me yell. Hell, the vet heard me when he climbed out of his car parked near the house nearly one hundred feet away. Anyway, when she found out I was injured, she went out of her way to wait on me hand and foot. It touched my heart that she was so concerned about me. I guess she really does love me.

Jordan was staring into space when she heard a knock on the door.

"Jordan, dinner is almost ready."

Jordan closed the diary and placed it on the stool beside the tub. "Thanks, Andi. I'll be out in a few minutes."

"Do you need any help?"

"No, I think I'll be okay."

"All right. Kale just came in from the barn and is setting the table."

Fifteen minutes later, a freshly bathed Jordan maneuvered herself into the kitchen. "I need to go out to the barn," she announced.

"What do you mean, you need to go to the barn? Right now?" Kale asked as he placed a plate of food in front of Jordan.

"Hmm, this smells good. No, after dinner is soon enough," she replied.

"What's so interesting in the barn that you need to see it tonight?" asked Andi.

"I'm not sure yet. There's something I need to check out. I may need your help, Kale."

Kale put his fork down and wiped his mouth with his napkin. "Sure. What exactly are you looking for?"

"That dream—or whatever it was last night—has been bothering me."

"Andi told you about it, huh? It was pretty freaky," Kale said.

"Did something in the diary prompt this sudden need to search the barn tonight?" Andi asked.

"After you told me about last night's fiasco, I thought I might find something about it in the diary. Specifically the 'barn incident' that Maggie mentioned. "

Kale frowned. "That incident happened more than eighty-five years ago. Do you really think you'll find new information that might shed light on the issue?"

"I don't know, but what have I got to lose by looking?"

CHAPTER 19

After dinner, Kale, Andi, and Jordan bundled up against the still-frigid April night and made their way out to the barn.

"You know, Jordan, Peter would not be happy to know you're spending so much time in this chair," he reminded her.

Jordan chose to ignore his gentle scolding.

As they approached the barn door, Jordan asked Kale to stop. Poised near the entrance to the barn, she turned around in her chair and mentally measured the distance between them and the house. She judged it to be approximately thirty yards. "Okay, let's go into the barn, please."

Looking confused, Kale followed Jordan into the center of the livestock area of the barn. The first thing Jordan did was look at the rafters.

"What are you looking for?" Andi asked.

"I'm not sure yet. It's too dark to see anything." She looked around a while longer before turning her attention to Kale. "Kale, would you mind standing on the porch steps?"

Kale put his hands on his hips. "What exactly are you up to? This is odd behavior, even for you."

Jordan grinned. "Just humor me. Please?"

He threw his hands up into the air. "And you call me a mad scientist."

Jordan laughed. "No, I said your hair made you look like a mad scientist. Now scoot. And leave the door open. Oh, and let me know when you're standing on the steps."

A moment later, she heard Kale's voice in the distance. "Okay, weirdo. I'm standing on the steps."

Suddenly, Jordan began to scream. "Help! Help me! Help!"

In a flash, Kale rushed through the doorway of the barn. "Jordan! Jordan, what is it?" he exclaimed in a panic.

Jordan grinned. "Hmm, I thought so. I assume you could hear me from that distance without a problem?"

Kale was obviously struggling to calm himself. "What the hell was that all about?" he asked angrily. "Of course I could hear you. I'm standing here, aren't I?"

"Cool," Jordan said. "Now, go back to the porch again if you would."

"Like shit I will. Tell me what you're up to. This isn't funny."

Jordan reached for Kale's hand. "I'll explain it all very soon. Please. I need you to do this for me."

Kale looked at Andi, who nodded slightly. "Okay. You're the one who'll have to wear the straight jacket, not me," he said as he returned to the porch steps.

"Andi, would you mind telling me when he's at the steps?"

Andi walked to the barn door. "He's there."

"Good. Now, if you would, please close the door."

"What are you up to?"

"I'll explain everything in good time. Okay. Here goes. Kale! Help, Help! If you can hear me, please come to the barn!"

A few seconds later, the barn door swung open. "You called?" Kale asked.

Jordan sat back in her chair and nodded. "Okay. I've got what I need for now. Besides, I'm freezing my ass off out here. Or at least I would be, if I could feel it. Let's go into the house."

Jordan retrieved the diary she had left on the stool beside the tub. When she returned to the living room, Kale was waiting for her.

"Okay, first things first. Out of that chair," he said as he scooped her into his arms and placed her on the couch. "And let me have your jacket."

Jordan made herself comfortable as Kale built a fire in the fireplace. Andi brought in three mugs of hot-spiced apple cider. "Here you go. I thought we could all use this to warm us up after that cold barn."

"You got that right. Thanks."

Andi made room at the end of the couch by lifting Jordan's feet and placing them in her lap as she sat down. Kale made himself comfortable in Jordan's hover-chair.

"Okay, Jord," Kale said. "You have a lot of explaining to do. Want to tell us what that little field trip was all about?"

"Don't you see?" Andi said. "With your help, she proved that Jan could have heard Maggie's cries for help with or without the door open."

Kale was skeptical. "Wait a minute. Are you saying you suspect Jan of foul play? Just because you're jealous of Maggie's relationship with Jan, that doesn't make her the bad guy. Besides, Maggie died in a riding accident, remember?"

Jordan sipped her cider. "I'm not saying that Jan has done anything wrong here. It just seems odd that she didn't hear Maggie's call for help. And for the record, I'm not jealous of Jan and Maggie's relationship."

"Bullshit you aren't."

"I'm sorry," Andi said, "but I've got to agree with Kale on this one, Jordan. Not that I blame you, though."

"Okay, okay. I'm jealous. I admit it. So shoot me. I'm sorry, but I can't help it. It sucks to be in love with a dead woman. Give me a break here."

Andi said, "I understand. I would feel the same way in your shoes. It's getting late. I think I'm going to take a quick bath then go to bed."

Kale intercepted her as she crossed the living room. "I'll be in soon, love," he said.

Andi kissed him gently then whispered, "No hurry. She needs you right now. Wake me when you come in."

Jordan waited until Kale returned to the couch and sat down beside her. "She's a wonderful woman, and she loves you very much, Kale," she said. "You're a lucky man."

"Yes, she is," Kale agreed. After a short silence, he said, "Jordan, if what you feel for Maggie is anything close to what I feel for Andi, I totally understand what is motivating you. You're right about the time travel experiments. I think between the three of us, we can figure out why the boot came back in an altered state. I won't promise you that we'll solve the problem quickly, but I'll work my ass off until we do."

Jordan touched the side of Kale's face. "Thank you. Now, why don't you go join that beautiful woman of yours? I'll head to bed after the fire dies down. Okay?"

"You're not supposed to be transferring yourself in and out of that chair, remember?"

"I'll be careful, I promise. Now go."

For the next half-hour, Jordan read from the final diary. The entry was dated approximately five months before Maggie's death.

Come to me, dream lover. You are the answer to my prayers. I have always prayed that I might one day find the one person in all the world who is right for me. The one person who will understand me, perfectly complement me, and be there for me regardless of the circumstances. The one person who will bond with me, body and soul—the perfect blend of physical and spiritual that will allow our lives to mesh together seamlessly. The one person to whom I can give all of myself without reservation, and who can accept that gift and return it to me. Come to me, my love. Soon we will be together and we'll start a journey that will take us the rest of our lives to travel. I can't wait to set off on that journey with you.

Jordan closed the diary and sipped the remainder of her cider as she watched the flames dance across the logs.

* * *

Jordan watched intently from her position on the bed as the four rats with prototype implants walked across the table. "There's something wrong here. Why are their movements so irregular? It's almost as though they aren't receiving a continuous flow of current. Like something is interrupting the flow."

Kale said, "I see what you mean. All four of the test subjects are displaying the same behavior, so it must be something fundamental in the design of the implant rather than a malfunction in any one of them."

"Either in the hardware design or in the software algorithm. This implant is smaller, but are there any fundamental changes in the hardware compared to the original?"

Kale thought for a moment before answering. "We can pull out the blueprints and do a point by point comparison. I believe the basic structural design of the implant is the same—just smaller."

"You were able to use the same basic hardware, but a smaller version of it?"

Kale frowned. "Exactly. Why the twenty questions?"

Jordan turned her attention to her computer screen. "I'm sorry. I'm not doubting you. I just need to be certain we're looking in the right place for the malfunction. I have a hunch. Give me a few minutes."

Kale waited as Jordan called up line after line of algorithmic code. Twenty minutes later, Jordan froze and stared at the screen. "Hmm… I wonder…" she murmured, paging back several screens.

"What? What did you find?"

Jordan looked at Kale. "Before I change anything, we need to record the rats with the current configuration of the implant for comparison's sake. Then, I want to spend some time reviewing the baseline until I either confirm or deny my hunch, okay?"

"You got it." Kale turned to the technician who was recording their observations on the rats.

"Chuck, turn on the video. We need to create a baseline behavioral record of the test subjects." He turned back to Jordan. "Come on. Let's get a coffee. I'll go out of my mind if we stand here and watch them for the next twenty minutes."

"No, you go ahead. I want to do a little more research into this algorithm. There's a lot riding on this. You can bring me back a coffee though. And say hi to Andi for me while you're at it, and if that should take longer than twenty minutes, I'll understand." Jordan winked.

Kale blushed and shook his head. "You know me too well. However, Andi is at the institute this afternoon, so I'm shit out of luck. I'll be back soon."

Kale handed a coffee mug to Jordan. "Any luck?"

"Actually, yes. I've viewed the tape several times, and I think I'm on to something."

"What do you think the problem is?"

"Significant digits," Jordan replied.

"Significant digits? Can you elaborate?"

"Sure. As you know, the algorithm supplies current alternately to each side of the injury. It appears the code which controls the timing for current delivery has a different number of decimal points for one side of the injury compared to the other. Because of that, there's a pause between the pulses. It's that pause that's causing the jerky movements."

"Hmm, I see," Kale said. "So all we need to do is change the line of code to reflect the correct number of significant digits and it should deliver a continuous current."

"Exactly. If you're ready to test it, I'll change the code right now and try it out."

"Go for it." Kale gave Chuck his instructions while Jordan made the algorithm changes and downloaded the updated software.

"All right, ready when you are."

The newly-programmed memory chips were placed in the rats, and the rats were positioned in their "starting gates" at the far end of the test field. Kale watched the table closely. "Okay, Chuck, open the gates and let them out."

Kale and Jordan held their breaths as the rats emerged from the gates. One by one they made their way across the table at an even, steady gait. All spasmodic movement was gone. Kale took Jordan's hand and squeezed tightly as the results spoke for themselves.

Kale couldn't stop grinning. "You did it! How the hell did you know?"

"It pays to be a computer geek."

"You're a genius! This is a momentous breakthrough. You, me, and Andi should celebrate tonight."

"I'm always in the mood to party. What did you have in mind?"

"Maybe dinner out? How does that sound?"

"Sounds like a plan."

*　*　*

"My stomach hurts. Why did you let me eat so much?" Jordan whined as Kale carried her back into the house and placed her on the couch.

"Like I was going to stop you? Every time we go there, you tell me not to let you eat so much, but you do it anyway."

"I can't help it. I love Indian food."

"It was really good," Andi said. "That was a first for me. I grew up in a meat-and-potatoes kind of family. Indian wasn't something I ever thought of eating, but it was fantastic. Thanks for suggesting it, Jordan."

"You're welcome. How about a nice warm drink while we wind down for the evening? I make a mean Kahlua coffee if anyone is interested."

"Tell you what. Kale, I'll give Jordan a hand with the drinks if you start a fire," said Andi.

"Sounds fair. One fire, coming right up."

Andi helped Jordan into her chair and followed her into the kitchen. She set up the coffeepot while Jordan poured a shot of Kahlua into the cups.

"That algorithm error was a huge discovery this afternoon. You should be proud of yourself for finding it."

Jordan was embarrassed by the praise. "It was nothing. I'm sure someone else would have found it eventually. No big deal."

"It certainly is a big deal, and I'm not so sure someone else would have found it as quickly as you did. That algorithm had been in use for several weeks, and no one even questioned the awkward movement of the test subjects. I think it may have cut weeks off the testing. We may be closer to implanting it in you than we thought."

Jordan was suddenly nervous. Andi reached for her hand. "Are you okay?"

Jordan looked down at their entwined fingers and squeezed gently. "I won't lie to you and say everything is great because I'm nervous as hell that this may not work. But if it does, the possibilities are staggering. There is so much going on in my life right now that depends on this. I'm not fooling myself about the time travel thing. I won't do it if I can't be completely mobile."

Andi smiled. "Kale and I are in your corner. We want only what's best for you."

The timer on the coffeepot beeped. Jordan smiled. "Fill 'er up!"

* * *

Jordan lay on her back and stared at the ceiling. "Damn caffeine. I shouldn't have had that coffee so close to bedtime."

Just then, the door to Jordan's room opened and a lone figure slipped in. Through the darkness, Jordan couldn't quite make out the person's identity, but it was unmistakably a female form. The figure quietly glided across the room and disappeared into the bathroom. The light shone from beneath the closed door, disappearing a few moments later as the door was opened. The figure moved into the bedroom and approached the side of Jordan's bed.

The woman pulled back the covers and slipped beneath the sheets. She smelled of patchouli and freshly-washed hair. Jordan froze as she felt an arm encircle her waist, and the woman's body mold against her. Very gently, the woman kissed her cheek and then burrowed her face into Jordan's neck, bending her leg to rest her knee on Jordan's abdomen.

"Good night, my love," the woman whispered in her ear.

"Maggie?" Jordan whispered.

"Hmm. I'm sorry I woke you, love. Go back to sleep."

"It's okay. I wasn't sleeping."

Maggie kissed her cheek again. "Are you okay?"

Jordan inhaled Maggie's heady scent. "I've never been better."

"I'm sorry it took so long. Unfortunately, bookkeeping is not one of my favorite things to do. Balancing the books might be easier if I did it more often. Maybe I can get you to help me. You're so much better at it than I am."

Jordan smiled. "Maybe I could write a computer program for you to keep track of all your accounts. One that you could balance with the push of a button. How does that sound?"

"It sounds wonderful. How is it that you're so good with computers?"

"Living nearly one hundred years in the future helps," Jordan joked. "In my time, I was known as the queen of significant digits."

Queen of significant digits... significant digits.... significant digits....

Jordan snapped awake. "Kale! Kale," she shouted.

Kale burst into Jordan's room, followed closely by Andi. He flicked on the light switch. "What is it? Are you all right?"

Jordan struggled to sit upright. "Oh, my God! I've got it. I know why the boot came back altered."

CHAPTER 20

Kale took Jordan by the shoulders and shook her gently. "Jordan, wake up. You're dreaming."

Jordan shook off Kale's hands. "No, no I'm not. I know the answer. I know the answer. Significant digits!"

"Jordan, its 3:00 a.m."

Andi placed a restraining hand on Kale's arm. "No, Kale, listen to her. Let her talk."

Jordan looked at Kale and then Andi. "I know why the boot came back altered. Significant digits. Don't you see? Being off by even 0.001 seconds in time, multiplied by the difference in years between Maggie's time and ours, returned the boot to us that much younger."

Kale sat down on the edge of Jordan's bed.

"Think about it. If we were off even one one-thousandth of a second, it would make all the difference. Think about what that would mean multiplied by the number of seconds in a year, and then multiplied by the number of years between 2018 and today. No wonder the boot came back changed. It's all about significant digits, Kale. That's the answer. Don't you see?"

Kale stood and began to pace back and forth across the bedroom. As he paced, he held his hands in front of his mouth as if in prayer. Finally, he stopped and faced Jordan. "How exactly do we test your theory? We'll need a test subject that will allow us to determine its age before and after each trial."

Jordan frowned.

"Why not use a newspaper?" suggested Andi.

"Great idea," Kale said.

Jordan threw the covers off her legs and shifted to the side of the bed. Kale stopped her from reaching for her chair. "Just where do you think you're going?"

"To the lab."

"Jord, it's the middle of the night. Surely this can wait until morning. You need to sleep."

"I have to agree with Kale on this one," Andi added. "With yesterday's breakthrough on the implant, it might be ready sooner than any of us anticipated, so you'll need to do whatever's necessary to speed your recovery. That means getting plenty of rest."

Jordan released an exasperated sigh. "All right. You win. But I'm working on it as soon as the lab crew calls it quits tomorrow afternoon."

"Deal," Kale replied as he lifted her legs and swung them back onto the bed. "See you in the morning."

Alone again, Jordan sighed deeply and stared at the ceiling. Soon, she drifted off to a place replete with images of red hair, green eyes, and a warm feminine form molded against her.

* * *

"What are you looking for?"

"I'm not sure yet," Jordan replied as she looked up at the rafters of the barn. "What I think I'm looking for might no longer be here, or if it is, it might not be obvious. To be honest, I'm not sure I'm even looking in the right spot." Jordan scanned the barn roof for a few more moments before giving up. "I was hoping I'd see more in daylight, but I guess not." She turned to Andi. "Maybe we'd better get our butts into the lab before Kale sends out a search party."

"Good idea." Andi kept a hand on Jordan's chair as they crossed the livestock section of the barn and into the lab where Kale and Peter were viewing the videos of the test subjects.

"Peter, I'm surprised to see you here," Jordan exclaimed.

Kale walked over and lifted Jordan from her chair. Carefully, he laid her on the bed and wheeled it over to where Peter was viewing the videos. Peter turned his attention to Jordan.

"I understand congratulations are in order," he said. "That was quite a discovery, Jordan."

Jordan could feel the heat of her blush. "I'm not sure why everyone is making such a big deal about it. It was a minor timing adjustment to the algorithm."

"As a scientist, you're aware that some of the world's biggest successes were accomplished through baby steps. I would venture to guess that the implant will now be ready for human testing in a couple of weeks." Peter took Jordan's hand. "How are you feeling? Do you think you'll be ready for the implant by the time it's ready for you?"

"I am so ready to be out of this bed," Jordan replied. "I feel great, and Andi says the wound is healing nicely."

Andi agreed. "Yes, it does look good. It stopped seeping a while ago, and it's pretty much scabbed over now."

Kale made a face. "Eww! I'm so glad I'm not a hottie," he exclaimed.

Peter raised his eyebrows as Jordan and Andi chuckled.

"Trust me, Peter , you don't want to know," Jordan said.

Peter retrieved his jacket from the back of the chair. "On that note, I guess I'll head back to the institute. Jordan, don't forget your checkup the day after tomorrow. We can talk then about scheduling the implant surgery."

He slipped on his jacket and walked toward the door before turning once more to address the group. "Oh, and by the way, there's a staff meeting at 3:00 p.m. tomorrow afternoon to review the overall status of the implant testing and the development of the self-charging energy storage unit. I'll see you all there."

"Okay," said Kale. "Back to work."

* * *

Jordan glanced at the clock as the last technician left for the day. Try as she might, she was unable to stifle a loud yawn.

"Long day or short night?" Andi asked.

"A little of both," Jordan confessed.

"Maybe we should skip the testing tonight," Andi suggested.

"Not on your life. I'm looking"—Jordan paused to fight another yawn—"forward to testing my theory on significant digits. I have several ideas on how to approach the testing."

"It looks to me like you could use a good night's sleep. Maybe we should get some dinner and call it a day. We can resume the testing after the staff meeting tomorrow," Kale suggested.

Jordan was crestfallen, but after failing to stifle a third yawn, she admitted defeat. "Maybe you're right. But I would at least like to discuss my theories with you over dinner."

"I can live with that. What do you think, Andi?" Kale asked.

"Works for me. Any suggestions for dinner?"

"Chinese," Kale and Jordan chorused.

Kale helped himself to some pork fried rice. "So, Jordan, how do you think we should approach the testing?"

Jordan took a long drink of her beer. "Let's look at what we know. The boot came back relatively new, so logic tells me that we retrieved it too soon."

Andi nodded. "That makes sense, but how much later do we attempt the retrieval?"

"Good question. It may take several trials before we'll know. That's what makes your suggestion of using newspapers such a great idea. We should be able to narrow our test range down pretty quickly after a few trials by correlating the date on the returned newspaper to the number of decimal places used in our trials."

CHAPTER 21

Andi scanned the page of notes that Kale and Jordan had assembled. "I can see how you arrived at your estimate, but before we actually send and retrieve a newspaper through time, I think we need to carry out a preliminary test to determine if the estimate is even remotely close."

"Don't you think we can accomplish that with the newspapers?" Kale asked

"We probably can, but it wouldn't hurt to test it first."

Kale ran his hand through his hair. "I guess that makes sense, but what do we use as a test subject that would let us know if we're in the ballpark?"

"How about the other boot?" Jordan suggested.

Andi looked at Jordan. "Do you know where the other boot is?"

"I do," Kale replied. "Wait here, I'll be right back."

He returned a few moments later. "Here it is," he said. "It was by the horse stalls."

"Great. Put it on the platform while I reset the time on the power surge. If we're right, adding the additional 0.11 seconds will return the boot in the same exact condition as when it left."

Kale positioned the boot in the center of the platform and tied the grounding filament around it. He joined Andi at the control console and began programming the computer.

Andi reached out her hand to stop him. "Wait. Before we carry out the test, why don't we write something on the bottom of the boot? If it comes back with the writing on it, we'll know we're either dead-on with the date, or we're some time in the future. If it comes back without the writing, we'll know we're still retrieving it too soon."

Kale grinned at her. "That, my dear, is a brilliant idea. You can do the honors." He handed her a stylus.

Andi lifted the boot and penned a short message on the worn sole. She then placed it back on the platform and returned to the console. "Let 'er rip, Einstein!"

The trio watched the outer rings begin to gain speed. Kale initiated the program to begin the rotation of the inner spheres. When the rings had reached maximum velocity, the boot began to levitate in the center of the spheres.

"Jordan, let me know when the boot has reached the center."

Jordan stared intently at the boot until she was convinced all movement in the center of the sphere had stopped. "Okay, Kale. We're there."

They reached for their dark glasses and braced themselves for the implosion as Kale initiated the power surge. A moment later, it was all over, and equilibrium returned to the room.

Andi looked intently at the empty platform in the center of the still-spinning rings. "Go ahead and power the rings down, Kale. The boot is gone."

"All right, phase one successful. Now let's see if we can retrieve it." Kale reversed the direction of the rings and powered up the system once more. "We'll have to program the power surge at exactly 249.41 seconds, okay? Jordan, the ball is in your court. It's critical we get this right."

For a full four minutes, the trio stood motionless, watching the timer. When it reached 249.41 seconds, a reverse wave of energy swept over them.

Jordan struggled against the wave as she craned her neck to see the platform. "It's back, Kale. It's back. Power down the machine."

Andi turned the boot over in her hand. "The writing is gone."

"That means we still retrieved it too soon," Kale said.

"Let me see the boot," Jordan asked. Andi handed it to her. Jordan inspected it carefully. "Hmm. It looks pretty much like it did before the experiment. Here Kale, put it on the desk for me." As soon as the boot was on the desk, it bent in half at the well-worn crease.

"See what I mean?" Jordan asked. "It's unable to stand up by itself, just like before, so even though the writing is gone, I don't think we retrieved it significantly early. I think we're close enough to try with the newspaper."

Kale nodded. "Okay then. Let's give it a go."

May 27th, 2105, 8:47 pm.

First attempt to send and retrieve today's Burlington Free Press in order to identify the margin of error. If successful, the paper will come back with today's date on it. If unsuccessful, the age of the paper will narrow the scope of our search field and allow us to further refine the number of significant digits used in our calculation.

Jordan completed the entry in the electronic log and closed the file. She turned to her friends. "Are we ready?"

They stood behind the barrier and watched the rings spin as the newspaper disappeared, then reappeared.

"I guess this is the moment of truth." Kale walked toward the machine. Moments later, he carried the paper to Jordan and handed it to her. The date at the top of the page was December 18, 2014.

Jordan frowned. "December 18, 2014... That's almost exactly five months too soon. Wow, I'm surprised we're even that close."

Kale took the paper from Jordan's hands. He scanned the articles. "I agree that we probably won't get things exactly right, but we need to be closer than five months. Think about how your life might change if you relived the last five months. Remember our discussion about paradoxes? Well, this is one of them."

"How close is close?" Jordan asked. "How accurate do we have to be to make this work with only minimal impact?"

Kale paced the room for a few moments before answering. "I'm not sure I know the answer to that question, but I'd like to get the accuracy down to less than a day."

Jordan pulled the computer close to her and opened the algorithm. "I guess we have some more work to do then." Andi reached across Jordan and closed the projection system. "Yes—when we resume testing tomorrow."

Jordan sat back in her chair. "Tomorrow?"

"Yes, tomorrow. Look at how late it is. You're still under doctor's orders. Let's not lose sight of that. All of this will be for naught if you injure yourself again because you pushed too hard, too soon."

Jordan glanced at the digital clock on the lower right corner of the computer screen. 11:37 pm. "I didn't realize how late it was getting," she said. "Guys, we're so close. I really don't want to quit now. I'll rest tomorrow."

Kale immediately approached the control console and began powering down the computers. "Andi's right. We're calling it a night. No argument."

Jordan spun her chair around. "You're enjoying this way too much, Kale," she said, a tinge of frustration in her voice.

"Enjoying what?" he asked.

Jordan's hands flew into the air. "This... this power trip you're on!"

Kale cocked an eyebrow. "Power trip?"

"Yes, power trip. You hold all the cards here, and you're using that fact to manipulate me into doing what you want," Jordan complained.

Kale walked away from the console toward Jordan. He stopped in front of her chair and placed his hands on the arms. Jordan leaned back as Kale invaded her personal space.

He spoke in a low, even tone, his gaze never wavering from Jordan's. "Don't you dare accuse me of manipulation. I am doing everything in my power to help you realize this half-crazed idea of yours to travel nearly one hundred years into the past because you have fallen in love with a dead woman. I am doing this against my better judgment because I happen to love you and because I want you to be happy. If it sometimes seems to you that I'm moving too slowly, that I'm using my power against you, then so be it, but someone has to look out for you because you are doing a piss-poor job of looking out for yourself. Someday, Jordan, someday you'll appreciate all of this, and you'll be happy that I was around."

Kale stood up and reached his hand out to Andi. "I'm heading to bed. Care to join me?"

Jordan was speechless as she watched Kale and Andi walk to the door. Just before leaving the room, Kale turned to Jordan once more. "Don't forget to shut the lights off when you leave."

* * *

"Jordan, do you know where my saddle is?"

Jordan turned to see Maggie stroll toward her from across the barnyard. She stopped working on the repairs to the front porch to give the red-haired woman her full attention. As always, Jordan felt the rush of desire pass through her abdomen. "Your saddle? It's not in the barn?"

"No. I put it on the stand yesterday when Shawny and I returned from our ride, but it's not there today. I was wondering if maybe you moved it."

"No, I didn't. In fact, I haven't been in the barn yet this morning. The saddler came yesterday, didn't he? Maybe he thought it needed repair and took it back to his shop."

Maggie stopped in front of Jordan and tilted her head to one side. Her curls escaped in all directions from beneath her cowboy hat. "Hmm. That's possible, I suppose. I'll call him to find out. This really stinks. I need to check on the horses in the north pasture, and you know Shawny doesn't do well with saddles he's not used to."

Jordan looked into Maggie's eyes and smiled. "Why don't you take my horse? I'm sure Sally won't mind the exercise."

Maggie smiled back. "You're so sweet. I just might do that." She stood on tiptoe to place a kiss on Jordan's lips. Jordan's arms immediately circled Maggie's waist as the kiss deepened. She pulled Maggie close to her.

"Hmm," Jordan moaned. "I want you, my love."

Maggie pulled back to catch her breath and to allow Jordan easier access to the sensitive skin of her neck. "God! If you keep that up, I'll never get out to the north pasture."

"You could always send Jan out to check on them while we make better use of your time right here," Jordan suggested slyly.

"I would, but she doesn't seem to be around right now. I'm having second thoughts about keeping her on. One moment she's stuck to me like glue, and the next, she's nowhere to be found."

Jordan picked up her hammer and dropped it into the sling on to her tool belt. "If you ask me, I think she's trying to win you over."

Maggie blushed then gently punched Jordan's shoulder. "Get out of Dodge. She is not."

Jordan locked eyes with Maggie. "Trust me, love, she wants you. She gets that same puppy-dog look on her face that I do when I'm around you. You have that effect on people, you know."

Maggie pulled Jordan close. "Well, lover, you have nothing to worry about. She can try all she wants. It's you I love, and nothing she can do will change that."

"The feeling is mutual. Now go on. Take Sally to the north pasture. I'll call the saddler for you while you're gone, okay?"

"Okay. I'll see you in a few hours."

A few minutes later, Maggie emerged, riding Jordan's horse. She waved her hat in Jordan's direction as she galloped toward the north pasture. When Maggie was finally out of sight, Jordan entered the house and called the saddler. "Are you sure you don't have it? She left it on the rail by the horse stalls. It wasn't there this morning, and I thought maybe you picked it up by mistake. No? Okay. I'm sure it's in the barn somewhere. Thanks, anyway."

Jordan hung up the phone and went into the kitchen for a glass of water. As she stood in front of the sink, she caught a glimpse of a figure leaving the barn. Jordan quickly moved to one side of the window so as to not be seen as she watched the figure move across the barnyard and into the bunkhouse. Suspicious, Jordan decided to investigate.

She sauntered toward the barn. Once inside, she paused to allow her eyes to become accustomed to the dark. She searched the horse stalls but found nothing unusual. She petted Maggie's horse, Shawny. As she left Shawny's stall, she saw that Maggie's saddle was hanging on the rail, right where it belonged.

Jordan inspected the saddle. It looked okay, but then something caught her eye. Grasping the saddle with both hands, in one quick movement, she lifted it, spun it around, and placed it back on the rail so that the left side of the saddle was facing outward.

Jordan lifted the stirrup and threw it over the top of the saddle, then reached down to grasp the belly strap. "What the hell? How did this get here?" Jordan released the buckle holding the belly strap. With the strap in her hand, she crossed the barnyard and banged on the bunkhouse door. "Open this goddamned door!"

Seconds later, the door flew open, and Jordan stood face to face with a petite woman with short blonde hair, green eyes, and a deep cleft in her chin. Jordan thrust the belly strap toward her. "Care to explain this?"

* * *

Jordan shut off the alarm and stared at the ceiling for a long time.

"Jordan? Are you awake?"

"Come in. The door's unlocked."

The door to Jordan's room slowly opened, and Kale entered.

"Truce?" he asked.

Jordan reached for the spare pillow on her bed and threw it at him. "You big dummy. Of course, truce. Get your ass in here."

Kale grinned, picked the pillow up from the floor, and threw it back at her. He sat down on the bed beside her. "I'm sorry for leaving you all by yourself in the barn last night."

"Don't worry about it. I deserved it. Sometimes, I get caught up in what I'm doing, and I end up with tunnel vision. I just want this so much there's nothing I wouldn't stop at to get there, even if it means neglecting my health. I'm the one who should apologize."

Kale extended his hand to her. "Apology accepted."

Jordan tried hard to smile but managed only a cursory effort.

"Okay," Kale said, "spill it. What's on your mind?"

She turned her gaze to the ceiling and tried hard to hold back the tears.

"You had another dream, didn't you?"

Jordan could only nod, too choked with emotion to speak.

"Take your time. I'll wait."

It was several minutes before Jordan finally spoke. "It wasn't an accident. I know it. Maggie's death was no accident."

"You don't know that for sure."

"No, I don't know for sure, but it's something I feel in my gut. All of these dreams, these visions... Maggie is trying to tell me something. She's trying to warn me—to give me clues."

"What happened in this last dream?"

"For starters, she knew me, spoke to me, kissed me, and she told me she loved me. It was as though I had always been part of her life. Anyway, she came out of the barn where I was working and said she couldn't find her saddle. She ended up taking my horse to do chores. While she was gone, I went to look for her saddle myself and found it in the barn in the very place she always put it. I thought that was really odd, so I inspected the saddle and found a sharp spur on the inside of the horse's belly strap—you know, the strap that goes under the belly of the horse to stabilize the saddle. Oh, I forgot to mention that right after Maggie left to do chores, I saw someone sneak out of the barn. It was Jan. When I found the spur on the belly strap, I went straight to the bunkhouse to find her."

"Are you suggesting that Jan planted the spur?"

"I guess I am. Who else would have done it? I can't help but wonder if Maggie's trying to warn me about something."

"Just be careful not to confuse jealousy with guilt, okay?"

Jordan fell silent as she thought about Kale's words.

Kale changed the subject. "Are we ready for the next round of experiments?"

Jordan perked up considerably. Kale reached for the spare pillow and swatted her with it. "Well, then, I guess you'd better get your butt out of bed and get dressed. Andi went out and picked up bagels and cream cheese this morning, and the coffee's brewing. Let's get the ball rolling here, okay?"

Jordan saluted. "Aye, aye, captain!"

Kale stopped in the doorway. "Hey, don't you have your checkup with Peter today?"

Jordan's eyes grew wide. "Damn, you're right. I forgot all about it. It's sometime this afternoon. Thanks for reminding me."

"I think Peter wants to discuss the implant schedule with you. He's anticipating it will be ready to go in two weeks, but I think we're actually ahead of schedule. I'd give it one more week."

Jordan drew one leg and then the other off the side of the bed and prepared to transfer herself to her hover-chair. She glanced at Kale. "The sooner, the better."

"Here, let me help you with that," he said.

Jordan maneuvered the chair toward the bathroom. "Let me take care of business here, and then I'll be right out."

* * *

Jordan saved the final changes to the algorithm. "Okay, the new code is installed. Let's give it a try." Andi placed the newspaper on the platform and wrapped the grounding wire around it. She looked over her shoulder to Kale, who was standing at the control console. "All set, Kale."

"All right then. Come over here behind the barrier," Kale instructed. "Okay, ladies… here we go."

Kale ran the machine through the sequences. Several minutes later, the scientists stood looking at the paper sitting on the platform.

Kale was the first to speak. "I suppose we should see how close we are, huh? I just hope we haven't gone too far and retrieved news that hasn't happened yet."

"If the original calculations are correct, we should never send anything to the future," Andi said.

"No time like the present," Jordan declared. She maneuvered her chair toward the platform, retrieved the paper, and looked at it closely. "May 26, 2105. That was two days ago. We're so close!"

Jordan returned to the computer and called up the algorithm. Kale and Andi watched as she made changes to the code.

"Be careful how much you add to the time. We want to be within twenty-four hours of the send date, no more than that," Kale said.

"I intend to do just that." Jordan typed a few numbers into the code. "There. That should just about do it. Let's give it a try."

Once more the hum of spinning rings filled the lab. This time, without hesitation, Kale leaned into the machine and read the date on paper. "May 27, 2015. We're now within one day." Kale turned and grinned at Andi and Jordan. "This is amazing. One more adjustment should do it."

As Jordan approached the time machine, Kale prepared the control panel for the next trial run. She reached in and lifted the paper from the platform, detaching the grounding wire. "No," she said suddenly. "No more trials."

Kale's head snapped up. "What do you mean? We wanted to get within twenty-four hours, remember? That means the paper has to be dated May 28 for us to claim victory."

Jordan grinned. Andi took the paper from her and looked at it carefully.

"Andi, when did you purchase this paper?"

Andi looked at the paper closely. "I bought it yesterday. I bought it on May 27."

CHAPTER 22

Peter sat in the chair beside the examination table and looked through paperwork.

"Despite all that you've been through, you seem to be in great shape," he said. "All of your vitals are in the normal range, and I think that by the time the implant is ready, there shouldn't be any question about your fitness to accept it." Peter closed Jordan's chart and looked up at her. "The whole team is counting on you to help us cross the finish line on this implant project. Are you up to it?"

Jordan placed her hands on the edge of the examining table and leaned forward. "I have never been more ready for anything in my life. Kale tells me the implant is actually only a week away from being ready. Is that true?"

Peter nodded. "Indeed, it is. I've already arranged for the procedure—one week from today. Assuming the implant stays on the accelerated schedule, that is."

"Kale seemed pretty confident that it would." Jordan fell silent for a moment. "Wow. I can't believe it's only a week away."

"Are you nervous?"

Jordan grinned sheepishly. "A little I guess." Peter sat in the chair beside her. "Okay, Jordan, there's something on your mind. Tell me what you're thinking."

Jordan took a deep breath. "I've been without tactile feeling in the lower half of my body for the past sixteen years. Hell, I don't even remember what it feels like to have legs."

Peter reached forward and touched Jordan's knee. "If it calms your fears at all, you should know that feeling will return gradually, not all at once. It will take some time for the nerve endings to grow, and eventually regenerate, over the injury site. I predict that the process will be so gradual that you won't even notice it happening. One day, you'll spill something hot on your leg, and it will occur to you that you can actually feel the heat—to some degree, at least."

Jordan nodded as she absorbed Peter's explanation, but remained quiet.

"Is there something else on your mind?"

As Jordan looked at Peter, a blush crept across her face.

"As your doctor, you know you can ask me anything," he said.

Jordan chanced a quick glance at Peter then looked away again. "Well..."

"Yes?"

Jordan threw her hands up in frustration. "Oh, hell. It's the sex. There, I said it. Will I be able to feel it?"

Peter's eyebrows shot up. "Sex?"

"Peter, I was sixteen when the injury occurred. I was an innocent farm girl. I hadn't yet begun to experiment sexually."

Peter cleared his throat. "Ahem... I see. If all goes well with nerve regeneration, you should feel everything quite normally."

Jordan noticed that she wasn't the only one embarrassed by the conversation. "Maybe we should save this conversation for a later time. After the sensations begin to return."

Peter said quickly, "Yes, that sounds like a good idea."

* * *

Jordan set the table while Kale and Andi worked side by side, slicing meatloaf and dishing up mashed potatoes.

"So, Jordan," Kale said as the trio settled in at the table. "How did your checkup go this afternoon?"

Jordan put a large piece of meatloaf into her mouth. "Hmm, this is good," she exclaimed. "Peter gave me a clean bill of health. He said I could go back to work. Oh, he also scheduled the implant surgery for a week from today."

"Next week?" asked Andi. "That's pretty soon."

Kale said, "Jordan cut a significant amount of time off the testing when she found the algorithm error a few days ago. We feel pretty confident that the implant will be ready in a week. The power pack is another story, though. There are at least a couple more weeks of work to complete before that will be ready."

"Peter thinks the recovery period will be roughly two weeks. Is that enough time to complete the testing on the machine?" Jordan asked.

Kale frowned. "Jordan, I refuse to work to a set schedule with the time travel experiment. There's too much at stake here to rush things. I won't play with your life like that. We have several experiments to carry out on other test subjects before we can even think of trying it on you."

Andi reached across the table and covered Jordan's hand. "I know you're anxious to do this, but Kale's right. Your safety has to be our first concern."

"And besides," Kale added, "even if we're successful with other test subjects, I don't want to use you until the energy storage unit is ready."

"Why not?" Jordan asked.

"Because we have no way of knowing if you'll be able to recharge the old-style unit when it runs out of juice. Don't forget—we're sending you back eighty-seven years. Who knows if their solar electrical systems are even compatible with the ones we use today."

As much as Jordan wanted to argue with Kale's logic, she had to admit he was right. "Well then, I guess I need to focus my efforts on the storage unit. I'll do anything to shorten the schedule."

"I'm sure the lab guys would welcome your help." Kale sat back and rubbed his stomach. "Great meatloaf, Andi. Now, if you ladies will excuse me, I'm going to load the sonic cleanser and then turn on the football game."

Jordan grinned. "That's a great idea."

"Do you want to join me?"

"Not on your life. I'm actually trying to get rid of you so I can talk to Andi in private."

Kale raised an eyebrow.

Jordan laughed. "Girl talk. You're welcome to stick around if you'd like, but you really don't look good in blush."

Kale jumped to his feet. "Ah, no, I don't think so. I'll be in the other room."

Jordan and Andi laughed.

"Girl talk?" Andi asked.

"Are you telling me you've never had an orgasm?" Andi said, clearly surprised.

"Beats the hell out of me if I have or not," Jordan replied. "Think about it, Andi. I haven't had any feeling in the lower half of my body for the past sixteen years. Everything still works down there, or at least, I think it does, but since I can't feel anything, I wouldn't know an orgasm from a hole in the wall!"

Andi frowned. "Wait a minute. Kale told me you had a girlfriend."

"I did. Her name was Susan."

"And didn't you and Susan... you know?"

"Did we have sex? Yes, of course."

"Okay, I'm having a little problem processing this one." Andi looked at Jordan. "Forgive me for being a little uncomfortable with this, but we're talking about oral sex here, right?" Andi waited for confirmation before continuing. "Did she ever do it to you?"

"She tried, but like I said, I have no sensation below the waist. I always felt uncomfortable with her doing it because I couldn't give her the response she was looking for. I mean, I couldn't even feel her mouth on me, never mind any potential orgasm."

"So was your love making one-sided?"

Jordan sat back in her chair and sighed. "In the beginning she was pretty persistent, but after a while she gave up, and yes, at that point, it was pretty one-sided."

"That must have sucked for you."

"Yes and no. I would have loved to have felt those waves of orgasm I've read about in so many books, but on the other hand, it was something I had never experienced before, so I guess I didn't know what I was missing. I still don't know. I mean, I understand the physiology behind an orgasm, but I have no idea how it feels."

"Did you ever experiment with masturbation before your accident?"

Jordan could feel her face reddening. "Of course I did, but it was so long ago, I don't remember how it felt, and I certainly didn't know enough about it to reach orgasm. I lived a pretty sheltered life."

"Have you talked to Peter about it?"

Jordan raised her eyebrows. "Would you talk to Peter about sex?"

"Hell, no, are you kidding? Oh, right. I see your point."

"That's why I need to talk to you."

"I'm not sure how much I can help you."

Jordan placed her hand on Andi's. "Andi, you're a woman, a woman in a relationship. Don't tell me you don't orgasm with Kale because I can hear you guys loud and clear."

Andi turned red to the roots of her hair. "Oh, my God. Tell me you can't!"

"I can share a few examples with you, if you'd like," Jordan teased.

Andi's blush deepened. "No, spare me. I believe you."

Jordan leaned in closer. "So, tell me—what does it feel like?"

"What does sex feel like, or what does an orgasm feel like?"

"Both."

"Well, there's sex and then there's making love. Having sex is one hundred percent physical, but for me, making love is twenty percent physical and eighty percent emotional. The experience is so much better when you're in love. And if you're really lucky, you will not only be in love, but you'll connect with your partner on a deeper level."

Jordan frowned. "Does that make the orgasm better?"

Andi smiled. "Does it make it better? Oh, yeah! Kale and I share a connection I've never felt before in my life. The first time I laid eyes on him, I felt as though someone had punched me in the stomach. Each time I had to work beside him in the lab, the need to touch him was so strong it felt as if I were magnetically drawn to him. Before we got together, I would lie in bed at night and nearly have an orgasm just thinking of him. He was all I could think about. I would make excuses just to be in the same room with him. When he was near, I felt an overwhelming urge to touch him, to map his body with my fingertips. I was driving myself crazy with desire. Thank God it didn't take much to convince Peter to let me work on the project with him. It makes me laugh now when I think how we wasted time skirting around trying not to look too obvious."

Andi drifted away, lost in thought.

Jordan waved a hand in front of Andi's face. "Hello? Earth to Andi."

"Oops. Sorry about that. Where was I?"

"You were describing how connecting on a higher level makes the experience better," Jordan reminded her.

Andi smiled. "Oh, yeah. It's so much better when you connect with the person on an emotional or spiritual level. It makes the intensity of the orgasm greater, especially if you can reach orgasm together. It's the emotional connection that qualifies it as making love rather than just having sex. Making love for me means sharing not only my body, but my heart, mind, and soul. For me, the moment of orgasm represents not only a physical release, but a state of synchronicity. You become one with your partner. You literally lose yourself in that person."

"You lose yourself? How?" Jordan asked.

"Imagine for a moment that not only is the burning sensation in your abdomen, it's also in your mind and your heart. Imagine the intensity of passion, both physical and emotional, amplified a thousand times over. Imagine nearly losing consciousness while your mind disconnects and is overtaken by a state of pure sensory intensity as wave upon wave of pleasurable spasms ripple through your body. Imagine being able to feel your partner's heartbeat blend with your own, almost to the point where you swear there is only one heart between you. Imagine the final moments of release being so intensely emotional that it brings you to tears. Imagine lying together afterwards, listening to his heartbeat returning to normal as you feel every cell in his body scream out love for you. That, Jordan, is making love."

The intensity of Andi's description made Jordan's breath catch in her throat and her eyes turn misty. "Thank you, Andi. I understand so much more now. If it's even half as wonderful as you describe, it's an experience I look forward to. Thank you."

Andi smiled and nodded, but remained silent.

Jordan grinned. "Go on, get out of here. He's watching the football game, but I think he can be convinced to change his plans."

Andi laughed heartily. "Okay, I'll go, but on one condition."

"What's that?" Jordan asked.

"That you wear earplugs when you go to bed tonight."

* * *

The next morning, Jordan rode to the lab with Kale and Andi to begin working on the self-powered energy storage unit. Peter greeted them at the door.

"Good morning," Jordan said lightly.

Peter bent over and placed a light kiss on Jordan's head. "Good morning, Jordan." He shook hands with Kale and Andi. "It's good to see all of you this morning—especially you, Jordan. Are you up to helping us collect baseline data for the new power pack?"

Jordan grinned. "That's why I'm here. Point me in the right direction."

Peter looked at Kale and Andi. "You're welcome to come along if you'd like."

"Actually, we're helping Chuck write the code for the energy storage unit this morning, so maybe we'll catch up with you later," Kale said.

"Okay then. We may have some information for you to use in that code by the end of the day."

* * *

"All right, Jordan, our goal is to digitally record the electrical activity of your muscles in order to determine your body's normal patterns for generating electrical currents when your muscles are active."

Jordan listened carefully to Peter's explanation as he attached the electrodes to the skin above her hip flexors and quadriceps muscles on her legs. "There's only one thing about this theory that concerns me."

"What's that?"

"What happens while I'm sleeping or just sitting still? It almost sounds as though my muscles have to be in motion in order to generate these electrical impulses."

"That's a very good question. Andi came up with the solution: building additional storage capacity into the power pack, similar to how solar panels work. Energy generated while you're physically active can be stored and used on demand at times when physical activity is low."

"Let me see if I have this straight. When the new, self-generating power pack is ready, it will be surgically inserted and the external power supply will be removed. Then, after a time, when feeling actually returns, the self-powered pack will also be removed, and I will basically be cured. Did I leave anything out?"

Peter smiled. "I'd say your explanation is adequate. Now, I'm sure the question on your mind is how long will this healing process take?"

"You took the words right out of my mouth."

"By the time we install the new energy pack, the implant will have been in for about two weeks. Although improbable in your case, it is conceivable that there might be a slight amount of feeling returning by then."

"Two weeks? Wow, I didn't realize it could work that fast."

"Whoa, slow down there. I said it was conceivable. Your injury is sixteen years old. While it's possible that feeling could return quickly, I don't believe it will actually happen that way for you. In your case, I estimate it might take upwards of a year or more."

Jordan's eyes opened wide. "A year?"

"Or more," Peter repeated. "You need to be realistic about this. Although your muscles haven't atrophied, the injury site has remained unchanged for the past sixteen years. The odds in favor of a speedy recovery would be so much higher if the injury were fresh. You've been aware of that fact right from the beginning of the R&D on this project."

Jordan sat dejectedly for several moments before looking at Peter. She sighed deeply. "I know you've warned me about this, but damn it. We're so close, and this has been so frustrating. I'm really hoping things will happen quickly."

"I won't lie to you. Do I think the new implant will work? Yes, I do. It might take longer for you than for someone with a new injury. It's up to you whether you want to proceed or not."

Jordan closed her eyes and fought back tears of frustration. As she looked inward for the courage to go on, a vision of creamy skin, curly red hair, and green eyes came into view. An intense feeling of peace suddenly filled her heart.

Jordan opened her eyes. "Let's do it. I can't give up now. I have a date to keep with a wild Irish rose."

Peter frowned, but he motioned for the lab technician to approach. "All right then. I think you've made the right decision. Jason here will take you to the rehab center where you'll be hooked up to the oscilloscope and then put on a recumbent bike. You'll be there for a couple of hours. After that, you're free to go home."

CHAPTER 23

Kale led Andi by the hand toward the barn. "I'm so glad Jordan was too tired to join us tonight."

"It seems the time she spent in the rehab center today took more out of her than she thought it would. She nearly fell asleep at the dinner table," Andi said.

"Regardless of why, I'm just glad she chose to go to bed early."

Andi grinned shyly. "Why this sudden need to be alone?"

"Because I don't want her involved in the initial time travel testing with the non-human subjects." Kale glanced at Andi, who had fallen silent. He thought for a moment and realized that she might have been hoping for a different explanation. "Ah, sheesh, Andi. I didn't mean it like that. It's just that Jordan can be a real pain when it comes to following the scientific method. When she thinks it's in her best interest, she cuts corners like crazy." Kale watched Andi's face carefully. His heart sank when his explanation didn't alleviate her disappointment. "Andi, you know that I love you, and you know that I love being alone with you."

Andi smiled at him. "Oh, hell. You're just too damn cute to stay angry with. Come on, let's get some work done. You can make it up to me later tonight."

* * *

Andi's heart was in her throat as she watched the platform carefully. "Kale, stop the rings and put them in reverse. The rodent is gone."

Kale loaded the retrieval algorithm.

"God, Kale. My heart is beating a mile a minute," Andi admitted. "I hope the little guy survives the transfer."

"Here goes," Kale announced as the rings began to spin once more. "Countdown to surge. Nine, eight, seven, six, five, four, three, two, one... surge!" The computer initiated the counteractive wave. Seconds later, an object appeared on the platform.

"Power down," Andi said. "It's back."

Andi ran to the machine before the rings came to a complete stop and stared at the object on the platform. She was still staring when Kale joined her a few moments later.

"Damn," Kale said. "Damn it all to hell."

On the platform was the cage, and at its bottom lay the lifeless body of the rat.

Kale turned abruptly and walked to the control console. He powered down the system. Andi remained where she was.

"That's it. It's over. I'm not going any further with this thing. It's too risky. Jordan can be pissed as hell at me if she wants to, but at least she'll be alive to be angry."

Kale threw a drop cloth over the console. "I'm going into the house. Are you coming?"

"Power the computers back up. I think I know why the rat died."

"You know why the rat died? Okay, I'm game. Why?"

"Take a close look. What do you notice about the rat?"

Kale stared at the animal. "Help me out here. I don't see anything unusual."

"Touch it."

Kale reached into the cage. He pulled his hand back almost immediately. "It's hot," he said. "Well, I'll be. We forgot to ground it."

Andi smiled. "That's right. We grounded the cage, but didn't ground the rat to the cage. I'm surprised it didn't spontaneously combust."

Kale kissed Andi full on the lips. "You're a genius. Do you think we have time tonight for one more trial?"

"We'll take the time. You power up the computers, and I'll get the next test subject."

*　*　*

An incessant pounding on her door roused Jordan from a deep sleep. "This had better be good," she said. "Stop pounding, will you?"

The door to Jordan's room swung open and Kale and Andi came in and climbed into the bed, one on each side of Jordan. She looked at them. "Do you mind telling me why you're invading my room at such an ungodly hour?"

Kale reached under his shirt and pulled out a black rat. He thrust the rodent in Jordan's face. "Meet Rupert the Rat, time traveler extraordinaire!"

"What?" Jordan maneuvered into a sitting position. "Are you telling me it worked? Kale, talk to me. Oh, my God! Oh, my God! Are you telling me what I think you're telling me?"

Kale was giddy with excitement. "I am definitely telling you what you think I'm telling you. We did it, Jord. We sent our little friend here through time without a scratch."

Jordan looked at Andi and both women screamed spontaneously.

"I can't believe it. I can't believe it." Jordan began to cry.

Andi took Jordan into her arms. "Go ahead, sweetie, cry it out. You deserve it. We're almost there. All we'll need to do now is wait for the power pack. While we're waiting, we do some repeat testing. We're almost there, Jord. We're almost there."

* * *

Kale rose to his feet when Peter entered the room. "How is she?"

"She's fine. Everything went like clockwork. They're closing right now. She'll spend a couple of hours in recovery, and she'll be in her room after that."

"How soon before she can come home?" Andi asked.

Peter slid the surgical cap off his head. "We don't have to worry about pain at the surgery site since she won't have any feeling for a while. We need to give it a couple of days for the wound to begin to heal. Then she can go home, but you'll need to keep her stationary."

Kale's eyes flew open. "Yeah, right. Like we were successful doing that last time."

Peter chuckled. "Well, this time, she'll be allowed to move around, but she shouldn't be doing any bending at the waist or she'll risk reopening the incision. There shouldn't be any problem with her walking around. I'd say about a week of taking it easy should allow the wound to heal enough to eliminate the risk."

Kale grinned. "A week of confinement for Jordan will be a month of hell for Andi and me, but we've done it before. I guess we can do it again."

* * *

"I want to go to physical therapy as soon as possible. I've been in that chair for too long. If I want to get back on my feet without a walker, I need to exercise these muscles." Jordan sat on the edge of her hospital bed and massaged her thighs.

"I agree, but your surgery was only yesterday. Let's wait until you've been home for about a week before we schedule PT, okay? Go ahead and walk around all you want, but I insist you use the walker for at least a week."

"No time like the present," she replied. She placed her hands on the support bars of the walker and pulled herself into a standing position. As she stood, she came face to face with Peter, who had been holding the walker steady. She grinned.

"This feels wonderful!" she said. "Do you know how tiring it is, always having to look up at people from that damn chair?"

Peter stood to the side. "If the implant works the way it's supposed to, you'll never have to do that again." He waited as she regained her balance. "Okay, you know the routine. Lift the walker and move it forward, then step toward it."

"Yeah, yeah, I got it." Jordan took two tentative steps toward the walker. She repeated the routine several times until she had walked the distance between her bed and the door. Peter followed close by her side. As she stepped into the hallway, she noticed Kale and Andi getting off the elevator. "Hey, guys!" she called.

A wide grin split Kale's face when he saw her. "Way to go, Jord!"

"Wow, I didn't realize how tall you are," Andi commented.

"The last time I was measured, I was five-foot nine."

"And I'm only five foot three," said Andi.

"Shrimp," Jordan teased.

"How does it feel to be on your feet again?" Kale asked.

"It feels wonderful. Come, walk with me," she encouraged her friends.

"As long as you have company, I'll take my leave and head back to the lab," Peter said. "Kale, be sure she doesn't overdo it, okay? One trip to the end of the hall and back, Jordan, and then off your feet. No argument. You'll have plenty of opportunity for long walks around the farm when you go home tomorrow."

* * *

Kale pulled his vehicle close to the front door of the farmhouse and turned off the ignition. "Stay where you are. I'll come around and help you out." By the time Kale made it around to Jordan's side of the vehicle, she had already swung the door open and planted her feet firmly on the ground. "Damn it, woman. You're the most stubborn individual I've ever met."

Jordan feigned a look of innocence. "What?"

"Don't give me that look. Here—hold on to my shoulders while I help you stand. Peter said no bending at the waist if you can help it. The last thing you need is to pull out your stitches."

"Nag, nag, nag," Jordan said as she allowed Kale to assist her.

"Okay, hold onto my arm while we walk to the door."

"I can do this by myself."

"Maybe you can, but not on my shift. I know you too well, Jordan Lewis. The moment I turn my back and leave you alone, you'll be skipping rope or something equally stupid."

"Do I look like an idiot?" Jordan asked.

"Do you really want me to answer that?"

Kale ignored Jordan's attempts to look insulted as he led her into the house and helped her into a reclining position on the couch. "You stay right here. I need to unload the vehicle." He pointed directly at her. "No sitting up."

Kale turned to leave and felt a sudden thud on the back of his head. He stopped short and bent down to pick up the pillow that had landed on the floor behind him. The moment he met her eyes, Jordan stuck her tongue out at him.

"You are so lucky you are recovering from surgery," he said in mock anger. He threw the pillow back at her.

Kale retrieved the bag of Jordan's personal items and her walker, which had been folded flat. He also removed her chair from the storage compartment and guided it into the house. When Jordan saw the chair, she narrowed her eyes. "I hope I never have to use that thing again." Just then, the sound of a beeping horn came from the barnyard.

"That would be Andi," Kale said. "She has the lab animals with her. I need to give her a hand transferring them to the barn. I'll be right back."

"I'm coming with you," Jordan said.

Kale stopped. "You really should be resting."

"Peter said I could walk around all I wanted as long as I didn't overdo it. I don't think walking from here to the barn will be too strenuous."

Kale reached for Jordan's walker. He carried it over to her and planted it on the rug in front of her. "He also said you needed to use the walker for the next few days."

Jordan looked distastefully at the walker. "I don't really think I need it," she said.

Kale folded his arms across his chest in a stubborn pose. "Then I guess you don't really need to come out to the lab either."

"You are a pain in my ass. You know that, don't you?" she said.

"Looks who's calling the kettle black," he responded. "You've got the market cornered on pains in the ass. Your choice, walker or couch."

"Grr!" Jordan replied. "Okay, have it your way. Give me the goddamned walker."

"I knew you'd see it my way," Kale snickered as he helped her to her feet.

* * *

"Hi there, Rupert. How's my little time traveler today?"

Rupert sat back on his haunches, eating the treats Jordan fed him. Rupert's survival during the time travel experiments had elevated him to the status of pet. Satisfied her little friend had eaten his fill, she turned her attention to the new specimen Andi had brought to the lab. "Hi there, little man," Jordan cooed as the monkey grabbed the finger she offered him through his cage. She looked at Kale, who was busy at the control panel. "Our little friend here has been fitted with the implant, right?"

"Yes he has, at the L1 vertebra, just like you. We were fortunate enough to have access to the same lab animals used to perfect the implant. Because of that, we'll be able to test the functionality of the implant during the time transfers."

Kale glanced at Andi who was working at a table on the opposite side of the room. "How are you doing over there, Andi?"

Andi turned to face Kale and Jordan. In her hand was a small vest-like garment. "I'm ready to put this on the little guy. I might need some help," she said, approaching the cage.

"What is it?" Jordan asked as she inspected the garment.

Andi turned it over in her hand. "See this right here?" She pointed to a small box attached to the front of the vest. "This is a micro-camera. We're going to attempt to film the transfer process. If we're successful, we'll know what happens during the transfer, and we'll be able to see everything."

"Are you recording the process on a disk or is it more like a webcam?" Jordan asked.

"We're attempting to do both. We really don't expect the webcam approach to hold up, but with any luck, the recording will," Andi said.

Jordan felt intense excitement rise in her chest. "I really hope this works. It would be great to know what I'll be facing when its time for me to make the trip."

"That's the plan, sweetheart. That's the plan."

* * *

Kale placed the chimp's cage on the platform. He secured the grounding hardware to both the cage and its occupant. Jordan and Andi waited behind the barrier near the control console.

"Is the webcam working?" Jordan asked.

Andi glanced at the small monitor next to the computer. It showed the chimp's view of the lab as he moved around in his cage. "Yes, it is. Let's hope it continues to work."

"All right, then. I guess we should start," Kale announced as he set the rings in motion. Within moments, both sets of rings were spinning and the cage containing the chimp hovered in the center of the spheres. The chimp chattered noisily.

"One minute to surge," Jordan said. "Ten, nine, eight, seven, six, five, four, three, two, one, surge!"

The force of the surge was felt by all as they clung to the table, which was anchored to the floor. Finally, when it was obvious that the subject was no longer on the platform, Kale powered down the rings.

Jordan was breathing heavily, and her heart beat wildly. "Reverse the rings, Kale. Bring him back."

"It looks like we've lost the signal. I suspected we would. I'm hoping it continues to record on the other side," Andi said.

"Okay. We're ready to retrieve. I'm going to start the rings," Kale said. He initiated the program.

"Get ready. We're almost there—now!"

Once again a surge of power washed over the lab as the cage containing the chimp reappeared in the center of the sphere. The chimp was screeching wildly as Kale powered down the rings and the cage gently floated down onto the platform.

"Look at the monitor," Andi said. "The webcam is working again. Quick, Kale, I need the camera."

The trio sat in front of the blank monitor. Jordan sat closest to the table, her hand inside the chimp's cage, gently patting the animal's back as he slept. It appeared the trip through time had taken more out of the chimp than they anticipated. They attributed his exhaustion to the hyper-excited state he was in when they retrieved him from the past.

"Are you ready?" Andi asked. She pressed "play" on the remote control.

The disk played scenes of the lab from the moment the cage was placed on the platform to the point of the first surge. Then, suddenly, the screen was covered with streaks of light, bright colors racing toward them. The speed and direction of the light streaks gave them the impression that they were moving down a thin tube at high speed—a tube filled with a million twinkling Christmas lights.

"It's so beautiful," Jordan whispered hoarsely.

Then, just as suddenly as the streaks appeared, they were gone. The barn came into view.

Andi frowned. "What's happening? It looks like the barn, only newer."

"That's because it is the barn—eighty-seven years ago. In-fucking-credible! I can't believe it," Kale said, excitement in his voice.

The image began to move. The chimp had regained his senses and was moving gingerly around his cage.

"It looks like the cage landed behind a stack of hay bales," Jordan said.

"Maybe that's a good thing. It wouldn't have been good for someone to come into the barn and discover the cage sitting in the middle of the floor. That might have caused all kinds of paradoxes," Andi said.

For the next hour, they sat glued to the TV monitor, observing different angles of the barn as the chimp rolled over, swung from the ceiling of the cage, and turned around in circles.

Kale finally sat back in his chair and rolled his shoulders. "This is starting to get boring," he complained.

"I can fast forward through this part if you'd like," Andi suggested.

Just as Andi pushed the fast forward button, Jordan cried out, "Wait! Stop! Give me the remote. Give it to me, quickly," she said with such urgency that Andi handed it over immediately.

Jordan put the reader in reverse. Seconds later, she found what she was looking for. She stopped the recorder and pushed the option for frame-by-frame playback. The monitor came to life and very slowly displayed what Jordan had seen flash by quickly just moments before. Tears filled Jordan's eyes as she paused on one particular frame.

"Maggie!" Jordan rasped.

CHAPTER 24

All three friends stared at the woman on the screen. Maggie appeared only briefly in the corner of the screen, well behind the hay bales as she entered the barn, but her image as captured by the high-tech camera was clear and crisp.

"She's beautiful," Andi choked out through her own tears.

Kale just stared at the screen, totally incapable of speaking, as he suddenly understood why Jordan was so intent on this journey. He watched Jordan run her fingertips across the frozen image of Maggie on the TV monitor in a gesture so intimate he could feel the depth of her love for this woman.

Jordan looked at Kale and an unspoken promise passed between them. Kale nodded. He wiped the trail of tears from Jordan's cheek, then took her hand in his.

"We need to watch the rest of the disk. I promise I'll make a copy for you. Right now, we need to see what happens, okay?" Andi said.

Andi returned to the spot just prior to Maggie's entrance and pushed play. Maggie's only appearance on the disk was the brief moment it took for her to walk by the lens. Nearly a half-hour more of scenes within the barn ended when a "disk full" message appeared on the screen.

Jordan frowned. "What happened?"

Andi rose to her feet. "I guess that's all we get to see for now."

"But the camera was still working when we retrieved the chimp," Jordan said.

"Yes it was, but apparently only in live webcam mode. The disk was already full by then, so it stopped recording," Andi said.

Kale sat staring at the blank TV screen. "Hmm... so that means we have no idea how long the chimp was actually there. He was only gone from here for what, ten or fifteen minutes? But a two-hour disk is full of images, none of which include the trip back to

184

the present. We don't know how many hours, days, or weeks passed in that time zone for those minutes."

"But the chimp came back healthy, so it couldn't have been that long," Andi said. "I mean, if he was gone for too long, he would be showing signs of dehydration or malnutrition. I'm guessing the time lapse on the other end wasn't any more than a day."

"I guess we'll have to figure that out when we send me into the past," Jordan said.

"I'm not sure I'm comfortable with that idea," Kale said.

Jordan dropped her chin to her chest and reached up to rub her temples. She sighed deeply then looked up. "Kale, sometimes we need to take risks. I, for one, am ready to do this as soon as I'm healed. I don't want to do anymore testing. Rupert came back okay, the chimp came back okay. He was obviously conscious when he got there. We have recorded proof of that. Enough is enough. I have faith in you. I have faith in both of you." Jordan looked back and forth between her friends. "I can't wait much longer. I need to be with her. It is physically painful for me not to be."

* * *

For the next two weeks, Jordan, Kale and Andi worked diligently on the self-charging power pack for the implant. As the two-week mark neared, Kale became more and more nervous about sending Jordan back in time. The night before Jordan's surgery, the three were enjoying a dinner of baked chicken, garlic mashed potatoes, and steamed asparagus.

"Jordan, I'm having second thoughts about this. What if something goes wrong?"

Jordan put her fork down on the table. "Please don't start, okay? We agreed to do this. You promised to do everything in your power to help me realize my dream."

Kale closed his eyes. He inhaled deeply then looked back at Jordan. "I'm afraid. I'm afraid of losing you. I'm afraid of failing you, I'm afraid of never seeing you again, but most of all, I'm afraid something will go terribly wrong and you'll die in the process. If that happens, I'll never forgive myself."

Jordan covered Kale's hand. "I know the risks, and I'm willing to take them if it means I have even the smallest chance of being with Maggie. We're so close. Don't take this away from me now."

"Jordan, I have no idea what may happen to you during the transfer. I don't know if you'll be aware of what is going on. I don't know if it will be painful. I don't know what will happen to your body. When we attempted to send the boot, molecule movement was so high it made parts of it unbearably hot to touch. Imagine what that might do to human flesh!"

Jordan frowned. "Don't give me that bullshit. You resolved that problem by grounding the test subject. You're trying to scare me into backing out. I won't let you do it."

Kale exhaled, deflated. "I just don't want to lose you," he admitted softly.

"Don't you understand that this is a win-win situation for me? If we're successful, I get to be with Maggie in life. If we fail, I get to be with Maggie in death. I'm prepared for both eventualities. Either way, I get what I need. I get to be with the one I love with everything I am. Don't you see?"

"Do you really love her so much that you're willing to risk dying to be with her?"

"Imagine for a moment that Andi was taken away from you for some reason. Then imagine you were given the opportunity to be with her again, but it meant leaving everything and everyone you know forever. Imagine the very process of reaching her again put your life in danger. Would you still risk it?"

"I would risk it in a heartbeat. I love Andi with everything that I am," he replied.

Jordan nodded. "All right then. I'll assume there'll be no more talk of backing out of this, okay?"

Kale looked at Andi as he answered Jordan. "Okay."

"Well then," Jordan said, "I guess I'll hit the sheets. I have a big day ahead of me tomorrow with the power-pack surgery. Thank you both for a wonderful dinner." Jordan stood and carried her dish to the sink.

"Leave that. I'll take care of it," Andi said.

"Thank you. Good night," she said. "Sleep well."

Kale watched Jordan exit the kitchen then returned his attention to Andi, who was staring off into space. "Are you okay?" he asked. "You look preoccupied."

Andi smiled. "I'm fine. There's something I'd like to talk to Jordan about."

"Is it anything I can help with?"

"No, love. It's just girl stuff."

"Okay. Why don't you go ahead and I'll take care of the dishes?" he said.

Andi cocked her head to one side. "Have I told you today that I love you?"

Kale placed a gentle kiss on Andi's lips. "You may have, but I have short-term memory problems, so I guess you'll just have to tell me repeatedly so I don't forget."

"Well, I do," Andi replied. "I'll be right back.

* * *

"Jordan, may I come in?"

"Sure, the door's open."

Andi pushed the door to Jordan's bedroom open just enough for her to slip through.

Jordan put down the book she was reading. "What's up?" she asked.

"Jordan, there's something you need to know about the physics of time travel... something I really don't want Kale to realize, because if he does, he'll probably refuse to send you."

Jordan frowned. "What is it?"

"Over a hundred years ago, an experiment was carried out with four atomic clocks."

"Oh, I know about that. Kale described it to me at dinner a while back. He said something about four atomic clocks flown on planes traveling in opposite directions and compared to one on the ground. He said that the clocks on the plane came back with different times than the one on the ground."

"Yes, exactly. The planes were flying at a speed faster than the rotation of the Earth. The clock flying in the same direction as the Earth ran faster and the one flying the opposite direction ran slower than the clock on the ground," Andi said.

"What about that concerns you?"

"In theory, if you gain time by going backward, traveling into the past may have an effect on the aging process. It's never been proven—primarily because time travel by humans hasn't been accomplished yet—but it is a possibility. I want you to be aware of the risks," Andi said.

Jordan smiled. "I meant what I said at dinner. There is no risk too great that I would be unwilling to do this. I need to do this. I can't live without her."

* * *

Peter completed his post-op examination of the incision on Jordan's back before signing her release papers. "Okay, Jordan. You're free to go. Just remember to take care of the wound site for the next few days. It should heal quickly, since the surgery was minor and relatively noninvasive. It's very important to let me know if you feel anything besides pain, or if the implant appears to fail in any way."

Jordan smiled. "I am so looking forward to this. No more plugging in at night. No more worrying that rolling over in my sleep will cause instant paralysis. Peter, I don't know how to thank you."

"No thanks necessary. Now go on, get out of here."

Jordan dressed herself as soon as Peter left the room. She was soon in her vehicle and heading home. As she rode through the business district, she was delayed by a traffic signal. Waiting for the light to turn, she looked around and realized she was sitting in front of her lawyer's office, the same lawyer who handled her parents' estate. As the light turned, she made a quick decision and turned into the driveway of the office.

* * *

"What's this?" Kale asked.

"Open it," Jordan said.

Kale read the return address on the envelope Jordan had handed him. "Stuart Benjamin, Attorney at Law, Shelburne, Vermont. What is this about?"

"Just open it," she repeated.

Kale opened the envelope and unfolded the document inside. A shocked expression settled on his face. His hands shook as he refolded the letter, returned it to the envelope, and handed it back to Jordan. "I can't accept this."

Jordan handed it back to him. "Yes, you can. I don't want any shit about it either, okay?"

"Jord, this is morbid. Don't do this. You'll jinx us all," Kale said.

"May I?" Andi asked.

Jordan handed Andi the envelope. "Sure. Maybe you can talk some sense into him."

Andi began to read. "In the event of my death, I, Jordan Marie Lewis, leave my 250 acre farm located at 1029 Pheasant Hill Road,

Shelburne, Vermont, to one Kale Lyndon Simmons, currently in residence at that location. The property and the entire contents of the house and barns, currently deeded solely in my name, will be transferred to him without lien. Also upon my death, all assets and income associated with the property, as well as any balances remaining in my savings and checking accounts will become the sole property of Mr. Simmons. If at such time, Mr. Simmons is deceased, or unable to assume ownership of the above-mentioned property, ownership will pass to Andrea Mae Ellis. If at such time, both Mr. Simmons and Ms. Ellis are deceased, or unable to assume ownership of the above mentioned property, it is to be sold, and the proceeds donated to the Spinal Cord Institute at the University of Vermont, in honor of their memory. Jordan Marie Lewis, July 1, 2105."

Andi looked at Jordan. "Wow!"

Kale looked at Jordan. "Don't do this. It doesn't feel right."

"What doesn't feel right about it?" Jordan grasped Kale's hand. "If something does go wrong, and I don't make it, I want you and Andi to be taken care of. None of this would be possible without you two. Both of you are risking so much to help me realize my heart's desire." Jordan sat back and grinned. "Besides, I need a place for my ghost to haunt, and quite frankly, I couldn't choose more suitable hosts than you two." Jordan took the letter back from Andi and thrust it toward Kale once more. "Take it, Kale. Please?"

Kale nodded his head slightly and accepted the letter. "You're amazing, Jordan. You don't have to do this, you know."

"I know I don't, but I'd rather see the two of you have the farm than let the state take it over and turn it into commercial development property. I want you to have it. You deserve it."

'Thank you," Kale replied softly.

Jordan rose to her feet and began to collect the empty dinner dishes from the table. "Now that that's settled, why don't we go into the living room, pour some wine, and talk about this time travel thing?"

Kale made himself comfortable at the far end of the sofa with Andi tucked under his arm. Both of them enjoyed a glass of merlot while Jordan crouched in front of the fireplace and tended the embers until the kindling wood she had placed on top began to burn. Her own wine glass was perched on the mantel. As the kindling burned, Jordan watched the flames dance to and fro along the wood.

"Are you going to stare at those flames all night?" Kale asked.

"Sorry about that." Jordan placed a larger log on top of the kindling and rose to her feet. She reached for her wine glass and sat in the chair nearest the sofa. "Okay, let's talk about when we're going to do the time travel thing."

"When do you think we should do it?" Kale asked.

"Tomorrow. Definitely tomorrow."

"Is that wise?" Andi asked. "I mean, you just had surgery today to install the power pack. Don't you think we should give it a few days?"

"I don't see any reason why we can't start right away. I mean, yeah, I had surgery today, but it was outpatient. Hell, Peter gave me a clean release and sent me home just a few hours after it was done."

"Andi's right. It's too soon. The power pack was just installed. At the very least, we need to give it a few days to be sure it's functioning properly before subjecting it to something like this," Kale said.

Jordan frowned and tried her best to look menacing to her friends.

Kale chuckled. "Give it up. Pouting won't work with us. You're just going to have to deal with it. Three more days, or not at all. Your choice."

Jordan threw her hands up in the air. "No fair. Why am I always outnumbered?" She looked at Kale and Andi one more time, but realized they were not going to change their minds. "Okay. You win." Jordan rolled her eyes and released a sigh of frustration before continuing. "All right, so hear me out. We need a way to communicate between now and Maggie's time."

"Communicate?" Kale asked.

"Yeah. I need a way to contact you if I need for you to bring me back quickly. For example, if Jan comes after me with a loaded shotgun because I stole her hot red-haired girlfriend away from her."

"If you'd learn to curb your libido, you wouldn't have to worry about things like that," Kale said dryly.

Jordan feigned surprise. "You're asking me to do the impossible. Hell, you've seen her picture. Would you be able to resist her?"

Kale grinned. Andi gave him a clearly disapproving look.

"Yes, I would be able to resist. Yes, indeed. Why wouldn't I when I have the most beautiful woman in town to share my life?"

Andi kissed Kale on the cheek. "Good answer," she said.

Jordan and Kale traded a grin as Andi looked away. "So, like I said, we need a way to communicate. I've been giving this a lot of thought, and I think I should leave something in the barn. Maybe there's a nook that would have been there eighty-seven years ago that's still there today. It would have to be a place that's relatively well-hidden, so that whatever I leave in there wouldn't be found by anyone who might own the barn between Maggie's time and now. Also, we need to use some medium that will withstand the amount of time it would be there," Jordan said.

"So we need to avoid things like paper," Andi said.

"Exactly. Anything biodegradable runs the risk of turning to dust over time period separating our eras. Maybe we could use rocks, or metal of some sort," Jordan suggested.

"How about we use a rock to mean 'retrieve me now', and maybe a nail or a horseshoe to let us know you're okay?" Kale asked.

"Sounds good. Now, all we have to do is find this nook." Jordan jumped to her feet and headed for the door.

"Where are you going?" Kale asked.

"To the barn to look for the nook. Care to join me?"

* * *

The three friends stood in the center of the barn and looked around. None of them moved.

"Who knows what was actually here eighty-seven years ago and what's been modified? I would hate to use a spot that's here now, but not back then. We need to find a place that's out of the way. I would think it would have a greater chance of being original," Kale suggested.

"Original? Out of the way? Follow me," Jordan said.

Andi and Kale followed Jordan to the small tack room located at the end of the horse stalls. Jordan went directly to the workbench, dropped to her knees and began to clear away the hay and dirt from an area under the bench. Kale also dropped to his knees to help her. Soon, they had a large area cleared away.

"What is it?" Kale asked as she struggled to lift one of the floorboards.

"It's stuck." Jordan grunted as she looked out from beneath the bench. "Andi, do you see a screwdriver or something up there that I can use as a lever?"

"There's a long spike. Will that do?"

"Perfect. Would you mind handing it down to me?"

Jordan took the spike from Andi and used it to pry the board loose. Soon, she exposed a relatively small opening in the floor. "There. What do you think?"

Kale looked into the hole. "It looks like this compartment was put here on purpose. Any idea what it was used for?" he asked.

"My dad thought this might have been a working tack shop at one time, and the owners might have used that space as a type of safe," Jordan replied. "I used to hide all my treasures in it when I was small."

"It looks like it might have been here from the beginning." He turned to Andi. "We need to check it at regular intervals while Jordan's gone so we'll know if she needs to come home."

"All right then. We have our communication portal." Jordan grinned.

* * *

Three days later, Kale embraced Jordan as tightly as he could while his heart beat wildly in his chest. "This scares the shit out of me," he whispered in her ear.

"I know. In a lot of ways, it scares me too," Jordan confessed in a choked voice.

"Please, let us know if you made it all right. If all goes well, you should be arriving in Maggie's barn, just as the chimp did."

Jordan chuckled. "Just don't send me to some alternate universe somewhere, okay?"

"I'll try not to," Kale said.

Kale released Jordan and walked toward the console, where he tried his best to focus on the computer screen through the veil of moisture that clouded his eyes.

Andi was openly crying as she clung to Jordan. "Whatever happens, I love you, Jordan," she whispered before releasing her and joining Kale at the console. Andi wrapped her arm around his waist and buried her face in his shoulder.

Jordan carefully climbed into the center of the sphere and sat cross-legged on the platform. With shaky hands, she reached for the grounding filament and secured it around her ankle. "I love you, guys," she called out before she pulled her knees up, wrapped her arms around her legs, and buried her face on her thighs below her knees.

Kale's hand shook as he initiated the time travel program. The whooshing sound of the rings grew louder as they picked up momentum. Within minutes, both sets of rings were at critical velocity.

Andi and Kale looked at the spheres and noted Jordan's body floating effortlessly in the center of the rings—her arms still wrapped around her legs, her face buried deeply into her thighs. Andi wiped the tears from her eyes as she monitored the speed of the rings and began to count down the seconds before surge.

Tears fell steadily from Kale's eyes as he listened to Andi count down the last few seconds. A wave of energy passed over them as a blinding light filled the room. After the energy wave passed, Kale looked at the platform. It was empty save for the filament that had been secured around Jordan's ankle.

CHAPTER 25

Jordan fought hard to remain in the fetal position as she felt herself slowly drift off the platform. Then, without warning, she felt a tremendous force exerted on her body, and she found it nearly impossible to breathe. She fought for oxygen. Immobilized by the force, she was unable to move even a finger. A terrible tingling then spread through her body as though every muscle had fallen asleep and was now awakening.

Jordan found herself in utter darkness—the kind of darkness that supports no sound and no sensory feeling. The feeling was claustrophobic, and a deep fear welled up in the center of her being. Then, just when she believed she would die from fear, the space around her exploded into a spectacular light show. Before her appeared a multicolored mass with a dark center. The colors moved in and around each other like a giant kaleidoscope.

Jordan felt herself being drawn toward the hole in the center of the mass. Curiously, the fear she had felt just moments before evaporated as she neared the center of the mass. The colors appeared to press against the edges of the hole, creating a wider opening for her to pass through. Each of the colors touched her in different ways. She could not only see them, she could feel them as well. Red was warm. Yellow was soft and silky. Green was tart, and blue felt like a gentle breeze. Lavender smelled like the air after a rainstorm. Jordan's senses were stimulated at every angle by the colorful beams of light.

As the center of the hole widened, it formed a funnel like the tail of a tornado. Jordan's funnel was calm and peaceful. She looked around as she gently floated through the gravity-less passage. Beyond her protective sheath of semi-transparent color, Jordan could see an infinite display of stars shooting around her. Her heart and mind filled with a sense of tranquility as she wondered if she had died during the time travel transfer and was now being transported to heaven. A feeling of serenity filled her as she closed her eyes and accepted her fate.

"Humph!"

Jordan lay face down in the dirt, clenching her stomach as the impact knocked the wind out of her. "Breathe, Jordan, breathe. That's it, relax and just breathe."

After a time, the cramps in her stomach subsided enough for her to elevate her upper body with her hands and look around. The room was very dark as the last remnants of daylight were fading away. "We're not in Kansas anymore, Toto. Where the hell am I?"

Jordan looked around. The air was heavy with the odors of hay and animals. "I'm definitely in a barn. I just hope it's mine." She paused when she realized what she was doing. "Great. Now I'm talking to myself." Jordan raised one hand to her face and brushed off the dirt from her fall to the ground. "Okay, Jordan, get your shit together and find out just where you are."

Jordan attempted to get her knees under her so she could stand, and realized her legs weren't moving. "What the fuck?"

* * *

"You can power down the machine now. She's gone," Andi said.

Kale powered the rings down. He approached the machine and stood staring at the platform. An intense sadness filled his heart, and he feared he would never see Jordan again. "What did we do, Andi? What did we do?" he asked softly.

Andi approached Kale and wrapped her arms around him. They held each other close. "You're helping her realize her dream. She's right. Regardless of what happened during the transfer, she would be with Maggie. One way or another."

"Then why can't I feel happy for her?"

"Because you're sad for yourself," Andi replied. "For you, the enormity of your loss outweighs her gain."

Kale lowered his forehead to touch Andi's. "How is it that you're so smart?" he asked.

"Believe it or not, I learned it from Jordan. In the short time I've been part of your lives, I've learned the value of love. For Jordan, no sacrifice is too great to be with the one who owns her heart. If she were here right now, she'd be kicking your ass for feeling so sad. It's because of your courage that she has this chance.

You've given her the most precious gift life has to offer. Be happy for her."

Kale smiled and kissed the end of Andi's nose. "If I only knew that she made it safely, I would feel so much better about it."

Andi pulled her head back and looked at Kale, then reached up and hit his forehead with the palm of her hand.

"Hey, what was that for?" Kale rubbed his forehead.

"Duh! The communication portal," she exclaimed.

* * *

"Son of a bitch!" Jordan slapped the dirt floor with her hand. "Goddamn son of a bitch!" She reached behind her to feel the implant and energy unit through the skin on her back. Both were easy to locate as they protruded noticeably under her skin, however the familiar vibration of the unit was absent. "How can this be? The rat and the chimp both came back with functional implants. Mine should remain functional as well."

Jordan pushed herself onto her back and looked around her surroundings. "Okay, Lewis, get a grip. You need to know exactly where you are, and you need to get a message to Kale." The light was fading rapidly, making it nearly impossible for Jordan to assess the situation. Feelings of panic began to grow in her chest.

Jordan strained to see in the darkness. She was just able to make out a horse stall nearby. With all her strength, she dragged herself into the stall and pulled the horse blanket down from the rail to use as a cover. Thoroughly exhausted, she quickly fell asleep.

* * *

"Okay, Shawny, time for your morning run. Maggie would take you, but she had an accident in the barn yesterday, so I guess that chore falls to me today."

Jordan's eyes flew open. She lay as still as possible so as to not draw attention to herself. *Did she say Maggie? Wasn't Maggie's horse named Shawny?*

Jordan strained to see through a gap in the boards separating the stall she was in and the one where the voice came from. As she watched, a petite woman threw a blanket over a beautifully groomed mustang marked by a star-shape in the middle of his forehead. Next came the saddle. As the woman secured the saddle to the horse,

Jordan caught glimpses of her appearance—short blonde hair, slim, but toned. *Jan?*

"Okay, big guy, let's go for a run," the woman said as she mounted the horse.

Jordan pulled the blanket over her head and remained as still as possible. She held her breath. The woman rode the horse through the barn. Jordan didn't relax until she heard the sound of hoofs galloping away.

Jordan threw the horse blanket to one side and, with great difficulty, she dragged herself toward the area where the tack room should be. As she passed each horse stall, she prayed that she would not be discovered. After nearly an hour, she reached her goal. Her shoulders and neck ached from the strain of dragging herself across the dirt floor. To her delight, beyond the door, she indeed found a tack shop. Spurred on by her discovery, she expended one last concerted effort to drag herself across the room to locate the secret compartment under the workbench.

Jordan worked her fingers around the edge of the board and with very little effort was able to work it free. She lifted the board and searched the floor around her. Now to find a stone...

* * *

Kale threw open the door of the tack room and nearly dove under the workbench in an effort to reach the secret compartment as quickly as he could. He tried in vain to work the cover free. "Damn it!" he exclaimed in frustration. He climbed out from beneath the bench and was frantically searching through the tools on top of it when Andi finally entered the tack shop.

"You could have waited for me, you know," she said.

"No time. I need to know if Jordan is okay," Kale said. "Got it," he said when he finally located a screwdriver and dove back under the workbench. Kale pried the wooden cover from the compartment.

"Is there anything in there?"

Kale reached into the box and searched around with his hand. Suddenly, his eyebrows rose sharply as he encountered an object. "Yes. Yes, there's something in here." A moment later he emerged from under the table and held the object out for Andi to see.

"What is it?" Andi asked.

"Damned if I know," Kale replied.

"Is it metal? Metal means she's okay."

The object in Kale's hand was rectangular in shape with a rough, granular surface. It was obviously manufactured, not something that appeared in nature. Kale turned it over in his hand. "I don't think it's metal. It's gritty. I would expect metal to feel smooth."

Andi looked at Kale. "Hon, we don't even know if Jordan put this object in the box. It could have been there already."

"The compartment was empty. Jordan put this in there. I think she's calling for help."

Andi looked around the tack room. "Maybe we can find an object similar to it in here that might give us a clue as to what it is," she suggested.

"Good idea." Kale rummaged through the tools on and around the workbench.

Andi began going through a drawer that contained old documents and catalogs. After a few minutes, she pulled an old, worn catalog from the back of the drawer. "Kale, look at this. It's a catalog from a company called "The Tack-L Box." It looks like a place for ordering tack shop supplies. Maybe we can find a clue or two in here."

Kale took the catalog from Andi. He cleared a space on the workbench to lay out the catalog then placed the object from the compartment on the bench next to it. He combed the document page by page, carefully examining the photographs on each page. About halfway through the catalog, a photograph caught Kale's eye. "This is it."

"It looks really similar. What is it?"

Kale read the description under the photograph. "This product is perfect for sharpening knives, axes and a variety of other cutting tools. The Tack-L Box keeps only top of the line whetstones in inventory."

Andi grasped Kale's arm. "Jordan is in trouble. It's a stone... a whetstone."

* * *

Jordan slowly dragged herself back to the main part of the barn, assuming she had to be retrieved from the same location. That meant looking around the floor to find her original drag marks in the dirt. She only hoped she could make it to the transfer zone before being discovered.

198

Kale's heart beat rapidly as he loaded the retrieval algorithm into the computer. "Come on, load already."

"Kale, honey, rushing won't get her back any sooner. Don't shortcut anything. We can't afford to make a mistake."

Kale stepped back from the computer and inhaled deeply to calm his nerves. He closed his eyes for a moment, then opened them again and looked at Andi. "You're right. I'm sorry, but I'm worried about Jordan."

"I understand." Andi glanced at the computer screen. "Okay, the algorithm load is complete. Go ahead and start the rings."

They focused intently on the spheres as both pairs came to critical velocity.

"All right, Kale. I am starting the countdown. Five, four, three, two, one—now!"

Kale felt the wave of energy pass over them. When the wave had passed, he glanced at the time machine. It was empty.

* * *

Jordan had managed to drag herself past all but the last horse stall when she heard voices outside the barn doors. With every ounce of strength she had left, she pulled herself into the stall and, once again, hid under the horse blanket.

"John, please take Shawny to his stall, give him fresh water and feed, and brush him down. You know how special he is to Maggie, and we don't want to disappoint the boss."

"Yes, ma'am," said a masculine voice.

Jordan held still, listening to the sound of heavy boots thudding against the dirt floor and the clippity-clop of horses' hooves. John led the steed to his stall, right next to the one Jordan was hiding in. Jordan closed her eyes and forced herself to breathe slowly and quietly. She listened as John brushed down the horse and filled his water trough and feedbag. Finally, the farmhand left and she was alone once more. Jordan waited for a few more minutes before she dared to venture out of the stall again. When she was ten feet from her goal, a blinding white light suddenly filled the room and then disappeared as fast as it came.

* * *

"No!" Kale screamed. "I knew this would happen. We've lost her. She's gone. I knew I shouldn't have let her talk me into this."

"Kale. Stop and think for a moment," Andi said. "What are the two things Jordan has that the chimp didn't?"

Kale narrowed his eyes. "I'm really not in the mood for riddles."

Andi sighed. "I'm going to let that one pass because I know you're scared. What she has that the chimp didn't are mobility and intelligence. The chimp was locked in a cage. He could move around inside it, but he couldn't move around the barn. Jordan can go anywhere she wants."

Kale stopped pacing. "Jordan may have ventured away from the retrieval site?"

"Yes. Jordan is smart. She'll figure this out. I think we should try again."

* * *

Jordan couldn't believe her eyes as she dragged herself the final ten feet. "Kale, please don't tell me that white flash was you. Please don't tell me I missed it." Jordan placed her forehead on the ground and rested for a moment. "I can't possibly drag myself to the tack room and back again today. I just don't have the strength."

Suddenly, the room was filled once more with a brilliant white light. Moments later the only occupant in the barn was Shawny.

* * *

"Jordan! You're back." Andi ran toward the spinning spheres as Kale powered down the rings.

Jordan was clearly furious as she swung her legs over the side of the platform and walked away from the machine. She turned to Kale, hands on her hips. "Want to tell me what happened here?"

Kale's first concern was for Jordan's health. "Please, sit down. Are you okay?"

Jordan walked up to Kale and looked him in the face. "No, I don't want to sit. I'm fine. But I do want to know what the hell happened."

Kale narrowed his eyes. "I honestly don't know what you're talking about. What exactly happened during the transfer? What happened when you arrived in the past?"

Jordan pivoted on her heels and walked away. Then she turned to face Kale once more, obviously upset and frustrated. "I'll tell you what happened, Kale. The implant failed."

"It failed?"

"What part of failed don't you understand?"

Andi interrupted the conversation. "Look, Jordan. Something obviously went wrong that you know about, but we don't. We're not mind readers, and we can't help to fix something unless we know what's broken. Now, I think we all need to calm down and talk reasonably about this."

Jordan rubbed her face vigorously with her hands, inhaled deeply, and released the breath slowly. "You're right. I'm sorry. Okay, I'm calm. When I arrived in the past, I couldn't move. I had no mobility in my legs at all, and the implant had lost its 'hum.' It wasn't working."

"But it's working now," Kale observed. "That means something happened in the transfer process that reversed itself during the retrieval."

"No shit, Sherlock," Jordan exclaimed.

*   *   *

Jordan sat at the kitchen table nursing a cup of coffee as Kale and Andi prepared a quick lunch.

"Thank you," Jordan said as Andi placed a bowl of soup in front of her. "I'm starved. I haven't eaten since we started all of this yesterday."

Kale carried the sandwiches to the table. "Whoa, say that again?"

Jordan was confused. "I haven't eaten since you sent me back yesterday."

Kale exchanged a look with Andi. "We sent you back this morning. In fact, you were gone for less than two hours."

"No way," Jordan exclaimed.

"It's true," Andi said. "Maybe you should tell us what happened."

Jordan took a large bite of her sandwich. She paused to swallow before continuing. "Like I said earlier, when I got there, it didn't take me long to realize the implant had failed. It was really dark, and I wasn't even sure it was my barn. I knew it wouldn't be wise to move around too much when I couldn't see, so I dragged myself to the closest horse stall and fell asleep. In the morning, I was startled by a voice talking to the horse in the next stall. I think it was Jan."

"How do you know?" Andi asked.

"I was sort of able to see her though the slats. She fit Maggie's description of her in the diaries. She also called the horse Shawny, which is what Maggie called him in one of my visions." Jordan spooned soup into her mouth as she recalled what happened next. "Jan was talking to the horse and said something about Maggie having an accident in the barn the day before. I wonder if she was talking about the accident Maggie mentioned in the diaries."

"If it was the accident she referred to in the diaries, then at least we'll have a frame of reference relative to exactly when you landed in the past," Kale said.

"True. Anyway, after Jan left with the horse, I dragged myself to the tack room and left the stone in the communication portal."

"By the way," Kale said, "a real stone would have saved us some time. We had no idea what that thing was. It took some pretty intensive investigation to figure it out. We had almost convinced ourselves that the object was put in the box by some previous owner rather than by you."

Jordan looked incredulously at her two friends. "Are you telling me neither of you know what a whetstone is?"

"You're looking at city folk here, Jordan. We were clueless," Kale admitted.

"Well, it was the only thing I could find in the room that was even remotely stone. Maggie keeps a pretty clean shop."

"Go on. What happened next?" Andi prompted.

"After leaving the whetstone in the box, I dragged myself back toward the spot in the barn where I first arrived. I was almost caught by the farmhand that brought the horse back. I had to hide until he was gone. Then, as I was making my way to the exact arrival point, a bright flash filled the room. I knew you guys were trying to retrieve me."

"We were devastated when the first attempt failed to bring you back. I thought we had lost you for good," Kale said.

"I thought I might be stuck in the past forever, which would not have been a bad thing had the implant not failed, but I hoped you guys would try again, and you did."

Kale retrieved a pad of paper and stylus, and returned to the table. "We really need to figure out the difference between how fast time is passing here versus there, so we can coordinate the transfer and retrieval process better. Otherwise, it will be hit or miss."

"Good point," Andi said. "Obviously, there's a big difference between the two. Jordan, you were only gone for about an hour and a half, but your description spans eight to ten hours. Does that sound right?"

"That's pretty close," Jordan said.

Kale scribbled a few notes on the paper. "If we assume that ninety minutes here is roughly nine hours there, we get the time ratio. Now divide the amount of time that passes here by that ratio, and it should tell us how long you've been in the past the next time we send you back."

"We're not going to do this again until we understand and fix the reason the implant failed," Jordan insisted. "I'll be useless to Maggie without my legs."

Kale nodded. "You're right. We saw on the recording that the chimp's implant worked in the past, so it must be the power pack. Tomorrow is Monday. Why don't we visit the Electrical Engineering department at the university and do a little research?"

CHAPTER 26

Andi, Kale, and Jordan walked across campus to the Engineering building. They had arranged a meeting with Professor Clayton Hibbs to discuss possible interference devices for the implant. As they walked, they discussed their game plan.

"We need to understand any external factor that might cause the power pack to fail electrically," Kale said. "Here we are." He held the door to the Engineering building open for the ladies.

It took only moments for them to locate the office of Professor Hibbs, where they made themselves comfortable in the reception area until he emerged for their meeting. The professor was a scholarly looking man with a thick shock of graying hair, a bushy mustache, and glasses.

Kale extended his hand. "Professor Hibbs, my name is Kale Simmons. This is Jordan Lewis and Andrea Ellis. We're from the University's spinal research clinic."

"Yes, I've heard of you," Hibbs replied. He shook Jordan's hand firmly. "Dr. Lewis, you're quite well-known around campus. I understand your kinesiology class is very popular with the students."

"Please, call me Jordan," she said.

Hibbs turned to Andi. "Miss Ellis. It's so nice to meet you. Are you new here?"

"Yes, I am. I've only been here for three months, but already I'm in love with the area and the people." Andi shot a quick sideways glance at Kale and smiled.

"Come in. Have a seat." He turned directly to the matter at hand. "To what do I owe the pleasure of your company?"

"Well," Kale began, "I'm not sure if you've heard, but about a month ago, Jordan was the recipient of a spinal implant that not only provides her with normal mobility, but also promotes nerve growth. Eventually, this will result in sensory feeling returning to the injury site."

Hibbs raised his eyebrows. "So you're the pioneering young lady I read about in the campus newsletter. Congratulations. I would never have known you had a spinal cord injury by observing your movement. It's quite impressive."

"Thank you, Professor," Jordan replied.

"How can I help you?" Hibbs asked.

"As you might have guessed," Kale explained, "it's imperative for the implant to have an uninterrupted power supply in order for Jordan to maintain mobility and to promote continuous cell growth. We're here because we need to understand what factors could interfere with the electrical function of the energy storage unit. The unit was designed to work with the body's natural electrical generators. It's basically self-charging."

* * *

Kale looked at Jordan in the rearview mirror. "Looks like we'll have to shield the power pack." He steered the vehicle into the long driveway between the main road and the farmhouse. "Who would have thought that electromagnetic fields would cause it to fail?"

"That's assuming electromagnetic waves are really the culprit," Jordan said.

"True, but at this point, we don't have any other leads. We'll just have to test it."

"How do we shield the power pack?" Andi asked.

"We use metal, just as Hibbs suggested," he replied.

Kale turned off the ignition, and the three climbed out of the vehicle and entered the house.

"Who wants a beer?" Jordan walked to the refrigerator. "Beer," she said, "quantity three." A slot in the door opened and three bottles slid into the compartment below. Jordan grabbed the bottles and handed two to her companions. "Cheers," she said. "Ah, that's good. Okay, let's get to work."

"Why don't the two of you head out to the lab?" Andi said. "I'll throw together some sandwiches and join you in a few minutes."

Kale and Jordan sat in front of the computer reading research material. Andi rejoined them, bringing a plate of sandwiches and a bag of potato chips. "Any progress yet?"

"We need to build a Faraday cage," Kale replied. "That will reroute the current generated by electric fields away from what's inside it."

"That makes sense," Andi said.

Kale sat back in his chair. "Let's do it, then."

* * *

"I feel like a real geek in this thing," Jordan complained.

"It's either this belt or no legs," Kale replied.

Jordan grinned. "I know, but I don't have to like it."

Kale snapped the buckle in place on the front of the belt and stepped back to admire his handiwork. "Hmm... you're right. You do look like a geek."

Jordan looked down at the belt. "All I need is a cape, some knee-high boots, and a spandex suit with 'Faraday Girl' written across the chest, and I'll be ready for action. Are you sure this will work?"

"In theory, yes," Kale replied.

"In theory? It would be nice to have something a little more substantial to go on."

"That's all I can offer right now. Besides, the time machine was just a theory at one time, and look what we've accomplished."

"Point taken. When do we test it?"

"Whenever you're ready," Kale replied.

Jordan clapped her hands. "No time like the present—let's do it!"

Jordan sat on the platform in the middle of the rings and pulled her knees into her chest. The Faraday belt made it a little uncomfortable for her to curl into the fetal position she'd used for the previous transfer. She wrapped her arms around her legs and lowered her forehead to her knees. "Okay, Kale. I'm ready."

"Wait!" Andi cried before Kale could put the rings in motion. She fished a rock out of her pocket and ran toward the platform. "Here. No guesswork this time. Put this in your pocket and use it if you need to." She kissed Jordan and took a step back. "We love you," she said before joining Kale at the console.

Jordan slid the rock into her pocket. Within moments, she had assumed the fetal position again. She gave Kale the "thumbs-up" to begin the transfer.

* * *

"Humph!" Jordan hit the dirt floor with a thud. "Ow! Damn, that hurts. Kale, old buddy, you really need to work on that landing." Jordan elevated her upper body with her hands and looked around to be sure her entry was unnoticed. Gingerly, Jordan rose to her feet and took a few small, tentative steps across the room. Her legs appeared to be fully functional. *Kale, you're a genius!*

Suddenly, she heard a voice nearby.

"Hey, Shawny-baby. How's Mommy's good boy this morning?"

Holy shit! Jordan quickly hid behind a cluster of hay bales. She crouched low and stayed as still as possible.

"How about a ride, sweetie? It's a beautiful morning. The air is crisp, and the sun is shining off the snow. A nice fast ride will do us both some good. That's a good boy."

Is that Maggie? Shawny is her horse. It has to be her.

Jordan slowly shifted her position so that she could see just beyond the edge of the bales. The woman had her back to Jordan, but the unruly red curls told her that it was Maggie. Jordan wanted desperately to make her presence known, but how would she explain appearing literally out of nowhere? She waited, mesmerized, while Maggie saddled her horse. Maggie slipped her foot into the stirrup and swung her lean frame up and into the saddle. Shawny danced happily in a circle, affording Jordan a frontal view of the beautiful woman sitting astride the horse. She gasped, suddenly finding it impossible to breathe.

My God, she's beautiful!

"Okay, dumpling, let's go for a ride." Maggie gently prodded the steed. Soon, she was out of the barn and gone.

Jordan sat on the floor with her back against the bales as she caught her breath. *What the hell am I doing here? She's magnificent. I can't imagine what she would see in me.*

After a few moments of self-pity, Jordan realized she had not yet removed the Faraday belt. *Kale! I need to let them know I'm okay and that things are working well.* Jordan grabbed the Faraday belt and covertly made her way to the tack room. She hid the belt in the back of a cabinet and then climbed under the workbench to expose the communication portal. After she removed the cover, she climbed back out from beneath the bench and looked around for a metal object—a horseshoe for its symbolism. Finding one in the tack room, she deposited it in the portal and replaced the cover. *There, that should send the right message.*

She poked her head out of the room. As she stepped into the barn, she heard footsteps running toward her. She quickly slipped back into the tack room and hid out of sight as a farmhand ran past the door. Moments later, a horse and rider raced past. Jordan stepped out and watched the rider speed across the barnyard. *That looks like me. I must be seeing things.*

Seeing that the coast was clear, she walked into the main room again and looked around. Having just seen Maggie ride off, she knew she had time to kill before her return, so for the next hour, she explored every nook and cranny of the barn, picturing it as it was in her own time.

The barn was spotless, a fact that spoke clearly of Maggie's organization. Jordan could see subtle touches of style and wondered if they reflected Maggie's personality. To her, a barn was a barn, but Maggie had painstakingly added her own flare: decorative benches with scenic pictures of the Vermont countryside hanging above them; old quilts adorning the walls; milk cans filled with dried grasses and flowers. Everywhere she looked, Jordan could see Maggie's attempts to make the barn feel homey.

In the barnyard was a shiny new red pick-up truck. The personalized license plate was grass-green. It read WLDRDHED.

WLDRDHED? I wonder what that means? Oh, Wild Redhead, of course. That's clever. Maggie's truck. It looks brand new. I wonder if she's really that wild?

Jordan pressed herself against the inside wall of the barn and began to formulate a plan. *Okay, Lewis, you need to get your head together here and come up with a way to introduce yourself to Maggie. That's the whole reason you're here, so get your butt in gear and come up with a plan.*

Jordan decided she had to sneak out of the barn and make her way across the property to the main road, where she could nonchalantly saunter up to the farmhouse and ask the mistress if she needed a hired hand. She made her way to the back of the barn and slipped out into the pasture. Over the next half-hour, she carefully circled around the house and across the field to the main road. By the time she reached the end of the driveway, she was quite winded.

"Damn. I'd forgotten how far away the main road was from the farmhouse. Now I've got to walk that entire distance back again," she complained.

Jordan wished she could transport herself down the driveway as quickly as she had been transported back in time, then chided herself for being so foolish. *You're out of shape, Lewis, that's the problem. You've spent all those years using your handicap as a crutch to avoid exercise. Now you have to walk a quarter of a mile and you're whining like a baby.*

She began the trek down the long driveway. As the house came into view, Jordan saw that some type of commotion was brewing in the barnyard. She slowed her step as she watched the scene unfolding before her.

An older man was running across the barnyard, leading a saddled horse by the bridle. He was calling out loudly. "Miss Safford! Miss Safford!"

A petite woman with short blonde hair came running out of the barn. "What is it? What happened, John?" she demanded loudly.

The man was clearly distraught. "I found Shawny running around loose in the north pasture. Maggie was nowhere in sight," he explained.

Jordan's heart sank. *Oh, my God. What day is it?*

"Quickly, saddle me a horse. I have to go look for her," Jan said.

"Why don't you just take Shawny?" the man suggested.

"Shawny's no longer fresh. I need a fresh horse to get to her faster," Jan explained impatiently. "Please, just do as I ask. Quickly!"

John directed Shawny to the barn and emerged five minutes later with a freshly-saddled mare. Jan grabbed the reins and mounted the horse. Within seconds, she was nothing but a speck in the distance as she galloped across the field toward the western ridge.

Jordan felt ill. She hid herself in the tree line that ran along the driveway and vomited. *God no! I'm too late. Please don't let it be so,* she begged any deity that would listen. *Please let her be okay.*

Jordan hoped against hope that Maggie was all right, but she remained hidden and waited for the inevitable. She didn't have long to wait.

The sound of galloping hooves could be heard long before Jan returned to the farmhouse. Her hair was windblown, and her cheeks were chafed from the cold winter wind, but most distressing was the unspeakable pain in her eyes as she fell from the horse and sank to her knees, wailing Maggie's name.

The farmhand helped her to her feet. "She's gone, John. She's dead!"

"Don't say that, Miss Safford. She can't be dead!"

Jan pushed John away. "She's dead, I tell you. I saw her. She's lying on the shore off the cliff on the west ridge. She must have fallen. Maggie!" she wailed again as John led her into the house. .

Jordan was beside herself with grief. She sat there for what seemed like an eternity, chastising herself for poor timing, until the ambulance arrived. Soon, Jan and John climbed into the back of the ambulance and accompanied the paramedics to the west ridge. When they were gone, Jordan emerged from her hiding place and walked sadly to the barn. She needed to go home.

CHAPTER 27

Jordan sat in the middle of the platform, wearing the Faraday belt. She was crying.

"Kale, she's back. Power down the rings."

As soon as Kale brought the rings to rest, Andi ran to Jordan, whose shoulders were shaking with powerful sobs. "Sweetie, tell me what's wrong."

Jordan looked at Andi with eyes full of sorrow "I could have stopped her, but I didn't. I watched her saddle her horse and ride off to her death. I was a coward. I hid myself from her, and now she's dead."

Kale came up behind Andi, who stepped aside to let him in. He scooped Jordan into his arms. "Come on, let's go into the house," he said in a low, soothing voice.

Kale carried Jordan to the house, Andi following closely behind. In Jordan's bedroom, Kale laid her gently on the bed and unhooked the Faraday belt.

"All right, tell me what happened," Kale said.

Jordan clasped Kale's hand tightly. "I failed her. I arrived just moments before she went out for that last ride. Instead of stopping her, I let her go. I was afraid of being found out, and so I hid while she saddled her horse and rode off."

"Jordan, don't blame yourself. Keep in mind that you have no control over exactly when you arrive in the past. I'm actually surprised we got you that close," Andi said.

Jordan wiped the tears from her face with the back of her hand and inhaled deeply. "I know. Intellectually, I know it's not my fault, but I was close, so close."

Kale squeezed her hand. "I guess we'll just have to try again. We can change the timing a little so that you arrive a bit further in the past. How much further will be hard to predict, but I'm fairly certain we can deliver you early enough to prevent Maggie from riding off that morning."

Jordan nodded and closed her eyes. "I'm so tired," she said. "What time is it?"

Andi looked at her watch. "Around 9:00 p.m."

Jordan yawned. "Damn, why am I so tired?" She opened her eyes and looked at Kale. "Let's try again in the morning, okay? I need some sleep."

"Sounds good to me," he replied. "Sleep well. We'll see you in the morning."

Jordan was so tired, she slipped into slumber before Kale and Andi had left the room.

* * *

Jordan lifted the carafe from the warmer and filled her cup with coffee. She walked out to the front porch and leaned against the railing, sighing heavily. As she surveyed the barnyard, she tried to imagine what it would have been like back in Maggie's time, back when it was a real working farm instead of a private residence. She could picture Maggie's red truck parked in front of the house, surrounded by free-ranging chickens pecking for food in the dirt. She imagined farmhands exercising horses in the corral, while others unloaded bales into the hayloft. She could almost smell the wonderful aroma of freshly-baked bread coming from the kitchen. A little piece of heaven, she thought, especially with someone as wonderful as Maggie to share it with. Pangs of agony filled her heart as she realized how close she had been to making that dream a reality, but in the span of a few heartbeats, Maggie had ridden off, never to return.

"I'm sorry, my love," she whispered softly. "I won't give up, Maggie. I'll reach you in time, I promise."

"Hey, you. You're up early." Andi pushed the screen door open and joined Jordan on the porch.

"Good morning," Jordan replied. "If I recall, I crashed pretty early last night. I don't know what got into me."

"Do you feel better this morning?"

"I feel pretty good. My lower back aches a bit, but it might be the way I slept." Jordan lifted her coffee cup. "There's fresh coffee if you're interested."

"You're a life saver," Andi exclaimed. "Can I refill yours?"

"Nope, I'm right behind you."

Jordan and Andi found Kale cooking eggs and bacon. He smiled when he saw them. "My two favorite women. How do you want your eggs?"

Soon, they were sitting at the kitchen table, enjoying their breakfast.

"Are you ready to give it another try this morning, Jordan?" Kale asked.

"You bet, but before we do anything, I want to look at the time estimates again and make an adjustment. I've got to land further back in time. The last thing I want to do is miss another opportunity. Yesterday nearly tore my heart out."

Jordan sat in front of the computer in the lab and made the final changes to the algorithm. Kale looked over her shoulder as she typed. "What are you using for significant digits this time?"

"I'm adding 0.15 seconds to the power surge time. If you remember, 0.11 seconds resulted in a five-month error, so 0.15 seconds should give me at least six or seven months. That should be enough time to influence the series of events that led to her death." Jordan grinned. "Who knows, maybe she'll fall madly in love with me, and she'll spend that particular morning having wild monkey sex with me instead of falling off a cliff."

"Sounds like a plan. Let me know when the algorithm is downloaded," Kale said as he walked to the control console.

"Just one more line of code—there. It should finish downloading in just a few minutes."

The door to the lab swung open to admit Andi. "Here's the Faraday belt, Jordan," she said. "It was in your bedroom."

Jordan wrapped the belt around her waist. "Thanks."

"You're welcome," Andi replied. "Are you all set to go?"

"In a minute. The new code is downloading right now."

"Correction," Kale said. "The algorithm has finished downloading. We're good to go."

* * *

Jordan landed on the dirt floor of the barn with a thud. "Damn. That's a real downside to this time travel business." She sat back on her knees, removed the Faraday belt, and brushed the dirt from her shirt.

"Good Morning, John."

"Morning, Maggie."

Jordan climbed to her feet and quickly made her way to the edge of the horse stall, which gave her a clear view of the other end of the barn without revealing her presence. "Maggie," she whispered as she saw the redhead talking to the farmhand.

"John, I need you to unload the pallets of feed from the wagon and move them into the loft," Maggie instructed.

"Sure thing. Is the wagon in the barnyard?" he asked.

"Yes. I could bring it in for you, if you'd like."

"No, ma'am. I'll take care of it," John replied as he went to retrieve the wagon, leaving Maggie alone in the barn.

Maggie shoved her hands deep into the front pockets of her jeans and walked directly toward Jordan. "Hey, Shawny. How's my guy this morning?"

Jordan's heart was in her throat as she retreated around the corner of the horse stall and pressed herself against the wall. She closed her eyes and tilted her head back in an effort to calm her nerves. *Calm down, Lewis. Breathe!*

As Jordan peeked around the corner of the stall, her attention was drawn to a loud cracking noise from above. "No!" she screamed. Jordan launched herself at Maggie, catching her around the waist and tackling her, knocking them both down to the dirt floor. A fraction of a second later, a large metal winch hit the ground in the exact place Maggie had been standing.

Jordan covered Maggie with her own body until the dust settled.

"Get off me," Maggie demanded. She pushed Jordan away and scrambled to her feet. "What the hell happened?"

Jordan stood up and brushed herself off. She looked around awkwardly, not knowing how to react to Maggie's anger.

"John!" Maggie yelled. "John, I need you in here, right now!"

Maggie circled the heavy winch. She and Jordan both looked up at the rafters.

"Son of a bitch. I could have been killed," Maggie said.

John ran into the barn. He was followed closely by a petite woman with short blonde hair.

Jordan frowned. *Jan.*

"Maggie, what happened?" John asked.

Maggie pointed at the winch. "That's what happened. John, I need you to inspect the rafter this thing was hanging from. Something caused it to snap, and I want to know what."

"Yes, ma'am," John said.

Jan shot a questioning look at Jordan. "How did it happen?" she asked, placing a hand on Maggie's back.

Maggie rubbed her forehead. "I don't know. I was walking toward Shawny's stall when all of the sudden this woman"— Maggie gestured at Jordan—"appeared out of nowhere and tackled me to the floor. The next thing I knew, the winch was sitting in a crater on the floor, exactly where I'd just been standing."

Jan wrapped her arms around Maggie and hugged her. "Thank God you weren't hurt," she said. "I'll investigate this. I promise we'll get to the bottom of it."

Maggie smiled. "Thank you, Jan." She turned abruptly and looked at Jordan, extending her hand. "And you are?"

Jordan stepped forward and grasped Maggie's hand. "Jordan. Jordan Lewis," she replied. It felt as if a liquid fire was running into her body from Maggie's hand. Her eyes locked with Maggie's, and she found it difficult to look away.

Maggie smiled, clearly aware of the effect she was having on Jordan. "Well, Jordan, I guess I'm indebted to you. I can't thank you enough. If you hadn't come along when you did, that winch would have killed me."

Jordan realized she was still holding Maggie's hand. Awkwardly, she released it. She looked around nervously. *What the hell is the matter with you, Lewis? You're acting like a lovesick teenager. Buck up. You'll never win her over if she thinks you're an insecure idiot.*

Jordan inhaled deeply. "You're welcome," she replied. "When I heard the rafter crack, I pretty much acted on instinct."

"Thank God for instinct," Maggie declared. "The question is, who are you and what were you doing in my barn?"

Jordan paled. She hadn't planned for her first meeting with Maggie to be so sudden and uncontrolled. "Ah... ah... I was actually looking for work," she began, "and no one answered the door at the house, so I came to the barn."

Maggie smiled again. "Work, huh? Well, why don't you join me for a glass of lemonade while we talk it over?"

Jordan smiled back at her. "I'd like that."

Maggie filled two glasses and handed one to Jordan, who was seated at the kitchen table. Maggie leaned against the cupboard and was clearly assessing Jordan as she drank.

As Jordan accepted the drink, she allowed her own gaze to linger on Maggie. *I could drown in her eyes. The green complements that wild red hair perfectly. I wonder what it would be like to run my fingers through those curls.* Jordan felt an unfamiliar flutter in her abdomen and a pulsing between her legs. She shifted in her seat, but the feelings persisted. *What the hell?*

"So, Jordan, where are you from?" Maggie asked.

Jordan had to think fast. For some reason, "from eighty-seven years in the future" didn't seem like an appropriate response. "I'm actually from the area," she replied. *Lame, Lewis, real lame.* Jordan hadn't put any thought into how she would explain her roots if asked. *It's not like I can tell her I grew up right here on this farm.*

Maggie sipped her drink. "I see. What kind of work are you looking for?"

Jordan sat back in her chair and crossed her legs. "My parents raised horses, so I have experience in their care and training." *At least that's not a lie.* "And I'm pretty good with my hands," she added.

"Hmm," Maggie murmured. "Is it safe to say you'll need to bunk here, as well? I mean, assuming I hire you, of course."

Just then, the kitchen door swung open and admitted Jan.

"Did you find anything?" Maggie asked.

Jan shrugged. "Not really. I climbed into the rafters and examined the beams. Odd as it sounds, that particular beam snapped for no apparent reason. It was probably defective."

Maggie frowned. "That seems strange. The winch has been hanging from that beam for the past two years, and there's been no sign of failure. What did John have to say about it?"

Jan shifted her weight from foot to foot. "John didn't look at it. I told him I would take care of it."

"I'll call the contractor who erected the barn and have him repair it for me," Maggie said, still frowning.

"I can repair it," Jordan interjected.

Maggie raised her eyebrows. "You can?"

Jordan stood. "Like I said, I'm good with my hands."

Maggie grinned. "Okay." She turned to Jan. "Jan, this is Jordan Lewis, our new ranch hand."

Jordan extended her hand to Jan, who pointedly chose not to shake it. "I've got to get back to the barn. John needs a hand off-loading the feed." Jan abruptly turned and left.

"Humph!" Maggie exclaimed as she looked at Jordan. "That's not like her. She's normally so friendly. My apologies."

Jordan smiled. "No problem. I'm sure she's still just shaken up by your near-accident."

"Maybe," Maggie replied absently.

"If you'll point me in the direction of your tools and wood supply, I'll get to work on that rafter," Jordan offered.

Maggie smiled. "You don't waste any time, do you?"

"No, ma'am," Jordan replied.

Jordan set up a ladder on the floor of the loft and leaned it against a rafter adjacent to the break. Once the ladder was in place, she carried up a few pieces of two-by-six lumber and placed them across two rafters in order to create a scaffold for herself.

Jordan was nailing the last plank in place when Maggie appeared in the barn below.

"Hey there," she called up to Jordan. "How's it going?"

Jordan looked down and caught her breath. *Why is it I suddenly forget to breathe when she's around?* "I've just built the work platform. I'm about to inspect the beam now."

"Do you mind if I join you?" Maggie asked.

"Not at all. Come on up." Jordan climbed down the ladder and waited for Maggie to join her in the loft. "You go ahead of me. I'll hold the ladder," Jordan offered.

"Okay," Maggie said.

Jordan had to control her breathing as she watched Maggie's bottom shift side to side with each step she took. *Lewis, you've got it bad!* Once Maggie was standing securely on the scaffolding, Jordan climbed the ladder and joined her. The platform was relatively narrow, so Jordan had to embrace Maggie as she shimmied past her in order to get close enough to inspect the break. As Jordan slipped by, she could have sworn Maggie intentionally brushed up against her breasts. *Focus, Jordan... focus! Falling off the platform would not be a good thing.*

"Okay," Jordan said. "Let's see what the problem is here. Hmm... this is odd."

"What is it?" Maggie moved in for a closer look.

"After what Jan said, I expected to see a ragged break. If this was caused by a defect in the beam, the break would most likely be splintered, jagged, and at an angle." Jordan pointed to the end of the rafter still in place. "Look here. This beam has been cut with a saw. Look at how straight and clean this edge is."

"That is odd," Maggie said. "I wonder who did that... and why?"

Jordan's eyes narrowed. "What I'd like to know is why Jan said there was no apparent reason for the break."

Maggie frowned. "You don't suspect Jan, do you?"

Jordan shrugged. "I don't even know Jan, so I'm in no position to judge her. I just think it's odd that she inspected the break and found nothing strange about it."

"To tell you the truth, Jan is really good with the animals, but she doesn't know which end of a hammer to use to drive a nail. I doubt she would have realized the significance of this clean cut. I'll call the original contractor and ask him about it. Would you mind talking to him?"

"No," Jordan replied. "Sounds like a good idea. In the meantime, I'll repair this."

Maggie smiled. "Okay. I'd appreciate it."

"Consider it done." Jordan smiled sweetly.

Maggie's gaze lingered on Jordan for several seconds. Finally, she chuckled. "Forgive me for staring, Jordan, but I've never met such a competent woman, especially not one as attractive as you."

Jordan blushed and did the only thing she could think of to diffuse the tension—she made light of the situation. "Well, thank ye, ma'am," she said in a mock southern drawl. She tucked her thumbs into her belt. "Yer not such a bad looker yerself."

Maggie laughed. "And you have a sense of humor as well. A very nice combination. Good luck with the repair. I've got to get ready for a meeting with the Shelburne Selectmen in about an hour. If you need anything, ask John."

Jordan nodded at Maggie. "All right, then. I'll just take a few measurements here. Do you need help with the ladder?"

"No, I'll be fine. I should be back in a couple of hours. I'll show you around the farm and get you settled into the bunkhouse when I get back. Is that okay?"

"That's fine. Have a good meeting."

Maggie smiled once more. "Thank you. I'll be back soon."

Jordan watched as Maggie climbed down the ladder into the loft and then exited the barn. It was only then that she released the breath she hadn't realized she was holding.

CHAPTER 28

When Maggie returned to the barn later that day, she saw Jordan standing in the hook of the winch as John raised her to the rafters and lowered her again. "Okay, this time we'll hook onto a pallet of feed and see how that goes."

Maggie leaned quietly against the doorway of the barn. Jordan hooked the winch to the straps supporting the feed pallet before climbing on top of the bags.

"Okay, take it up."

Jordan held on to the rope just above the winch as John slowly raised her and the pallet to the level of the hayloft. "Looks good from here," she announced. "Take it down."

John slowly lowered the pallet to the floor of the barn. When it was stable, Jordan jumped off and turned to John. "Good as new," she said. "You should be able to unload the feed safely now."

"Thank you, Jordan. Maggie will be happy to know the rafter is fixed."

"Yes, I'm very happy," Maggie said from her position by the door.

"Maggie—you're back," Jordan exclaimed. "How long have you been standing there?"

Maggie walked up and linked her arm with Jordan's. "Long enough to watch your acrobatics. Do you always test out your own work like that?"

Maggie led Jordan out of the barn and across the yard.

"I do have a habit of using myself as a test subject. I figure if I put myself at risk, I'll do a better job."

"I like that level of personal commitment," Maggie said. "I think you and I are going to get along just fine."

"Here's the bunkhouse," Maggie said as they mounted the steps to the cabin. Maggie pushed the door open and stepped aside so Jordan could enter first.

"Wow, this is really nice," Jordan said. She looked around the well-furnished bunkhouse. It was built in an L-shape off one side of the farmhouse and extended behind the main house. *This bunkhouse must have been torn down before my parents bought the farm.* "Does anyone else live here?"

"No, you're the only one right now, so you get your pick of beds."

"I take it John and Jan don't live on the farm."

Maggie smiled. "John, no. He lives about a mile down the road. Jan? She does live here— just not in the bunkhouse."

Jordan turned red with embarrassment. "Oh... I... ah... well, that's really none of my business."

"No, I don't mind. In fact you should probably know that my lifestyle is a bit unconventional. You see, Jan is my... well, let's just say she's my significant other. Is that going to be a problem for you?"

The only problem I have is that it's not me that you're significant with.

Jordan said, "No. Why should it? What you do in the privacy of your own home is your business. I do have one question for you though."

"And that is?"

"Considering Jan's status in your household, am I to take instructions from her as well as you?"

Maggie grinned. "Absolutely not. Like I said, Jan is good with the animals, but not very proficient in other things. No, if there's something to be done around here, I'll be the one to direct it."

"That's a relief," Jordan replied.

Maggie cocked her head to the side. "How so?"

"Because judging by her reaction in the barn earlier today, I don't think she likes me very much."

Maggie chuckled. "Don't let her bother you. She tends to be a bit territorial, but she's all bark and no bite."

I'm not so sure about that.

"Take your pick of the bedrooms and make yourself comfortable. Look around, settle in, and let me know if you need anything, okay?"

Jordan shoved her fingertips into her back pockets. "I don't think I'll be needing anything right now... oh wait. Maybe some paper and a pen? I like to keep a journal, and I don't have anything with me right now to record today's entries."

"Not a problem. I'll go fetch it for you right now. I assume your diary is in your luggage?"

Jordan was caught off-guard by Maggie's question. *Shit! I don't have any luggage. Hell, I don't have any clothes with me at all, except what I have on my back.*

"Er... yes. My diary is in my luggage. Now that I have a job, I'll send for it. With any luck, it'll be here in a couple of days."

Maggie crossed her arms and cocked her head to one side in a gesture so endearing that Jordan was barely able to control the urge to kiss her. "I guess you'll need something to sleep in, as well?"

Jordan turned red and looked at the floor. "Well, I thought about washing my things out in the sink tonight and just sleeping in the nude."

"You'll do nothing of the kind. Come with me. I have several old T-shirts here that my dad left behind when they moved to Florida. Come pick out what you'd like to wear. He wasn't a very big man. There may even be some jeans and shirts of his that you can wear until your luggage arrives. As for the personal items, you're a few inches taller than I am, but it looks like we wear pretty much the same size jeans, so I'm sure I have some underclothes you can wear."

Jordan was taken aback by Maggie's generosity. "You don't have to do that, Maggie."

"No, I don't, but I want to. Come with me."

Jordan allowed her to lead the way from the bunkhouse into the kitchen of the farmhouse.

As they stepped into the kitchen, Maggie turned to Jordan and smiled. "Dinnertime is normally a community affair around here, and everyone pitches in. However, I must warn you, if you can't cook, you usually end up doing the dishes."

Jordan grinned. "Well, I guess I'll be sporting dish-pan hands, 'cause I burn water."

Maggie chuckled. "Luckily for you, I can cook. In fact, I usually end up doing most of the cooking around here."

Jordan followed Maggie from room to room as she pointed out areas of the house that were all too familiar. Eighty-seven years had made surprisingly little difference. After the tour of the living areas was complete, Maggie led Jordan down the hall to the bedrooms. "That's my room," she said, pointing out the first door they passed on the left. "The bathroom is right across the hall, and down here at the end is a suite of rooms that my parents used when they lived here."

Jordan wanted so much to tell Maggie that she knew exactly which room was hers, that she had found the diaries embedded in the walls. Jordan had occupied the very same room eighty-seven years later. Jordan also noted that the suite of rooms had sometime along the way been converted to two separate bedrooms—one that Kale currently occupied and a spare room that Jordan used as an office.

Maggie pushed the door open to her parents' suite. "Okay, let's see." She opened a dresser drawer and pulled out a few T-shirts. "Here, these should fit you. Also," Maggie pulled open another drawer, "here are some blue jeans that Dad sometimes wore. Like I said, he wasn't a large man. He was maybe three or four inches taller than you are, but he was pretty slim. If the cuffs are too long, just roll them up."

Maggie handed the pile of clothes to Jordan. Then she led Jordan back into the hall to her own bedroom. She pushed the door open and, instantly, the scent of patchouli reached Jordan's nostrils. Jordan inhaled deeply as she stepped into the room. "Hmm," she said.

"It's patchouli. Do you like it?"

Jordan looked into Maggie's eyes. She could have sworn she felt something pass between them. "It's my favorite scent," she replied.

Maggie smiled. "It's my favorite as well."

Maggie's gaze held Jordan's for a tad longer than would be considered conventional. After a moment, she inhaled deeply and seemed to regain her sense of awareness.

"Underclothes," she said as she pulled open a dresser drawer and pulled out a few pairs of panties, some socks, and a couple of bras. "I'm a 34C. Will that work for you?"

In more ways than one, sweetheart.

"Perfect," Jordan replied as she accepted the clothing. "I don't know how to thank you enough."

"No thanks necessary. After all, if you hadn't come along when you did, I probably wouldn't be here. That winch hit the floor exactly where I was standing. It surely would have killed me. I should be thanking you."

Jordan grinned and shook her head. "Like you said, no thanks necessary."

Again, a silence fell as they stared at one another for what seemed like an eternity. Finally, Jordan broke the reverie. "I guess I should be getting settled in."

Maggie snapped out of her trance. "Of course, of course. Oh, let me get you some paper and a pen before you go."

Maggie retrieved a small journal from the bedside table and handed it to Jordan.

"Here. This is a spare journal, one I haven't used yet. I keep diaries myself, you know. I realize how important it is to organize your thoughts at the end of the day."

Jordan grinned as she accepted the book and pen. "Thank you. You know, something told me you were the diary type."

"Really?"

"Yes, really," Jordan replied. She added the diary to the growing heap of things tucked under her arm. She looked at Maggie. "So, if you were writing today's entry right now, what would it say?"

Maggie looked up at the ceiling and squinted her eyes. She raised one hand for emphasis as she spoke. "It would say 'September 23, 2018. This is the day I almost died. Luckily, my beautiful blue-eyed guardian angel came to my rescue.'"

Jordan stifled a gasp as the date registered in her brain. She cleared her throat to mask her surprise. "Well, I guess I should go settle in. Thank you again."

"You're welcome. Can you find your way out?" Maggie asked.

"No problem," Jordan replied. "This place already feels like home."

* * *

"How long has she been gone?" Andi asked.

Kale looked at his watch. "About two hours. That would be roughly 12 hours for her."

"Maybe we should check the communication portal," Andi suggested.

"You're right. It's about time we checked it again, anyway." When Kale reached into the hole, he expected to find it empty. Instead, his hand made contact with something. "There's something in here," he said as he grasped the object. It was a bottle. He handed it to Andi as he climbed out from under the bench.

Andi held the bottle up to the light. "There's something inside. Look!"

Kale looked at the object, now backlit by the ceiling light. "It looks like paper. Jordan, you're a genius."

Kale took the bottle and pried off the cap. A few firm shakes and the edge of the paper protruded from the opening. Carefully, he extracted it from the bottle. He unrolled the paper and laid it flat on the workbench, holding the curled corners down with his fingers. Andi read the note over Kale's shoulder.

Kale and Andi: I arrived safely. As luck would have it, I also arrived just in time to save Maggie from a winch that had fallen from a rafter to the floor of the barn in the very place she had been standing. This particular incident is described in one of Maggie's diaries under the date September 23, 2018. By the way, I need you to find that diary and tell me what the first couple of lines of the entry are for that day. Kale, I know you're probably thinking that I'm messing with the past by preventing accidents that were supposed to happen, but I just couldn't help myself. I acted on instinct. Anyway, I ended up introducing myself to Maggie by tackling her to the ground. Very suave, Lewis, very suave. I don't have a lot of room to write, but suffice it to say that I'm fine and have figured out a way to be close to Maggie. What I need you two to do for me is to send a bag of clothing sturdy enough for farm work, and, of course, please include a piece of paper containing the diary entry for September 23, 2018. Don't worry about me. I'm fine. I love you guys. Jordan.

"Jordan, you're playing with fire," Kale said.
Andi furrowed her brow. "Farm work?"

* * *

Maggie kicked off her boots, stripped off her blue jeans and flannel shirt, and threw everything into a heap by the side of the bed.
"Wow," Jan said, entering the bedroom. "Now that's what I call a nice welcome."
Maggie slipped a tank top over her head.
Jan frowned. "I take it you're not interested in making love tonight."
Maggie stood in front of the dresser mirror and tousled her curly hair. "It's been a long day, and not a little frightening."
"How so?"
"For starters, having a three-hundred-pound metal winch nearly fall on my head this morning. Do you realize I could have been killed? Thank God Jordan was there."

"There's something odd about that one," Jan said.

Maggie turned to look at her. "Why do you say that?"

"What do you know about her? Where does she come from? What did she do for a living before she came here? Have you asked her any of those questions yet?"

"I know that her family raised horses. I know that she's from somewhere around this area, but she hasn't specified exactly where, yet. I know she seems to know what she's doing on a farm. I know she's good with her hands, and I know that if she hadn't been here today, I wouldn't be standing here talking to you right now. For me, that's all I need to know."

Jan snorted. "I'll bet she's good with her hands."

Maggie stomped up to Jan and stopped within inches of her. "What exactly to you mean by that?" she demanded.

"Don't tell me you haven't noticed how attractive she is," Jan said. "Are you going to pursue her like you did me when I first came to work for you?"

"The way I remember it, that pursuit went both ways," Maggie replied.

"Yeah, well, I'm not sure she's going to be a welcome addition to the crew. She has kind of a know-it-all attitude."

"Oh, really? Just how much time have you spent with her to come to that conclusion?"

"I don't need to spend time with her. I think I'm a pretty good judge of character, and she doesn't look like a farmhand to me. She looks more like she should be sitting behind a desk or teaching school or something like that."

"Well, I'll have you know that she's very capable of working a farm. She inspected the rafter after you said it was probably a weak point in the wood, and she found where someone or something had mechanically cut through the boards."

"What?" Jan said. "How the hell did she come to that conclusion? I looked at the boards myself and saw no such thing."

"Well then, either you didn't really look or you didn't know what you were looking at because she showed it to me. It was obviously sawed—not broken and not splintered."

Jan paced back and forth across the bedroom, clearly agitated. "I don't like what you're implying, Maggie. You shouldn't be letting this Lewis character put those kinds of thoughts in your head. She'll be nothing but trouble for us. Mark my words."

Maggie intercepted Jan's path as she crossed the room. "Let's get one thing straight, Jan," Maggie said in a stern voice. "When it comes to this farm, there is no 'us.' This is my farm, and I will run it the way I see fit. Is that clear?"

* * *

Jordan, your "message in a bottle" approach was a brilliant idea. I guess I don't need to nag you about interfering with the past. Just know that everything you do there will change something about the future. Please be careful. We're checking the communication portal several times a day, so be sure to let us know how things are going, and especially when you need to come home. You asked for an excerpt from Maggie's diary. Here it is: "September 23, 2018. This is the day I almost died. Luckily, a beautiful blue-eyed guardian angel came to my rescue." I assume you had something to do with that particular entry? Again, Jord, please be careful. We love you. Kale and Andi.

"Wow, I guess Kale is right. Everything I do here has the potential to change history, so to speak," Jordan said out loud as she rummaged through the bag of clothing Kale had sent.

"Thanks, guys. This is perfect." She zipped the bag and carried it to the bunkhouse.

* * *

"No sir, I inspected the board myself. In my opinion, it looks as if it were cut mechanically. The break was straight and clean instead of jagged and angled, as I would expect it to be if the board had snapped under the weight of the winch."

Jordan listened as the contractor reacted to the information she'd just given him.

"Okay then," she said. "I'll let Miss Downs know one of your carpenters will be here today around noon to inspect the board. All right. Thank you. Good-bye."

Maggie had entered the house at the end of Jordan's conversation. While Jordan finished her call, Maggie sorted a handful of mail. "What did he say?" Maggie asked without looking up.

"He's sending a man over at noon to inspect the beam."

Maggie threw the last envelope into the bill pile and then looked up at Jordan. "Wow. Daddy never looked that good in those jeans."

Jordan blushed. "Stop that. You're embarrassing me," she said. She couldn't tell Maggie that they were actually her jeans, courtesy of Kale and Andi.

"Hey, how would you like to accompany me to an auction?"

Jordan shrugged. "Sure. If you want me to, I'm game."

"All right then. Give me a minute to freshen up, and I'll be right with you. Help yourself to some lemonade while you wait. I won't be long."

"Take your time, I'm on the clock," Jordan joked. She watched Maggie ascend the stairs. Then she went to the kitchen and took the pitcher of lemonade from the refrigerator. As she was pouring herself a glass, Jan walked in.

"Does Maggie know you're helping yourself like that?" she asked curtly.

"As a matter of fact, she does. I'm waiting for her to freshen up. We're going to a horse auction," Jordan replied.

Anger sparked in Jan's eyes. "I guess it will be a threesome then," she stated.

Just then, Maggie breezed into the kitchen. "Okay, I'm ready." She stopped short when she saw Jan. "Jan, I'm glad you're here. The building contractor is sending a man over in about an hour to inspect the damaged rafter. I think it might be beneficial for you to meet with him. I'm taking Jordan with me to the Mustang auction. We'll be back later this afternoon."

Jordan locked eyes with Jan. If looks could have killed, Jordan would be dead on the spot.

CHAPTER 29

Jordan sat in the passenger seat of Maggie's pickup truck. She couldn't help but steal glances at the redhead driving.

"Okay, I give. What do you find so interesting that you feel compelled to stare at me?"

Jordan felt herself turn red with embarrassment. She covered her face with her hands. "I'm sorry. I can't help myself," she confessed.

"No, really, I'm flattered, actually. But why can't you help yourself? I do want to know."

Jordan was surprised. "You mean you don't know?"

Maggie glanced at Jordan quickly then turned her attention back to the road. "Know what?" she asked.

Jordan shook her head. "Well, I'll be damned. Maggie, you are a beautiful woman. In fact, you're more beautiful in person than in print." Jordan realized her slip of the tongue as soon as it left her mouth.

Maggie frowned. "When exactly did you see me in print?"

Damn it, Lewis, you screwed up big time! Think before you open your mouth.

"Well, I did a little research on you and your farm before I came to apply for the job. I found a picture of you that was taken at some county fair a few years back."

Maggie appeared to be deep in thought. "I see. Do you really think I'm beautiful?"

"I'm surprised you have to ask that question. I would think you'd have suitors lined up for a mile."

Maggie chuckled. "It's pretty much common knowledge around town that Jan and I are a couple, so there haven't really been any offers for quite some time now."

"Did you date much before Jan?"

"A little, but I had a bad experience with a girl named Jess when I was in my twenties, and that pretty much turned me off relationships for a while. Jan is my first serious relationship in a long time."

"How long have you and Jan been together?"

Maggie thought for a moment before answering. "For about four years."

"Hmm," Jordan said.

Maggie tossed her a sideways glance. "What is that supposed to mean?"

Jordan looked down at her booted feet on the floor for a moment or two before answering. "Well, I guess I just don't see that she's your type."

"And why do you feel you're qualified to know what my type is? Hell, you've only been here for two days."

Jordan wanted desperately to tell Maggie that she knew practically her entire life history, at least from the time she was sixteen years old, but she decided to play her cards close to her chest. "You're right. I apologize, but it doesn't feel right to me. Don't ask me why. It just doesn't."

"I don't appreciate you talking about Jan that way. I'll decide what my type is, not you. Jan suits me just fine, thank you very much."

Maggie and Jordan rode along in silence for a few moments. Finally, Maggie broke it. "What exactly do you think is my type?" she asked.

Jordan thought for a moment. *How do I say this so it doesn't seem self-serving?* "I guess your type would be someone who was your intellectual equal, someone who could give you good advice yet know when not to cross boundaries. That person should complement you physically as well. You're a very beautiful woman. Don't take this the wrong way, but your feminine nature doesn't fit the profile of someone who can run a farm all by herself."

Maggie glared at Jordan. "Let me get this straight. First you tell me my partner is stupid and she gives bad advice, and then you have the audacity to imply I can't run a horse farm properly because I'm too feminine?"

Jordan smacked herself in the forehead with the heel of her right hand. *Damn it, Lewis. You can give Kale advice on how to win women over, but you suck at it yourself.*

"No, no. That's not what I meant." She looked at Maggie's shocked and angry expression. "Look, I'm digging a hole for myself that I won't be able to climb out of if I keep running my mouth, so let's just forget I said anything."

"Oh, no, you're not getting off that easy. Now, explain what you meant."

Jordan placed her hands on her thighs and dropped her head back to look at the ceiling of the truck. She inhaled deeply then turned her head to look at Maggie. "Okay. Let me just say that most of the feminine women I have known in the past are pretty high-maintenance, and quite frankly, they tend to prefer someone more on the butch side to take care of things for them."

Maggie slammed her foot down hard on the brake, bringing the truck to a grinding halt on the dusty country road. Jordan nearly went through the windshield—she was only able to stop herself at the last minute by quickly placing both hands on the dash.

"What the hell?" Jordan exclaimed.

"Get out," Maggie demanded.

"What?"

"I said, get out. You're fired."

Jordan turned in her seat to face Maggie. "Why am I fired?"

Maggie leaned across the seat toward Jordan. "You're fired because anyone who doesn't respect who I am and what I can do is not welcome on my farm. Now get your ass out of my truck!"

"When did I say I didn't respect you?" Jordan spat back.

"You called me high-maintenance." Maggie's voice had risen an octave.

"Like hell I did."

"You said that feminine women look for butch women to take care of them," Maggie said.

"Wrong," Jordan shouted back. "I said you don't fit the profile of someone who can run a farm alone. Sheesh, woman. Do you always look for a fight where there isn't one?"

Both women fell silent. Jordan reached for the door handle. She had one foot on the ground before Maggie took her arm.

"Where are you going?"

Jordan looked down at Maggie's hand on her arm, then up at Maggie's face. "I'm fired, remember? I'm going back to the farm to collect my things."

"No. Don't go. Please get back into the truck."

Jordan looked at her for a few moments, then shifted her weight back into the vehicle and closed the door. She stared straight ahead.

Maggie had both hands on the steering wheel as she looked out over the hood of the truck. "I'm sorry," she said.

Jordan's pride would not allow her to respond, so she continued to sit silently, staring out the windshield.

Maggie turned in her seat to face Jordan. "I said I'm sorry. I misunderstood what you said. Forgive me?"

Jordan tilted her head down and to the left so she was looking at Maggie out of the corner of her eye. "Only if you rehire me," she said, trying to hide a grin.

"Done," Maggie replied.

"And give me a raise," Jordan added.

Maggie's anger immediately erupted again. "Why you..."

Jordan grinned. She pointed her index finger at the angry redhead. "Got you," she teased.

"Jesus Christ, you are exasperating."

"Yeah, but I'll grow on you."

"Like hell you will," Maggie replied, smiling.

Jordan and Maggie sat staring at each other for several long moments. Finally, Jordan broke the standoff.

"I think we're going to be late for the auction."

Maggie's head snapped back. "Shit, you're right. Hold on. It's going to be a wild ride."

* * *

"Hi, Mom. How are you and Dad doing tonight?" Maggie paced back and forth across the living room as she held her cell phone to her ear. "That's good. Is Daddy's cough getting any better? Great. I'm sure it's just a cold. If it's not gone in another week, promise me you'll take him to the doctor's and have it checked out. Okay? All right. I'll talk to you in a few days then. Give Daddy a big hug for me. Okay, Mom. I love you both. Goodnight."

Jan placed the book she was reading in her lap. "How are Mom and Dad?" she asked as Maggie sat on the couch with one leg curled under her.

"They're doing okay. Dad still has a cough, but Mom says it's getting better."

"That's good. Have they said any more about putting the farm in your name?"

"Not really. I know Dad hired a lawyer to set things in motion, but it'll take a few months before anything is finalized."

"Still, your parents aren't getting any younger," Jan said.

"I said Daddy is taking care of it. Now, I don't want to discuss this anymore."

Jan threw her hands into the air. "Fine. Whatever you want."

A tense silence fell between the women. Jan broke it. "How was the auction?"

"Things went great. We were able to secure about a half-dozen mustangs. It appears our Jordan knows her animals. Those horses came from quality stock."

Jan cocked an eyebrow at Maggie. "*Our* Jordan?"

Maggie sighed deeply. "Why do you always have to nitpick everything I say? I don't want a fight. I'm going to bed."

"Suit yourself," Jan said as Maggie stomped away.

By the time Maggie had reached their bedroom, she was furious. *Why does she always have to have the last word? Sometimes I regret ever becoming involved with that woman.* Maggie turned on a small bedside lamp. She pulled her boots off and slipped her blue jeans down over her hips, letting them fall to the floor. She kicked them away with one foot and unbuttoned her shirt. A second later, Maggie was wearing only a sports bra and low-cut panties.

"Eww! I need a shower."

* * *

I was fired today. Yes, fired after two days on the job. Kale, forget everything I ever told you about women. Obviously, I didn't know what I was talking about. We were on our way to a horse auction, and, well, I quite readily opened my mouth and inserted my foot when I told Maggie she looked too feminine to run a farm by herself. Apparently, that was not a good thing because she pulled the truck over, fired me, and told me to get out. Damn, she's feisty! Of course, I held my ground (would you expect anything less?), and used my charm to wriggle my way back into her good graces.

Anyway, I've been here for two whole days and so far, things are tense with Jan; the other farmhand, John tolerates me, and Maggie... Maggie and I are getting along okay, except for her firing me today.

I'm living in the bunkhouse, and it's bugging the shit out of me knowing Jan is in there sleeping beside her every night. I know. Don't do anything to change the course of history. I can hear you nagging me from eighty-seven years away. I'm trying very hard not to do too much of that.

Okay, it's late and I need to rise early to mend fences in the north pasture, so I'll say goodnight for now. I hope all is well with both of you. I love you lots. Jordan.

Jordan placed the pen beside the pad of paper and pushed her chair back. She rose to her feet and walked to the window. From her vantage point, she had a clear view of the back of the farmhouse, and a clear view of Maggie's bedroom. As she stood there, the light suddenly came on. Common courtesy urged her to close the blinds and give Maggie her privacy, but Jordan couldn't tear herself away from the sight of the slender redhead. Jordan stood immobile as Maggie flitted in and out of view.

Maggie, why do you enchant me so? I ache to touch you. I so need to kiss you. I ache to hold you in my arms while you sleep. I love you. Sleep well. Long after the light from Maggie's room was extinguished, Jordan continued to stare into the darkness.

* * *

The next morning, Jordan rose early and headed to the north pasture to mend fences. She worked in the hot sun all day, and by the time she returned to the house, she was in desperate need of a shower. She rode her horse into the barn and dismounted, then led the animal into its stall. After feeding and watering the horse, Jordan meticulously brushed him until his coat was gleaming. As she turned to leave, she was startled by Maggie who was standing in the entrance to the stall.

Jordan jumped. "Jesus, you scared me. How long have you been standing there?"

Maggie leaned against the post with her arms crossed in front of her. She grinned. "For about five minutes," she replied. "You really do a nice job with the animals, Jordan. You have a knack for it."

Jordan took her hat off and dusted it as she spoke. "Like I said before, I had horses while growing up. Mustangs, in fact. They're beautiful animals."

"Yes, they are. You've been in the north pasture all day, right?"

"Yeah, mending fences. And now I need to shower. I'm kind of filthy and smelly."

Maggie's eyes roamed up and down Jordan's tall frame. Jordan was wearing a plaid button-down shirt with the sleeves rolled back to her elbows and the tails tucked into soiled blue jeans. She had on a brown leather vest, a bandanna around her neck, and a well-worn pair of cowboy boots. Tucked in her back pocket were the leather work-gloves she'd used to handle the barbed wire fencing. Her shoulder-length brown hair was damp with sweat. She'd tucked the wayward locks behind her ears.

Jordan shifted uncomfortably under Maggie's scrutiny. "I really should shower. I'm a mess."

Maggie grinned. "I happen to think you look fine. I like a woman who isn't afraid to get dirty doing a hard day's work."

Jordan smiled. "Looking fine and smelling fine are two different things. If you'll excuse me..." Jordan walked past Maggie into the main part of the barn.

"Jordan?" Maggie called out. Jordan turned around. "Would you care to join us for dinner? At the risk of sounding full of myself, I'm a pretty good cook."

As if on cue, Jordan's stomach replied for her, loud enough for Maggie to hear. Jordan felt herself blush.

Maggie laughed. "I'll take that as a yes. Dinner is at six o'clock sharp."

*　*　*

At precisely 6:00 p.m., Jordan knocked on the front door of the farmhouse. She looked around nervously as she waited for someone to answer the door. Just as she'd convinced herself that her knock would go unanswered, the door swung open.

"Hey, Jordan. Come in. You clean up real nice," Maggie said. Jordan's hair was freshly washed and she wore clean, well-tailored slacks and a shirt.

Jordan stepped across the threshold and handed a bouquet of wildflowers to Maggie. "I, ah... I saw these out in the north pasture this morning while I was mending fences. I ran out and picked a few. I hope you like them," she said, feeling as awkward as a schoolgirl.

Maggie accepted the flowers, inhaling their aroma. "They're beautiful. Thank you." She closed the door behind Jordan. "Jan is pouring wine in the living room. Go on and join her while I put these in water."

Jordan didn't relish the idea of spending time alone with Jan while she waited for Maggie to join them, but having no other option, she pushed open the door between the kitchen and living room and passed through.

Jan was standing by the fireplace looking pensively at the flames while she sipped a glass of wine. She looked up when Jordan entered the room. She smiled and extended her hand. "Jordan. It's so nice you could join us."

Jordan was taken aback by Jan's polite and friendly manner, but offered her hand anyway. Jan's handshake was firm.

"How do you like the job so far?" Jan asked.

Jordan's dislike of the woman increased significantly as she realized Jan was using her relationship with Maggie to establish a hierarchy in the farm's chain of command. "I like it just fine. I appreciate Maggie giving me a chance."

"Good. Maggie and I have great plans for this farm. We've been thinking about opening a riding school for handicapped children. Maggie just loves kids. In fact, we've considered having one of our own, or maybe adopting one or two in the near future."

Jordan wanted to puke. The very thought of this woman spending the rest of her life with Maggie and raising their children sent waves of revulsion through her.

"I'm sure Maggie would make a great mother," Jordan replied.

Maggie entered the room carrying the bouquet of flowers Jordan had given her. "Jan, look at the beautiful flowers Jordan picked." She placed the vase on the fireplace mantel then turned to face them. "So— is anyone hungry?"

"Famished," Jan replied. She directed Jordan into the dining room.

Jordan held Maggie's chair for her, then she chose the seat to Maggie's left. The table was nicely set for three, and a crisp garden salad waited in the center of each plate. An array of salad dressings was clustered in the center of the table.

Maggie gestured toward them. "Help yourselves."

When they'd eaten the salad, Maggie excused herself, returning a few moments later with a food-laden platter. "I hope you like chicken," she said to Jordan.

"I love chicken. It all looks so delicious," Jordan said as she filled her plate.

As soon as they had served themselves, Jan reached into the back pocket of her jeans and pulled out a folded envelope. "Oh, Maggie, I forgot to tell you that this letter arrived by registered mail today. It's from your father's lawyer."

Maggie's eyes narrowed as she reached for the letter, and her eyebrows arched high on her forehead "You opened it?"

Jordan's gaze moved from Maggie to Jan.

Jan behaved as if opening Maggie's mail was something she did on a regular basis. "Yeah. I thought it was important enough to read right away. You were gone to town, so I opened it. It's actually good news," she said.

Maggie rubbed her forehead. Jordan recognized the gesture as one of frustration and disapproval. "I really wish you hadn't opened it."

"What's the big deal?" Jan asked. "You would have read it to me anyway. After all, it concerns me as well."

Maggie put both hands down on the table hard. "I fail to see how this letter concerns you," she said firmly.

Jan shrugged. "We've talked about getting married. I think the fact that your father has signed the deed of the farm over to you definitely concerns me."

Jordan's eyes opened wide as Jan threw out the reference to marriage. *No!*

Maggie took the napkin off her lap and put it on the table beside her plate. She rose to her feet. "Jan, could I please see you in the kitchen?"

"Sure," Jan said brightly as she followed Maggie.

Jordan sat alone in the dining room, feeling like she was intruding on a private conversation as loud voices came from the kitchen.

"What the hell was that all about?" Maggie asked in a high-pitched voice.

"I don't know what part of it you don't understand, Mags. Your father transferred the deed of the farm to you. It's all yours now."

Jordan could hear Maggie pacing back and forth across the kitchen as she spoke.

"And what does that have to do with you?" Maggie asked.

"You and I have talked about getting married some day. When that happens, we'll want to add my name to the deed. That way, the farm is protected in the event something happens to either one of us."

A pregnant pause filled the air as Jordan strained to hear what Maggie would say next.

"Look, Jan. We have company. This is not the time to have this conversation. I am going back into the dining room, and I am going to enjoy dinner with Jordan. You're welcome to join us if you want, but I don't want to hear another word from you about this deed. Is that understood?"

"I thought you'd be glad to hear the news. Forgive me for living."

"That doesn't even warrant a response. Now, I'm going to finish my dinner. You can come with me or not. Your choice."

Jordan quickly grabbed her fork and transferred a bite of mashed potatoes into her mouth as Maggie came into the room. Jordan waited for Jan to appear behind her but soon realized she would be dining alone with Maggie.

"Jan sends her apologies. She's decided to have dinner later."

"That's too bad. Is she feeling okay?" Jordan asked, hoping she sounded sincere.

Maggie sat down and spread her napkin in her lap. "She's fine. Let's just enjoy our dinner, okay?"

After dinner, Jordan excused herself and stood to leave.

"Do you have to go so early?" Maggie asked in a wistful tone.

"I promised John I'd help him unload the hay crop in the morning. We're meeting at seven, so I really should get settled in for the night."

"But you haven't had dessert yet."

"That's okay. Dinner was so good, I ate too much anyway. Maybe I'll take a rain check on dessert?"

"Deal," Maggie said. "Let me walk you to the bunkhouse."

"You don't have to do that," Jordan said.

Maggie grinned. "I know I don't."

Jordan offered her arm to Maggie, who slipped her hand into the crook of Jordan's elbow.

A few minutes later, they stopped in front of the bunkhouse door and Maggie released Jordan's arm.

Jordan shoved her hands into her pockets. "Maggie, I want to thank you for dinner. It was the best fried chicken I've had in a long time. I appreciate the invitation."

Maggie looked into Jordan's eyes and smiled. "You're welcome. I enjoyed having you. However, I must apologize for Jan's behavior." Maggie crossed her arms in front of her and hugged herself close. "Brrr. I can't believe it's getting cool at night already," she complained.

"Are you cold? Sheesh, how inconsiderate can I be? Let me get you a jacket. Wait right here," Jordan said as she slipped into the bunkhouse, emerging seconds later carrying a jeans jacket. "Here, put this on." Jordan helped Maggie into the jacket and then rubbed her upper arms to warm her up. "Is that better?" she asked.

"Much. Thank you."

Maggie took a step closer and looked up at Jordan.

Jordan felt as though all the air had been forced from her lungs. She stared at the beautiful face before her. *I could easily drown in her eyes.* "I need to kiss you," she whispered, lowering her mouth to Maggie's.

As Maggie's lips parted, Jordan's tongue explored the moist cavern within. A wave of liquid desire coursed through Jordan as the kiss deepened. It was a full minute later that Jordan finally broke the kiss and leaned her forehead against Maggie's so they could both catch their breath.

"Oh, my God!" Maggie whispered hoarsely.

Jordan took a step back. "I'm sorry. I shouldn't have done that."

"You didn't do that. We did," Maggie said, "and I'm the one who should apologize."

"No, I take full responsibility. You have a partner, and I should know better than to interfere with your relationship. Jan doesn't deserve that," Jordan insisted.

Maggie placed her index finger on Jordan's lips. "You're right. She doesn't, but I'm sure you can see that things aren't perfect with her. In fact, things have been a little shaky for some time. Maybe you were right earlier... she is assuming." Maggie wrapped her arms around her middle and walked a few feet away. "I don't know, Jordan. I need time to think about Jan. I need to process what I'm feeling for you. I'm sorry if I'm sending confusing signals. Please, forgive me."

Jordan inhaled deeply and nodded, releasing a breath she hadn't realized she was holding.

Maggie smiled and stood on tiptoe to place a gentle, chaste kiss on Jordan's lips. "You need to sleep. I'll see you tomorrow. Good night," she said.

Jordan's heart flipped in her chest as she watched Maggie walk across the barnyard and into the house.

CHAPTER 30

Early the next morning, Jordan directed pallets of hay bales into the loft as John lifted them with the hoist and pulley. She had a perfect view of Maggie sauntering into the barn wearing Jordan's jacket.

Maggie greeted John brightly. "Good morning."

John tipped his hat with one hand while maintaining a firm grip on the pulley rope with the other. "'Morning, Maggie."

"Nice jacket," Jordan called down from the loft.

Maggie looked up. Her face lit up happily as she grabbed the sides of the jacket, spreading them out while turning around in a circle as though modeling a coat. "Thank you. Do you like it?"

"It's great. You have good taste," Jordan responded.

Maggie smiled. "Are you almost finished? I was hoping you'd be free to ride with me to the north end of the property. I'm meeting my carpenter up there to go over plans for a new barn."

Jordan looked down at John. "How many more do we have, John?"

"Looks like two more. Why don't you go ahead with Maggie, and I'll finish up here."

"No, a promise is a promise. We're going to finish this before I leave," Jordan said. She looked again at Maggie. "Give me about twenty minutes, and I'll be with you. Okay?"

"Sounds good. I'll go straighten up the tack room while I wait." Jordan stepped into the hook of the winch and rode it down to barn level to help John secure the next pallet.

John watched Maggie nearly skip away before he looked at Jordan with raised eyebrows.

"What's that look for?" Jordan asked.

"I'm surprised she didn't blow a cork," John replied.

"What do you mean?"

"Maggie sometimes isn't very patient when she wants something."

"Really?" she asked. "Has she ever lost patience with you?"

"Nope, not me, but Jan's been on the receiving end a few times. Let me tell you—what they say about redheads and tempers is true in her case."

"Hmm... interesting." Jordan wondered to herself what Jan had done to provoke Maggie's ire. "I know what you mean. She seems to lose her temper quite easily. I can't imagine it would have taken much for her to blow up at Jan."

John eyed her conspiratorially over the pallet of feed. "To tell you the truth, if it was me, I'd have been mad too."

Jordan grabbed the hook and stepped onto the edge of the pallet. "Take her up, John."

John winched Jordan and the load of feed to the level of the loft. Jordan stepped onto the platform and pulled the pallet over far enough to settle lightly on the deck as John slowly released the tension on the rope.

"Okay. That's enough." Jordan unhooked the straps from the pallet and once more slipped her foot into the hook. When John had lowered her to the floor, she handed the straps back to him. Curiosity got the best of her as she waited for him to thread the straps through the final pallet. "What did she do to make Maggie so angry?"

"Maggie was away for a couple of days about a month ago, showing some of the mustangs at a horse show in the next town. One of Maggie's favorite mares took sick while she was gone. Jan was supposed to be keeping an eye on the place, but instead of taking care of chores, she pretty much lorded it over the farm like she owned it. When Maggie came home and saw the shape her mare was in, all hell broke loose."

Jordan tried to imagine how she would feel if Kale had neglected her horses when she was in the hospital. "Wow. Maggie must have really been upset."

"I was in the barn here, cleaning stalls when she returned. I could hear her yelling at Jan from here, not that I blame her none. Jan really should've been taking care of things while she was gone instead of playing king of the castle."

Jordan pulled the straps through the bottom of the pallet and looped them over the hook. "That must have put a strain on their relationship."

"Climb on. She's going up." John pulled the slack out of the winch rope.

Jordan stood on top of the pallet while John winched it into the loft. Once the pallet was safely settled in the loft, she unthreaded the straps from the pallet and hung them back on the hook. "Winch it up, John."

By the time John had taken care of the winch, Jordan had descended the stairs of the loft and met him at the bottom.

"Why does Maggie keep her around?" she asked John.

John looked at her. "I reckon she loves her," he replied.

Jordan's brow furrowed into a deep frown.

John shook his head "I thought as much," he said, almost sadly.

"What?" Jordan prompted.

"You're in love with her, aren't you," he stated rather than asked. "I've seen how you light up when she walks into the barn."

Jordan looked everywhere but at John. "Ah... I don't even know her yet."

"Doesn't matter how long you've known her," John replied. A few moments of silence fell between them before John spoke again. "You know Jan won't be happy about this."

Jordan's attention was suddenly drawn away from her conversation with John. She turned to see Maggie standing nearby with her arms crossed impatiently in front of her. She wondered how long Maggie had been standing there.

"How long are you going to keep me waiting?" she asked.

Jordan grinned. "Patience woman," she said teasingly. "Some of us have work to do around here."

Maggie swatted Jordan's behind with the leather gloves she was holding. "Mind who you're talking to, Missy. You're liable to get yourself fired again."

"Yeah, yeah," Jordan replied dryly. "Whatever."

Jordan looked at John and winked. "John, did you say you needed some help with the feed bags next?"

"Oh, no you don't." Maggie locked her arm with Jordan's. "You're coming with me to the north pasture, remember?"

Jordan slapped her palm on her thigh. "Oh, yeah. I almost forgot. You know, Maggie, I think I'll be needing that raise now, considering how valuable I am around here."

"I'll give you a raise you little shit—right at the end of my foot if you don't shape up." Maggie laughed.

Jordan looked at John and shook her head. "Women," she said, which earned her a quick kick in the pants from Maggie.

* * *

Jordan rode beside Maggie on the way out to the north pasture. "I've always though this is a beautiful farm," Jordan said.

Maggie looked at Jordan and frowned. "Have you seen the farm before?"

"Huh?" Jordan asked. "What do you mean?"

"You just said you've always thought the farm was beautiful. That sounds like you've seen it before."

Shit!

"I meant I always thought Vermont was a beautiful state. It goes without saying the farmland is the best part of it." *Lame, Lewis. Real lame.*

"I couldn't agree more," Maggie replied.

Jordan released an almost audible sigh of relief. They rode in silence for the next minute or two before Maggie posed another question.

"Have you lived in Vermont long?"

"Yes I have, all my life in fact. I've traveled a lot, but my heart is right here. This is where I want to spend the rest of my life." Jordan fell silent as she realized the double meaning of her words.

"What did you do before you came to me looking for work?"

Think fast, Jordan.

"I was affiliated with the University of Vermont. I worked in the lab there."

Maggie looked at the field ahead of her as she spoke. "Doing what?"

How am I going to get out of this one?

"I did some work with injured animals." *Not a total lie, at least.*

"It sounds interesting. You'll have to tell me about it some time. But right now, I'm going to kick your butt in a race to that outbuilding over there."

Maggie dug her heels into the side of her horse and galloped across the field.

"Hey, no fair," Jordan called. She kicked her own horse into gear. Jordan pushed her horse as fast as she dared and slowly closed the distance between them, but was unable to catch up before Maggie reined her horse to a stop at the hitching post in front of the barn. She was out of breath by the time she, too, reached the barn.

Maggie grinned broadly. "Not bad for a femme, huh?"

Jordan pulled her horse alongside Maggie's and leaned forward until their faces were only inches apart. "A sneaky femme, maybe. That was no fair!"

"I never claimed to be fair," Maggie replied. She climbed out of the saddle and tied her horse to the hitch.

Maggie glanced at Jordan. "Are you coming?"

Jordan shook herself out of her reverie. She dismounted and tied her horse next to Maggie's.

Maggie waited for Jordan to join her before entering the barn. "We've set up an office of sorts in this barn for the contractors. They are also storing the raw materials in here." Jordan allowed her eyes to adjust to the darker interior then looked around at the rough lumber that was organized by board width and length. There were piles of boards stacked neatly in each of the horse stalls as well as in the loft.

"I take it you don't use this barn for livestock?" she asked.

"Not right now. It's kind of small for what I'm planning," Maggie replied.

"What exactly are you planning?"

"A breeding center for Mustangs. The new barn will be large enough to board several studs and mares, and will include a special birthing wing."

"Where will it be erected?"

"Right next to this one. I'll reuse this space as a supply shed. It's not really big enough for anything else," Maggie said.

"I see," Jordan remarked as she walked around. When she reached the opposite side of the room, she turned and faced Maggie. "I have a question for you. The Vermont state horse is the Morgan. Why the passion for mustangs?"

Maggie's smile brought a twinkle to her green eyes. "I like their spirit. They remind me of me, actually—fiery disposition and hard to tame."

Jordan cocked an eyebrow and walked toward Maggie. "Hard to tame, huh? I've broken a few spirited fillies in my time."

Maggie took two steps forward and stopped directly in front of Jordan. She looked up into Jordan's face. "You have, have you?"

"Yes, I have."

"Maggie, are you in there?" came a decidedly male voice from outside the barn.

"Shit. It's Dave," Maggie said.

"Dave?"

"The contractor. I said I was meeting him here, remember? Why else did you think I asked you to come out here with me?" Maggie looked toward the barn door. "I'm in here, Dave."

Jordan shifted under Maggie's scrutiny. "Well..."

Just then, the door to the barn swung open and admitted a large, lumberjack-looking, barrel-chested man. "There you are," he said. "Sorry I'm late."

"I'm not," Jordan said under her breath, just loud enough for Maggie to hear.

Maggie gently kicked Jordan's shin.

"Ow." Jordan's complaint drew Dave's attention.

Maggie immediately stepped in. "Dave, this is Jordan Lewis. She started working for me a few days ago. She's the one who checked out the rafter that broke in the main barn."

Jordan extended her hand to meet Dave's. "Nice to meet you," she said as her hand disappeared into the much larger one presented to her.

"Likewise," Dave said as he released Jordan's hand. He then turned to Maggie. "I have the new plans if you'd like to go over them."

"Yes, please," Maggie replied as Dave unfolded the blueprints on a nearby desk.

For the next hour, the three of them poured over the plans, and made minor changes to the location of a few walls and windows. Jordan made her recommendations based on how that actual barn looked in her day. It was nearly noon by the time they completed their review.

"Okay, I'd say that just about wraps it up," Dave said.

"Good. When do we break ground?" Maggie asked.

"I can have a crew here on Monday. Is that soon enough?"

Maggie clapped her hands. "Wonderful." She glanced at her watch. "It's already noon. Where does the time go? You're welcome to come back to the house for lunch if you'd like, Dave."

"Thanks for the offer, but I have another appointment at one." Dave extended his hand to Jordan once again. "Jordan, it was nice meeting you. Oh, and by the way, I agree with your assessment on the rafter. That board was cut mechanically. Natural weak points in wood don't break that cleanly. I'm not sure if the cut was made before or after the rafter was up, but it was definitely created manually."

Jordan nodded. "That's exactly what I thought. Thanks for verifying it."

"No problem. I've got to run. I'll be here with the crew first thing Monday morning."

"Thank you, Dave," Maggie said. "Have a great weekend."

Jordan and Maggie watched Dave leave. As soon as the barn door closed behind him, Jordan looked at Maggie pensively. "Why did you ask me out here?"

"Maggie? Maggie, where are you?"

Maggie threw her hands into the air at the sound of Jan's voice. "Is this freaking Grand Central Station?" she said angrily. "In here, Jan," she called.

Jan pulled the barn door open and stepped inside. When she saw Jordan, she crossed her arms in front of her and addressed Maggie. "Humph. When I saw two horses tethered outside, I kind of figured she was with you."

"Jordan and I just went over the blueprints for the new barn with Dave. She made several good suggestions. What brings you here?"

"I was in the house pouring a glass of lemonade when the phone rang. I let the answering machine pick it up and couldn't help but overhear the message being left. Your father's lawyer called. He left a message for you to call him back. It has something to do with the deed to the farm."

Maggie frowned. "Hmm. I wonder what that's all about."

"I don't know, but I thought you might want to call him back right way. Maybe Dad needs some information from us or something."

"Maybe," Maggie said.

An uncomfortable silence fell over the trio as Maggie waited for Jan to leave. When it became obvious that no one was moving, she addressed Jan directly. "Is there anything else you need, Jan?"

Jan shifted from foot to foot. "I was wondering if you're coming home for lunch."

"I have a few more items to go over with Jordan. We'll be along soon. Why don't you get a head start?" Maggie suggested.

Jan approached the table with the blueprints spread out on it. "Actually, I'd like to see the changes you've made in the layout. After all, the design needs my input as well."

Jordan shifted nervously at the uncomfortable tension in the room. "I'm going to head back to the house," she said. "John could use some help with the feed delivery."

Maggie tried to stop Jordan from leaving. "Why don't we ride back together and get some lunch?"

"No, I think I'm going to skip lunch today. I'll see you back at the house."

Maggie watched Jordan leave while Jan remained bent over the blueprints with a self-satisfied smirk on her face.

* * *

"Mr. Pritchard, I don't see why my father needs to name a second beneficiary on the deed. Yes, I know none of us will live forever, but I still don't see why he... look, just send me the paperwork, okay? I want to see exactly how it's worded. All right. Thank you."

Maggie hung up the phone. A deep frown creased her forehead.

"What did he want?" Jan asked anxiously.

"He said Daddy added a second beneficiary to the deed. Apparently, someone put it into his head that he needed backup in the event I died before he did. Where on earth did he get that harebrained idea?"

Jan shrugged. "Beats the hell out of me, but I guess it makes sense."

"Well, it makes no sense to me. If he deeds the farm to me, it's up to me to name my own beneficiary, not him. I'll review the paperwork, and if I don't like what it says, I'll get Daddy to change it." Maggie yawned loudly. "Damn, I'm beat. I'm going to bed."

Jan looked at her watch. "It's a little early for me to turn in. I think I'll read for a while. I'll be in soon."

"Suit yourself," Maggie replied.

Maggie paced back and forth across the bedroom trying to decide how to break the news to Jan. In her heart, she knew their relationship had been on a downhill spiral for some time, but she hadn't been able to summon the courage to end it. She was still pacing when Jan finally came to bed.

"You're still up? I expected to find you asleep," Jan said as she entered the room. "What's wrong?" Maggie wrapped her hands around her middle. "Jan, we need to talk."

Jan's face grew ashen. "I've been expecting this. You're attracted to her, aren't you?"

"This isn't about Jordan. It's about our relationship no longer working. It's about you being presumptuous... it's about you taking me for granted... it's about you taking liberties you shouldn't be taking."

"What the hell does that mean?"

"I feel like you're trying to control me. It seems that you're making plans and decisions that clearly I should be making—or at the very least, we should be making together."

"You're talking in riddles. What decisions are you talking about?"

"Let me give you a few examples. You told Jordan we were getting married and planned to have a baby. You're being oddly persistent about the deed to the farm. What are you up to? Something doesn't feel right."

Jan paced back and forth, clearly agitated. "This isn't about us getting married, and this isn't about the deed to the farm. This is about Jordan, and you know it! You're attracted to her, aren't you?"

Maggie sighed. "I don't know what to say. Yes, I'm attracted to her. I can't help it."

"Goddamn it! I knew it."

"I tried to resist what I was feeling, but I couldn't. There's something about her that draws me in. I feel like we've known each other forever."

"Have you slept with her?"

"How can you even ask me that question? No, I haven't slept with her."

"What does this mean for me?" Jan asked. "I love this farm. I've put my heart and soul into training the horses for the past few years. In some ways, I feel like this place is my own. Please don't ask me to leave all of this behind."

Maggie rubbed her hands across her face in a gesture of frustration. "Jan, I appreciate everything you've done for me, and I have nothing but good things to say about what you've done for the farm, but I don't know if it's fair to ask you to stay, especially considering..."

"Especially considering how you feel about Jordan?" Jan finished Maggie's sentence.

"Like I said, this isn't about Jordan. I'm sorry. I never wanted to hurt you."

"Do you want me to leave?"

"I'm not asking you to leave if you don't want to. You're right—you have worked hard to make this farm a success."

Jan walked to the closet to retrieve a suitcase that she carried to the bed. "Okay. I'll respect your wishes. Like I said, I don't want to walk away from everything I've worked for over the past four years, so if it's all right with you, I'll move into the bunkhouse with Jordan for now."

Maggie's eyes grew wide. "Do you really think that's a good idea?"

Jan paused on one of her several trips back and forth between the chest of drawers and suitcase. "If this truly isn't about Jordan, then that shouldn't be a problem. And besides, if I want to stay, I don't see that I have any other choice."

"Okay," Maggie said softly before leaving the room.

*   *   *

Jordan felt a chill in the air as she made her way across the barnyard. She pushed the bunkhouse door open and stepped into the warmth and immediately turned her back to the room to take her jacket off and hang it on a hook beside the door. When she turned around, she met Jan face to face. Her eyes widened with surprise.

"Hey, roomie," Jan said.

Jordan frowned. "Roomie?"

"That's right. Thanks to you, Maggie has no use for me in her bed anymore."

Jordan walked to the refrigerator and took out a beer. "I don't know what you're talking about," she said, taking a swig from the bottle.

Jan rose to her feet. "No matter. Just know I have my eye on you. Don't make the mistake of getting in my way, understand? I don't take kindly to anyone who gets in my way."

Jordan walked directly up to Jan and leaned over the shorter woman. "I don't know what's up with you and Maggie, but don't make the mistake of threatening me. I don't take kindly to anyone who threatens me." Jordan walked away and went to her room. Once inside, she leaned against the door and closed her eyes.

Maggie, what are you up to?

CHAPTER 31

Jordan turned off the water and drew back the shower curtain. As she squeezed the water out of her hair, she heard a loud, incessant pounding on the front door of the bunkhouse. She wrapped a towel around herself and cautiously made her way to the door. "Who is it?" she called out.

"Maggie. I've brought a few things that Jan forgot at the house. May I come in?"

Jordan opened the door and stood there, one hand holding the towel together above her breasts.

Maggie's eyes opened wide. "Oh. I see I caught you at a bad time. I'll come back later," she said, turning to go.

"No, it's all right. Come in." Jordan stepped aside and allowed Maggie to enter the bunkhouse.

Maggie held a bag of clothing in front of her. "Jan left these at the house last night. Is she here?"

"No, she's already gone to the barn. That was a nice little surprise you sent my way last night."

"I'm sorry about that, but she offered to stay in the bunkhouse, and I wasn't going to pass on the opportunity to break things off with her without a fight."

"You really put me in an awkward situation. What were you thinking?"

"I'm sorry, Jordan. I had to do it. It wasn't fair to continue the charade. Things haven't been good between us for a while now."

"So why here? Why didn't she just leave?"

"She didn't want to go, and to tell you the truth, she's good at what she does. I really didn't want to lose her. She's helped a lot with this farm. I feel like I owe her something for that."

Maggie, you don't know what you've done by keeping her around. A shiver of fear ran through her.

"You're cold. As much as I like seeing you in just a towel, you should dry yourself off and get dressed."

Jordan smiled. "You're right. Make yourself comfortable. I'll be right back." She turned around and began to walk toward the bedroom.

"God, Jordan! What happened?" Maggie asked.

Jordan stopped short. She looked at Maggie questioningly. "What do you mean?"

Maggie took several steps toward Jordan. "Turn around," she said.

Jordan did as asked and turned her back to Maggie. The towel hung loose and low on her back. She stood as still as possible as she felt Maggie's breath very close to her still-wet skin.

"What happened to you?" Maggie whispered as she traced the length of Jordan's scar from the middle of her back to where it disappeared behind the towel just above her bottom.

Jordan shivered, more from Maggie's touch than from the cool air on her back.

"Horse riding accident. I was sixteen at the time," Jordan replied truthfully.

Maggie traced the scar once more, but this time, ventured beyond the towel barrier. Jordan stood very still, not wanting Maggie to stop her exploration. Suddenly, Maggie's hand became very still as her fingers encountered a foreign object. Jordan closed her eyes and wondered how she was going to explain it to Maggie.

"What's this?" Maggie asked as she pulled the towel down lower on Jordan's back. "It vibrates," she exclaimed. "What is it, some kind of sex toy?"

Jordan chuckled as she reached back and held Maggie's hand against the implant bulging through her skin. "The vibration you're feeling is due to an alternating electrical charge coming from an energy storage unit, kind of like a power pack. The small box-like structure bulging from the skin is a spinal implant."

Maggie quickly retracted her hand. "A spinal implant? You mean like bionic parts?"

"Kind of," Jordan replied. "The horse riding accident I mentioned a moment ago? I was paralyzed from the waist down. The implant restores mobility."

"You're paralyzed?"

"I was until the implant. I guess you could technically say I still am."

"Do you have any feeling below your waist?" Maggie asked.

"So far, no. No sensation on the skin, at least. I will admit however, that when you kissed me, I felt some very distinct fluttering deep within my abdomen."

"I... I never knew something like this was possible. You're paralyzed, yet you can walk. I didn't know science had advanced that far already."

Jordan breathed deeply and slowly let out her breath. "Maggie, there are things you don't know about me that I promise I will explain when the time is right. Please, just trust me for now, okay?"

Maggie frowned. "Trust you? Hell, I don't even know you. This is a major deal. How long did you think you'd be able to hide this from me?"

Jordan looked hurt. "I wasn't trying to hide it. It's just not exactly dinner conversation, you know?"

Maggie looked apprehensively at Jordan.

Jordan took several steps toward Maggie, but stopped abruptly when Maggie put her hand up. "Don't, please. I need time to digest this."

Jordan stepped back. "I'm sorry. Would you like me to pack my things and leave?"

Maggie walked toward the door then turned to look at Jordan. "Do I want you to leave? No, not unless you want to."

Jordan looked down at the floor. "I don't want to," she said softly.

When she looked up, Maggie was gone.

*　*　*

For the next several weeks, Jordan fell into a routine of chores as well as repairs to fences, outbuildings, and grounds. During that time, Maggie made herself conspicuously absent and communicated with Jordan through notes left on the bunkhouse door or through messages hand-carried to her by a very smug Jan. It was obvious to Jordan that Jan sensed the tension between her and Maggie and reveled in her role as messenger, but she rarely engaged Jordan in conversation. Instead, she spent the time she did share with Jordan watching her and doing her best to make Jordan uncomfortable.

Jordan had free access to Maggie's home, but rarely encountered Maggie. When their paths did cross, Maggie always had board meetings to attend or chores to be done, and excused herself with little more than a cursory goodbye.

Jordan spent most evenings standing by the window waiting for the light to come on in Maggie's bedroom so she could catch a glimpse of the redhead. Her heart was heavy with regret. Maggie's revulsion with her condition was not something she had anticipated, and it broke her heart to know she would probably never be truly accepted by the woman she loved. She even considered telling Maggie the truth about where she had come from, but then the voice of reason stepped in and convinced her that Maggie would probably banish her from the farm if she were to divulge that kind of information. So she pined away for lost love in silence. Despite Maggie's rejection, she still loved her with all of her heart and vowed to prevent her untimely death.

Three weeks after Maggie discovered the implant, she asked Jordan to help with the barn raising. Jordan looked forward to it, as she knew Maggie was deeply involved in the project and would no doubt be a frequent visitor on the jobsite. By the time she joined the crew, the footing had already been poured and the wall frames erected. Jordan arrived at the jobsite with her tool belt in hand and immediately climbed the staging to assist with the rafter assembly.

From her vantage point in the rafters, Jordan could see Maggie moving around the site, reading blueprints with Dave, and assisting in various ways.

"Wow, that redhead down there is really hot," said the carpenter working at Jordan's side.

Jordan glanced down at Maggie, who was talking to Dave several yards below them. "Forget it, Don. Somehow, I don't think she'd be interested in you." Jordan chuckled.

Don looked offended. "And why not? I'm a good-looking guy. What is she, a dyke or something?"

Jordan raised her eyebrows. "You do realize she's the boss, right?"

Don snorted. "I don't care who she is. I answer only to Dave."

"Whatever," Jordan replied as she drove a spike into the rafter Don was holding level. "Okay, your turn."

Don retrieved a spike from his tool belt and began to hammer it into the wood. When he realized Maggie was looking up at them again, he took his attention off what he was doing for a brief moment to smile at her and promptly lost his footing.

"Whoa!" he yelled as he struggled to maintain his position on the beam.

Jordan tried to reach him, but in his attempt to catch himself, he released his end of the rafter. It pivoted toward Jordan as it was being held aloft only by the spike she had driven into it moments earlier. Jordan had all she could do to maintain her own balance on the beam as she avoided the swinging rafter and watched helplessly as Don fell to the floor of the barn.

Maggie screamed as he narrowly missed landing on her.

"Don't touch him," Jordan said loudly as she scrambled across the beam toward the ladder. "Please, don't move him!"

Jordan climbed down the ladder as fast as she could. "Call an ambulance, quickly!" She fell to her knees beside the fallen man and touched the side of his face gently. Maggie, Dave and several of the crewmembers circled them helplessly.

"Don? Don, can you hear me?" she asked.

Don blinked his eyes and tried to nod his head.

"Don't move your head, Don, okay? Help is on the way. Can you breathe? Blink twice for yes, once for no."

Don blinked twice.

"Good." Jordan looked up at Dave and Maggie. "I need something soft to stabilize his neck, towels, pillows, rolled up blankets, anything. Please hurry!"

"I have some blankets and towels in the truck." Dave turned and ran out of the barn.

Maggie squatted down next to Jordan. "What can I do to help?" she asked anxiously.

Dave returned carrying a blanket and several towels. He handed them to Jordan. "I'm afraid they're not very clean," he said.

"I don't think he'll care at this point." Jordan reached up for the blankets and gave one to Maggie. "Cover him up while I stabilize his neck. It will help to prevent shock."

Maggie and Dave worked together to drape a blanket over Don while Jordan rolled two of the towels and placed them on either side of Don's neck and held them there to prevent him from moving his head back and forth. She then lowered her ear to his mouth to monitor how laboriously he was breathing. Satisfied that his airway was unobstructed, she smiled at the man.

"Help is on the way, Don. Hang in there, buddy. Are you feeling pain anywhere?"

Don blinked his eyes twice.

"Is the pain in your neck?"

Two blinks.

"How about your arms and legs?"

One blink.

"Can you move your fingers and toes? Do it gently... don't lift your hand or foot."

Jordan watched as Don wiggled his fingers and moved his foot. "That's good, Don. Just lie as still as possible. I think I hear the ambulance coming."

"I'll flag them down," Maggie said as she rose to her feet and ran out of the barn.

Moments later, two EMTs rushed into the room carrying medical instruments. Maggie followed close behind. One EMT took over Jordan's position by Don's head while the other assessed his bodily injuries.

"What happened?" asked one of the EMTs.

"He fell from the rafter," Dave replied.

The EMT looked upward. "That's at least fifteen feet."

The EMT who was kneeling beside Don's head looked up. "What's his name?

Once more, Dave replied, "His name is Don. Don Feldman."

"Who secured his neck?" he asked.

"I did," Jordan replied. "I also assessed his respiration, which appears to be even. There doesn't appear to be any radiating pain. Most of the pain is centered in his neck. He is also able to move extremities such as fingers and toes. With any luck, the injury will be isolated to muscle pain and not affect the vertebrae beyond C2."

Maggie's eyes grew wide as she listened to Jordan speak with the emergency personnel.

The EMT attending at Don's head glanced up at Jordan. "You seem to know a lot about spinal injuries. I take it you're either a doctor, or you've had such an injury yourself?"

Jordan shrugged. "Something like that," she replied as she met Maggie's gaze.

"Okay. Jim, we'll need the backboard, neck brace, tape and gurney," the EMT instructed his partner. He then looked down at Don. "We'll have you out of here in a jiff, Don. You're in good hands."

Over the next ten minutes the EMTs worked to carefully secure Don to the backboard before loading him into the ambulance.

"I'd better follow them to the hospital," Dave said.

"Yes, of course," Maggie replied quickly. "Do whatever's necessary. I'll cross my fingers that his injuries aren't too extensive."

Jordan, Maggie, and the remaining carpenters watched as the ambulance drove away. While Maggie dismissed the rest of the crew for the day, Jordan walked away and collected her tools, then headed toward the old farm truck she had driven to the construction site. As she climbed into the driver's seat, Maggie ran toward her. "Jordan," she called out.

Jordan remained in the truck and waited for Maggie to reach her. She sat quietly looking out the windshield.

Maggie stopped by the driver's door. "Hey," she said.

Jordan nodded but continued to look straight ahead.

Maggie kicked the dirt around gently with her toe. "Look, I know you're angry with me, and I don't blame you, but that was quite a bombshell you dropped on me a few weeks ago."

Jordan looked at her. "I had hoped it wouldn't matter."

Maggie shrugged. "I don't know if it matters or not. It... it just took me by surprise."

"Well, for that, I apologize," Jordan replied stoically.

"Don't be that way!" Maggie exclaimed.

Jordan's turned her head sharply in Maggie's direction. "How the hell do you want me to be?" she asked angrily.

"Honest, for one," Maggie replied.

Jordan could feel the anger rising in her chest as she gripped the steering wheel tightly.

Maggie sighed deeply. "Look, Jordan, I don't want to argue with you."

Jordan shook her head. "You just don't understand."

Maggie put both hands on the window frame and leaned forward. "Then why don't you explain it to me?" she suggested.

Jordan reached across the bench seat and threw the passenger door open. "Get in."

Jordan and Maggie drove to the western fringe of the property to where the land abruptly fell off to the lake. As Jordan turned off the ignition and looked around, she realized they were very near the spot where Maggie would fall to her death in a few short months. The thought sent shivers up her spine.

An uncomfortable silence settled over them as they both stared out at Lake Champlain.

Maggie turned in her seat to face Jordan. "Tell me about your accident."

Jordan dropped her hands from the steering wheel and allowed them to fall into her lap. She stared at them for several minutes before she looked at Maggie. "Like I said, I was sixteen at the time. I was riding my horse, Sally, who, by the way, was a mustang.

Anyway, I was riding Sally across the field and she stumbled and threw me. I landed pretty hard at an angle that broke my back at the L1 vertebra, just below the small of my back. I was in a hover... ah, I mean, a wheelchair until I was thirty."

"Oh, my God! How old are you now?" Maggie asked.

"I'm thirty-two, almost thirty-three."

Maggie was obviously calculating in her head. "You were in a wheelchair for fourteen years? How awful for you."

"Awful doesn't even begin to describe it. I grew up on this... er, I mean, I grew up on a farm very much like this one, and I felt so incredibly useless stuck in that chair. I spent a significant amount of time after school in the barn with my father. I helped as much as I could with the horses, and we enjoyed small carpentry projects together, but I didn't venture far from the property. I was an only child and my parents were somewhat older than those of other kids, so it was a pretty lonely childhood."

"Where are your parents now?" Maggie asked.

"They died in a car accident when I was twenty-six."

"I'm sorry," she whispered softly.

"Thanks," Jordan replied without looking up.

"How did you come to have the implant?"

Jordan lifted her head and pressed it against the headrest. *Should I tell the whole truth... or a partial truth?*

"I volunteered for a spinal implant development project being conducted at the University of Vermont Spinal Institute. They almost didn't accept me because my injury was so old, but I persisted, and eventually, they gave in. This is actually the second implant. The first one lasted for two years then failed several months ago. So far, this new one is working well."

Maggie tilted her head to the side. "How does the implant work? I mean, you walk like there's nothing wrong with you."

"The implant sends alternating electrical pulses to both sides of the injury site, and, in theory, it encourages the nerve endings to begin growing toward each other. Hopefully, some day soon, they will bridge the injury site and grow together. In the meantime, I have restored mobility, and with any luck, at some point, the nerve endings in my skin will wake up and smell the coffee too," Jordan explained.

"I had no idea that medical science has progressed so far. It's like a miracle," Maggie said.

Jordan closed her eyes and berated herself for being so ambiguous. She felt like a total wretch for deceiving Maggie.

Several more moments of silence passed as Maggie apparently digested the information Jordan had given her. Finally, she touched Jordan's hand.

"Jordan, close your eyes," she said softly.

Jordan turned her head to face Maggie and drew her brow into a frown. "Why?"

"Humor me, please," Maggie replied.

Jordan dutifully closed her eyes and waited for Maggie's move.

"Can you feel this?" Maggie asked as she rubbed Jordan's knee with her hand.

"No." Jordan's eyelashes fluttered.

"No, no, no. Don't open your eyes. Do you feel this?" Maggie ran her hand along Jordan's thigh.

Jordan concentrated hard but failed to feel anything. "No," she said impatiently.

Maggie allowed her hand to roam across Jordan's abdomen and into the crevice between her legs. "How about this?"

Jordan dropped her chin to her chest without opening her eyes. "No. I don't feel anything."

"Surely, you can feel this," Maggie said as she slipped her hand into Jordan's shirt.

Jordan stiffened, but kept her eyes closed.

"Yes, you can feel that. How about this?" Maggie reached far enough inside Jordan's shirt to feel her left breast and capture her nipple between her fingers.

"Ah!" Jordan exclaimed as a sudden bolt of desire shot directly to her core. Her eyes flew open and she pressed her own hand into her abdomen. She looked at Maggie. "Do that again."

Maggie applied pressure to the hardened nipple. Once more, Jordan nearly doubled over.

"Damn!" Jordan quivered as ripples of pleasure ran through her. She looked at Maggie. Her eyes were wild with wonder and desire. "I can feel that deep within my core. It feels incredible."

Maggie smiled. "This is your first time, isn't it?" she asked softly.

Unable to speak, Jordan just nodded. To Jordan's dismay, Maggie retracted her hand from inside her shirt.

"Well, your first time won't be in the front seat of a beat up old truck. Drive us home."

CHAPTER 32

Jordan left a large cloud of dust in her wake as she accelerated the old pickup truck across the plains and brought it to a screeching halt in front of the farmhouse. She jumped out of the driver's side and quickly ran around the front of the truck to open Maggie's door for her. Maggie took her hand as she stepped out of the truck. Together they ascended the porch steps and came to a halt at the top.

Jan was standing inside the house, just behind the screen door. "Well, well, well. Isn't this interesting," she sneered.

Jordan took a step toward the door, but was stopped by Maggie who glanced at her and silently communicated that she would handle the situation.

"Don't start, Jan. Has the hospital called yet?" she asked.

Jan narrowed her eyes. "Hospital? Why would the hospital call?"

"Because one of the carpenters fell out of the rafters directly to the floor of the new barn. We had to call an ambulance to come after him. Jordan stabilized his neck until they got here. I hope he's going to be okay," Maggie said.

"No, they haven't called yet."

Maggie reached for the screen door handle and pulled it open. Jan stepped aside to allow them to enter. Maggie nervously paced back and forth across the room as she spoke.

"Jan, I need you to go to the hospital to follow up on this for me. This is very important. I'm afraid the carpenter might hold the farm liable, and I need to be sure he's going to be okay. The last thing we need is a lawsuit, never mind losing the farm in the process."

"We'll lose the farm over my dead body!" Jan exclaimed angrily. "Who was it?"

Maggie tried to remember the man's name. "Don... Don..."

"Feldman," Jordan supplied. "Don Feldman."

Jan was clearly surprised. "Don Feldman? I know him. Quite the ladies' man, or at least he thinks he is. Which hospital did they take him to?"

"It was the Shelburne Rescue Squad. I would assume they'd take him to Fletcher Allen," Maggie replied.

"Okay, I'll go check it out. I'll be back in a few hours," Jan said.

"Take the truck. The keys are still in it," Jordan called after her.

Maggie and Jordan watched as Jan ran down the porch steps and jumped into the truck. Seconds later, all that remained was dust. Maggie closed the house door and leaned her back against it. She reached a hand forward and beckoned to Jordan. Jordan walked toward Maggie and, without touching her, leaned forward and placed a forceful kiss on the redhead's lips. She then took one step back and extended her hand, into which Maggie willingly slipped hers. Jordan gently pulled her away from the door and led her toward the bedrooms.

Jordan pushed the bedroom door open and allowed Maggie to pass through before her. She closed the door behind them and pulled Maggie into her arms. They stood there for what seemed an eternity, with Maggie's face pressed close to Jordan's chest. "You're trembling," Jordan said. "Are you okay?"

"I'm fine. I just want you so badly," Maggie said.

Jordan released her hold and took Maggie's face between her hands. "You are so beautiful," she whispered as her mouth descended once more. She gently teased Maggie's lips, caressing them with her tongue, asking for permission to enter. Maggie was hardly able to breathe as she parted her lips and readily accepted Jordan's tongue into her mouth.

"I want you," Jordan rasped.

Maggie's ardor grew as she pulled Jordan's hair to force her closer. "Make love to me," she insisted breathlessly before plunging her tongue into Jordan's mouth, tasting and caressing in a duel for dominance before breaking for air.

"I will," Jordan replied as her hands wandered freely over Maggie's body. She placed her hands on Maggie's bottom and squeezed. Maggie sighed aloud. Jordan emitted a low growl as she pulled Maggie's shirttails out of her jeans and ran her hands under the shirt and over the creamy white skin of her back. Maggie arched her back in an effort to press herself into Jordan's touch.

Within moments, Jordan released the clasps of Maggie's bra. She then unbuttoned Maggie's shirt, and pushed it off her shoulders only far enough to trap her arms in the process. Her lips explored Maggie's neck as she continued to push the shirt down and off her arms. The shirt drifted to the floor, followed closely by Maggie's bra.

Not to be outdone, Maggie deftly made short work of the buttons on Jordan's shirt as her garment joined the growing pile on the floor. She ran her hands over Jordan's deltoids, across her collar bones, and down over her breasts. Within seconds, Maggie pulled Jordan's sports bra off over her head and threw it on the floor. Skin to skin they embraced. Nipples hardened against each other.

Jordan pulled back for a moment and gently led Maggie to the side of the bed. She lowered her mouth once more to Maggie's neck and nuzzled her ear as her hands teased and squeezed her nipples to full erectness.

"Jordan!" Maggie moaned as she grasped Jordan's hand and encouraged more.

Jordan's hand left Maggie's breast to unbuckle her belt and jeans. She eased the zipper down and slipped her hand inside Maggie's pants. Jordan nearly doubled over with lustful hunger as she found the evidence of Maggie's passion.

"Maggie, you're so wet. My God, what you do to me."

"Please, baby, I need more," Maggie begged as she reached between them to unzip Jordan's jeans and push them off her hips.

Jordan kicked her jeans off then lowered herself to one knee as she pulled down Maggie's jeans and panties and helped her to step out of them. She then dropped to both knees and pressed her face into Maggie's abdomen and firmly gripped the curves of Maggie's bottom.

"Maggie, I need you," Jordan whispered.

Maggie grasped the sides of Jordan's arms and encouraged her to stand. She pushed Jordan's panties to the floor. Eagerly, they embraced and lowered their entwined bodies to the bed, where they lay in each other's arms kissing, exploring and breathing common air.

"I am so in love with you," Jordan confessed.

Maggie rolled on top of Jordan and placed one finger on her lips. "Shh. Don't say that. You barely know me."

Jordan smiled. "I have known you for a hundred years, and I will love you for a hundred more," she replied as she reached down between them and slid two fingers inside Maggie.

Maggie moaned loudly. "Jordan, baby, that feels so good."

Jordan rolled Maggie onto her back. She continued to plunge into her lover as she grasped a handful of Maggie's hair and devoured her mouth. Maggie's moans became louder and Jordan could feel the vibration of her voice echo between their mouths.

Jordan suddenly retracted her fingers. Maggie moaned in protest. "Jordan... no, please, I need you."

"Shh, relax, my love," Jordan whispered as she placed gentle kisses along the length of Maggie's collarbone.

Maggie placed her hands on Jordan's head and pushed her downward.

Jordan chuckled. "All in good time, my love. All in good time."

Jordan continued to place butterfly kisses across Maggie's breasts until she reached her nipples, which she captured between her teeth one at a time. With the sensitive nub gently held captive, Jordan flicked each one with the tip of her tongue until Maggie shuddered with delight. Jordan allowed her hands to run freely over Maggie's abdomen as her mouth slowly made its way southward. Maggie's hips rose to meet Jordan's mouth, demanding satisfaction.

Then, just as Jordan captured Maggie's sweet spot between her teeth, she drove two fingers once again deep into Maggie's core. Maggie's chest arched off the bed and a scream of desire erupted from her throat.

Maggie's body began to stiffen as her muscles tightened around Jordan's fingers. "Harder, baby, please!" she begged as Jordan increased her rhythm. Jordan held her close as Maggie's body arched off the bed and she cried out her release.

"Let it go, baby. Let it go. I want all of you, forever," Jordan whispered gently as Maggie's orgasm subsided. Jordan gathered Maggie into her arms and held her close as her breathing returned to normal and the pleasurable tension left her body.

Several moments later, Maggie rolled Jordan onto her back. "Your turn," she said. "I want this first time to be special for you."

"Just being here with you makes it special," Jordan replied.

Maggie dropped a delicious kiss on Jordan's lips then licked her way along Jordan's jaw line to her ear. Her tongue gently invaded the cavity. Jordan moaned as she felt a wave of desire invade her abdomen. The intensity of the invasion was unsettling and ecstatic. She had never felt so out of control in her life. She began to tremble.

Maggie raised her head and looked at Jordan questioningly. "Are you all right?"

Jordan forced a smile to her lips, but was unable to chase away the tears at the corners of her eyes. "I'm okay. A little nervous... and a little scared, maybe, but I'm okay."

"Do you want me to stop?"

Jordan reached up and tucked a lock of wild red hair behind Maggie's ear. "No, love. Don't stop. I want you to make love to me. Please?"

Maggie smiled and placed another deep kiss on Jordan's lips. "Anything you want, lover. Anything you want."

Jordan tilted her head back as Maggie kissed her throat. With her tongue, Maggie traced her flesh to the indentation where Jordan's collarbones met above her breastbone. The erotic feel of Maggie's tongue drove Jordan crazy and she grasped the sheets on both sides of her body and arched herself closer to Maggie's body.

Maggie took her cue from Jordan and moved downward, biting Jordan's skin along the way. Each gentle strike brought a spasm of desire to Jordan's abdomen. Maggie stopped at Jordan's breasts and gently ran circles around each erect nipple before sucking them one at a time into her mouth and capturing the hardness between her teeth. She flicked the sensitive nub with her tongue repeatedly.

Jordan's hands flew up to Maggie's head. Maggie looked up. "Harder, please," Jordan urged. Veins protruded from Jordan's neck and her face and chest were flushed crimson as she strained against the ripples of desire spreading through her.

Never before had Jordan felt such intensity of desire and emotion. Her experiences with other women paled in comparison to what Maggie was doing to her. "Maggie... I need you. Please release me," she begged.

Maggie once more moved downward, not stopping until she could smell the aroma of Jordan's readiness. "Hmm, lover, you are ready for me, aren't you?" she cooed as she slipped her tongue between the folds of Jordan's womanhood.

Jordan felt as though she would burst, but to her dismay, she had absolutely no feeling from Maggie's caresses.

Maggie continued her efforts for the next few minutes until she realized there was no change in Jordan's demeanor. She raised her eyes and looked at Jordan over the expanse of her abdomen and saw the apology in her lover's eyes as she mouthed the words, "I'm sorry." Maggie raised her head and cocked it to one side.

"I'm sorry, love. I... I don't feel anything. I'm so sorry." Jordan began to cry.

Maggie was confused. Didn't she say she felt the burn of desire in her abdomen? Not wanting to admit defeat, without warning Maggie plunged two fingers deep inside of Jordan. Curling her fingers upward, she thrust in and out of Jordan, massaging her most sensitive spot with each thrust.

Jordan's head slammed back into the pillow. "Ah!" she screamed out. "Don't stop! Please, don't stop!"

Tears rolled down both women's faces as Jordan's thrusts matched Maggie's. Jordan grasped the bed sheets on both sides to anchor herself as her hips rose higher and higher off the bed. Waves of desire pummeled her body as Jordan's orgasm raced through her, setting every nerve ending on fire.

For what felt like an eternity, ripples of aftershocks ran through Jordan's body as Maggie held her close. Finally, the spasms subsided, and Maggie gently slid her hand out of her lover then wrapped her arms around Jordan, who was crying uncontrollably. "It's okay, baby. You're safe. Let it go, lover. Relax. Sleep."

Jordan was nearly incapable of speech as sobs tore through her chest. "I love you, Maggie," Jordan said as she burrowed her face into Maggie's neck.

"Hmm," Maggie replied as she continued to hold the fragile woman.

Before long, Jordan relaxed and drifted off to sleep in Maggie's arms. Maggie turned her head and placed a delicate kiss on Jordan's forehead. "I love you too, Jordan," she whispered.

* * *

Maggie glanced at the digital clock and saw 3:04 p.m. flash on the LCD. *What time did Jan leave for the hospital?* It must have been just after noon. She turned her head slightly and placed a gentle kiss on the back of Jordan's head, then wrapped her arms around her as she spooned herself behind Jordan. "Wake up, lover," she whispered softly into Jordan's ear.

Jordan moaned and rolled over to face Maggie then took the redhead into her arms and held her close. "I don't want to wake up. I want to stay like this forever," she replied without opening her eyes.

"I, too, would like nothing more, but Jan will be back soon. Our attraction is difficult enough for her to accept without her seeing us this way."

Jordan rolled onto her back and threw her arm over her eyes. "I forgot about her." She sat up. "I guess we'd better get dressed."

Jordan stood beside the bed and stretched her arms high above her head. Unable to resist temptation, Maggie rolled to Jordan's side of the bed where she climbed to her knees and wrapped herself around a naked Jordan from behind. Jordan's arms immediately came down to reach behind her and pull Maggie close.

"God, you feel good, Maggie," Jordan said huskily as the flames of desire once again began to flicker within her.

Maggie's hands roamed freely around Jordan's abdomen as she pulled herself closer to her. One hand slipped lower to cover Jordan's mound, where she stroked gently.

Jordan looked down and saw where Maggie's hand rested, and although she could not feel her hand from a tactile standpoint, the psychological effect was overwhelming as a spasm tore through Jordan. "If you keep that up, we'll never get out of here before Jan returns," she warned.

Maggie kissed Jordan's back. "I know, but you make me feel so alive. All I want to do is make love to you." Maggie placed a trail of kisses along the scar running down Jordan's back. Finally, she sat back on her heels and ran her hand over the area where the implant protruded from Jordan's skin. "Does it hurt?" she asked.

Jordan couldn't feel what Maggie was doing but knew instinctively what she meant. "No, I don't feel it at all. In the beginning, the constant vibration kind of drove me crazy, but I hardly notice it now. It's a small price to pay for mobility."

Maggie patted the mattress beside her as she settled herself into a seated position on the edge of the bed. "Sit. Talk to me for a bit."

Jordan sat beside Maggie, then reached up and tucked an errant lock behind Maggie's ear. "Yes, my love?" she asked.

Maggie looked directly into Jordan's eyes. "When my mouth was on you, you didn't feel anything, but when I entered you it was amazing how you reacted."

Jordan smiled. "I know. I was so afraid that I would feel nothing at all, but when you were inside of me... I... well... it felt so intensely overwhelming I thought I might explode. When the orgasm hit me, I nearly lost consciousness it was so intense. I have never felt anything so wonderfully satisfying in all my life. I don't know how to thank you enough for helping me experience that, especially for the first time."

Maggie leaned in and kissed Jordan tenderly. "No thanks necessary, sweetheart. You're an incredible lover. You've made me feel more alive in the past two hours than I've ever felt. Thank you for coming into my life."

Both women's attention was suddenly drawn toward the open window as the sound of a vehicle approaching broke them out of their desire-induced haze.

"Shit," Maggie said. "That's probably Jan."

Maggie quickly jumped up and grabbed her robe from behind the adjoining bathroom door. "I'll intercept her in the kitchen while you get dressed," she said.

Maggie donned her robe and ran through the living room to the kitchen as Jan walked in the door.

Jan raised her eyebrows. "A little afternoon delight?" she asked accusingly.

"What I was doing is none of your concern," Maggie replied.

Jan narrowed her eyes. She walked to the bar and poured herself a drink. Maggie tied the belt of her robe tighter around her.

"What did you find out at the hospital?"

Jan rested her backside against the bar and crossed her ankles. She casually sipped her drink.

"The doctors say Don is a lucky man. It appears he landed directly on his back and fractured a few vertebrae, but the X-rays don't show any permanent damage. He'll be laid up for a while, but they predict a full recovery."

"That's great news," Jordan said from the hallway leading to the bedrooms.

Jan sneered as Jordan came into view. "Got my answer," she said as she downed the rest of her drink and placed the glass on the bar with a resounding thud. "I've got work to do. I'll catch up with you two later," She turned and walked toward the barn.

* * *

Hi guys,

First, my apologies for not writing over the past few weeks. Things have been pretty crazy here. More on that in a minute.

Let me start with the most important part. Andi—you were right. Orgasms are awesome! Maggie and I made love for the first time today. I still don't have feelings in my legs, but man... when Maggie was inside of me it was the most incredible feeling in the world. I know, Kale. You're probably covering your eyes right now and screaming "too much information." What a wonderful feeling. More than anything guys, I am so in love! I never knew love could be so wonderful.

Kale—don't get your panties in a wad when you read this, but I told Maggie about my accident and the spinal implant. She doesn't know yet where I came from, but she knows about my paralysis. She wouldn't talk to me for three weeks after she first found out (I think it freaked her out a bit), but I finally explained the accident to her and how the implant works, and she is quite amazed at how medical science is so much more advanced than she thought it was. I hated lying to her but it will all come out in good time.

Maggie has broken things off with Jan. Neither of us felt comfortable beginning a relationship while she was still committed to Jan. She came clean with Jan about her feelings for me and Jan voluntarily moved into the bunkhouse to give her some space. Yep, Jan and I are now roommates. Go figure. I'm not real crazy about the idea, but it gives me an opportunity to keep an eye on her. Kale, I know you've encouraged me to give her the benefit of the doubt, but I still don't trust her. Anyway, things have been interesting with her living in the same bunkhouse.

Okay, it's late and I have early chores in the morning, so I'll sign off for now. I love you both. Know that I'm safe and I'm happy. I'll write again soon.

Jordan

CHAPTER 33

Early the next morning Jordan stepped into the common room of the bunkhouse just as Jan entered their living quarters from outside. After setting the coffee pot to brew, Jordan turned around and leaned against the counter and crossed her booted feet at the ankles. Her hands rested on the countertop on each side of her reclining torso.

"Are you always up and about this early?" Jordan asked.

Jan diverted her eyes from the mail she was reading to glance at Jordan. "Only when I have business to attend to," she replied abruptly. She returned to reading her letter.

Jordan allowed the next few moments to pass in silence as the coffee brewed. It wasn't long before a beep at the end of the brewing process signaled that her much-needed morning energy was ready for consumption. Jordan turned and retrieved two mugs from the cupboard and filled them both. She held one out to Jan.

Jan looked up from her letter once more and cocked an eyebrow at Jordan.

Jordan continued to hold the cup out to her. "Look, Jan. These past few weeks have been awkward at best. It seems we're going to be roommates for a while, so we might as well make an effort to at least be civil to one another."

Jan accepted the cup from Jordan. "Thanks," she said tersely.

An awkward silence fell between the women as they each sipped their coffee. Finally, Jan cleared her throat. "I, ah, I have some correspondence to take care of. Thanks again for the coffee."

Jordan nodded and watched as Jan retreated to her bedroom and firmly closed the door behind her.

* * *

Maggie was waiting for Jordan in the barn when she arrived a short time later.

"Hey you." Maggie greeted her with a smile. "Sleep well last night?"

Jordan grabbed her saddle and threw it across the back of a regal Mustang mare she had affectionately named Sally in honor of her own childhood horse. "I slept okay."

"Where are you going?" Maggie asked as she watched Jordan secure the saddle in place.

"Out to the new barn raising. I was thinking last night that it won't be long before snow falls. We don't have much time to finish the shell before that happens. I thought I'd get a head start before Dave and the rest of the crew shows up."

"Well then, I'm going with you," Maggie replied as she saddled her own horse. "Surely there's something I can do to help."

Jordan traced her gloved finger along the side of Maggie's face. "Sweetheart, I will have no problem finding something for you to do."

Maggie smiled and raised her eyebrows seductively. "I think you'll find me to be an efficient helper."

Jordan placed her foot in the stirrup and gracefully swung herself into the saddle. "Come on, then."

A moment later, the two women were making their way to the site of the new barn where they released their horses to graze in the corral then entered the old barn to retrieve Jordan's tools.

Maggie looked on as Jordan draped her tool belt over her waist and adjusted it into place. "You look very butch in that tool belt," she said suggestively.

Jordan grinned devilishly and retrieved a screwdriver from her belt. "Let me know if you need something screwed. I'd be happy to oblige."

Maggie reached forward and grabbed the front of Jordan's shirt, pulling her close. "I definitely have something you can screw," she said as their mouths met.

Maggie explored Jordan's mouth for several moments before she pulled back and smiled. "Well, lover, as much as I'd like to sample your handyman wares right now, we're bound to get caught if we take this much further. I will, however, hire your services later tonight."

Jordan chuckled and kissed Maggie passionately once more. "Tonight? A midnight rendezvous?"

"Once I have you in my bed, there's no way I'm letting you leave. Call it a sleepover, imprisonment, confinement, a hostage situation—call it anything you want, but you're not leaving."

"Sounds like fun, but aren't you worried about Jan missing me when I don't come home tonight?" Jordan asked.

"I broke things off with Jan nearly a month ago. She has to get used to it some time."

Jordan took Maggie's hand and placed a delicate kiss in the palm. "I like the way you think," she whispered hoarsely.

In the distance Jordan and Maggie could hear sounds of vehicles approaching. The hum of the motors grew louder as they neared. Finally, the sound of male voices competing with each other signaled that the work crew had arrived.

Jordan leaned in to kiss Maggie deeply once more before stepping back to allow Maggie to exit the barn before her.

*   *   *

Over the next several weeks, Jordan worked side by side with the carpenters to complete the outer structure of the barn while Maggie split her time between supervising the finishing touches inside the new barn and, with Jan's help, maintaining the day-to-day workings of the farm. Jan was uncharacteristically stoic during those weeks.

The relationship between Maggie and Jan became distant. Their communication focused on the workings of the farm. The relationship between Jan and Jordan was strained but polite, a fact that both surprised and unnerved Jordan, considering the veiled threats Jan had delivered to her the day she moved into the bunkhouse.

Just before Christmas, the barn was finished. To celebrate the occasion, Jordan erected a small Christmas tree inside the main foyer of the barn. The entire construction crew and their families were invited to a holiday celebration, which began with a wine and cheese social in the grand room of the new barn followed by a home-cooked dinner at the farmhouse.

The farmhouse was gaily decorated with lights and garland and a large Christmas tree stood proudly in the corner of the living room beside the fireplace. The tree was festively adorned with lights and ornaments, new and old, including several that Maggie had made as a child.

Dinner was a huge success, followed by a gift hunt for the crew's children in the main barn. Partway through the evening, Jan claimed she had a headache and returned to the bunkhouse.

It was well into the evening before the last guests departed. Jordan and Maggie walked them to their cars then returned eagerly to the house to take advantage of the blazing fireplace. They threw blankets and pillows on the floor near the romantic flames.

"Make yourself comfortable while I pour us some wine," Jordan suggested.

"Okay, love. I'll tend the fire," Maggie replied.

When Jordan entered the living room carrying two glasses of wine, she found Maggie sitting in front of the flames, surrounded by pillows. She approached Maggie and handed her one of the glasses.

Maggie smiled up into Jordan's face. "Thank you. Come sit with me," Maggie added as she patted the floor next to her.

Jordan sat on the floor next to Maggie and sipped her wine. She couldn't help but stare at the woman beside her.

"What are you thinking?"

"I'm thinking that I'm the luckiest woman in the world. I'm thinking that you are so beautiful you take my breath away. I'm thinking that I want to spend the rest of my life showing you how much I love you."

Maggie smiled and looked down into her wine glass, apparently deep in thought.

"My turn to ask you. What's on your mind?" Jordan said.

"I guess I'm waiting to wake up and discover this is all a dream. I've never known anyone like you. There's something so mysterious about you, yet I feel like I've known you forever. I feel safe with you, yet I hardly know anything about you. Who are you, Jordan Lewis?"

Jordan leaned in and kissed Maggie tenderly. "I am the woman who loves you with all her heart. I'm asking you to trust me. I promise I'll tell you everything you want to know in time. Just know that I will never hurt you."

Maggie yawned loudly.

"You're tired, love. It's been a very long and hectic day. Here, let me take your wine," Jordan said as she took Maggie's glass and placed it on the hearth. "Come here, lie with me. Close your eyes and enjoy the warmth of the fire."

Maggie rested her head on Jordan's shoulder and draped her arm across Jordan's mid-section as they lay together on the pillows. Jordan kissed Maggie's forehead. "Close your eyes. Relax. I'll keep you safe." Moments later they were fast asleep, caressed by each other and by the slow, flickering glow of the fire.

* * *

The next morning, Jordan woke up alone among the pillows strewn in front of the fireplace. She sat up and looked around groggily. When she realized where she was and how she came to be there, she smiled broadly.

"Are you going to sleep all day?" Maggie teased as she walked into the living room, fully dressed. She scooted away as Jordan playfully reached out for her legs. "Oh, no you don't," Maggie said.

"No fair," Jordan said as she lay back down among the pillows. A glance at the clock told her it was only 7:00 a.m. She watched Maggie button the cuffs of her shirt. "Where are you going so early this morning?" she asked.

"I'm going to take a ride out to the north pasture. Want to come?"

Jordan placed her hands behind her head. "Actually, I thought I'd fix the broken spindles on the porch then start breakfast while you're gone."

Maggie smiled. "You won't get an argument from me, but make it brunch if you would. I'll probably be gone for a few hours." She squatted down beside Jordan and kissed her. "I'll be back in a while, lover."

Jordan watched Maggie leave, then climbed to her feet and tried to iron out the wrinkles in her clothing with her hands before heading into the kitchen to set up the coffee pot. While the coffee brewed, she showered and dressed in clean clothes then went out to the porch to assess which spindles needed to be replaced.

"Jordan, do you know where my saddle is?"

Jordan turned to see Maggie strolling toward her from across the barnyard. As always, Jordan felt a rush of desire pass through her whenever Maggie was around. "You're still here? I thought you headed to the north pasture."

"I can't find my saddle. I've been looking for it for the past half hour."

"It isn't in the barn?"

"No. I put it on the stand yesterday when Shawny and I returned from our ride, but it's not there today. I was wondering if maybe you moved it."

"No, I didn't. In fact, I haven't been in the barn yet this morning. The saddler was here yesterday, wasn't he? Maybe he thought it needed repair and took it back to his shop."

Maggie stopped in front of Jordan. Her curly red hair splayed in several directions from beneath her cowboy hat. "Hmm. That's possible, I suppose. I need to check on the horses in the north pasture and you know Shawny doesn't do well with saddles he's not used to."

"Why don't you take my horse? I'm sure Sally would love the exercise."

Maggie smiled. "You're so sweet. I just might do that." Maggie stood on tiptoe and placed a kiss on Jordan's lips.

Jordan's arms immediately circled Maggie's waist and her hands found their way into the waistband of Maggie's jeans as the kiss deepened. Jordan's hands delved deep, firmly grasping Maggie's buttocks and pulling the woman close to her own heated core.

"Hmm," Jordan moaned. "I want you again."

Maggie drew her lips away from Jordan's to catch her breath. "God! If you keep that up, I'll never get out to the north pasture."

"You could always send Jan out to check on the horses while we make better use of our time," Jordan suggested slyly.

"I would, but she doesn't seem to be around right now. She's been behaving pretty erratically. One moment she's stuck to me like glue and the next, she's nowhere to be found."

Jordan picked up her hammer and dropped it into the sling attached to her tool-belt. "If you ask me, I think she's trying to win you back."

Maggie blushed then gently punched Jordan's shoulder. "She is not."

Jordan advanced one step in Maggie's direction and took the Maggie's face between her hands as their eyes locked. "Trust me love, she wants something. Why else would she stay?"

"Well, lover, you have nothing to worry about. She can try all she wants. It's you I love and nothing she can do will change that."

"The feeling's mutual. Now go on, take Sally to the north pasture. I'll call the saddler for you while you're gone, okay?"

Maggie turned to head back to the barn. "Okay. I'll see you in a few hours."

Jordan's eyes were glued to Maggie's swaying hips as she made her way back to the barn. After a few minutes, Maggie re-emerged riding Jordan's horse and waving her hat in Jordan's direction as she galloped toward the north pasture.

When Maggie was finally out of sight, Jordan entered the house and called the saddler. "Are you sure you don't have it? She left it on the rail by the horse stalls. It wasn't there this morning so I thought maybe you picked it up by mistake yesterday. No? Well, okay. I'm sure it's in the barn somewhere. Thanks anyway."

Jordan hung up the phone then went into the kitchen for a glass of water before continuing the repairs on the front porch. As she was filling her glass, she caught a glimpse of a figure covertly exiting the barn on foot. Suspicious, she decided to investigate.

So as to not call any attention to herself, Jordan sauntered toward the barn as she had done countless times before. She searched the horse stalls, but found nothing unusual. She even spent a short amount of time petting Maggie's horse, Shawny. Strangely, upon exiting Shawny's stall, she immediately noticed that Maggie's saddle was hanging on the rail, right where Maggie said she always put it.

Was this saddle really not here earlier today or are you losing your marbles, girlfriend?

The saddle was hanging over the rail with the right side facing the rider. Jordan inspected the saddle, then turned to walk away, but stopped when something caught her eye. She turned back and in one movement, she lifted the saddle, spun it around, and placed it back on the rail so that the left side of the saddle was facing outward.

Jordan lifted the stirrup and threw it over the top of the saddle, then reached down to grasp the belly strap. "What the hell? How did this get here?" Jordan reached under the saddle and released the buckle holding the belly strap. With the strap in hand, she crossed the barnyard toward the bunkhouse. She stopped before the bunkhouse door and banged loudly. "Open this goddamned door!"

The door flew open and Jordan came face to face with Jan. Jordan thrust the belly strap toward her. "Care to explain this?"

CHAPTER 34

Jan looked at the belly strap Jordan held in her hand. "It's a belly strap. Surely you know that," Jan said sarcastically.

Jordan turned the strap over in her hand. "No, I mean this."

On the underside of the strap was a metal burr, embedded deep in the leather.

Jan took the strap from Jordan and looked at it closely. "It looks like a burr to me."

"That's exactly what it is. Care to tell me how it got there?"

"How the hell am I supposed to know that?" Jan replied.

Jordan grabbed the strap from Jan and folded it in half. "This strap came off Maggie's saddle, which, by the way, went missing this morning and then miraculously reappeared just after I saw you sneak out of the barn. If she had ridden Shawny with this burr in the belly strap, he would have thrown her. She could have been seriously hurt—or worse."

Jan crossed her arms and cocked her head to one side. "So? Why are you telling me this?"

Jordan leaned in close. "Because if anything happens to Maggie, I will hold you personally responsible," she answered vehemently.

"Why would I want to harm Maggie?" Jan asked.

"That's the part I haven't figured out yet. I would have half-expected me to be your target, not her," Jordan replied.

Jan stepped in defiantly close. "Then I guess maybe you're the one who should watch her back."

"What's going on here?"

Jordan turned to see Maggie standing on the bunkhouse porch behind her. She turned back to Jan and stared directly into her face while addressing Maggie's question. "Nothing. Everything's fine. Jan and I were just making sure we're on the same page."

Jordan looked down at the strap in her hand then shoved it inside her jacket before she turned to face Maggie once more. "Are you ready for brunch?"

Maggie smiled broadly. "You bet I am. I'm famished." She looked over Jordan's shoulder. "Would you like to join us, Jan?" she asked.

"No, thanks," Jan replied. "I've had breakfast already."

Maggie linked her arm into the crook of Jordan's elbow. "All right then, let's eat."

* * *

"Hmm, this is wonderful. I thought you said you couldn't cook," Maggie said as she chewed a forkful of French toast.

Jordan chuckled. "This happens to be one of the few things I can make without poisoning myself. My friend Kale taught me how to make it."

"Kale? That's an unusual name. Male... right?"

"Definitely male," Jordan replied. "He's my best friend in the world, and my surrogate little brother. He's such a sweet guy. He's kind and considerate. We shared a house together for a couple of years. For the longest time he was convinced he was in love with me, until Andi came along."

"Andi? Pretty androgynous name. Male or female?"

"Andi is all girl. A very beautiful one at that, and smart. She's a physicist. Andi, Kale, and I all worked together at the lab." Jordan smiled wistfully as she thought about her friends.

"You haven't seen them in a while, I take it?"

Jordan pushed her food around on the plate as she shook her head. "No... and you're right, it's been a while. I didn't realize until now how much I miss them."

"Maybe we can invite them to visit. Do you think?"

Jordan looked at Maggie and smiled. "Maybe," she replied.

"When I came back from the north pasture, I noticed you found my saddle. Where was it?"

"Actually, I didn't find it. It was right where you always put it."

"No way. I swear to you, it was not there when I went to saddle Shawny this morning."

"For what it's worth, I believe you," Jordan said.

"Who would have taken it? And who brought it back?"

"I'm guessing it was Jan." John is on vacation until after the holidays and she's the only other one around besides you and me."

"What would she want with my saddle?" Maggie questioned.

"That's what I was trying to find out when you interrupted us a while ago."

"What I interrupted was some type of confrontation. I'm not blind, you know. I could have sworn Jan was dealing okay with the breakup. Want to tell me what you were discussing?" Maggie prompted.

Jordan sat back in her chair. "Nothing, really. I was just making sure she and I understood each other."

Maggie narrowed her eyes at Jordan. "Why don't I believe you?"

Jordan stood and collected their dishes, then placed an inviting kiss on Maggie's lips. "Trust me, sweetheart. I'm just looking out for things, especially for you."

"I don't need looking out for. I'm a big girl, and I can take care of myself."

Jordan carried the coffee pot back to the table and refilled their cups. "I'm sure you can, but it never hurts to have help. Tell me about your ride this morning. How are the horses?"

"I stopped at the new barn to check on the foals. They're doing really well."

Jordan sat down and enjoyed her coffee as Maggie talked excitedly about the foals, the farm, and life in general. For Maggie's benefit, she maintained the smile on her face, but inside, she was seething.

Jan, I won't let you screw this up. That's a promise.

* * *

Maggie sat at the kitchen table studying several official-looking documents. As she read, she jotted notes on a pad of paper nearby. She looked up at the sound of stamping feet on the porch just outside the kitchen door.

Jordan pushed the kitchen door open and stepped inside. "Damn, it's colder than a witch's tit out there," she cussed as she bent over to remove her boots.

Maggie chuckled. "And just how cold is a witch's tit?" she asked coyly.

"Cold enough to produce milkshakes." Jordan grinned. "Sometimes I think your parents have the right idea. Florida in

January sounds like a wonderful thing." Jordan hung her coat up on one of the hooks by the door then rubbed her hands together as she approached Maggie. She stood behind her and looked over her shoulder.

"What are you reading?" she asked.

Maggie glanced up at Jordan. "I'm just reviewing the Planning Commission guidelines before I draft the proposal for the riding school," she said, returning her attention to the documents.

"I can imagine there will be a lot of rules and regulations we'll have to follow and safety upgrades to make the farm safe and suitable for the kids," Jordan said.

"I'm afraid you're right. The problem I'm having, though, is trying to put limits on the definition of 'handicapped' that don't exclude too many of the more disabled children. I really don't want to limit any child with a disability from taking lessons, but I guess it will be unavoidable if we can't make it totally safe for them."

Jordan leaned over Maggie as she read and nuzzled Maggie's neck.

"Yeeow!" Maggie screamed as she squirmed away. "Your nose is cold."

Jordan laughed evilly as she shoved her cold hands into the neckline of Maggie's shirt.

Maggie jumped up from the table. "Jordan Lewis," she shouted. "Stop that!"

Jordan was apologetic as she opened her arms to Maggie. "I'm sorry, love. Come here and I'll make it up to you."

Maggie stepped into the circle of Jordan's arms. After a few moments, she relaxed and returned the hug.

Without warning, Jordan pulled Maggie's shirt up and planted her cold hands in the middle of Maggie's back.

"Ah!" Maggie protested as she wiggled out of Jordan's embrace. "Why, you little shit," she yelled.

Jordan grinned. "Uh-oh. Time for a hasty retreat." She made a quick exit into the living room with Maggie hot on her tail. Once in the living room, she threw herself on the couch and put her arms up to protect herself as Maggie grabbed a throw pillow and pummeled her with it. In between hits, Jordan managed to work a pillow out from behind her to enter into the battle. Before long they were both on their feet and engaged in a full-fledged pillow fight. Many minutes later, and laughing so hard their sides hurt, the two women dropped side-by-side onto the couch.

Jordan moved to the end of the couch and half-reclined. She beckoned to Maggie. "Come here, you."

Maggie delved into Jordan's arms. They lay there entwined with Maggie's cheek resting on Jordan's chest.

"Hmm, this feels good," Maggie said. "I love listening to your heart beat."

Jordan kissed the top of Maggie's head. "It beats only for you, love."

"How is it that you so easily walked into my life and stole my heart?" Maggie asked.

"Actually, I didn't walk into your life... I transported into it. You see, I'm really a scientist from the future and I traveled here via a time machine to intentionally invade your life," Jordan replied. She waited for what felt like an eternity for Maggie to absorb what she had just said.

Maggie raised her head and looked directly into Jordan's eyes. She smiled widely. "You're such a kook sometimes," she said. She leaned in and kissed Jordan on the nose then laid her head back onto Jordan's chest. "Don't ever change, sweetheart. I love you just the way you are."

* * *

February 16th, 2019

Dear Andi and Kale,

Damn, it's cold here! I don't remember it being this cold in 2105. I never thought I would say thank God for global warming. Anyway, time is becoming shorter with each passing day. We're only six weeks away from Maggie's death. I find myself being very protective of her. I am so in love with her, she owns me, heart and soul. She is the most beautiful creature on the face of the earth. How is it I'm so lucky to have found her? How is it I'm so lucky that she actually loves me too?

Guys, I've said this before, but I don't think it's a coincidence that I found those diaries. I truly believe Maggie had been trying to contact me for several years, even way back when I was a kid and having nightmares. The diaries provided a portal for her to reach out to me. Kale, you'll remember when the dreams first started they were just that—dreams. I was more of an observer than anything else. I think Maggie was planting those dreams in my mind in an attempt to contact me. Later on, they became more like visions and I appeared to take a more and more active role in them. Well, several of those visions have happened while I've been here. I can't help but think that I dreamed about them because my traveling back in time made me part of Maggie's past. Does that make sense? Anyway, talk about déjà-vu!

Okay, I just wanted to keep you up-to-date on what's going on with me. I am in love... way over my head in love and I'm enjoying every minute of it. I have never been happier and I owe it all to you. You have my undying love and gratitude. I'll write again as D-day approaches. I love you guys, and I miss you lots. Later!

Jordan

* * *

Maggie and Jordan had chosen to spend a cold winter evening reading in bed. Maggie lowered the book she was reading into her lap and looked at the woman sitting in bed beside her. "Jordan?"

Jordan looked away from her book. "Yeah?"

"Will you marry me?"

Jordan's head snapped back. She was surprised by Maggie's unexpected question and was left speechless.

"Don't look so shocked."

"Uh... Um... I'm sorry. Your question just took me by surprise," Jordan replied.

"I don't know why it should. I mean, you've been here for five months now, right? I don't know about you, but I pretty much felt the attraction the minute I set eyes on you."

Jordan nodded. "I think I was in love with you before I met you," she said.

"Come on," Maggie said. "How could you possibly have loved me before you met me?"

Jordan was so tempted to confess all to Maggie at that very minute. "Let's just say an angel visited me in my sleep. She had wild curly red hair, and looked an awful lot like you. She told me everything about you. I couldn't help but fall in love the moment I saw you."

Maggie smiled. "I love you so much. I've never felt this way about anyone before. I can't begin to tell you what your smile does to me. There are so many emotions that run through me when you look at me. It seems that you can see deep into my soul."

Jordan leaned in and placed a delicate kiss on Maggie's lips. "I'm so glad you love me, Mags. I've wanted this for so long. You have no idea what I've been through to get here."

Maggie blinked rapidly to clear the moisture from her eyes. "I do love you. I love you beyond anything in my life's experience. I want so badly to be the object of your desire, your partner in heart and in soul. I dream of a life together in body, in spirit, and in name."

Jordan took Maggie's hand and kissed it. She felt Maggie quiver as she looked up into her eyes. "I want to share your life, my love. I want to laugh with you and cry with you. I want to help you achieve everything you've ever wanted in life. I want to be by your side through all the good things, and the bad things too. I want to spend every day of the rest of my life looking into your beautiful green eyes, even when we're old and gray and rocking beside each other in our chairs on the front porch, even when we have just one tooth between us and you have to change my diapers. If that isn't love, I don't know what is."

Maggie wiped a tear from the corner of her eye as she laughed at Jordan's words. "You're such a goofball sometimes. So, as one member of the mutual admiration society to another, does that mean you'll marry me?"

Jordan grinned. "Yes, I'll marry you."

Maggie squealed as she threw her book on the bedside table and stood on the bed. She danced around joyously as Jordan laughed.

"Now who's the goofball?" Jordan exclaimed.

Maggie threw herself at Jordan and straddled her lap. She kissed Jordan soundly. "I love you so much, Jordan. Thank you for loving me, too."

"That's so easy to do. I was gone the first time you visited me in my dreams."

Maggie looked confused. "You're a complicated woman. You talk in riddles sometimes. I realize there are things about you I don't know, but my heart is telling me to trust you anyway."

Jordan nodded. "Thank you."

Maggie grinned. "I'll call the justice of the peace tomorrow and—"

"Whoa," Jordan said. "Slow down a bit. Why don't we plan this out? I want it to be special, not just the two of us standing in front of a total stranger saying 'I do.'"

And besides, I still need to save your life before we can spend the rest of it together.

"I don't want to put it off forever."

"Neither do I," Jordan replied. "Let's wait until the weather breaks, say, maybe April or May?"

Maggie nodded. "Okay. I'll compromise. My birthday is April 16. That's about a month from now. I'm still going to call the justice of the peace tomorrow though. It's not too early to begin planning!"

Jordan smiled. "What am I getting myself into here?" she teased. "I hear redheads are notorious for determination and hot tempers."

Maggie leaned down and whispered into Jordan's ear. "I'll show you hot, but it won't be my temper."

"Oh, God!" Jordan exclaimed as she scooted down in the bed, taking Maggie with her.

CHAPTER 35

Jordan walked across the yard and stepped into the barn. She stopped short when she heard voices.

"Did you hear the news?"

Jordan recognized John's voice as she waited for the reply to his question.

"News? No. I'm pretty much out of the loop these days."

Jan. Jordan's interest was piqued as she covertly listened to the conversation.

"Maggie was in here about an hour ago to take Shawny for his morning ride, and she told me she and Jordan are getting married."

"What?" Jan shouted. "Say that again!"

"I said Maggie and Jordan are getting married. Apparently, she proposed last night and Jordan said yes. Maggie was all smiles this morning. I haven't seen her that happy in a long time."

"Jesus Christ," Jan said. "Did she say when?"

"She said something about having it on her birthday." John replied.

"April 16," Jan whispered.

John looked at the date on his watch. "It looks like we're going to have a party in about a month."

"Damn," Jan said.

"Look, Jan. I know you and Maggie used to be together, but maybe you should just accept that she's in love with Jordan now and let it go."

"I don't have to accept anything, old man. I knew that Lewis woman would be bad news the moment I laid eyes on her. I won't just sit back and let her take everything away from me."

Jan's attempt to intimidate John apparently did not sit well with him. "Well, I reckon I wouldn't be making an enemy of Jordan seeing as she'll be your boss soon."

"We'll see about that," Jan spat.

Jordan heard footsteps coming in her direction, so she quickly stepped out of the barn and pretended to enter for the first time, just as Jan was leaving. "Good morning, Jan," she said cheerily.

"Fuck you." Jan stamped past Jordan and headed to the bunkhouse.

Jordan watched her go as she continued to enter the barn. Stopping face to face with John, she asked, "What's up with her?"

"She isn't very happy with the fact that you and Maggie are getting married."

"I see," Jordan replied.

"I think it's grand," John said and extended his hand to Jordan. "Congratulations."

"Thank you John." Jordan looked around. "What can I do to help you today?"

"You don't need to help me with anything, Miss Jordan," John replied.

Jordan put her hand on John's shoulder. "John, I'd appreciate it if you cut the 'Miss Jordan' shit, okay? I'm still just Jordan, and I still want to pull my weight around here. So, what do you say you and I clean the stalls together?"

John smiled. "You got it, Jordan."

* * *

Jordan spent the entire day in the barn with John, cleaning stalls, stacking hay bales in the loft, and doing general repairs. When the sun began to set, she called it a day and sent John home. As she crossed the yard toward the house, she noticed a truck approaching the barn from the north pasture.

The truck was soon close enough to read the name on the door. J. T. Robinson, Artesian Well Drilling.

The well in the north pasture! Maggie, do you realize what you have just done?

Jordan immediately went in search of Maggie. "Maggie, where are you?" she called when she entered the kitchen.

"In here," Maggie replied from the living room.

Jordan found her in the far corner of the living room, sitting at the desk organizing paperwork. Maggie turned to face her, smiling broadly.

"Hey, baby," she said.

Jordan forced herself to remain calm. She realized that there was no way Maggie could have realized the ramifications of placing the well in the north pasture. "Hi, love. I just saw an artesian well-drilling truck come out of the north pasture."

"They're finished already? That was fast," Maggie replied.

"I didn't realize you were having a well drilled."

Maggie shrugged. "I almost didn't remember about it myself," she said. "It's been scheduled since last fall. It was supposed to be finished at about the same time the new barn was, but Jack Robinson fell behind due to some health issues. By the time he was able to get back to work it was winter, so it had to wait until now."

Jordan nodded. "I see. Where in the north pasture did you have it dug?"

Maggie continued to sort her paperwork while talking to Jordan. "That's the unfortunate part. It's pretty far from the barn. Jack couldn't find a spring to tap into any closer. I'm afraid we'll have to lay pipeline between the new well and the barn for it to be useful."

"So, it's out in the middle of the field?" Jordan asked.

"Unfortunately, yes." Maggie stopped what she was doing and turned to face Jordan. "Why the sudden interest in the well?" she asked.

Jordan recalled the present location of the working artesian well on the property nearly one hundred years in the future as being within ten feet of the new barn's location, and wondered if the contractor had even tested for springs closer to the barn. Claiming dry land in the immediate vicinity of the barn was certainly a way to make additional money off Maggie by laying pipeline.

"Did the contractor produce evidence that the land is dry near the barn?"

"No. I just assumed he was right. What are you implying?"

"I'm working on a hunch here. Could I ask you to humor me by getting another opinion?"

"I... I guess so," Maggie replied hesitantly, "but I just paid $3,000 to have that well dug."

"If my hunch holds true, it will cost a lot less money to have the well re-dug than it will to hire Robinson to lay pipeline."

"Okay. You're the boss on this one."

"Thank you, love," Jordan replied as she kissed the top of Maggie's head. In doing so, she glanced at the paperwork laid out across Maggie's desk. "What are you doing?" she asked.

"Ugh. Tax time. Every year I have to sort out receipts and bills in preparation for having the taxes done. I hate it."

"How about next year, I set up a spread sheet on the computer so you can keep track of debits and credits as they occur? Then, at the end of the year, all you'll have to do is print out reports in any flavor you want. Sound good?" Jordan asked as she glanced again at the paperwork. As she looked away, something caught her eye. It was a letter from Pritchard and Yeats law firm, the firm that handled Maggie's father's estate.

"That sounds wonderful. But I'm afraid I'm not very computer literate," Maggie replied.

Jordan continued to stare at the paperwork—at one document in particular.

Where have I seen that logo before?

Jordan replied, "It's easy. I wouldn't mind holding your hand through it until you're comfortable doing it yourself."

Maggie grinned. "I'm game. Any reason to hold hands with you is good."

Jordan committed the name above the logo to memory in the event it came to her later. "Okay. I'm going to leave you alone so you can finish what you're doing. How about I start dinner?"

Maggie was immediately on her feet. "Baby, no offense, but I think I'll make dinner."

Jordan tried to look offended, but was secretly glad. The last time she tried to make dinner, they ended up ordering takeout. "I really don't mind."

"The paperwork can wait. I'll make dinner," Maggie said.

"Well then, let me help, okay?"

"Only if you promise not to burn the water this time," Maggie teased.

"Deal." Jordan chuckled.

* * *

As March 29 approached, Jordan became increasingly agitated. She felt very frustrated by the knowledge that Maggie was about to die. She had to find a way to prevent it, yet she couldn't change the events leading up to it. All she could do was keep herself busy and hope she was prepared when the time came.

Jan had made herself scarce since she discovered Jordan and Maggie were to be married. She spent a great deal of time training and exercising the horses and avoided the immediate area of the farmhouse during daylight hours. Jordan did, however, notice that Jan spent a significant amount of time in the barn after John left for the day and after Jordan and Maggie retired to the house. Each morning, Jordan rose early and went to the barn to search for evidence of what Jan was up to, but each time, she failed to find anything. Finally, on Wednesday, March 27, only two days before Maggie's death, Jordan allowed her suspicions to get the best of her. She sought out Jan in the bunkhouse to confront her.

Jordan knocked loudly on the bunkhouse door and waited for Jan to answer. After several moments of silence, Jordan knocked again. Still no answer. Finally, she reached down and turned the knob. The door opened easily.

The bunkhouse was dark. Jordan stepped inside and turned the light on. Everything was neat and orderly. Jordan walked across the common room and pushed open the door to Jan's bedroom. She stepped inside and turned on the lamp that was on top of a nearby dresser. Again, Jordan found nothing out of place in the room. With paranoia running rampant in her brain, Jordan began searching drawers for anything that appeared suspicious. A thorough search of each dresser drawer yielded nothing. She sighed deeply and was about to leave the room when she noticed the bedside table had a built-in drawer. She quickly crossed the room and pulled the drawer open.

Jordan stared at the contents of the drawer for several moments before reaching in to extract an envelope. She held the envelope up and realized it was addressed to Maggie, but what was most disturbing were the return address and the familiar logo below it— Pritchard and Yeats, Attorneys at Law. Jordan's hands shook as she opened the flap and removed the letter inside. The letter was dated October 29, 2018.

Damn! That was more than four months ago.

Jordan closed her eyes and tried to remember back four months and suddenly realized why the logo looked so familiar to her. This must have been the letter Jan was reading the morning after she moved into the bunkhouse. *That's where I've seen the logo before.* She read the letter and became angrier and angrier with each line of text.

"Maggie needs to see this," she decided as she folded the letter and placed it back in the envelope.

Jordan closed the drawer of the nightstand and turned the lights out behind her. She left the bunkhouse then charged directly toward the house. Maggie was in the kitchen preparing dinner.

"Hey, baby," Maggie said. "Good news. The new well contractor just called and said they hit pay dirt, or pay water as the case may be. They found a water source exactly where you told them to drill, just off the corner of the new barn. How did you know?"

"That is good news," Jordan replied. "I hate to minimize it, but I have some news of my own that's more important, but unfortunately, not as good."

Maggie frowned. "What is it?"

Jordan handed the letter to Maggie.

"What's this?" she asked as she opened it.

"Read it," Jordan encouraged.

Maggie extracted the letter from the envelope and read it out loud.

October 29, 2018

Miss Downs, please find below a description of the information you requested relative to a recent change made to the deed of the horse farm in Shelburne, VT, based on the wishes of your father, Gary Downs.

Based on the addendum, ownership of the farm is hereby transferred to Miss Margaret Michele Downs, with secondary ownership transferred to Miss Janneal Safford in the event Margaret Downs predeceases her. Since Gary Downs is the author of the above-mentioned addendum, any changes to the intent and contents must be requested only by him, until he is deceased, at which time, changes may be made by Miss Margaret Downs and approved by Miss Janneal Safford.

Please feel free to call our office if you have any questions about this document.

Sincerely,

Jeffrey Pritchard

"Oh, my God!" Maggie exclaimed when she finished reading the document. "This is the document I asked them to send to me months ago. I totally forgot about it. Where did you find this?"

"In the nightstand drawer next to Jan's bed," Jordan replied.

"Jan? How did she get it?"

"She must have intercepted the mail, Maggie. That's the only thing I can think of. She obviously has a vested interest in making sure the deed stays exactly as it is."

Maggie folded the paper and angrily shoved it back into the envelope. "Well, she has another think coming to her. I'll call Daddy right now and insist he has this changed immediately. How dare she?"

"Do you have any idea where she is right now? I have a thing or two I want to discuss with her as well," Jordan said.

"Unfortunately, you'll have to wait a couple of days. She's visiting friends out of town. She should be back on Friday. At least that's what she told me."

"Damn," Jordan responded.

* * *

After dinner that evening, Jordan made excuses about a project she was working on in the barn and left Maggie to work through the tax papers. Jordan secreted herself in the hayloft and waited. She had a hunch that Jan was not really out of town. Near 9:00 p.m., as Jordan fought to stay awake, the door of the barn slowly opened. Jordan had positioned herself such that she had a clear view of the main area of the barn and sat as still as possible so as to not call attention to herself in the loft.

Jordan watched as Jan crept slowly into the barn and walked directly to Maggie's saddle. Jordan's view of the saddle was blocked by Jan's body, so she was forced to wait patiently until Jan covertly exited the barn before she could investigate what she had done. She wanted so badly to rush Jan, tackle her to the ground, then pummel her senseless with her fists, but she had promised Kale not to mess with any events other than rescuing Maggie from the edge of the cliff.

When the barn door closed behind Jan, Jordan descended from the loft and approached Maggie's saddle. She inspected it carefully. Jan had cut the right stirrup strap nearly clean through. It was hanging by barely a quarter of an inch of leather.

"Damn you, Jan," Jordan said. She was shaking violently and had to consciously stop herself from going after the woman. Instead, she paced back and forth across the barn to calm down and think.

Finally, Jordan made a decision. She took Maggie's saddle and put it into the repair pile for the saddler to collect. She would call him in the morning and ask him to collect it right away and return it by the end of the day on Thursday. She decided not to tell Maggie what had happened. She hoped that by removing the saddle from use, she could also eliminate the possibility that Maggie would die. Satisfied that she had an effective plan, Jordan left the barn and returned to the house.

CHAPTER 36

On Thursday morning, Jordan dropped Maggie off at the new barn then drove the old truck across the north pasture. The sound of shovels rattling in the back kept time with each bump she encountered. Her mind was occupied with the events of the previous night when she had witnessed Jan sabotaging Maggie's saddle. She was thankful Maggie didn't argue with her about riding to the new barn instead of taking Shawny out on her usual morning run. She was hoping the saddler would keep his word and collect the saddle that morning and return it by the end of the day as he promised he would.

Finally, she spotted a mound of dirt in the distance and steered the truck in that direction. After a few minutes, she pulled the truck along side the dirt mound, turned off the ignition, and climbed out. Jordan walked over to the mound and peered over it to see the hole that had been dug in the earth by the well drillers. It was approximately three feet in diameter and was so deep that she couldn't see the bottom.

"It's not going to fill itself, I guess." Jordan walked back to the truck to retrieve a shovel from the bed. Within moments, she was hard at work shoveling dirt from the mound into the hole. For the first hour she was unable to hear the dirt hit the bottom. Several hours later, the bottom of the hole became visible.

Jordan pulled a bandana from her back pocket to wipe the sweat from her brow. She looked up and guessed from the position of the sun that it was near 2:00 p.m. She had been shoveling for five hours. Two hours later, she scooped up the last shovel of dirt and held it above the filled-in hole.

"This one is for you, Sally."

Jordan tipped the head of the shovel and allowed the dirt to slowly slip to the earth. She then stood on top of the small mound covering the hole and packed the soil firmly with her boots.

Covered with sweat and dirt, Jordan carried the shovel back to the truck and tossed it wearily into the bed. She then climbed into the cab and drove away.

Twenty minutes later, Jordan parked the truck in front of the barn and climbed out of the driver's seat. She went directly to check out the saddler's handiwork on Maggie's saddle. To her dismay, the saddle was still in the repair pile.

"Damn it," she shouted.

She headed toward the house and climbed the two steps leading to the porch. Jordan removed her cowboy hat as she pushed the kitchen door open and stepped inside. The tempting aroma of freshly baked cookies was stronger than her willpower as she reached for a cookie. Next to their cooling rack on the countertop, Jordan spotted a note from Maggie.

Jord—the saddler called and apologized for not making it out today. He had a family emergency. He said he'd be here by noon tomorrow.

Jordan read the note and cursed again under her breath. "Damn. I'll just need to get up with Maggie tomorrow and convince her to take Sally out again since her saddle won't be usable on Shawny."

"Jordan, is that you?" Maggie called.

"In the kitchen."

"Hey, you'll ruin your dinner," Maggie said as Jordan took a large bite of the tasty cookie.

"No chance of that happening. I'm famished."

Maggie approached Jordan and tried to wrap her arms around her waist. Jordan took a step back. "Whoa. I'm dirty and sweaty from working in the field."

Maggie crossed her arms. "Well then, get in the shower. Dinner will be ready soon."

Jordan saluted while clicking her heels. "Yes ma'am!" She kissed Maggie on the cheek. "I'll be back shortly."

In their bedroom, Jordan stripped off her dirty clothes and threw them into the hamper. She reached behind the shower curtain and turned on the water. Once in the shower, Jordan relished the pulsating warm liquid. She basked in the feel of the needle-like spray as it massaged muscles worn sore by what seemed like endless shoveling.

Jordan remained under the spray for a long time with her eyes closed and her hands braced on the sides of the shower as the water rinsed the dirt and grime from her body. Suddenly, she felt a presence behind her. She willed her eyes to remain closed as she felt hands slide across her hips and abdomen while a soft, supple body molded itself against her from behind. One hand slipped downward, coming to rest in the curly patch below her navel while the other hand pressed firmly on her abdomen.

Whoa, this feels way too familiar. Didn't I dream this? Did I dream it because I'm now part of Maggie's past and this really did happen? Jordan allowed her forehead to contact the shower wall as Maggie's fingers slipped between her folds. She moaned loudly. *Oh, God, that feels so good. Just enjoy it, Lewis. Shut up and enjoy it.*

* * *

Jordan reached over to silence the offending peal when the alarm went off at 6:00 a.m. As she rolled back into bed, she noticed a hollow in the pillow beside her, an indentation that clearly indicated someone had been sleeping in that spot. She smiled and reached over to discover the pillow was still warm.

You haven't been gone long, my love, have you?

An intense feeling of déjà vu washed over her. She stared at the ceiling trying to remember when she had experienced this sequence of events before. Suddenly, she sat up in bed.

"Maggie!"

Jordan realized she had slept too long and had missed the opportunity to ensure that Maggie took Sally instead of Shawny for her morning ride. Jordan grabbed her robe from the back of the bedroom door and headed toward the kitchen.

"Maggie? Maggie, where are you? Clothes... I need clothes." She started rummaging through the dresser. After a moment, she found a pair of jeans and a button-up flannel shirt that she hurriedly put on as she sat on the edge of the bed. She slipped on a pair of cowboy boots that had been sitting partially under the bed.

Jordan ran to the kitchen and grabbed her jacket from the hook by the door. *Please don't let me be too late, please!* Jordan shrugged into her jacket and headed for the door when she noticed the note sitting on the counter. With intense dread, she opened the note and read the all too familiar words.

My Dearest Jordan,

I awoke this morning and saw your beautiful face beside me. Last night was so incredible. How did you have the energy to make love after working so hard yesterday filling the well? I wanted desperately to wake you with kisses and make love to you all day long, but I knew you needed to sleep. Thank you for filling the well. You were right. Putting it in the middle of the north pasture was a bad idea. How did you become so wise, lover? I've decided to take an early morning ride along the west ridge. I anticipate making love with you upon my return.

I love you with all my heart, Maggie.

Fear settled into the pit of her stomach as a searing pain shot through her temples. She grabbed the edge of the counter to steady herself as a loud ringing filled her ears and dizziness caused her balance to falter. Her knuckles were white as she held on. She closed her eyes to lessen the wave of nausea that invaded her stomach while the room seemed to spin. Suddenly, a vision rushed in and sent shock waves deep to her heart. In her mind's eye, she saw Maggie lying at the bottom of a cliff.

"Why did I sleep so late? I've got to stop her. Please tell me she didn't use her defective saddle."

Panic clenched Jordan's heart. She jumped to her feet and hurriedly made her way out into the yard. Within moments, she had run the distance between the house and barn and flung the barn door open. It resounded with a bang as it flew into the side of the nearest horse stall. She checked the repair pile and realized Maggie's saddle was no longer there.

Damn it! Damn it all to hell!

Jordan desperately searched several empty stalls until she came across one containing a magnificent mustang steed.

Jordan talked soothingly to the animal as she first threw a blanket and then a saddle over the horse's back. "Come on, big guy, we've got a job to do." Ten minutes later, she led the horse out of the stall and climbed into the saddle. With a quick jab to the horse's ribs, she was out of the barn and on her way in a full gallop across the barnyard heading for the western edge of the property bounded by Lake Champlain. As Jordan rode across the plains, she agonized over how long it was taking to cover the distance between the house and the lake. In her desperation, she was oblivious to the biting cold that chafed her cheeks as she rode.

I've forgotten how large this property is. God, please let me reach her in time.

Nearly a half hour later, the frozen lake came into view. The sight encouraged Jordan to dig in her heels and push her steed nearly beyond its limits as their speed increased and she felt airborne.

Maggie, please stay away from the edge. Please! I'm coming, my love, I'm coming. Please let me reach her in time.

Suddenly, Jordan heard a shot ring out. Intense fear filled her mind as she dug in her heels and urged a faster gait from her steed.

A few moments later, Jordan approached the last knoll between herself and the cliffs. As she crested the knoll, the sight she saw robbed her of breath. There before her was a rider-less horse. Jordan's heart fell within her chest.

"Maggie! Oh, my God, no," she screamed. Again, she dug in her heels. Within seconds, she reached the edge of the cliff and brought the steed to an abrupt stop. Jordan's feet hit the snow before the animal was fully settled. The impact of hitting the ground so suddenly caused her to tumble into the snow.

Jordan climbed to her feet and limped to the edge of the cliff. She threw herself to the ground as she reached the edge and peered over the side. At the bottom, among snow-covered boulders and rocks, lay a decidedly female form. Her arms and legs were askew at odd angles and her long red curls splayed out around her head.

"Maggie," she whispered breathlessly.

Jordan looked around desperately for an easy way down the cliff and spotted a worn trail about thirty yards away. She scrambled to her feet and made her way along the edge of the cliff until she reached the path. Clumsily, she began her descent, falling several times along the way on the slippery downhill slope. Jordan was terrified that she was already too late. "Maggie, baby, please hold on. I'm coming. Please hold on."

It seemed like an eternity before Jordan finally reached the bottom. She struggled to climb over the rocks and boulders that lay in her path and slipped several times on the ice-covered obstructions. Finally, Maggie was but a few feet away. Jordan called out to the injured woman as she closed the distance between them. "Maggie, Maggie, talk to me, sweetheart. Say something, please." She could see the woman's labored breathing rise from her mouth in a cloud of steam as her chest rose and fell unevenly.

Finally, Jordan reached Maggie and knelt by her side. She took special care not to move her, in order to avoid further injury to her neck or back. Instead, she gently brushed the curly locks from Maggie's brow and gently held Maggie's face. She leaned forward so that she was but a hair's breadth away. "Maggie, I'm here. Hold on, my love. Please don't leave me. John will find your horse. Help will be here soon. Please hold on."

Maggie's green eyes fluttered open.

Jordan gasped and fought back the sobs as renewed hope filled her heart. She took Maggie's hand in her own and brought the bloodied appendage to her lips to kiss it tenderly. Jordan's eyes never left Maggie's.

Maggie smiled. "Jordan," she rasped.

Jordan leaned down so she could more clearly hear what Maggie was saying. "I'm here, love."

Maggie took a ragged breath and her brow furrowed in pain, but her eyes remained locked with Jordan's. Finally, she spoke once more in a low, raspy breath. "Jordan, I love you. I always have... through all time."

Jordan's throat was nearly closed with emotion as she held back a sob. "I love you too, Maggie. I always will. Please don't leave me. I need you, my love. Please don't leave me." Tears fell from Jordan's eyes as she lowered her face to Maggie's and tenderly kissed her lips. As she raised her head, she watched the life ebb from the beautiful green eyes below her. Still holding Maggie's hand, Jordan fell back onto her knees. Her head fell back and a long, painful wail escaped her.

"No!"

* * *

Jordan's heart was shattered as she crawled out from beneath the workbench in the tack room and slowly made her way to the other end of the barn. She stopped several times to steady herself when the sobs made it difficult for her to breathe. Finally, she reached her destination and fell to her knees on the dirt floor. It felt as though an eternity passed before she found herself floating along the tunnel.

"She's back," Andi said as she watched Jordan's form appear on the platform. It was obvious from Jordan's body language that she was in a great deal of pain. Andi waited for the rings to become still before she reached into the sphere and helped Jordan climb down from the platform. Jordan immediately wrapped her arms around Andi while heart-wrenching sobs tore through her.

"It's okay, Jordan. Cry it out," Andi said as she rubbed her friend's back. "Sweetie, we missed you so much!"

Kale approached the pair after powering down the machine and wrapped his arms around both women. The trio of friends stood in their embrace for several long moments while Jordan regained her composure. Finally, she was able to speak.

"I failed," Jordan began. "I was so close. I rode after her, but I was too late." Jordan looked at Kale with haunted eyes. "What will it take, Kale? Why is this so hard?"

Kale inhaled deeply. "Jord, I know you don't want to hear this, but maybe you can't save her. Maybe she was supposed to die when she did."

Jordan shook her head vigorously. "No. I won't accept that. I need to try again."

"Well, the first thing you're going to do is have something to eat and then tell us what happened while you were gone. Maybe we can learn something from it to get the timing right the next time."

* * *

While Jordan picked at the salad Andi prepared for her she relayed her heartbreaking account of why she was too late to save Maggie.

"I overslept. Do you believe it? The love of my life died because I overslept. I was exhausted after filling the well in the north pasture, that's why. I was being selfish, thinking only of myself, and now Maggie is dead."

Andi reached out to cover Jordan's hand with her own. "Don't think that way."

Kale shook his head. "I warned you about playing with the time continuum. Everything you undo in the past has the potential to affect thousands, if not millions of lives in the future. Hell! Just you being there is displacing molecules that weren't displaced before. Your presence alone can change the course of history, never mind you intentionally changing something that happened back then. That's the primary reason I'm worried about you trying to save Maggie. Her not dying when she was supposed to could have significant consequences."

Jordan put her fork down and removed the napkin from her lap. "All I know is that I have to try again. Forget what I may or may not have changed in previous visits. I need to go back again, and this time, do things differently. And as far as not saving Maggie is concerned, that's not even an option. End of discussion."

Andi patiently listened to the conversation between Jordan and Kale while trying to stay neutral. She understood that Jordan was approaching things from an emotional angle and couldn't quite grasp the technical points Kale was making. Andi saw an opportunity to inject her own opinion when Jordan sat back and crossed her arms before her in a gesture of defiance.

"Jordan, I know how you're feeling and I realize how important it is for you to do what you can for Maggie, but Kale has some valid points. You've already gone back three times, and each time you've had an impact on that time frame. From what you've told us, the first two visits were relatively harmless, mostly because you didn't come in contact with anyone, but this last time is another story. You interacted with people, built relationships, and yes—you changed history."

Jordan frowned as she listened to Andi. She opened her mouth to speak, but was interrupted.

"Before you say anything, let me finish. My biggest concern about sending you back a fourth time is that since you spent five months there this last time, there's a very good possibility you'll actually run into yourself this time. That would not be a good thing."

Jordan's eyes suddenly opened wide. "Run into myself? Oh, my God! I think that's already happened."

"What do you mean?"

"The second time you sent me back, I was exploring the barn on what turned out to be the morning Maggie died when I heard footsteps running from the house to the barn. I hid in the tack room so I wouldn't be seen, but about ten minutes later, a woman rode a horse through the barn like a mad woman. When I stepped out of my hiding place to watch her ride away, I remember thinking that she looked just like me. Are you saying it was me?"

"It's not only possible, but probable that it was you from the third and last time we sent you back," Andi replied.

"How can that be?" Kale asked. "I mean, how could the third time we sent Jordan back create the chance encounter that she'd meet herself from the second time we sent her back? Wouldn't she have been gone already from the second visit?"

"No, because the time frame we sent her back to the third time overlapped the time frame from the second time."

Jordan rose to her feet and began to pace the floor. "Wait a minute here, guys. When I go back again, it will also overlap the time from my last visit. Are you saying I have to avoid myself when I get there?"

"Yes and no. You see, the laws of physics dictate that the same matter cannot occupy the same physical space more than once at the same time. You can't be standing here in more than one form in the very same place at the very same time. Physics also dictates that you cannot occupy the present and the past at the same time nor the present and the future at the same time. A problem could occur if you run into yourself in the past because you already exist there. The only way to get around that is to avoid yourself or somehow avoid touching your past self."

"This is creepy. I mean, I guess I can avoid contacting myself physically when I go back, but what would happen if I did?"

Andi shook her head. "I don't really know. I would assume that since it's an impossibility to exist twice in the same space then both of you might cease to exist altogether. That's only a guess. This stuff is based on scientific theory more than anything else."

"What about the other Jordan?" Kale asked. "Will she know what's going on?"

Andi frowned. "I'm not sure what you mean."

Jordan pointed to herself. "Well, this Jordan right here will obviously know what's going on, but I would assume the Jordan from the last transfer won't, right?"

"Correct. You see, this Jordan has already lived through what the previous Jordan has, and she'll go back once more with knowledge the previous Jordan doesn't have. In effect, this Jordan will have the ability to actually change the previous Jordan's future. She'll be able to influence the outcome of events differently," Andi said.

Jordan stopped pacing. "I'll be able to influence what happened during the last visit? Is that what you're saying?"

"Essentially, yes."

"Then I know what I have to do. Kale, I need to go back." Jordan yawned loudly as she completed her statement.

CHAPTER 37

The next morning, Kale and Andi sat at the kitchen table waiting for Jordan to wake up. Andi had set the second pot of coffee to brew when she commented on Jordan's absence.

"Maybe we should check on her. It's nearly ten o'clock. It's totally unlike her to sleep past seven," Andi said.

"You're right." Kale rose to his feet and headed to Jordan's room. He stopped in front of her door and called her name.

"Jordan? Jordan, you're going to sleep the day away if you don't get your lazy butt out of bed."

Kale listened for a response, and became alarmed when none came. By this time, Andi had joined him in the hallway.

"She isn't answering me," Kale said. He reached for the handle and pushed the door open. Inside, Jordan lay in the same position she had fallen asleep in when they left her the night before. He frowned and approached the bed.

"Jord?" he said. She didn't reply. He glanced at Andi helplessly.

Andi touched the side of Jordan's face with her palm. Jordan's skin was warm, but not hot. She leaned in closer.

"Jordan. Sweetie, wake up." She gently patted the side of Jordan's face. "Come on, time to get up."

Jordan turned her head to the side to escape Andi's touch.

"Oh, no you don't. You're not getting off that easily," Andi said. "Come on, wake up," she repeated, patting the side of Jordan's face again.

"No," Jordan moaned. "Go away."

"Not a chance. The day is almost half over. We have work to do."

Jordan brushed Andi's hand away but Andi persisted. Finally, Jordan pushed herself into a seated position. "Okay, Okay, I'm up. Sheesh! Can't a girl get any sleep around here?"

"We woke you because we were worried. You've been sleeping for over twelve hours."

Jordan looked at him. "Are you serious? What time is it?"

"Nearly 10:00 a.m.," he replied.

Jordan threw herself back onto the bed and covered her eyes with her hands. "Why am I still so tired?" She sat up once more. "All right. I need to get up." Jordan swung her legs over the edge of the bed and placed her feet on the floor, then leaned forward to stand up. She rose halfway and then grasped her thighs. "Oh, my God!"

Kale and Andi were immediately by her side. Kale wrapped his arm around her back. "Sit," he said

"No, wait a minute. Just let me hold on to you for a minute," she replied as little by little, she forced herself to stand erect.

With one hand on Andi's arm and the other on Kale's, she took a tentative step forward and grimaced. Her eyes suddenly flew open.

"What is it?" Andi asked.

"It hurts," she replied. A grin split her face. "It hurts! My legs actually hurt."

Kale stared at her intently. "Are you telling me you feel pain in your legs?" he asked.

"Yes, that's exactly what I'm saying." Kale frowned. "That's a good thing, isn't it?"

"A year from now, it would be a good thing. Two weeks after the implant surgery, I'm not so sure. It's too soon for the implant to be working."

Jordan released her friends' arms and walked gingerly across the room to her bathroom. She stopped at the door and looked back. "I, for one, refuse to look a gift horse in the mouth. Give me a few minutes, and I'll join you for coffee."

Kale and Andi interpreted the dismissal for what it was and left Jordan's room. On their way back to the kitchen, Kale was deep in thought.

"Are you okay?" Andi asked.

Kale shook his head. "Something about this isn't right. Her injury is sixteen years old. There's no way the implant could restore synapse connection after only two weeks. Hell, even if the injury were brand new, it would take longer than that."

"Maybe it's phantom pain. I've heard amputees say countless times that they still feel pain in limbs that are no longer there. Maybe that's what she's experiencing."

"I guess that could be it, but still, something doesn't feel right about this."

* * *

Jordan stepped into shower and allowed the water to cascade over her body for several minutes. She leaned against the wall of the shower and reveled in the feel of the needle-like spray bombarding the skin on her legs with endless tingles of sensation. Tears mingled with water as the alien feelings overwhelmed her, yet she was reluctant to turn off the water for fear the sensation would also cease. A loud knock on the bathroom door shook her from her reverie.

"Jordan? Are you okay?" Andi called through the door.

Jordan turned off the spray and reached for her towel. "I'm fine. I'll be right out." She stepped out of the shower and methodically dried her body from the top down. When she reached her legs, she very slowly messaged them with her towel and was amazed at how soft the terry cloth felt against her skin.

This is fricking awesome!

Jordan stood in front of the vanity and tossed her hair with her fingertips. As she manipulated her wet hair into place, she saw something that disturbed her. "What the hell?" she said out loud as the leaned in closer to the mirror. "Gray hair? That's odd. Mom didn't gray until she was nearly fifty. God, I hate getting older." She scrutinized herself closer.

Lewis, you need to take better care of yourself. I can see the beginnings of wrinkles here. Get a grip, girl, you're only thirty-two. At this rate, you'll look like Grandma Moses by the time you're forty.

A second knock at the door interrupted her scrutiny. "I'll be out in a minute, Andi."

"It's Kale. You've been in there an awfully long time. Are you sure you're okay?"

Jordan dropped her head back and looked at the ceiling. "I'm fine. Really. I'm coming out right now, so if you don't want to see me naked, you should get out of my bedroom. Here I come," Jordan warned.

She threw the door open just in time to see her bedroom door close behind Kale. She chuckled as she entered her bedroom to get dressed. Moments later, she joined her friends in the kitchen for coffee.

"What the hell took you so long?" Kale asked. "Usually, your morning routine takes half the time mine does."

"The truth?" she asked. "I couldn't resist the feel of the shower spray on my legs. Guys, it's the most amazing thing to actually feel again. I could have stayed in there all day."

Andi sat back in her chair and looked at Jordan. "Something's different about you. I can't quite put my finger on it, but something is different."

Jordan chuckled. "It's probably my gray hair. Can you believe it? Look," she said as she tilted her head for Andi to see the dense shock of gray beginning at the back of her head. "I don't remember seeing that there yesterday."

Kale suddenly put his coffee cup down and rose to his feet. He approached Jordan and swung her around to face him, chair and all.

Jordan nearly fell out of the chair at the sudden move. "What the hell are you doing?"

"Don't move," he told her as he carefully examined her face, and then the gray hair she pointed out earlier. "Bend over. I want to see your incision."

"What? Whoa," Jordan exclaimed as Kale pushed her head down between her knees and lifted the back of her shirt.

The next thing she knew, Kale was pacing angrily back and forth across the kitchen. "Goddamn it! Damn it all to hell. No wonder the implant is working already." He approached Jordan and dropped to one knee. "I hate to break this to you, but the time travel experiments are over. You got that? Over!"

Jordan's eyes opened wide. "Why?" she demanded.

Andi looked just as shocked as Jordan at Kale's declaration. "Kale, I don't understand."

Kale approached Jordan once more. "Bend forward again."

Jordan did as she was told and Kale once again lifted her shirt. "Andi, look at the incision on Jordan's back."

Andi looked at Jordan's back, frowned, and then leaned in for a closer look. "It's barely discernable," she exclaimed.

"That's right," Kale said. "Any doctor or nurse—hell, any mother who's put a bandage on her child's scraped knee would tell you that incision was made maybe twenty years ago, instead of two weeks."

Jordan sat upright and looked at Kale. "What the hell are you talking about?" she demanded.

"Come with me," Kale said as he took her hand and led her into the bathroom. Andi followed them and leaned against the bathroom door. "Here, stand with your back to the mirror. Now look." He gave her a hand mirror.

Jordan angled the hand mirror so that she could see the area around the incision on her back as Kale lifted her shirt yet again. "Oh, my God," she said in nearly a whisper. Jordan put the mirror down and faced Kale. "What does this mean?" she asked.

Kale ran a hand through his hair. "It means that each time we send you through time your body ages by God only knows how many years. That's why the implant is working so quickly. The time travel is adding years to your body, giving the nerve endings adequate time to grow over the injury site."

Jordan sneaked a look at Andi. A knowing gaze passed between them as she recalled the conversation they had earlier about how traveling back in time might have a potential affect on the aging process.

"From Einstein's experiments, we know time is gained when traveling backward and lost when traveling forward. I can only assume that each time we send you back, the actual transfer process accelerates time for you. Once you arrive there, time moves at a normal pace, but during the actual transfer, it moves faster," Kale said.

"Then why wouldn't the aging reverse on the return trip?" Jordan asked.

"I can answer that one," Andi interjected. "There probably is some amount of reversal, but theory dictates that time gained by traveling backward is much larger in magnitude than time lost traveling forward, so the amount of reversal would be minute compared to the aging."

"Jordan, we can't risk sending you again. Judging by the change in your physical state just since the last transfer, it's almost as though the aging effect is cumulative. In other words, it increases with each transfer. At this rate, you'll die from old age in no time."

"I have to go back," Jordan insisted.

"I can't do it, Jordan. I won't risk it. Look at you! You look like you've aged at least fifteen or twenty years over the past three transfers. You had surgery just two weeks ago, and yet the implant site has the appearance of a scar that healed years ago. Hell! It's obvious to me that you don't even need the implant anymore. I'm sure if Peter opened the injury site up right now, all synapse connection would be restored. If we could have accomplished that one thing without causing you personal harm, all of this would be worth it, but I'm not willing to risk your death or be the cause of your premature death from old age."

Jordan walked directly up to Kale and grabbed the front of his shirt. "Well I'm willing to risk my death and old age because without Maggie in my life, it won't be worth living anyway."

Kale put his hands on his hips and closed his eyes. "Jordan, I don't want to lose you," he whispered.

Jordan released the front of his shirt and cupped his face. "Sweetheart, you will never lose me—regardless of where I am." She paused for a moment for her message to be absorbed. "Kale," she said softly, "I need you to do this for me. Please."

Kale closed his eyes as if to shut out the war raging in his mind between his own heart and Jordan's desires. He opened his eyes to find only desperation in Jordan's blue eyes.

"Please," she whispered once more.

* * *

"Okay, Kale. You need to use these time coordinates. They should land me very close to when I need to be there."

Kale took the piece of paper from Jordan and looked at it. "Remember, you promised to come back as soon as you've taken care of things, okay?"

"Yes, I remember," Jordan replied. "I don't break my promises."

"And then, no more time travel, right?" Kale reiterated.

"No more. Got it," Jordan replied nonchalantly.

Kale narrowed his eyes at Jordan. "Why is it that I don't believe you? What is going on in that mind of yours?"

Jordan adopted a surprise look on her face. "Who, me?"

"Jordan!" Kale said.

Jordan threw up her hands in frustration. "All right, all right. No more transfers. I got it."

Kale turned his attention back to the control console as he typed in Jordan's time coordinates. "Good. I'm just about ready to go."

Jordan took her queue from Kale and climbed onto the platform. Just then, the door to the lab opened.

"Wait. Don't you dare leave without saying good-bye to me," Andi shouted as she entered the barn and hurried over to the time machine. She reached forward and embraced Jordan warmly, then kissed her full on the lips. "Take care of you, girlfriend. I love you."

Jordan smiled. "I love you too, Andi. And you too, you pain in the ass," she shouted across the room to Kale.

"Yeah, yeah, whatever," Kale responded teasingly.

Jordan drew her knees into her chest and wrapped her arms around her legs, then lowered her forehead to her knees. "Okay, blastoff," she shouted as Kale powered up the rings.

Moments later she was gone.

"I love you, Jordan," Kale whispered.

* * *

As usual, Jordan landed on the dirt floor of the barn with a thud. She pushed herself into a seated position and looked around to be certain she had not been seen. Suddenly she heard a voice.

"Hey, Shawny-baby. How's Mommy's good boy this morning?"

Maggie!

Jordan crept toward a cluster of hay bales near Shawny's stall to get a better look. Half way there she stopped and stared at the woman already hiding behind the cluster of bales.

Damn, it's me. That's where I was hiding the second time Kale sent me back. I can let her... er... I mean... I can't let me see me.

Jordan hid behind a nearby saddle rack and watched as Maggie saddled her horse.

"How about a ride, sweetie? It's a beautiful morning. The air is crisp, and the sun is shining off the snow. A nice fast ride will do us both some good. That's a good boy."

Jordan waited impatiently as the scene she'd witnessed before unfolded.

"Okay, dumpling, let's go for a ride," Maggie said as she gently prodded the steed forward through the barn. Soon, she was gone.

Jordan watched her other self remove the Faraday belt and make her way to the tack room. As soon as she was out of sight, Jordan emerged from behind the saddle rack and ran as fast as she could to the house. She threw open the kitchen door and ran directly through the house and into Maggie's bedroom.

"Jordan! Jordan, get your ass out of bed." She flung the door to the bedroom wide open. It hit the wall behind it with a resounding bang.

"What the hell?" the sleeping Jordan exclaimed as she quickly sat up in bed.

"Go after her, now! Quickly, or you'll lose her forever," Jordan screamed.

"Who are you, old woman?" Jordan demanded as she scrambled out of bed and pulled her jeans and boots on as fast as she could.

"Never mind who I am. Just hurry. For God's sake, please hurry. She just rode off. You have very little time." She scurried out of Jordan's way as quickly as she could to avoid the two of them making bodily contact as the younger Jordan ran past her.

Without stopping, Jordan grabbed her canvas barn jacket on the hook by the kitchen door. Within moments, she had run the distance between the house and barn and flung the barn door open. She ran directly to the pile of tack being held for repair and realized Maggie's saddle was no longer there.

Oh no! Maggie, please don't tell me you are using the defective saddle.

Jordan desperately searched several empty stalls until she came across one containing a magnificent mustang steed. She talked soothingly to the animal as she first threw a blanket and then a saddle over the horse's back.

"Come on, big guy. We've got a job to do."

Minutes later, she led the horse out of the stall and climbed into the saddle. With a quick jab to the horse's ribs, she was on her way in a full gallop across the snowy fields, heading for the western edge of the property bounded by Lake Champlain.

On her way through the now-empty farmhouse, the old woman stopped in the kitchen and retrieved the note Maggie had left for Jordan. Without reading it, she folded it in half and slipped it into her pocket, then stepped onto the porch outside the kitchen door. From her vantage point, she could see Jordan speeding across the plains.

"Godspeed, Jordan. Please reach her in time. This is her last chance. This is our last chance."

Then she slowly descended the stairs and walked toward the barn.

As Jordan rode across the plains, she anguished over how long it was taking to cover the distance between the house and the lake. In her desperation, she was oblivious to the biting cold that chafed her cheeks as she rode. Nearly a half hour later, the frozen lake came into view. The sight encouraged Jordan to dig in her heels and push her steed nearly beyond its limits as their speed increased and she felt airborne.

Maggie, please stay away from the edge. Please! I'm coming, my love, I'm coming. Please let me reach her in time.

Jordan pushed her mount as hard as she could and almost gave up hope until she spotted Maggie on the horizon, galloping freely across the plains, directly toward the edge of the cliffs.

"Maggie!" she screamed. "Maggie, stop!"

Jordan's screams were ineffective. The distance between them and the sound of the crashing surf below the cliffs drowned out any chance that Maggie would hear her.

Jordan silently asked her horse for forgiveness as she dug her heels in once more in an attempt to get just a little more speed out of the animal. Her efforts paid off as she began to close the distance between them. Again, she attempted to call out to Maggie, and again, her efforts were for naught. Finally, when she had closed the distance to within thirty feet, she heard a shot ring out. Maggie's horse suddenly reared up very close to the edge of the cliff.

*   *   *

"Kale, Jordan left us a message. It's time to bring her home," Andi said as she entered the lab.

"Okay. Let's do this," Kale replied, powering the system up.

"Two minutes to surge," Andi said. "Ten, nine, eight, seven, six, five, four, three, two... ready... surge!"

*   *   *

Maggie stood in the saddle in an attempt to steady herself and calm the animal as it continued to rear up.

"Maggie!" Jordan shouted once more. She was now only twenty feet from Maggie.

Maggie looked up and saw Jordan just as she lost her footing and began to tumble off the horse.

"No," Jordan screamed, reaching for anything she could cling to. Just as her fingers made contact with the collar of Maggie's jacket—the same jacket that Jordan had lent to her on the steps of her bunkhouse so many months earlier—she felt the now-familiar tingling in her body as though every muscle had fallen asleep and was now awakening. She realized immediately what was happening. "Kale! No, not now. For heaven's sake, not now!" she screamed.

* * *

The power surge passed over Kale and Andi as they watched Jordan appear on the platform. Then, the unthinkable happened. Jordan's figure began to fade again as though she were somehow resisting the retrieval.

"Do something," Andi shouted.

"I... I don't know what to do," Kale said.

They stood by helplessly as Jordan began to fade away. Then, as suddenly as it began, the process reversed itself and Jordan appeared once more on the platform.

"Power down," Andi ordered, running toward Jordan.

Kale powered down the rings as fast as he could. Moments later, he ran toward the machine where Andi had climbed onto the platform and had gathered Jordan into her arms. She was rocking the frail, gray-haired Jordan back and forth while cradling her close to her breast.

"Andi?" Kale said softly.

Andi looked at Kale with tear-filled eyes. "She's gone, Kale. She's gone."

EPILOGUE

Kale glanced up at the lab technician assisting him. Then he returned his gaze to the rodent trying furiously to escape his grasp. "Okay, Dave, I'll hold the little bugger while you slightly increase the current to the implant. I'll tell you when to stop." Kale was in the middle of an experiment on a rat in which damaged musculoskeletal nerves were replaced with synthetic fiber optics. Just as Dave completed the first incremental step, Kale's communicator chimed loudly.

"Hello?"

It was a hysterical Andi. "Kale! Jordan is hurt. Come quickly!"

Kale felt like someone had punched him in the stomach. "Andi, slow down. Tell me what happened. Where are you?"

"We're at the hospital. She was on the bus. It went off the road and rolled over. She's in the hospital. Please, come quickly."

"I'm on my way. Hold on, love. I'm on my way."

Kale grabbed his jacket and ran from the building. The University of Vermont was affiliated with the Fletcher Allen Health Care teaching hospital, and the laboratory was located just on the other side of the parking lot opposite the emergency room. Realizing he could cover the distance between the lab and the hospital quicker on foot than by trying to find his vehicle in the vast parking lot, he set off running, making it to the emergency room within five minutes of Andi's call. Andi met him at the door. He grabbed her by the shoulders. "Where is she?" he asked desperately.

Andi was barely able to speak as she pointed to the door of an examination room. "They took her in there."

Kale was frantic as he ran toward the door, only to be stopped by a resident who would not permit him entry.

"I'm afraid you can't go in there," the resident informed him.

"I'm afraid I don't care," Kale responded as he tried to push his way past the man. "Let me by," he said.

"I said no. You'll need to see the doctor if you want a status."

Just then, Peter Michaels exited the room Kale was attempting to gain access to. "Peter! Peter... how is she?" By this time Andi had joined Kale and was clinging tightly to his arm.

Peter took Kale by the arm and walked him a few feet away from the door. Andi followed closely. "She's stable. As stable as she can be considering her condition."

Andi stepped forward. She was clearly distraught as she wiped the tears from her cheeks. "Tell me, Peter. How bad is she?"

Peter looked back and forth between Andi and Kale. "Judging by the severity of her injuries, it's apparent she was violently thrown around the bus." Peter ran his hand through his hair then looked at his friends and coworkers once more. "All indications are that she's broken her back and probably severed her spinal cord completely."

Andi nearly collapsed and Kale supported her with an arm around her waist. "No," she moaned.

Kale felt he needed to be strong for Andi's sake, and tried hard not to cry. "Can we see her?"

Peter nodded. "Of course. They'll be prepping her for surgery soon to further stabilize her spine, so you'll only have a few moments. We'll let you know as soon as she's been settled into Intensive Care."

Kale nodded. He tightened his arm around Andi and led her into Jordan's room. Peter followed close behind. Andi was shaking uncontrollably. "She looks so small and helpless!"

Kale nodded, unable to speak for fear of losing control. As they approached the bed they separated, with Andi on one side and Kale on the other. Kale leaned over the small form lying in the bed and kissed her on the cheek. "Jordan, honey, Daddy's here. Mommy's here too, baby." Andi rubbed the back of the girl's hand as Kale spoke. "You're going to be all right, sweetie. Mommy and I will be right here waiting for you to wake up, okay?"

Andi inhaled deeply to control the tears that cascaded down her face. She too leaned in close to the injured child. "We love you, sweetheart. You'll be better soon. Just wait and see."

Peter motioned to them that time was up as the technicians entered the room to wheel the child to the operating room. Andi looked at Peter and nodded, then turned back to her daughter. "Jordie... the doctors are here to take care of you, but we'll be here when you come back, okay? Mommy and Daddy love you, honey."

Andi and Kale kissed their child tenderly then stood together by the window as they watched the technicians move the five-year-old Jordan from the room.

*   *   *

Andi paced back and forth across the floor of the waiting room as Kale sat hunched over with his head in his hands. Every few moments Andi blew her nose, left runny by nonstop weeping. Kale felt totally helpless as his baby girl lay clinging to life on the operating table and his wife paced worriedly across the floor in front of him. Few words passed between them as they waited for news of their child.

Finally, after what seemed like an eternity, a man wearing a white lab coat entered the room. He looked at the clipboard in his hand before addressing Kale and Andi. "Mr. and Mrs. Simmons?"

They were on their feet immediately. Together, they approached the man who extended his hand to them. "My name is Dr. Lewis. I'll be evaluating your daughter's condition."

Kale looked at the man's nametag as he firmly shook his hand. *Dr. Jordan Lewis. What the hell?*

His eyes moved from the nametag to the man's face. He appeared to be around fifty years old, and something about him felt familiar to Kale. "Dr. Lewis," Kale replied as he shook the man's hand and then stepped aside to afford the same courtesy to Andi.

"How is she?" Andi asked.

Dr. Lewis smiled. "She made it through surgery just fine. I won't be sure about the extent of her injuries or her chances for recovery until I've had a chance to examine her holograph."

"When can we see her?" Kale asked.

"They're moving her to the ICU right now. You should be able to see her in a couple of hours."

Andi noticed the doctor's nametag as Dr. Lewis answered Kale's question. She gasped and gently elbowed Kale in the ribs to call his attention to the badge. Kale briefly glanced at his wife and acknowledged that he was aware of it.

Dr. Lewis scribbled a few comments on his clipboard. "I encourage you to get something to eat while you wait. There's a cafeteria downstairs that serves hot meals. Neither of you will be of any use to your daughter if you don't take care of yourselves. You can stop by the nurse's station at the ICU afterward and they'll be able to direct you to your daughter's room. I'll check on her as soon as she's settled in."

Kale stopped the doctor as he turned to leave. "Dr. Lewis?"

The doctor stopped his retreat and turned back to Kale. "Yes?"

"We couldn't help but notice your nametag." Kale looked at Andi, then back at the doctor. "We... we knew a Jordan Lewis. In fact, we were very close to her." He cleared his throat before continuing. "We loved her very much. So much that we named our daughter after her."

Dr. Lewis simply nodded, then left the room. Outside the waiting room, he stopped and leaned against the wall. After taking a deep breath, he scanned the papers attached to his clipboard.

Simmons, Jordan. Age 5. Parents: Kale and Andrea Simmons.

Dr. Lewis pressed the back of his head into the wall and closed his eyes.

It's them!

* * *

Kale stood at the window of Jordan's room and looked out over the city. A canopy of stars stood guard over the night and streetlights dotted the scenery below. Andi sat at her daughter's bedside and hummed nursery tunes in time to the various monitors that beeped in harmony with her voice. Both parents waged internal battles between hope and desperation as they waited for their daughter to regain consciousness.

After a time, their vigil was interrupted by Peter's arrival. Andi looked up at him with expectation and hope on her face.

"Peter?"

Peter walked over to the bed and placed his hand on Jordan's forehead. He addressed Kale and Andi without taking his eyes from Jordan. "She's a beautiful child, very much like her namesake."

Kale approached Peter and placed a hand on his shoulder. "What can you tell us?"

Peter turned to address Kale and Andi. "As you might guess, she's in pretty rough shape. We know her spinal cord is severed, but we have yet to determine just how catastrophic her injury is. I assume you've met Dr. Lewis?"

"Yes," Kale replied. "Do you realize his name is Jordan Lewis? How odd is that?"

Peter's eyebrows rose on his forehead. "Yes, I know. What's even stranger is that he's rapidly building a reputation for new spinal cord regeneration techniques—techniques that are supposed to restore complete sensory communication and feeling in a matter of months rather than the years we would have realized from our research. He's apparently been doing independent research for the better part of his career, largely funded through private organizations."

"Do you think he can be trusted?" Andi asked.

"I checked out his credentials thoroughly. He has an excellent reputation and from all reports, his patients are doing exceptionally well. From what I can tell, he's little Jordan's best chance at this point."

"When do you think we'll know if he can help her?" Kale asked.

Peter inhaled deeply. "Well, Dr. Lewis and I examined her while you two were having dinner. Hopefully, we'll know better tomorrow morning after Dr. Lewis has reviewed the test results."

Kale and Andi nodded as they absorbed Peter's statement. Peter headed toward the door, but stopped and turned around. "The two of you should go home and rest. She'll be sedated throughout the night, so I don't expect she'll be aware of your presence at least until morning."

Andi shook her head. "I can't leave her."

Peter looked at Kale. "I'm staying as well," Kale added.

Peter nodded. "All right. At least take turns napping, okay? You two need to take care of yourselves in order to help your daughter through this."

* * *

Dr. Jordan Lewis entered the Intensive Care Unit the next morning to find Andrea Simmons sleeping with her head resting on her daughter's bed. Kale was pacing the floor.

Kale's attention was immediately drawn to the door as it opened. He reached out to shake the doctor's hand. "Dr. Lewis, good morning."

Andi stirred at the sound of voices in the room. "Kale?" she asked groggily.

Kale walked over to the bed and rubbed Andi's back. "Sweetheart, Dr. Lewis is here."

Dr. Lewis walked over to the bed and shook Andi's hand then he pulled up a chair and sat down. He motioned for Kale to sit as well.

"Please, sit. I have some news for you."

He waited for Kale to sit on the arm of Andi's chair and place his arm around Andi's shoulder to both give and receive emotional support.

"I believe I can help your daughter."

Andi began to weep softly.

Dr. Lewis continued. "I've been working for the past thirty years on a revolutionary method for restoring spinal function in a completely severed spinal cord." He stopped speaking for a moment both to allow Kale and Andi to absorb what he had said and to prepare himself for what he had to say next.

"We can't thank you enough," Kale said, wiping the tears from his face.

Dr. Lewis reached into his breast pocket and retracted an envelope. "Before you thank me, you need to read this. You see, there's a reason my first name is Jordan. I was named after my grandmother."

Kale's knees buckled and he slowly lowered himself to the edge of the hospital bed. "Oh, my God. Jordan," he whispered.

Jordan smiled. "Yes, Jordan—your Jordan. She and Grandma Maggie wed in 2020. My father, Kale, was born two years later through artificial insemination, followed by my aunt Andrea a year after that."

Kale and Andi looked at each other. They were speechless as Dr. Lewis continued.

"You see, I know about how you two helped her transcend time so she could be with Maggie." Dr. Lewis stared off into the distance as he fought the mist that was forming in his eyes. "They were the happiest two people I have ever known in my life. Grandma Jordan lived to the ripe old age of ninety. Grandma Maggie died a year later."

He looked back at Kale and Andi as he continued. "Thanks to you, she was not only a happy woman, but she also brought into the past all of the knowledge and talent required to advance stem cell and spinal regeneration research a century before it would otherwise have been discovered. So, as you can see, it's her you should be thanking."

Dr. Lewis smiled as he watched Kale and Andi attempt to compose themselves.

I can't believe it." Kale knelt in front of Andi. "Sweetheart, he's Jordan's grandson. She made it. I always felt like she had, and now, thanks to her, our baby has a chance to live a normal life."

Kale lowered his head into Andi's lap while he cried. Andi lowered her cheek to rest on top of his head and spoke soothingly to him.

Dr. Lewis stood and looked at the couple before him. "I can clearly see why Jordan loved you two so much. Here, she wrote this for you before she died, more than thirty years ago. My wife found it a few years ago in some old papers that were in a trunk my grandmothers owned. It was enclosed in a larger envelope that had my name on it. With it was a note to me in which she asked me to hand-deliver it to you. I didn't expect it to be under these circumstances, but it seems appropriate. Considering what you three meant to each other, it's only fitting that she continues to help you across time."

Dr. Jordan Lewis handed the envelope to Andi. "I'll check back with you later today to discuss little Jordan's treatment." He then smiled at the couple and left the room.

* * *

Kale and Andi walked hand in hand across the pasture toward the tall oak tree. To the right of the tree was a small cemetery where the remains of the Lewis family had been interred. Jordan, as well as both her parents, were buried there. The couple approached Jordan's headstone and sat side by side, with their backs leaning against it. Kale pulled out the letter Dr. Lewis had given them and gingerly opened it. It was several hand-written pages long. Andi entwined her fingers with his and laid her head on his shoulder as he held it before them and began to read.

My Dearest Kale and Andi,

I don't know how to begin except to say that I dearly love you both with all my heart. Because of your love and sacrifice, I have lived a long and prosperous life with the one person who completes me. I will be forever thankful that you came into my life. I know you compromised everything you believed in to help me realize the love of my life. For that you have my undying gratitude.

Kale—you once told me that someday I'd be happy that you were around. My dear friend, I was always happy that you were around. You are the closest thing I have ever had to a brother. Did you ever learned to comb your hair?

Kale and Andi both chuckled through their tears as Jordan teased him from beyond the grave. They continued to read.

Andi, I am so happy you came into Kale's life. You are the main reason I felt comfortable leaving him. He needs you. You are the other half of his soul. Please take care of him.

I cannot possibly rest until I tell you how I came to be so happy. As it turned out, the final trip back was the charm.

Kale, I realize now that I took a terrible risk—I filled the old well. I wasn't thinking. I might have created a time paradox—I might never have met you! But I did. Maybe there are parallel realities.

On the morning Maggie was supposed to die, I almost slept through my opportunity to save the love of my life. An old woman that looked strangely familiar woke me in the nick of time. At the time, I didn't know who she was, but as I write this and see my own visage in the mirror, I can only thank you for obviously indulging me one final time.

Loving Maggie is the most important thing I have ever done in my entire life. I don't know how I could ever live without her. She is even more beautiful in person than she was in my dreams. The first time we made love, it was so incredibly life altering. I was changed forever.

As I suspected, her death was not an accident. I knew the reports of her death in the Free Press sounded odd. An accomplished horsewoman just doesn't fall off her horse over a cliff. You see, having arrived five months before she died, I worked my magic and made her fall in love with me. (Not that it was hard. As you know, I'm incredibly charming, wink, wink!) Being that close to her, I was able to observe the day-to-day events, and soon realized that her demise was being carefully planned and staged by Jan. Remember her? Reading about Maggie and Jan's relationship while I was in the hospital upset me terribly. Now I know why. I knew there was something evil about that woman.

Jan made a show of running the farm and making sure I knew my place. I would catch her in the barn when she wasn't aware I was there. She seemed to have a fascination with the saddles, especially Maggie's. It turns out she had cut the stirrup on the right side of Maggie's saddle so that it was barely attached. Considering horsemen mount from the left side, Maggie wouldn't have noticed it until it was too late, until she had already mounted and was speeding across the plains. I moved Maggie's saddle to the pile of tack that was going out for repair the next day. The last thing I wanted was for Maggie to be injured.

Unfortunately, the saddler was unable to pick up the damaged saddle on time and it was still there the morning of March 29. On that morning, Maggie decided to take her horse on her usual early morning run along the cliffs, bordering Lake Champlain. Once awakened, I immediately ran to the barn looking for Maggie and realized her horse was gone. I also realized her defective saddle was no longer in the repair pile. As fast as I could possibly move, I saddled another horse and rode after her.

I was sure I would be too late as I scanned the horizon hoping for a glimpse of her. Finally, I saw her, galloping directly toward the edge of the cliffs. I pushed my horse as hard as I could and came to within thirty feet of her when I heard a loud shot. It sounded like a rifle or shotgun. Maggie's horse suddenly reared in fright. She stood in the saddle in an attempt to calm the animal, then the defective stirrup snapped and she began to tumble directly toward the cliff. I barely reached her in time and grabbed the back of her denim jacket.

By the way, she was wearing the jacket you sent to me. Apparently, denim in the future is much more durable, because it held without ripping. Anyway, here I was, barely hanging on to my own saddle with one hand, while holding her by the collar with the other. I swear her feet were dragging the ground. She nearly pulled me off my own horse as I half-dragged, half-carried her away from the edge of the cliff.

When we had cleared the cliffs by a good distance, I dropped her to the ground and stopped my horse. I dismounted and ran toward her. We fell into each other's arms and cried for what seemed like an eternity and we clung to each other like there was no tomorrow. We must have knelt there for a good half hour just holding each other. The reality of what might have happened came crashing down on us.

Maggie's horse had run off back to the barn as I knew it would, so we both mounted my horse. She wrapped her arms around me and clung so tightly, I could hardly breathe. It was the sweetest bone-crushing grip I had ever known. I never wanted her to release me. It was both the most uncomfortable, yet most wonderful ride back to the farm. Before we headed back to the farm, I directed my horse to the spot where Maggie's mount had reared. There, on the ground, was a brightly colored bag. It was empty.

The following day, I returned to the cliff and searched around, both on the precipice and on the ground at the bottom of the cliff. I found a 10-gauge shotgun shell among the rocks—directly under the location where Maggie's horse reared. I am convinced Jan was responsible for that gunshot. Jan would have known Maggie would be drawn to the colorful sack so oddly out of place on the snow covered plain, and planned the gunshot at the precise moment Maggie was closest to the edge.

After it was all over, I learned from the other farmhand, John, that Jan had saddled Maggie's horse for her that morning. Obviously, she used the saddle she had tampered with. Kale, her plan would have worked if I hadn't discovered those diaries. This was meant to be, of that I am certain.

Jan turned out to be Janneal Safford, the woman who owned the farm immediately following Maggie's parents. As it turned out, Jan had convinced Maggie's father to leave the farm in both Maggie's and her name. She would assume ownership if Maggie died before she did. Jan had been planning Maggie's death for several months. As you know, she succeeded, at least until I appeared on the scene. With me in the picture, Jan's plan failed. Curiously enough, Jan disappeared that very evening, but not before I cornered her in the barn and kicked the shit out of her. Even though I had no real proof, I made her well aware that I knew what she had done. We never saw her again.

Oh, jumping ahead for a moment, Kale—do you remember the land records said there were several owners between Maggie's parents and mine? Well, I needed to find a way to assure you and Andi ended up with the farm, so I convinced Maggie to hold on to it until 2071, when my parents came along, and we sold it directly to them. Let me tell you, it was very odd meeting them before I was even born. They both stared at me in the oddest way, like they thought they should know me. I wanted so much to tell them who I was, but that might have just given them both heart attacks, then I would have killed my parents before I was even born. Talk about the ultimate paradox!

Anyway, Maggie asked me how I knew she was in danger. I had no choice but to tell her about my life and my journey into the past to be by her side. Quite frankly, she thought I was insane at first. I tried to prove it to her by recounting word for word, things she had written in her diary. She immediately accused me of finding *the diaries and stealing them, which I readily confessed to doing... one hundred years later. She actually made me tear the walls down in our bedroom to prove to her they were still there. She pretty much freaked out when I told her the whole story. I don't think she totally believed me until I was able to predict historical events that occurred over the next few years, but eventually, she relented and admitted that I was such a wing-nut, I could only have come from another time. She was just too cute.*

Maggie and I were married a year later, and thanks to the wonders of science, we had two children, a boy we named Kale, and a daughter named Andrea, after the two people I love with all my heart. The two of you made all of this possible for me. I will forever be in your debt and will watch over you and your loved ones for the rest of eternity. That is my promise to you.

Kale, you warned me about not creating paradoxes with my presence in the past, but as I see it, impacts of a positive nature would surely be welcome. So, as you probably know, I continued our spinal cord regeneration research. It is my sincere hope that by taking the knowledge back one hundred years, SCI healing will have advanced at a phenomenal rate. It's the least I could do to repay the two of you, and Peter, for all you did for me.

If you're reading this letter, then you have met our grandson, Jordan. We are so proud of him. He has known about where I came from since he was a child. In fact, our children, Kale and Andrea, as well as all six of our grandchildren know. Jordan chose to enter the field of spinal cord regeneration to follow in my footsteps. When I realized he might have the opportunity to meet you in person, I penned this letter and gave it to him for safekeeping until he had the opportunity to deliver it personally. It is my sincere hope that he carried out my wishes.

Well, my dear friends, I am tired and must rest. It is unfortunate that time travel cannot erase the ravages of age. My body is old, but my spirit is still young. I have little time left in this world and look forward to the day that Maggie will join me and we will be together again for all eternity. I am not afraid to die. I know there is something more beyond this physical state. One day, Maggie will join me, as will both of you. I will miss my Maggie when I go, but we have had fifty-eight wonderful years together thanks to you. There is nothing in this world that I could ever do to repay you. Know that I love you both, and I look forward to seeing you again one day. Give my best to Peter. Take care of you...

Love, Jordan

Andi clutched at her heart. "It hurts so much. I miss her."

Kale made no attempt to stem the flow of tears from his eyes. He brought the letter to his lips and kissed it tenderly.

"I love you too, Jordan. I always have." He reached over to take Andrea's hand in his own. "It warms my heart to know she was happy."

Andi smiled through her tears. "Me, too."

Kale held the letter in front of them both. "Jordan," he said out loud. "You said there was nothing in this world that you could do to repay us. Well, my friend, you were wrong. You are giving our child's life back to us. That is a greater repayment than we could ever ask for."

"Amen," Andi chimed in.

Kale leaned over and kissed Andi tenderly. "Have I told you today that I love you?"

Andi inhaled deeply. "I believe you have, but I never tire of hearing it. I love you too, Kale, across all space and time."

"Across all space and time."

Kale carefully folded Jordan's letter and placed it in his pocket, then rose to his feet and offered his hand to Andi. Soon, they were walking hand in hand back to the farm.

At that moment, if Kale and Andi had looked at Jordan's headstone they would have seen that it now mysteriously read:

Jordan Marie Lewis, age 90. Born September 20, 2073, died July 4th, 2077. Free from the bonds of time and held by the arms of love. Thank you, Kale and Andi.

Photo Credit: Brad Fowler, Song of Myself Photography

About the Author

Karen D. Badger, better known to her online fans as "kd bard" is the author of *On a Wing and a Prayer* and *Yesterday Once More*, both of which are published by Blue Feather Books, Ltd. Born and raised in Vermont, Karen is the second of five children who were raised by a fiercely independent mother, who remains one of her best friends to this day. Karen earned her B.A. in 1978 in Theater and in Elementary Education, and in 1994, earned a B.S. in Mathematics.

Ten years ago, writing became an escape when Karen underwent a much-needed lifestyle change, and reinvented herself as an independent woman. Her sons remain the pride of her life. In April of 2005, a beautiful baby boy came into her life when her first grandchild was born. Kyren is the apple of his Nona's eye. Just 18 months later, a beautiful granddaughter made her appearance. Ariana is Nona's little angel. Granddaughter Elise is due in the fall of 2008. Karen considers herself blessed to be living in Vermont and surrounded by the love of her family and friends. She has learned to put the past behind and to move on, never looking back. She firmly believes that "If you keep looking back, you'll trip over what's in front of you."

Karen currently works as an Engineer in the semiconductor field and still lives in Vermont with her partner, Barb. She fills her spare time with writing, and spending time with family and friends. She is currently editing the Billie/Cat series for publication.

Look for the exciting first story in the
Billie/Cat series,

THE
COMMITMENT

Available soon, only from

www.bluefeatherbooks.com

Printed in the United States
119292LV00002B/382-417/P

9 780979 412035